THE INVISIBLE EYE

Also by Sparrow Hall

TWO BLUE WOLVES & NIGHTWORK

THE INVISIBLE EYE

SPARROW HALL

HYDROGEN MEDIA

VALATIE | NEW YORK

www.sparrowhall.com

Library of Congress Cataloging-in-Publication Data
Names: Hall, Sparrow, author.
Title: *The Invisible Eye* / Sparrow Hall.
Description: First edition. | Valatie, New York : Hydrogen Media LLC, 2025.
Identifiers: LCCN 2025909635 | ISBN 978-0-9825780-4-9 (US open market)
| ISBN 978-0-9825780-5-6 (ebook / Kindle) | ISBN 978-0-9825780-6-3
(ebook / EPUB)

Cover design by Sparrow Hall
Rune symbol artwork "Dagaz," "Uruz," and "Wunjo" by Sparrow Hall

First Edition

Hydrogen Media, LLC
P.O. Box 424, Valatie, NY 12184
www.hyd01.com

For those who share their gifts.

CONTENTS

CONTENTS *(Continued)*

ACKNOWLEDGMENTS

To those who offered their unwavering love and support throughout the writing process—RA, JD, GDM, LD, EH, JTK, JL, LM, MN, AO, NP, LR, and ER—your faith in this project has been an enduring source of inspiration.

A special acknowledgment to my editor, WM, and copy editor, AM, for their invaluable expertise in refining this work.

And to J—whose love, insight, and encouragement carried this book to completion—your thoughtful feedback helped shape this story into what it has become. I am forever grateful.

A person's shadow or silhouette is always present. Because of this, Egyptians surmised that a shadow contains something of the person it represents.

—Ancient Egyptian conception of the soul,
  Wikipedia

The reverse side also has a reverse side.

—Japanese proverb

THE INVISIBLE EYE

PROLOGUE | MONSTERS

I stand at the side of the bed and nudge my father's shoulder until he flinches awake, rubs his eyes, and reaches for his glasses. "Hey, sweetie, what is it?" he mutters. I step back from the bed, motioning for him to follow. He regards me for a moment, squinting in the purple darkness, then folds back the covers and gently tucks them back in around the sleeping mound of my mother. I put a finger to my lips and lead him down the hallway, halting him at the threshold of my bedroom. I scan the room.

The moonlight beams in from the window over the bed, fanning a milky blue across the floor, making shadows of things. My father rests a hand on my shoulder and steps around me. He moves to the window and checks the latch, peering out into the night. "Did you see something?" he asks.

I shake my head no.

"Hear something?"

No.

"Feel something?"

I nod.

He looks for my eyes, to read something in my face, then sits down on the edge of the bed. He pats the covers beside him. I remain at the door, judging the distance between here and there, and then, cautiously, tiptoe forward, one foot in front of the other, arms at my side, fingers spread wide. I feel something in the air, a breath of static, humming along the hairs on the back of my hands. I hurry to my father's side and push up against him. He puts an arm around me, keeping his voice low. "What do you think it is?" he asks.

I look at the length of my forearm, the little hairs standing up like white fur.

"A monster?" he asks.

I nod.

He considers this, then leans into me. "Can I tell you a secret about monsters?"

I coax up a shrug, still watching the room.

"They don't want you to know this," he whispers, "but you've got it backwards."

I look up into his spectacled face.

"The monsters are scared of you," he says.

"Of me?"

"You know when you lie down in bed and don't want to close your eyes because that's when they'll come to get you?"

I nod.

"They're thinking the same about you," he says. "Why else do you think they sneak around at night?"

"Because they're hungry?" I ask.

"No. Because they think you are."

1 | THE SUN IS ALWAYS SETTING

My eyes clenched tight, I imagine it there. A white pinpoint of light, pulsing like a beating heart in the black cavity of my ribs. A torch in a cave, it illuminates the dark walls of my organs, my bones. I focus on the light, my eternal self, sizzling and white, moving it up through me, up the long dark tunnel, into the dome of my skull, down the back of my neck, to the span of my shoulder blades pressed against the wall of the elevator. I smooth the front of my dress to feel my stomach breathing inside it, to know that I'm here. Here, now, in this moment. Here among others, and that I'm fine. I'm fine.

I breathe in through my nose and out through my lips, face tilted down, eyes closed and hidden beneath the brim of my hat.

My belly lifts and settles, billowing like a parachute as we descend through the floors, then wait, then descend again. I draw in one long, deep breath, filling my lungs, then slowly expel it through my lips as we touch down and the doors glide open. We pour out into the marble lobby, through the revolving glass doors, out into the white blast of Seventh Avenue at rush hour.

A mangle of sounds—delivery trucks and clattering carts and honking horns. I blink to get my bearings as a flood of people stream around me. And there, farther upstream, the soft, unfocused shape of a woman, charging straight at me. We edge from side to side, trying to avoid one another, until she's right on top of me, face to face, and the pale green pools of her irises blink into mine, and my inner self is sucked forward like a tissue in a vacuum tube, down into the black void of her pupil, into the swirling tunnel of her past—

> *Walls like quicksilver spin around me*
> *like water down a drain.*
> *Shards of images,*
> *still frames,*
> *moments,*
> *a hundred million filmstrips whipping by*
> *in beams of light.*
> *I clench myself to stop, to pull myself*
> *back, but it's like tripping forward with*
> *nothing to grab.*
> *I reach out*
> *into the light,*
> *and it seizes me,*
> *snatches me down*
> *into a moment,*
> *a scene,*
> *jump-cutting like a movie with the fast-*
> *forward button held down.*
> *A man in a suit passes me in a hallway*
> *of an office building.*
> *He ignores me.*
> *I turn to watch him go...*
> *Now I'm huddled in a bathroom stall,*

making a whispered phone call.
I'm in tears,
the saltiness dripping down my face,
into the corners of my mouth...
Now I'm in an apartment,
a bedroom.
I'm staring into a closet crammed with
clothes.
I drown my sorrow with things.
I buy away my pain...
And then, I'm standing in front of a
medicine cabinet,
gazing at my reflection—
her reflection,
the woman on the street.
She looks deep into her eyes,
and I wonder, does she see me there?
Does she see me looking out?
Suddenly I'm thrust backward,
back into the lightning curl.
Down farther,
faster.
So fast and so far that the flashes streak
into white-blue beams of light,
lifetimes screaming by.
I'm snared by a slash of light,
ripped down into another body in
another time:
My arms ache, my legs heavy,
bare feet the color of ash,
caked in mud.
My palms are scarred, rock-hard, a
man's hands.

I'm outside, in a farm field, rows of thick
stalks rising overhead, stretching to the
sun.
Dark figures move through the rows,
gathering leaves into woven baskets the
size of bathtubs,
their voices low, murmuring.
My head goes faint,
my face cold.
I sway, stumbling backward,
back into the light,
through the slipstream of time—

back into this moment, here on the sidewalk at rush hour, and the woman ducking past me, looking back over her shoulder like, *Crazy bitch.* I watch her as she marches off.

I try to hold myself here in this reality, but I can feel it shuddering, trembling apart—the white lines of the crosswalk, the edges of the buildings, glitching, switching, revealing other heres, other nows—street scenes shuffling like a deck of cards. I grip my phone, the date and time lighting up the screen—WED AUG 17 2011 5:13 P.M.—but the day, the time, the year keep switching, and the mismatched sounds of the flickering city come faster and faster, clipping together, rising up into a single, sharp, angry hiss bearing down on me like a giant snake. I put my hands up to shield myself as something like a wall screeches to a halt before me. I look up—at a man, a bus driver, blinking down at me. Someone takes me by the elbow, guiding me, a woman holding a giant iced coffee. "Holy shit, are you OK?" she asks. Another woman scuttles around our feet trying to collect something scattered in the street—the burgundy square of my purse, its contents dumped out. A crowd has formed, and I hear another woman's voice cry out, "That woman almost got hit by a bus!" She's pointing at me. I scan around, mortified—at the faces of the onlookers, the bus driver unbuckling and hurrying down the steps. I watch as the woman gathering my bag shovels everything back inside, wiping it off, holding it out to me. I lunge for it, snatching it away from her, completely freaking her out, then squeeze through the encircling crowd. I duck around the corner, under the scaffolds on 37th Street, where I stop and take a deep breath, gripping the brim of my hat, shielding me from the stares of the people streaming past.

I hurry down the subway steps, slipping in through the closing doors, squeezing into a seat, small and tight. I keep my head down, breathing in through my nose, out through my lips, white knuckles digging into my purse to keep my hands from shaking. Two women watch me from the seats across the way. One of them leans over to whisper in the other's ear. I pull my bag closer, wishing I could disappear inside it.

Today was meant to be an easy day—plenty of time to rest, to be alone, until a text buzzed in from my Chloé client asking if I could come in to meet the designer. *She's in town last-minute. Can you show her the forecast in person?* Which meant rushing from my 10 o'clock way out on 12th Avenue, and checking the presentation in the cab three times to make sure I swapped out all the names from one label to the other to give the impression that this forecast is all about them, their singular vision. They would die if they knew the truth—that all of this was prewritten. You just have to have the eyes to read it. That's what leaves me like this, too depleted to maintain my grip on the present, and all I'm left with is my bag of tricks, my last vestiges of control. "Gnittes syawla si nus eht," I recite under my breath."Gnittes syawla si nus eht." Until the train pulls to a halt at West 4th Street and I lurch forward, out onto the platform, up the stairs into the white blast of light.

I fish out my keys, pushing into the vestibule of my building, faking a cheerful hello to my neighbor Charlotte as she lugs her 10-speed down the stairwell. I grip the bronze rail, heaving myself upward, one flight, then another, to the fifth floor. Damp with sweat, I shove the key into the lock and push inside my apartment, shutting the latch, my knees shaking. I close my eyes and focus on the smell of home—the warm green scent of the fig tree baking in its patch of sunlight, the bitter black coffee grounds spilled in the kitchen sink. I steady myself down the hall into the living room, dropping my bag, my hat, and collapsing on the sofa.

I need to lie down, to lie flat, flatter than the sofa will let me, so I slide myself to the floor, splaying my legs and arms like a star. I need to be someplace else, someplace safe. I will my mind backward, back to another time, lying in the grass at school, the quad at night, the buildings and dorms rising up around me like the walls of a fortress…

"Do you ever think you'll go crazy?" I ask. I'm lying on my back on the shag carpet in Leslie's off-campus apartment, gazing up at a diaphanous tie-dyed sheet pinned to the ceiling. Streaks of white and green and indigo swirl together into a sea-colored cosmos.

"I hope so," Leslie mutters. She sits hunched over her sewing machine beside the window haloed in the sunlight, her unwashed golden hair pinned up in a loose bun. "But, like, sexy-crazy," she clarifies. "Like Edie Sedgwick, in one of those old WASP-y sanitoriums, drawing pictures of horses and then getting out and fucking Mick Jagger." She holds up the beginnings of a plaid skirt, pulling her glasses down from her forehead to inspect the seam, then leans forward, chugging the pedal.

"I feel like I'm always hiding," I say, gazing up at the canopy.

"Everyone's hiding," Leslie says with a sniff.

I roll my head to watch her work, the purposeful shape of her silhouette, perched forward on her stool.

"Maybe I need something like you have—like sewing," I muse half-heartedly. "Something to focus on."

"You just need some tricks." She ties down a stitch and snaps off the thread with her teeth. "When I was little, my brother showed me how if you play 'Stairway to Heaven' backwards, it sounds like a poem to the Devil. Honestly, it sounds like a bunch of garbled bullshit, but whatever. I had him play it backwards, and I sat there and read the liner notes in reverse, and you'll never guess what happened. All the Winks disappeared."

"Winks" were what Leslie called the ghosts that inhabited her childhood home, an old New York townhouse overlooking Central Park. The ghosts had resided there with her family as long as she could remember. When she was a baby, an old woman would sit in the rocking chair in the corner of the nursery and sing her to sleep. As Leslie got bigger, she realized the woman wasn't like the other people in the house. The nursery was the woman's room long before it was Leslie's, and they both were inhabitants, each in her own way.

Leslie called the ghosts Winks because of the way they flickered like eyelashes winking. She once described how she saw the world with two realities playing over each other—one of the living and one of the dead. Most people only saw the living reality, but Leslie saw both at once—to the point where the flickering was the only way to tell them apart.

"There were a couple of ghosts that lived in my brother's room," Leslie says, rummaging through a bin of ribbons and scraps. "They were from different times. One was an old man, the other was a little boy. The moment I read the lyrics backwards, they both went *poof!* Gone. Like I pulled a plug from the socket. But not just them. The whole house—every room. It was spookier than when they were there. I didn't know what a regular house sounded like. You get used to it—the voices and the sounds and the creaking floorboards. The ones that pass through walls like they're sleepwalking. For the first time in my life, I was experiencing what 'normal' was like."

"So then what happened?"

"The song ended, and they all popped back in. The whole house blinked back on. But something was different. The Winks, they were messed up—like, out of it. The old man was trembling. He had to hold on to the wall just to keep from falling down. And the little boy, he was an absolute mess, just completely freaked out. But I wasn't sad for them. I was sad for me. I was like, why are you here? This is my house." She chugs the pedal and the sewing machine comes back to life—she leans into a stitch. "I thought maybe if I kept it up, I could scare them out of the house. So I sang the song backwards every night until it was the only way I knew how to sing it. I'd lie in bed at night and sing myself to sleep."

"I don't understand. How did it work?"

She turns to me. "How did what work?"

"The song. How did it shut them out?"

She thinks about it. "I don't know, maybe it confuses your brain. Like, the part that tunes all that stuff in—it switches it off somehow."

"But why do they come back all messed up?"

"Maybe they needed me to be tuned in to them. And when I wasn't, they lost their connection."

"But where did they go?" I ask.

"Maybe they went to Heaven," she says with a shrug. "Maybe they saw where they were supposed to be and realized they were lost." She turns back to the machine and lines up another stitch. "All I know is you can recite anything backwards and it works the same way. But I like to use that song. It's kind of like my 'fuck you' anthem."

I lay on the floor, my mind lifting from the memory, back into my apartment, back into the now. A blare of car horns echo from the street below. I imagine crawling across the room, reaching up to the record player, and clicking the special switch that spins the record backward, letting the muddy slur of reversal fill the room, fill my mind. I think of Amy standing there that night, flipping through the record sleeves as I watched her from the kitchen. "I can't believe you have a record player!" she exclaimed, delighted. "Concrete Blonde! Madonna! True Blue! Oh my god, I stole this album from my sister. I literally wore this record out!"

I knew Amy from the gym, a part-time trainer who tended bar at a French bistro a few blocks away. I memorized her schedule so I could accidentally run into her on slow nights, and buy her a drink and talk and laugh at the end of the bar—until one night I mustered the courage to invite her back, a night like this, when all my other tricks had failed and I was desperate for the one thing that could tether me to the here and now. I stood in the kitchen, watching her select the perfect record and set it on the turntable, fitting the pin—my hands shaking as I poured our glasses of wine.

I think of how she looked across the table, the flash of her smile, her laugh, radiant and alive. And how I willed myself to be cool, to just let things happen—pop in a movie, prop up the pillows, feel the warmth of her beside me. And how, when she looked for my eyes, I wanted to let her see me, but knew I wouldn't have the strength to keep from falling into her gaze, tumbling into her past. So I concentrated on her mouth, the air between her lips, the way her legs felt as they pressed against mine. Unzipping, peeling off, the softness of her breasts, the warmth of her ribs, her stomach, her breath catching as I lifted her up to me, to my mouth, and the slow grind of her hips, finding her rhythm, commanding me not to stop as I held her there, at the edge, gripping her nails into the back of my head, pulling me in, to finish her. Her body flinching, shuddering, melting down the length of me, turning me, positioning me the way she wanted. How she held me there, feeding upon me, swallowing me down, until everything slowed—the air in my lungs, the light in the room—shifting, coalescing into a form, a diamond-shaped door, hovering there, shining into my hollow eyes, my gaping mouth, calling me to it, calling me home…

The whine of an ambulance siren breaks the spell, and I'm here again, lying on the floor. I pull my phone to me, wanting to text her, but the words won't come, so I dial instead. I'll know what to say when she answers. But it rings twice and goes to voicemail, and a wave of panic runs through me, a feeling like falling, the floor dropping out beneath me, pulling me backward into the void.

2 | FOOL IN THE TOWER

I slouch forward at the breakfast table, my face in my hands, listening to the coffee maker splutter. Drawing in a long, deep breath, I sit up straight and pull my laptop toward me, lifting the lid. A cascade of emails floods in—clients, designers, project managers, message threads overlapping one another. A calendar notification bings in the corner of the screen: *Dad's birthday*. I gaze at it for a moment as it hovers there, asking me to do something, but I don't know what.

I do the math to figure out how old he would be today…62. I subtract my age from that and realize I'm the age he was when he had me.

I picture him here now, seated across the table, his thick, wavy hair gone gray, his lean runner's frame still strong, his pale pink button-down shirt rolled up at the sleeves.

What a handsome couple he and my mother were. She could have been a model if she wanted. I'd watch her getting ready at her bathroom sink, doing her makeup in the mirror, her hand precise as she drew the lipstick across her lips. How she looked gazing at her reflection, alone with herself, as if I wasn't there. And then she would cap the lipstick and hand it to me with a wink.

Do you see me now? I wonder. *What do you think? Are you disappointed? I know you'd say no. But are you?*

A reminder chimes in the corner of the screen: *Gucci Fall Walkthrough—11 a.m.*

I close the lid and slide the laptop away.

Something catches my eye on the way to the subway: a hand-painted sandwich board propped outside a shop window. An open eye in the palm of a hand. It gazes back at me. Written beneath:

PSYCHIC
$10 READINGS

A bell *trings* over the door as I step into the vestibule, a tiny cubby of a space made smaller by a pair of hulking floor-to-ceiling bookshelves crammed with objects—religious icons, tiny woven baskets, ancient figurines depicting Hindu gods and goddesses, their arms fanning around them like rays of the sun. A glittering menagerie of crystals fills the front window, purple and emerald and pink, catching the daylight and reflecting it around the room. A thick curtain cuts across the front parlor—behind it, I hear the soft shuffle of house slippers. A plump, wrinkled hand pulls back the curtain, revealing Sofiya in her long woolen sweater, oblivious to the late summer heat. "Yes, hello?" she blinks up at me.

"It's me, Sofiya. It's Catherine."

"Oh goodness, what a surprise!" she gushes in her thick Ukrainian accent. But I know it's no surprise at all. I bend down to give her a hug and breathe in her sweet, powdery smell. Her embrace is warm and comforting, like a bowl of chicken soup.

"Turn the sign," she orders, waving to the door as she waddles to her chair and plunks herself down.

I flip the door sign from OPEN to CLOSED and join her in the opposite chair.

She pats my leg, smiling. "It has been *months* since I have seen you," she says, giving my hands a squeeze. "Let me see your eyes, dear. Please, look here. You will not fall in," she assures. "Please, look to me." I do, reluctantly, my gaze meeting hers. Her soft amber irises are flecked with shards of green. The muscles of my mind impulsively tense, trying to hold myself back from tumbling forward into her past—but nothing happens. I'm held in place.

"You've learned a new trick," I say. "What is it?"

"No trick, dear. A prayer. I have prayed for your eyes. For peace to find you." She pauses, examining my face. "But I see it has not. What can I do?" she asks.

"I have something for you, Sofiya," I say, digging through my purse. "This is a business card for Dr. Zimmer, the chiropractor I told you about. I want you to have him look at your knees. Will you do that for me?"

She tugs her reading glasses up from her bosom, holding them to her eyes, examining the card.

"He's in touch with Spirit," I explain. "I saw his other lives. He's been a healer for a long time."

She looks at me over her eyeglasses. "Is he handsome?" she asks.

"Well, yes!" I laugh. "But he's also—"

"Then I will go," she says flatly.

"Is that all it takes?"

"Is there a better reason?" she says with a grin, slipping the card into the pocket of her sweater. "I am very shallow, I know.

But I do not want to talk about me. What can I do for you, my dear?"

"I just wanted to sit with you, Sofiya. Just for a moment, if that's OK. Tell me how you are."

"Well, I have been very busy thanks to you!" she says, laughing. "All of these girls you send to me! They are like supermodels! Who are these girls? They are girlfriends?"

"Well, no." I blush, fumbling for an answer. "They're just—"

"My dear. Please," she stops me. "American girls, you call it 'experiment.' In Ukraine, we call it 'winter.'" She squeezes my hand with a wink. "Why don't you let me read you? Just tarot."

"Sofiya, I don't—"

"Just tarot!" she implores. "I know you don't like to see, but that is when you are doing the seeing. Here, you let me. Spirit protects us, you know this." She retrieves a large deck of cards from a basket beside her chair and places the stack in my hands. The cards have soft edges, worn down from decades of use. I shuffle the cards, cutting the deck into threes, then restacking them into a single pile. Sofiya gathers up the deck and flips the top card, snapping it down on the table, then another, then another, forming a horseshoe. I name the cards in my head as she flips them.

> Present Position: The Hanged Man
> Present Desires: The Tower
> The Unexpected: Death
> The Immediate Future: The Fool
> The Outcome: The Magician

I sigh as the arrangement takes shape. "This is why I don't want to be read."

"My dear, please," Sofiya insists. "It is important." She rests her hand on the first card, closing her eyes, as if listening to it. "Here now," she begins. "Present Position: The Hanged Man. You see how he hangs from one leg, but he is not in pain? He hangs by his own choosing. He is caught up in his own troubles, distracting thoughts, bad habits. He has complicated his life, and now he forces himself to stop. He hangs himself by the left leg, the leg that represents the higher self. And you see his right leg crossed over the left? This means a crossroads, a lack of decision. But look at his face. Calm. Because he knows the answers will come to him when he is still. His gold hair hangs down around his head like a halo. This is enlightenment. The knot at his foot. He has tied this himself, and he knows the more he struggles, the tighter it will get. But look how he hangs. At peace. He knows he can reach up and untie the rope and set himself free whenever he wishes…which leads us to Present Desires," she continues, moving her hand to the Tower card.

"The Tower in flames. Bodies falling from the sky. Lightning and wind and the sea crashing all around. We see this and it looks frightening. We think of terror and cataclysm. But this is only about change. A very big change. It is nothing to be scared of. Change is sudden. *That* is what scares us. But it is necessary. When we change we become better than before. It is a change handed down from God. You see?" She points. "The lightning bolt. This is how he touches our lives. To move us forward."

Her hand hovers over the next card. "And this will have a big effect, because here now we have Death," she says. "The Unexpected. This is not a death of the body. It is a death of what was. Do you see behind the figure? Do you see the sun rising? This is to remind us that when one thing dies, something else is born. Something new. The white flower. Purity and promise. Which takes us to the Immediate Future, the Fool."

"The Fool represents adventure. Going where others fear to go. The Fool has blind faith. He follows his heart. And to help him comes the dog. A loyal friend who keeps him safe from danger. The dog pulls at the Fool's robe, guiding him to safety. And look now at what he carries. The sack at the end of the stick. You see how it hangs, like testicles? This is his seed, which he will sow into the earth. And he will reap what he sows. This is the responsibility he carries with him…

"And now," she touches the final card, "the Outcome: The Magician. The one with power over reality. You see the infinity symbol over his head? And the snake around his waist? The infinite energy of the universe that cannot be created or destroyed. An endless cycle. He is a master of this energy, and he knows that how he shapes the energy has infinite consequences. He knows we come into this world with all the things we need to live the best life. These are represented by all the symbols of the tarot spread out before him. He reminds us that we are the master of our gifts and that we are not slaves to our circumstances." Sofiya turns her face to the light of the window, her eyes closed, sensing something. "My dear, what brought you here today?"

"My father," I say. "Today is his birthday."

She looks to me. "He hears your heart. You are asking him things. Things about his passing."

"I replay it in my mind—the night they died. The knock at the door. I was hiding at the top of the stairs. All I could see was their feet. The police officers' shoes and my Aunt Teri's slippers. My parents had gone to dinner and my aunt was watching me. There was a knock at the door. She went and opened it, and the officers stepped inside. She called up to me and said to wait in my room and that she'd be right up. But I stayed there, at the top of the stairs, frozen, listening. They went into the kitchen. And then I heard a shriek. I never heard a sound like that. It was like an animal screeching. Then Teri was shouting. One of the policemen was trying to say something to her, trying to calm her down, but she was screaming at them, pushing them out, these two giant men. One of them saw me at the top of the stairs. My aunt looked up and our eyes met, and something left me. It flew out of me, from the center of my brain, out of my face like a bat, down the stairs, into her wet, crying eyes, down into the tunnel of her past. And I saw her. I saw her with my father. As children. As teenagers. My dad behind the wheel, driving Teri to school. I could feel Teri's heart beating, how proud she was to have her big brother driving her to school, being seen with him. And then a flash, further back, younger. My father as a boy. He's furious because he's been grounded. Teri is sneaking him comic books under his door. And then a flash, further back. Teri as a baby, held in her brother's lap, and a warm feeling—of love and safety. And then I'm ripped back through the tunnel, out of her eyes, up the stairs into my body, and Teri is snorting back the tears, reaching up to me, telling me to come down."

Sofiya listens to the story as if she's feeling her way toward something. "They died together," she says. "Your parents. Water. I see water rushing in."

"There was an accident," I say.

"But you think it was not." She looks to me. A chill races through me. "A secret," she says. "In your heart. There is something calling you. There is something you must find. It is here, in the cards. You are being called." She touches one card, then another, closing her eyes. "You are the same age?" she asks. "As your father when you were born?"

"Yes, that's right."

She opens her eyes. "Then this is no coincidence. You see here," she points to the Magician card. "It is the cycle continuing. The infinite. The snake around the Magician's waist.

It is a message. Where your father's story ends, this is where your story begins."

"I don't understand," I say. "What story?"

She touches the Death card. "You see here? The sun rising behind you. The answer is there, on the horizon."

A faintness sweeps over me, a cold sweat. "I'm sorry, Sofiya, I have to go."

"Yes, go," she says, patting my knee. "Listen to your heart. It will give you clues."

I kiss her soft cheek, and she heaves herself forward, limping beside me to the door.

As I hurry up the block, I glance back to see Sofiya standing at the window, watching me go—then she flips the sign from CLOSED to OPEN, and her silhouette recedes into the dark.

3 | AN INWARD GAZE

"Oh, good! Catherine!" Raffaella cries, delighted, ushering me into the corner conference room, a sleek glass box with floor-to-ceiling windows overlooking the blue-black water of the Hudson. She makes a sweeping gesture to a tiny, leather-tan wisp of a woman with a shock of white hair. "Angela, this is our forecaster extraordinaire, Catherine Harper. Catherine, I'd like you to meet Angela Bronelli."

As Angela rises to greet me, I note her understated power outfit—black silk jumpsuit, Louboutin heels. She juts out a tiny hand. "Wonderful to finally meet you!" she says, beaming, perfect white teeth, super present, full eye contact. I clench my mind, chanting backward in a silent loop.

"Likewise!" I gush. "I don't know if Raf mentioned what a fan I am."

"*Really?*" she coos. "How wonderful! Thank you!"

I take a seat beside her at the glass conference table. "Your silhouettes," I say. "Every season I'm like a child waiting for Christmas."

"How very kind of you!" she says.

Raffaella seems delighted with everyone's delightedness. She nudges us along. "I had Catherine put some ideas together. Catherine, do you want to take us through them quickly?"

"Yes, I'd love to," I say, pulling out my laptop, patching it into the room's AV system.

"You may remember Catherine from her blog," Raf says, buying some time as I set up. "*In Stitches*?"

"No!" Angela gasps, gripping the edge of the table for dramatic effect. "Is it true? You actually exist?"

"Apparently so," I say with a laugh.

"I am amazed," Angela says. "How I loved your writing! It was like my drug. Why did you ever stop?"

"So she could work for us," Raf chides. "We brought her to the dark side."

"I know this will sound absurd," Angela says, "but I thought you were a gay man writing as a woman. How funny is that? No one knew what you looked like. You were such a mystery!" She sits back, arms folded, regarding me with pleased satisfaction. "Well, now I am even more excited," she says, gesturing to me. "I am working with a celebrity!"

The meeting wraps and Raffaella takes Angela on a tour of the office, which I use as my opportunity to slip away and set myself up at a workstation at the far end of the creative department, strategically positioned with my back to the wall so no one can see my screen. I need to send out the Helmut Lang deck by two o'clock, and Raf would shit a brick if she knew I was working on a competitor's forecast, in her office no less, but there's no time to head home.

A massive flat-screen monitor serves as the perfect block from the rest of the room—designers assembling layouts, team meetings around mood boards.

An intern with flamingo pink hair screeches to a halt beside my desk and asks if I want anything, they're ordering Thai. I tell him sure and reach for my purse, but he waves it off. "No worries, Raf's got it," he says, scooting away.

I periscope over the monitor for a final check of the room. All clear.

If you want to know what people will be wearing in the future, all you have to do is look at the past. The signals are everywhere; you just need to know what to look for. And when you've traveled through time as often as I have, the signals become a second language. The trick was to find a way to access the past without having to slip into another's gaze. I've never divulged my process to anyone, and no one has ever asked. I think they like it better left to the imagination. And how would I explain it anyway?

I begin by patching my laptop into the monitor and opening a browser window, then another, then another, six in all, arranging them into a three-by-three windowpane grid. In each pane I open a website: the Hong Kong stock exchange, Google News, the BBC, Instagram, the *Drudge Report*, and the Night Sky Map. From my purse, I retrieve a small spiral-bound notebook, a black pen, and a compact mirror. I set the pen and the mirror on the desk and the notebook in my lap. The notebook's pages are filled with jittery squiggles, scratched-in words, shapes, symbols. Arriving at a blank page, I uncap the pen and lay it in the crease, then pick up the mirror in my left hand and rest my right hand on the mouse.

I close my eyes and slow my breathing. My mind, a storm of images, dissolves into a single black dot.

My eyes flick open—pupils constricting in the monitor's white light.

My index finger whirls the track wheel, scrolling through the websites. A cascade of images, words, colors, blurring like paint in water, mixing into a message.

My left hand lifts the mirror in front of my face, and there in the reflection, my eyes gazing back at me. Black pupils pulling me in, swallowing me down, flashing into a scene—

A cobblestone street,
the clopping of horse hooves,
rattling carriage wheels.
I scan around me. Landmarks—where?
A small stone chapel. A bell tower.
The hollow chime of bells swinging
against a woolen sky.
People pass me in the street.
Dark shapes of men, top hats,
waistcoats, breeches, black as a raven.
A woman wears a bright yellow ribbon
tied around her hat.
The yellow sizzles like the sun
and swallows me,
down, down, down
and out:
An open field, farmland, hillsides rising
and falling,
withering with blight, the putrid smell of
rot.
No birds, no sound.

Storm clouds roll in from all sides,
gathering above me like a white tower,
crackling with light, a thunderclap.
And now the sky is changed,
clear and blue,
and below it,
the fields, alive now, a sea of golden
sunflowers, their black faces turned to
the sun.
brilliant and white
blinding in a flash,
then darkness:
a dirt floor
in a room,
a cave,
the glow of a fire hissing and popping,
flickering yellow light dancing across
the walls.
An old woman sits before the fire,
windblown cheeks, ropes of braided
gray hair.
She's wrapped in the skin of an animal,
a bear.
She cradles something in the fold of her
cloak.
She lifts the thing to me so I can see—
a baby
wrapped in a swaddling hide.
She braces it by the back of its head to
face me,
so I can see the baby's eyes,
my eyes,
sparkling green,

gazing back at me...
My knees go weak and I stumble
backward, reaching out, grasping, but
there's nothing to grab,
only smoke,
swirling,
swallowing me,
and within the smoke, blue flashes of
light,
images,
shards of lifetimes slicing past like
splintered glass—

Thrusting me back into the mesh of the chair.

My body slumps forward. The mirror tumbles to the floor.

I feel for the notebook in my lap, the pen, scrawling down a message left in the vision's wake:

2012
      black
            yellow
                  death
            rebirth
                sun
                      cycle
                          end

The hum of the creative department filters in, murmurs of conversations, the drone of a laser printer. I look down at the words scratched in a broken line down the page.

The flamingo-headed intern buzzes past my desk clutching a throng of take-out bags. "Food's here!" he announces.

I duck out of the office before Raf can find me, hailing a taxi out front and sinking into the back seat. I just want to be home, on the couch, smoking an enormous joint. I let my mind go soft, gazing at the passing buildings, the people hustling by, when something catches my eye. A figure standing on the far corner, his face shadowed by the sun glinting off the glass of the building behind him. He stands facing me with his shoulders square, as if waiting for my cab to pass. There's something familiar about him, the proportions of his frame, the cut of his pants and his shirt, tucked in with a belt. As we pull closer, I squint into the darkness of his face, the details materializing from the shadow, my father's chin and mouth and nose. I grab for the door handle, ready to fling it open, to dive into his arms as his face comes fully into focus—a stranger, oblivious, waiting to cross the street. My heart races as I turn and watch him recede, dissolving into the flow of the crosswalk. Without thinking, I turn to the driver and ask if he can take me to Jersey instead. "Yes, ma'am, no problem," he says, maneuvering the car. I sit back, watching the traffic siphon southward past the policemen waving us into the black mouth of the Holland Tunnel.

4 | A BOX WITHIN A BOX

Fluorescent lights blink to life down the corridor of the self-storage facility, a procession of red double doors stretching up the carpeted hall. I count the numbers on the doors to 16, then punch in the code and push inside. Lights pop on, illuminating a tomb of cardboard boxes and shrink-wrapped furniture.

The storage unit was my Aunt Teri's idea. After my parents' death, the house in Princeton was packed up and sold. The contents were moved to her and my uncle's two-car garage in Butler and eventually transferred here as a more permanent, out-of-the-way solution. The idea was that one day I would have my own house and I could fill it with all of my family's belongings, essentially picking up where I'd left off. The plan seemed to make sense at the time, but now, as an adult, I feel tethered by the unit to a moment in my life I should have moved on from long ago. Now it feels like I've missed my chance, and these boxes, these chairs and bookcases, have formed a kind of permanent bridge forever linking the past and the present.

I squeeze through the stacks of boxes tagged in faded black marker, my aunt's handwriting—BOOKS, PLATES & BOWLS, KNICKKNACKS, BLANKETS, CHINA. I pause at a box marked OFFICE and wiggle it forward, pulling open the flaps, its contents wrapped in brittle folds of crumpled newspapers. I unwrinkle one of the pages, smoothing it flat, a *New York Times* Arts & Leisure section from April 14, 1988. A black-and-white photo of Michael J. Fox gazes back at me, young and handsome in a blazer and wayfarers—a film still from *Bright Lights, Big City*. I feel deeper into the box, unearthing a bronze pen cup, a marble paperweight, a gray metal stapler, and an Oliver Peoples eyeglass case. There's something else, big and heavy, down at the bottom of the box, that feels like a giant dictionary. I heave it out. *Molecular Biology and Biotechnology: New Science, New Frontiers*, its pages bookmarked with a fan of colored tags. I turn to one of the flagged pages, scanning a highlighted section about the role of the endocrine system in vertebrate sleep patterns.

I set the book aside and wade further into the stacks of boxes, pulling out anything marked OFFICE. More books, science journals. A crayon drawing I made for my dad mixed in with his diplomas, certificates, awards. A National Medal of Science plaque and a photo of him shaking hands with Jimmy Carter.

The last box is the heaviest of all, piled deep with files, research folders, conference programs. Buried beneath them is a black metal box about the size of a small picnic cooler. I pull it out by its handle and unlatch the brass clamps, but the lid won't budge. I dig through my purse and pull out my "janitor's ring," an assemblage of keys of all sizes that my aunt and uncle collected around the house in Princeton, assuming one day I would figure out what they belonged to. I try each of the keys until one slides into the lock and turns, popping the lid. Inside the box are more folders, different from the others—crisp and organized, each labeled with an alphanumeric code and a red-ink block stamp: TOP SECRET, FOR PROJECT EYES ONLY. The folders contain documents, records—of military personnel enlisted in the Army, Air Force, Marines, Navy. Medical and psychological reports with numerical grades. One line is highlighted on each file, titled "PSY." Most of the subjects average about a 4 in this category, but a handful rate a 9 or 10. These reports are marked with green tags. I flip them over and look at the photos attached to the back—black-and-white headshots taken against a sterile cinder block wall. Men, women, some as young as 18, others in their 40s or 50s. The reports are accompanied by spiral-bound documents—research analyses written by scientists, for scientists, judging by the complexity of the language, the medical equivalent of legalese. I come to a folder titled NI-AST137-X369. Its contents date from January 1987 to March 1988, the month my parents died. I flip through the pages, attempting to glean the contents, something about serotonin. A diagram depicts a cross-section of the pineal gland, a node the size of a pearl nested in the center of the brain. I run a search on my phone and click a link to Wikipedia:

> The pineal gland (also known as the pineal body or epiphysis cerebri) is a small endocrine gland in the brain of most vertebrates. It produces melatonin, a serotonin-derived hormone, which modulates sleep patterns following the diurnal cycles. The shape of the gland resembles a pine nut, which gives it its name. The pineal gland is located in the epithalamus, near the center of the brain, between the two hemispheres, tucked in a groove where the two halves of the thalamus join.

I scan through the results to another link:

> The pineal gland has been compared to the light-sensitive, parietal eye present in the epithalamus of some reptiles, amphibians, and fish—also called the pineal eye. The 17th century philosopher René Descartes believed the pineal gland to be the "principal seat of the soul" and regarded it as the third eye in humans.

I flip through the reports in the file. A handwritten note flutters to the floor—on it, a list of names written in my father's bird-scratch handwriting. Each is written in a different ink, a different pen, as if he'd been jotting them down, one by one, over an extended period of time.

Dr. Allison Barnes (Biotech)
Dr. Margaret A. Koeffler (Neuro)
Dr. James Siegfried (C. Psych)
Dr. Colin Marsh (A. Math)
Dr. Peter Phillips (Q. Mech)

And beside the list of names, underlined: White Ladder 369. I run a search on my phone, but nothing surfaces. I hold the list in one hand and a black-and-white photo of a soldier in the other, his chart flagged and highlighted: PSY 9.7. His young eyes gaze back at me, soft and unaware.

5 | SMILING EYES

I pour a glass of red wine and type the list of names into a search, one after another. Of the five names, three of them take me to obituaries—Barnes, Koeffler, and Siegfried—which seems odd, since that would mean that all of them would have died at a relatively young age.

Dr. Allison Barnes. Deceased.
Exposure/Hypothermia. Grimentz, Switzerland,
1992.

There's an article from the *San Francisco Chronicle* reporting the death of Barnes and her college-aged daughter, Melissa, during a skiing trip in the Swiss Alps. Their car was discovered in a ravine off a mountain road. The two women appeared to have survived the crash and tried to find help on foot. Both died of hypothermia. I scan through the remaining search results. I find an article in *The Journal of Scientific*

Research and Development that lists Barnes as Executive Vice President of Research and Development, for a biotech company.

> Dr. Margaret A. Koeffler. Deceased. Myocardial
> infarction. Cambridge, Massachusetts, 1998.

I find an in memoriam page on the Harvard Medical School website mentioning Koeffler's work in the "genetic dissection of neural circuits that control stress-induced behavioral states." I hope they didn't write that on her gravestone. I find an archived obituary for her in *The Boston Globe*.

> Dr. James Siegfried. Deceased. Drowned. New
> York, New York, 2005.

Psychiatry practice on the Upper East Side, Vietnam vet—Siegfried worked extensively with veterans helping them reacclimate to civilian life through a program he founded called Arms Wide Open. He published articles on PTSD and served as a go-to pundit for the press. I find a clip from CNN where he's being interviewed by Anderson Cooper. Another from a *60 Minutes* special on American troops returning home from Iraq.

I plug in the last two names on the list—the living two:

> Dr. Colin Marsh. Professor of applied
> mathematics, Columbia University.

The Internet goes wild for this one—a stream of articles, TV interviews, NPR sound bites. An academic superstar, Marsh seems to be tied to everything from the World Economic Forum to the Mars Exploration Program.

In contrast, the last name on the list is no more than a blip in the ether. I can find his name listed only once:

> Dr. Peter Phillips. Chief researcher, Sellings
> Laboratory, Virginia Beach, Virginia.

The Sellings Laboratory website doesn't offer up any additional information. The only photo I can find is from a holiday gala at the White House in 2004. Phillips has the gentle, pudgy demeanor of a suburban dad in a rented tux. He's pictured with his wife, a tall, Carly Simon–looking woman in a long burgundy dress. They're both smiling for the camera. Her eyes are smiling, but his aren't.

I click back to the laboratory website, the contact link, a phone number—I dial it. The phone rings once, then pushes to an automated directory. I type in the letters P-H-I and it clicks over to a voicemail: "Hello, this is Dr. Peter Phillips. Please leave a message and I'll return your call shortly. Thank you."

I rise from the couch, pacing the room. "Dr. Phillips. My name is Catherine Harper. This'll probably seem completely out of the blue, but I think you may have worked with my father. Dr. Andrew Harper? I had…a question. I was wondering if you could give me a call when you have a moment. I'd appreciate it." I leave my number and hang up, then continue scanning through the Sellings Laboratory website.

> Established in 1962, Sellings Laboratory
> specializes in the theoretical aspects of
> nanoelectronic systems and engineered quantum
> systems. Our major research interests include
> quantum information processing and molecular
> electronics.

I bookmark the page and set it aside.

There's only one person left to look up. I hesitate, realizing I've never typed his name into a search before. I don't know why.

> Dr. Andrew Harper. Deceased. Automobile
> accident, Washington Crossing, Pennsylvania,
> 1988.

The first link sends me to his Wikipedia page, detailing his breakthroughs in serotonin modulation and receptor control, helping pave the way for a long line of anxiety and depression therapies. Next is a link to the *Washington Post* digital archive, a clipping from the Medal of Science ceremony with Jimmy Carter, followed by a handful of articles from *The American Journal of Medicine*. I find a mention on Princeton's former faculty roster with a picture taken in his office beside the window overlooking the courtyard. He must have thought he needed to wear something professorial. I'd never seen him so dressed up for work, but here he was, in a slightly rumpled corduroy blazer, his arms loosely folded with his glasses dangling in one hand—a look of ease, like he had just laughed at something. I wonder when the photo was taken. I don't remember him ever looking like this. I remember a darkness that followed him around like a storm. The photo makes me uneasy, like I don't know who this man is.

6 | WE'RE SISTERS NOW

I stare at the black box of files on the living room floor, not sure what to do with it. I need to talk to somebody about this, but I don't know who—or what I would say. There's only one person that comes to mind, but she has no connection to it, and there's no way I'm calling her at this hour. Still, I can't help wishing I were back at school—back when I could wander over to her house after midnight and see the lights still on, both of us quietly grateful that the other was awake and up for a chat. I lay on the couch and close my eyes, thinking of that first night we met …

I spot her in the organic food aisle at the Amherst Big Y, a few blocks from my dorm. She's perched on tiptoe, reaching for something on the top shelf, a thick wave of silver-white hair crested back from her forehead, a pair of black-rimmed glasses positioned on the tip of her nose. She wears a long wool sweater-coat cinched at the waist, enfolding her. She is the antithesis of the mostly stoned, late-night, pajama-wearing students roaming the aisles at midnight on a Thursday. And yet there's something instantly familiar about her. I find myself standing there waiting for her to recognize me, though I don't know why. She inspects a can of steel-cut oats and tosses it in her cart, noticing the random girl staring at her from the end of the aisle. "Hi," she says, point-blank. Her big, dark eyes pull me in, whisking me forward like a phantom, down the aisle, into the blackness of her pupil, down, down, flashing into her past, life before life, churning around me, flinching at what I see—

> *Flames peeling back layers of bubbling*
> *flesh.*
> *Then flash—to another life, another*
> *time—*
> *a girl thrashing desperately underwater,*
> *rope binding her hands and feet.*
> *Flash—*
> *gagging wet gasps as blood spurts onto*
> *her chest,*
> *a stake driven through her heart.*
> *Each scene, each lifetime, worse than*
> *the last.*
> *A repeating cycle of torment.*
> *I recoil, tripping backward,*
> *back through the lightning flash of time,*
> *whipping out of her eyes,*
> *down the aisle,*
> *slamming back into my body, back into*
> *the now—*

The woman catches herself on the handle of her shopping cart, woozy, putting a hand to her forehead. She looks back at me, confused.

"I'm sorry," I fumble, "can I—can I talk to you?"

She regards me for a moment, chin raised, eyes narrow, through the black circles of her eyeglasses. "Of course," she replies, hesitating. "But not here. Come by my house. I'm the big white one with the gardens next to the Episcopal church. Do you know it?"

I nod my head yes.

"Good," she says. "Come by tomorrow, in the afternoon, and we'll talk then." She casts a quizzical look my way, then turns her cart and wheels it to the checkout line.

I have no trouble finding the house—an immaculate white Victorian I've passed a hundred times on my walks into town. It gleams in the sun, bounded on all sides by luxuriant flower gardens, soft plumes of purple wisteria hanging from the columned porch.

I ring at the front door. Inside I hear the soft tread of footsteps, then the door being unlatched and heaved open.

"Why, hello there! You found me!" she says, beaming, ushering me into the wood-paneled entryway.

I'm instantly put at ease by the smell of her home, something like a professor's office: an underpinning of old books and clove tea—and a subtle hint of weed.

"Can I take that?" she asks, motioning for my jacket, then hangs it on a peg on a huge mirrored coatrack. She turns to me, her hand outstretched. "I don't think we've introduced ourselves properly. I'm Clara."

Her handshake is firmer than I expected. At the supermarket, she had seemed dark and intimidating, a towering presence, but I realize now how small she is, light and dancer-like, dwarfed by the grandness of her home. She's dressed in a man's periwinkle button-down shirt, linen trousers, and a pair of orange loafers. She's quite stunning in an unintentional way, and I can only imagine what she must have looked like when she was younger, someone's muse. She appears to be in her mid-50s, but I have a feeling she's older than that. She wears different glasses from the night before—big, red circular frames that make her look like a magazine editor. "I'm always excited to meet new people," she says cheerfully. "Can I offer you some tea?"

"That would be lovely, thank you," I say, not knowing what to do with myself.

"Wonderful, make yourself comfortable," she says, motioning to one of the adjoining rooms, then shuffles off to the kitchen.

I pause, marveling at the loveliness of her home. The rooms have a shimmering quality to them, the sunlight filtering in through wavy cathedral windows, dreamlike, like a library in heaven.

I step into the front room, a parlor, and take a seat on a tufted armchair. The room is home to a panoply of objects and art, stacks of books, exquisitely mismatched furniture. A handsome black grand piano gleams in the light of a bump-out window. And plants, plants everywhere—an improvised conservatory of waxy green leaves, tumbling jades, African violets, and frothy parlor palms.

Clara carries in a wicker tray and sets it down on a coffee table between us—a prim porcelain teapot, two flowered teacups, and a plate of macarons in Easter pastels. She curls herself onto a toffee-colored couch, tucking her legs beneath her. "Have a cookie," she urges. "The tea needs a minute."

I select a pink macaron. Its shape and color make it a morsel of modern art, almost too good to eat. "This cookie is amazing," I mumble through a mouthful.

"I'm glad you like it," Clara says with delight. "I love the colors." She selects a purple one and sits back on the couch. "Well, we know one thing," she smiles. "We both like a bit of late-night grocery shopping."

"Yeah, so—," I say as I sit up, preparing an explanation. "I'm sure that must have seemed a little awkward."

"When is the Big Y not awkward?" Clara says, laughing. "So what was it then?"

"What was…?"

"The—" she flutters her hand. "You know." She regards me, a look of knowing.

"Right, so this might sound a little odd…"

"Odd is good."

"…I felt like I recognized you."

"Did you?" she asks.

"Well, no. I mean, we've never met before. Have we?"

"We may have," she says, taking a bite of her cookie.

"When I say that I saw you…"

"Yes?" she asks. "What was it? That you saw?"

"It's kind of hard to describe. I see things…about people… Where they've been."

"OK."

"Their past lives."

"Really!" She brightens to this, perching forward. She takes up the teapot and pours our tea. "And what did you see in mine?"

I hesitate to answer. She notices.

"Uh-oh!" Clara says with a laugh. "From the look on your face—"

"I saw a pattern," I say.

"A pattern."

"Repeated over and over."

"Is that a bad thing?" she asks.

"For you it was."

She looks at me, through me, knowing something.

"You had a gift," I say.

"Well, that sounds nice," she says. I lean forward, taking up my tea, avoiding her glance. "Or not," she smirks, taking a sip of her own. "Tell me about this gift of yours," she says. "How long have you had it?"

"Since I was young—like nine or 10."

"But there was always something there," she says. "Even before that. Like a whisper in your ear."

A chill runs down my core. "Yes," I say, "something like that."

"But there was a moment when it really came through, wasn't there?" Clara asks. "Something brought it on."

I take another sip of tea, dodging the question. She sets down her cup and saucer, rising from the couch. "Can I show you something?" she asks. She glides across the room to the piano. Lifting the shiny black lid of the piano seat, she extracts a bundle of something swathed in a flowered pillowcase. She slips it off, revealing a long wooden box. She sets the box on the coffee table between us and tilts back the lid. Inside lies a thin, nubby branch, the length of a badminton racket, stripped of its bark and polished a bright honey-gold. "Tell me," she says, "when you looked into my past, did you see something like this?"

I can't believe what I'm looking at—if this is what I think it is. "Did you—make this?" I ask.

"Well, yes, that's how it works," Clara smiles.

"You mean—like a—"

She raises her eyebrows. "Yes?"

"Like a—witch?"

"Aha!" she says brightly.

"But you—I mean, you don't look like a witch."

"Well, thank God for that!" she says, laughing.

"But you are one."

"Are you surprised?" she asks.

"I mean—I've never met…"

"Oh, I'm sure you have." She smiles. "You just didn't realize it. We can be a bit stealthy when we want to be. A thousand years of persecution will do that to you." She closes the lid and tucks the box beside her on the couch. "Anyway, a little show-and-tell between us girls," she says with a wink. "But honestly, I'd much rather hear about you—this fabulous, gifted, young person in front of me! Tell me, what is it like having a window into people's souls?"

"Um, terrible?"

"Ha!" she shrieks. "I love it! Tell me more!"

"It's like TMI, nonstop."

"TMI?" she asks.

"Too much information. Like when someone opens up way too much. There's no small talk with the soul. It's like going from a total stranger to—*wham!*—knowing everything about them. Centuries of baggage. Every way they ever died. Every crime they committed. Every murder. Every fucked-up thing you could imagine."

"And you see all of this at once?" she asks.

"Not all of it. It's like a roulette wheel. You don't know where you're going to land. You move forward and back at the same time. It's insane."

"And how does it work, the seeing?"

"Honestly, I have no idea. But it's like a nonstop panic attack. You have no control."

"So you're watching it? Like a movie?"

"You're not just watching. You're in it. You go through this tunnel, like a storm of light."

"Like a near-death experience," she says.

"Like when people describe having their life flash before their eyes."

"So when you're in these lifetimes, can you touch things?" she asks. "Are they solid? Can people see you?"

"It happens so quick, I don't have much time to interact—not that I'd want to. Sometimes I feel like I'm being seen. Or felt. Like with dogs."

"Dogs can see you?"

"I think so. Anytime I'm in a past life and a dog sees me, it either freaks out or it can't stop sniffing me. The whole thing happens so fast, I have to scramble just to get my bearings and figure out where and when I am. There are clues if you look—sort of coded into the scene. Like a message that's trying to come through."

She sets down her tea. "A message."

"From the person's soul. It's how the soul speaks. It doesn't have a language with words. It speaks in images, in feelings. Like when a medium connects with the other side, it's like she's an antenna. Spirits realize she can pick up their signal, so they're drawn to her. They need her to translate for them. But those are past souls. The ones I experience are here, in a body, now."

"So they're separate, the body and soul?" she asks.

"The body is like…a vessel. It houses the soul. But it's a house with a door. The soul can leave and come back whenever it wants. But it can also get lost, so it leaves a trail. Not a trail, but a cord. A silver thread. Yogis will separate their souls from their bodies when they meditate. They'll walk their soul across the room, out the door, all around town and back again. We can all do it if we want."

"Is a body like a robot?" she asks. "And the soul just animates it?"

"It's more like a portrait. I think our bodies are made in the image of our souls. We might look a little like our parents, but that's just a signature. I think the soul designs the body based on where we've been, what we've done. I think that's what birthmarks are. They're like notes. Things our soul doesn't want to forget—or hasn't let go of."

Clara nods. "Like a scar from a past life. So the body is like a partner to the soul."

"Yes—and the two want to communicate with each other."

"But they can't."

"Not directly. Not consciously. Did you ever read the book *Conversations with God*?" I ask. "The author was this incredibly unlucky guy, this down-and-out writer. His house had burned down. His marriage had broken up. He got in a car accident and broke his neck."

"Oh my god."

"Yeah, he was like, 'You know what, I'm done. Just kill me.' So, anyway, that's when he starts writing these long letters to various people as sort of a coping mechanism, a way to vent. Except he'd never send them. He'd just write the letters and put them in a drawer. Then one day he was like, 'You know what, of all the people I've written letters to, I've never written one to God.' So he does. And guess what happens?"

"God writes back."

"Kind of!"

"Like a pen pal!" Clara says, excited.

"Like a voice in his head. His first letter to God was this list of questions. Why is my life so fucked? What am I doing here? What are any of us doing here? And as soon as he'd write the question down, he'd feel the answer in his head. Like a feeling you can hear. At first, he was like, 'Ummm, what? Like, am I having some kind of split personality episode?' And God was like, 'No, this is actually God answering you.'"

"I love it."

"But of course he didn't believe it."

"Well, come on—would you?" she asks.

"Fuck, no! So God had to keep being like, 'No, you're not crazy. This is God. Like, *God*-God. You're writing me a letter, and I'm answering you.' So they start having this long dialogue about the meaning of life, the universe, how and why everything works the way it does. Like some super-mind-blowing shit. And along the way, God teaches him about the soul—how your soul is actually the real you, the eternal version of you, and it's just inhabiting your body. And before you were in this body, the soul was inhabiting another body. But it's the same soul. It's the same you every time. It's not getting older. It's not learning and becoming more enlightened. It's perfect as is. It always has been, since the moment it was created. When you get a feeling in your gut about something, that's your soul being like, 'Yes, you know this. Trust that you know this.' It wants to talk to you—as a friend. It wants to live through your experiences. It wants to have fun."

"But we don't let it," Clara says.

"No, we don't. Because we're constantly looking for answers outside ourselves, when our soul is trying to give us the answer all along."

"When you look into my eyes…," Clara says.

"Your soul sees me. And it's like, 'Holy shit! You can get a message to my body, to my brain!' And it sucks me in."

She sits back, absorbing this. "That's wonderful," she says, sighing.

"If you say so."

She pauses a moment, considering something. "I'd like to play you something," she says, rising and crossing back to the piano. She takes a seat on the bench and pats the spot beside her, signaling for me to join her. I take a seat, and she opens a piece of sheet music. She begins to play gently, a simple melody that builds in complexity, rising to a lilting crescendo. Then, just like that, it's done. Short and sweet, like a haiku set to music.

"That was beautiful," I say. "What is it?"

She folds the music book closed, revealing the title in gold leaf script: "Clara's Suite."

"My husband, John, wrote it for our wedding," she says, fidgeting, smoothing her hair back with the palm of her hand. "I'd come to Northampton for a professorship. He was teaching economics at UMass. He'd been working for a hedge fund in New York and had a marriage that had fallen apart. He hated who he was becoming. So he left it. We met at a yoga retreat in the Berkshires. I felt that knowing feeling you talked about the moment I saw him. He was handsome, of course, but it wasn't that. I'd watch the way he spoke with the other women, the way he listened, his shoulders square, like he was there, and I just knew. It was funny, I actually felt jealous of the other women who were chatting with him. This prickly wave of bitchiness would come over me just as I was trying to be all Zen. I'm not usually like that. I couldn't care less about competition. But I had to work up the nerve to talk to him. What do you even talk about at a yoga retreat? I didn't want anyone talking to me, so why would he want me talking to him? He was wearing a class ring, and I complimented it in passing. I asked where he'd gone to school. Yale—of course. On a football scholarship—of course. I told him I was probably the least sporty person on Earth, but I found football charming. I liked the pants. He said he was probably the least flexible person on Earth, and that he'd forgive my lack of sportiness if I'd forgive his lack of balance. As it happened, we were staying at the same hotel, so we grabbed dinner that night and things just sort of happened quickly after that. He was the most beautiful, warm human being I'd ever met. He was mannered. You don't see that. You don't know what that is until you've been around it. It sounds so old-fashioned, doesn't it?"

"It sounds wonderful, actually."

"It felt like the sun had shone on me," she says, turning to the light of the window. "I don't know why, but I felt…guilty. Like I didn't deserve him. I would have a moment come over me and I would be like, is this what happiness is? Had I ever known this? I felt like I had stolen something. Something that was never mine. We were married a year from the day we met, in a little church outside Lenox, not far from the yoga retreat. We were older, so we didn't make a big deal about it. We just wanted to be together. John got a job teaching at the Montessori school here in town, and we moved into this house. I never thought of putting down roots in a place like this. I was just a naive girl from Vicksburg, Mississippi," she says, playing up a southern twang. "And here I was in Yankee territory masquerading as an intellectual! But John always made me feel like I belonged here. He was my biggest fan. We'd be at a party and he'd brag about me to everyone. It was horrendous—and lovely. He was proud of me, and that made me proud of myself." She glances at me, smiling. "How un-feminist of me, right? Oh, fuck it. Who cares? It was like I saw myself through his eyes, and for once I didn't hate what I saw."

She looks down at her wrist and fixes her watch, a man's watch.

"Anyway," she continues. "One day he came home and said he wanted to go for a drive. It was a Tuesday, so it seemed kind of strange, especially since he'd been sick. I didn't know why he wanted to go, but we did, and at one point I began to recognize the scenery—the foothills and the farms we loved so much, our old stomping ground. But John was quiet. I asked him if everything was all right and he said, 'Clara, do you remember what I read to you the morning we were married? That I felt like an angel was with us the weekend we met? That he wanted us to be together?' I told him yes, I remembered. And he said, 'Well, he's come back to us again.' But this time he was there to take John away. All through the winter he'd had this sickness he just couldn't shake, a weakness I'd never seen in him. He had tests done without telling me, of course. By then, the cancer had webbed through his body, his liver, his lungs, like dynamite wired into a mountainside. I went nuts. I was furious. I don't know what I was furious at. Just everything. We parked in a turnoff along the river as the sun was going down, and he took my hand and said, 'We're lucky, you know, that we won't have to go through some long terrible end. Some couples aren't so lucky.' The doctor's prediction was right. He was gone two months later."

She rests her fingertips on the keyboard lid, then closes it. "Now this is all I have of him—this house and our things. Sometimes I wish this house would burn to the ground. Sometimes I stay in here for days. I thought it was just me missing him. But it feels like something else."

"Your soul misses him," I say.

"Yes, my soulmate!" she blurts, pretending to brush it off. "That must be it."

"Can I ask you a question?"

"Anything," she says, turning to me, wiping her eye.

"How do you do it?"

"How do I do what?" she asks.

"Be—a witch?"

"Ha!" she cries, breaking the spell.

"I mean, do people…know?" I ask.

"Well, to begin with, I don't really think of myself as a witch," she says, moving back to the couch, getting comfortable again. "I'm not ashamed of what I am, but I don't relate to it the way you might think. It's just what I do. Teaching is part of me, but it's not who I am. I know why I'm here. Some people have their art. Some have their writing. I have my thing, whatever you want to call it. I guess you could say I'm like a consultant."

"So you just, like, get jobs as a witch?"

"Well, yes," she laughs. "I have clients."

"People just know what you are, and they're like, 'You know what? I could really use a witch right now.'"

"You'd be surprised," she says with a chuckle. "Everyone has their own name for it. Some people need a guru. Some need a guide. Some people just need a friend to talk to. And some need—"

"A straight-up witch."

"A straight-up witch," she says, nodding. "For instance, one of my clients is the town of Cornwall, Connecticut. Have you heard of Dudleytown? You should look it up. It's quite a story. The way it goes, there was an English nobleman in the 1700s, Edmund Dudley. He was beheaded for treason. Some pretty powerful people had it in for Dudley, it seemed, because cutting off his head just wasn't enough. Apparently, a curse was placed on the entire family—and it followed them when they fled to America. The Dudley clan settled in western Connecticut, and they built a town in their family's name. It wasn't long before the drama began. People started to lose their minds, seemingly out of nowhere. They'd commit suicide, just completely unravel. The sick would talk about the demons they saw from their windows walking the streets just before they died. To this day, people report weird things out there. Orbs of light swishing through the trees. And a silence—like an emptiness. No animals or chirping birds or insects. Just a blankness. Eventually, the neighboring township of Cornwall expanded its borders, engulfing what remained of Dudleytown, but it never officially brought it into the fold. Everyone knew the stories, and no one wanted to touch it. So they let the town die off on its own until there was no one left. Instead of maintaining the one road that leads in and out of Dudleytown, they let the forest take it back. If you look at a map of Cornwall now, you'll see an empty spot in the western corner where all the roads seem to end. There, under the vines and thickets, you'll find Dudleytown's crumbled remains. It's a bit of a mecca for curiosity seekers. The police had to put up road barriers and NO TRESPASSING signs, but it didn't stop anyone. People still get arrested going up there. A few months ago, the town of Cornwall put in a bid for the new Hartford Hospital expansion, and it had to show that it had enough property to develop it. And there was Dudleytown, just sitting under the brush. One of the councilwomen is a client of mine, and she put my name forward as someone who could help 'clean up' the area. And amazingly, they went for it. It's funny, when it comes to stuff like that, people just want it gone. It's like calling a plumber. You don't want to know what's in the pipes. You just want it out."

"So what did you do?"

"I'm still figuring it out, to be honest. It's a process—listening, walking in the woods."

"By yourself?"

"I usually have a couple of state troopers with me, but they mostly hang back by the road."

"Yeah, I bet they do!" I blurt.

"Whatever it is, it knows I'm there. I've never felt anything like it. It's like something's watching. It's not your normal curse. There's something else going on. It has the fingerprints of black magic. Amateur sorcery."

"How do you mean?"

"Something about it just feels off," she says. "Not just evil, but wild—predatory. It feels like someone was messing with something they didn't understand. You have to realize something about the craft—at its core, it's a science, even if we don't fully understand it. All of these things—sorcery, alchemy, quantum physics—they're all just different doors into the same room. I don't care if you're a scientist or a psychic, we're all trying out the same set of keys on the same lock. Now, if you're smart, you don't pull out those keys without being careful. But there are a lot of stupid people out there with the wrong motives. You've heard of Aleister Crowley, I'm sure. He was one of the most famous black magicians of all time. He had ties to some very powerful people. It's said that he taught Winston Churchill the victory sign." She makes a V with her fingers. "It was supposed to counteract the power of the swastika. Do you know Jack Parsons? The rocket engineer? The one who helped send us to the moon? He had a deep fascination with the occult. He was close with Crowley—he converted to his religious movement after the war. There are tons of stories about Parsons working with black magic. I wonder if he opened a door without even realizing it."

"A door to what?"

"Good question," she says, pausing as she thinks for a moment. "Imagine this: You're standing in a beautiful field in the countryside. It's a warm summer day. The sky is perfect and blue, the sun shining down. Now imagine, as you're standing there, you have a razor blade pinched between your fingers, and in one swift stroke you slice the air in front of you, leaving a black slit, a tear in the fabric of the sky. Now, with two hands you pull the edges apart like a mouth, and you peek through, and there, on the other side, you see the same field, the same hillside, but it's night. But how can that be? How can it be day and night at once? These are the questions that reveal themselves when you play with magic. Riddles wrapped in riddles, mirrors reflecting mirrors. A good magician will mend that tear before she leaves. But what if you were blind to your own magic and didn't realize what you had done? And then, what if something on the other side, the night side, happened upon that same field and saw a thin blue line hovering in the air and decided to come have a look? What have you just let in?"

"You think he let something in?"

Clara takes up the teapot, topping up our tea cups. "There are a lot of strange coincidences around that time," she says with a sniff, "and I'm not a big believer in coincidences. You know about Roswell, the famous UFO crash in New Mexico. I wonder if it was somehow connected to Parsons and what he was playing around with. There was a lot going on then. We were coming out of the most devastating war in history. We'd perfected the atom bomb. I think we were being watched—by something."

"OK, so wait," I say. "I'm trying to process this."

"Which part?"

"Well, the UFO part, for starters."

"You don't believe in UFOs?" she asks.

"I guess I've never really thought about it."

"Interesting," she says, squinting. "In all the years you've had this gift, you've never run into an alien?"

"Um, not that I know of."

"I suppose they have their ways of concealing themselves," she says with a shrug. "Even to eyes like yours."

"Like, we're talking *alien*-aliens?"

"Right. Not the Grays per se, although they're around," she says. "Mostly the Nordics. You wouldn't be able to pick them out if you saw them on the street. They're tall and blond. They look just like us, only more beautiful."

"Blond aliens."

"Yes!" She laughs. "It's ridiculous, but yes, blond aliens. You'd think they were Swedish supermodels."

"And you've seen them?"

"I've seen two, actually—together."

"Like, boyfriend and girlfriend?"

"I don't know what they were," she says. "I didn't talk to them."

"I'm sorry, but what—where was this?"

"Santa Barbara."

"Right. Of course."

Clara sips her tea. "I was there visiting my friend Louise. She's a clairvoyant. These aliens lived near her. They had a farm. Apparently, the man was teaching at the university."

"As a professor?"

"Exactly."

"What did he teach?"

"I have no idea. But if anyone would know an alien when she saw one, it would be Louise."

"Is there, like, a giveaway?"

"A giveaway?" she asks.

"Do they have an accent?"

"That's a good question," Clara says. "Can you imagine? 'Pardon me, do I detect an accent?'"

"This is crazy."

"It is crazy!" she says with delight. "There's another theory about them—that they aren't aliens in the way we usually think of them. Have you ever heard of the Watchers? From the Book of Enoch? Their story comes from the ancient texts, from before the time of Christ. They tell of a legion of angels that God placed on Earth to watch over the early humans. These angels eventually turned on God, giving forbidden knowledge to the humans, which led to our loss of innocence. The Watchers were said to have taken human wives and spawned a race of half-mortal, half-divine beings, the Nephilim. They're described as abominations—giants that wreaked havoc on mankind. But other texts associate the Nephilim with the heroes of ancient myths. Achilles, the Greek warrior, for instance—he was said to be the offspring of a king and a sea nymph, Thetis, who was herself a descendant of the gods."

"So what you're saying is, these aliens aren't really aliens—"

"Yes, go on."

"—but are actually…angels?"

Clara nods. "Or vice versa," she says. "I'm sure you'll come across one sooner or later."

"I don't want to come across one!" I cry, half-joking. "It's bad enough dealing with people. You have no idea."

"Tell me then," she says, selecting another macaron and taking a bite.

"People call this thing I have a gift," I tell her. "They don't know what they're talking about. It's a fucking curse. It disrupts your entire life. I can't just have a normal day like everyone else. I can't just go to a coffee shop. Everyone, every set of eyes, they're like open books. Everyone's *stuff*. It's just all out there. I have to shut it out."

"And you can do that?" Clara asks. "You can shut it out?"

"I can try. I have tricks that I use. But it's exhausting. It's like my brain is constantly working just to shut things out."

"Tell me one," she says.

"Of my tricks? Well, there's the one my friend Leslie taught me."

"She sees like you?"

"No, it's different. She sees ghosts—ever since she was a baby. When she was little, she couldn't tell the difference between the living and the dead. It wasn't until she started telling the kids at school about the people she saw—the kids in the classroom that no one else could see. It freaked people out."

"I'm sure it did!"

"So that's when she knew there was something different about her. She wanted to have friends and be normal, so she kept it a secret after that."

"And she's here at school with you?" Clara asks.

"We met in art history class. The first day, our professor was doing a slide presentation, testing us to see what we knew. He came to the painting *Joan of Arc* by Jules Bastien-Lepage. It's my favorite painting of all time. It hangs in the Met. I used to spend hours looking at it as a child. Joan's face—it's lifelike. These big, sparkling blue eyes. She looks like she's about to cry. And the saints hovering over her shoulder. Our professor said the painting was panned by critics. They thought that the saints made it feel too much like a fantasy—that they took away from the composition. But I disagreed. I spoke up. I said no, the saints *were* the painting. They're the secret only she can hear. That's the look in her eyes. That feeling. Of being suddenly alone. Because you can see and hear what no one else can. Leslie came up to me after class and asked how I knew that about the painting, and I said I knew how Joan felt. She asked if I ever saw things no one else could see. And for once I didn't hide it. I said yes, all the time. And she grabbed me by the hand and said, 'We're sisters now.' I'd never had a sister before."

"Well," Clara says, leaning across the table to squeeze my hand, "I guess you have two now."

7 | WORLDS COLLIDE

I wake on the couch, the room gently warmed by sunlight beaming in through the window, the leaves of the fig tree casting soft shadows across the floor. I reach for my phone and check the time. *Shit! Fuck!* I leap up and whip on a pair of jeans, tuck in a T-shirt, and shuffle into a pair of moccasins. I dart into the bathroom to brush my teeth, typing out a text as I sit on the toilet. *Running 10 min late sorry!* I check my face in the mirror and pull my hair back in a bun. A reply buzzes back: *No prob getting us a table.*

Jemma waves to me through the front window of Union Square Cafe. As I arrive at the table, she jumps up and pulls me in for a giant hug. She smells incredible as always, a sort of peach-fuzzy sweetness mixed with cardamom. She's wearing a hot pink silk blouse, a blaze of color that sets off her shiny black mane and her big, beautiful Indian eyes. "Cute outfit!" she says, beaming. She takes a seat across from me. "So, what's going on?" She scooches in. "I haven't seen you in…wait, have we not seen each other since the Prada launch?" She drops her voice to a whisper. "Did I tell you that I hooked up with the bartender? The one that looked like a dirty camp counselor? Oh my god, Cat, please, whatever you do, *do not* date an actor. It's like one step away from homelessness." She scans the menu. "I'm thinking we do something sweet and something savory and we share…wait." She pauses, switching gears. "Have you seen Jake? Is he back from his assignment?"

"I'm not sure," I sigh, feigning a lack of interest.

"You're not sure of what?"

"I'm not sure where he is. I told you. We're just—"

"Friends. Right. But the way you're 'just friends' makes me think I need some better fucking friends—like, stat. Doesn't he have some hot photographer buddies you could hook me up with? You need to get on that. By the way, before I forget, we have a mission today. I need to buy sneakers for my spin class."

"You're taking a spin class?"

"Oh my God, Cat, you of all people need to try it. You don't have to think. You just get on a bike and haul ass."

The waiter arrives and takes our orders and sweeps the menus away. Jemma leans in, squeezing my hand. "So what's been going on? I love you, by the way. I just want to say that right now, because it's Saturday, and I'm having brunch with my favorite lady, and I'm full of love."

"I love you, too!" I laugh.

"OK, so what's the deal then?" she asks. "'Cause I'm sensing something."

"It's nothing," I say. "Really. It was my dad's birthday yesterday…"

"Oh, sweetie." She squeezes my hand again. "Are you OK?"

"I'm fine, really. I just feel like…I don't know. Maybe I didn't actually know him. Either of them."

"What do you mean, you didn't know them?"

"I was super young, Jem. How could I have possibly *known* who either of them were?"

"But you were so close," she says. "How could you not—"

"I just feel like there was…something." I look at the people passing on the street outside. "Isn't it kind of weird that I still have all their stuff?"

"I mean, it's not like you have *all* their stuff," Jemma replies.

"Jem, I have an entire storage unit in New Jersey full of their shit. I feel like one of those hoarder ladies with a hundred cats and piss jars stacked in the corner."

"Cat, it's not like that, and you know it. It's just some things to remember them by."

"I went out there the other day. I was looking through my dad's stuff and I found something. It was strange."

"Strange how?" she asks. "Like what?"

"I don't know. Files. For these projects he was working on. Like, classified military shit."

"Seriously?" She glances at the table beside us, leaning in to whisper. "Like some *X-Files* shit? Like, what are we…?"

"I have no idea. Some kind of project. Everything's marked top secret."

"Get the fuck…"

"Seriously."

"Your *dad*? He was into some spy shit?"

"Of course not. I mean, I can't imagine him having anything to do with the military. I mean, seriously, how do you teach at Princeton, run a laboratory, *and* have some top secret side hustle?"

"Maybe they're not his?" she offers.

"His name is all over them. His notes, his handwriting."

"So what are you doing with them?"

"I don't know. Right now, I'm just poking around."

"Poking around for what?" she asks.

"I don't know. I'm just looking into it."

"OK, but what is there to look into?" she asks, seeming more concerned.

"I don't know, Jemma. I'm just curious. Wouldn't you be?"

"No, I get it," she says. "I'm just thinking, maybe you need to be careful."

"Be careful of what?"

"Sometimes you get swept up in other people's stuff."

"Jemma, this is my dad we're talking about. Not some stranger I'm bumping into on the street."

"I know," she says. "I'm just…"

"Do you think I like being sucked into other people's lives? Maybe I should focus on myself for once—my own family. Is that wrong?"

"No, it's not wrong. And yes, you should look out for yourself," she says. "But whatever you want to call it, this is still about you getting pulled into somebody else's life. Even if it is your dad's. You get sucked in, Cat. You *know* what happens. What was the last conversation we had? About the time traveler at the grocery store who's all up in your shit now? Because he feels like you're the only person he can talk to? You open yourself up to these situations, Cat. They draw you in, and then it starts breaking you down."

"Jemma, don't you get it? These people don't have anyone else to talk to. I see the things they keep locked away. You think this guy goes to a party and just strikes up a conversation about how he's a time traveler? Put yourself in his shoes for a second. You're some awkward 13-year-old kid, and your dad asks if you want to be part of a military experiment. Just that alone is completely fucked up. But it's the '70s, and you're 13, and it sounds cool, right? Like a comic book. So, fuck yeah. The next thing you know, you're walking through some rickety-ass stargate in a warehouse in New Jersey, and when you walk out the other side, you're standing in a cabbage field at night. *Wait, what?* So you turn around to look for the portal they said would be there ("Just walk right back through!"), but there is no portal. And you're like, 'Um, hello? Where the fuck is the portal? Can we open the fucking portal, please?' But the portal doesn't open. There is no portal. It's just a quiet summer night on a farm in New Jersey. And here you are. So what do you do now? Where do you go? You don't go anywhere, because you're scared shitless. You sleep there, in the field, for two days, just praying the portal reappears. But then you realize it's not happening. This is it. Welcome to the '90s. Have fun re-creating a life for yourself as a lost 13-year-old time traveler. Where do you even begin?"

Jemma processes this. "I'm just trying to imagine what it would have been like to have missed the '80s."

"It would have been fucking terrible," I reply.

"*Who's the Boss?*"

"*Charles in Charge?*"

"The '80s is, like, half the music on my iPod," Jemma says.

"This guy basically went directly from the Bee Gees to the Backstreet Boys."

Jemma looks aghast. "That's like a sandwich with no meat. And now he runs a bodega?"

"A greengrocer. He's got this whole setup. It's like some kind of witness protection program for time travelers. I can't follow half of what he tells me."

"The produce guy," she clarifies.

"The fucking produce guy."

"And you saw all this when you looked into his eyes?"

"That's the thing," I explain. "I didn't see anything. When I fell into him, there was a missing chunk of time. Like a library shelf with no books. I'd never experienced that before, and I needed to know."

"So you were like, 'Hey, listen, I just took a quick spin through your past, and it seems to be missing a decade.'"

"Basically."

"I love you," she says. "OK, and so he was just like, 'Funny you should mention it!'"

"That's just it—these people are dying to talk to someone. Can you imagine? Having a secret like that bottled up inside you?"

"And now he can't leave you alone."

"Jemma, honestly, he just wants to talk."

"Yeah, I'm sure he does. Is he cute?"

"OK, can we just—"

"I'm just asking," she presses. "*Is he hot?* Is he a hot time traveler? 'Cause that makes a difference."

"You know what, when someone is dealing with something that's on the same fucked-up level you are, it's like looking at your cousin."

"Do you have a photo of him?"

"Why would I have a photo of him?"

"I don't know. Describe him to me, then. Is he all '70s-ed out? Does he have a mustache?

"Yes, Jemma, he looks like Oates from Hall & Oates."

"Seriously?"

"Jemma, he looks like any guy from *this* decade. He's trying to blend in! It's not like he's wearing a brown leather trench coat and driving a Trans Am."

She considers this. "I need to meet this dude."

"That's not happening."

"Why not?"

"Jemma, you know why. Worlds collide."

"Please, you're talking about a time traveler and a psychic. Those worlds already collided. You need to hook a sister up." She plucks a blueberry muffin from the basket and cuts it in half. "Anyway, getting back to your dad and this top secret shit. Do you think your mom knew about it?"

This catches me off guard. "I mean…I can't imagine he would keep something like that from her."

"Didn't your mom work for the government?" she asks.

"She worked at Bell Labs as an engineer. I never really knew what she did. I just remember she always looked good. She'd wear these tailored suits, heels."

"Love it."

"The way people used to dress back then…"

"Oh my God," Jemma sighs. "The women were like, 'Fuck you. Pencil skirt. Heels. This is engineering, bitch.'"

"My mother was kind of a…mystery. She definitely wasn't like the other moms. She wasn't—I don't know… She was present. She looked right at you. She was like the cool, sophisticated friend you thought you'd have when you were older. I was always performing for her—anything to get her attention. And her laugh. Smart people have a different laugh. They laugh at things you didn't know were funny. I loved it when I made her laugh, the way her face would light up. Every mother loves her daughter, but it was something else with her. She *liked* me. I was different from her, and she liked that."

"Have you ever looked her up?" Jemma asks.

"Looked her up?"

"Have. You. Looked. Her. Up. On. The. Internet?" Jemma asks, emphasizing the obvious. "Maybe it would make you feel better," she says with a shrug. "Just to see her name. Like, proof she was real."

For everything I love about Jemma, this might be the ultimate—the way she can pull me back to Earth. I took to her the moment we met at our first job as junior editors at *Harper's Bazaar*. We were hired the same day—both fresh out of college, at the very bottom of the corporate ladder, and perpetually broke. We bonded over our mutual plight and tag-teamed any free event we could sneak ourselves into. The senior editors would throw us invitations for anything they didn't want to go to themselves: store openings, FIT runway shows, accessory conventions at the Javits Center. Anything that involved a cheese table and wine in plastic cups, we were there.

I'd never had a friend like Jemma, someone who was always up for whatever. Leslie was a soul sister, and the other girls at school were smart and funny and would always include me, but I always had the feeling they saw me as a loner. Jemma was my first girl's girl. She liked men, even dumb men. And parties. And sample sales. And spending an hour to achieve the perfect smoky eye. She liked being bought drinks by guys with expense accounts, and she taught me how to work my "feminine wiles." She had a thing she called her "responsibility switch," which she would turn off whenever she wanted to be totally uninhibited, which usually amounted to nothing more than an innocent groping session in the back of a packed bar, or making poor choices at a corporate Christmas party.

Jemma was a warrior in the majority of her past lives—a personal guard to Ghengis Khan, a samurai, an Afrikaner officer killed in the Boer War, and a kamikaze pilot who perished in the Battle of Okinawa. She had been men almost every time, although she had once been the Rani of Jhansi, an Indian princess known for her beauty and ferocity on the battlefield— a life Jemma takes particular pride in.

Jemma wasn't puzzled by how often she had been a man in her past lives. "I'm surprised I'm not into eating vag this time around," she mused one day over lunch. When I described my "gift," what it was like when I looked people in the eyes, she was completely unfazed. "My family is mystical as fuck," she kidded. "Believe me, this is nothing."

She once asked if I saw people naked when I looked back in time. "Honestly," I said, "most people wouldn't want to know what they looked like."

"Some *big* bushes back then."

"Insane bushes."

"I probably looked pretty good, though," she mused. "Being a warrior and all. I bet I was jacked as fuck. Wait, though, how does this whole thing work? You look into my eyes and you see all these other *mes*? Like a lineup?"

"It's like I see them in their own time," I told her. "Like a book of chapters. It's like the story of your soul. When I look at someone, I don't just see the color of their eyes, I see behind it, a light that's been there since their soul first came into existence. It has its own signature, almost like a Dewey Decimal number. When I go through your past, it's not just *your* past, I'm going back through history. But I'm receiving, like, pings from your lifetimes. It's hard to describe, because it doesn't work like you think it does."

"What doesn't?" she asked.

"Time. Everything we ever did, everything we're doing now, and everything that's yet to come. It's like everything is happening at once. All at the same time. Past, present, and future."

"So, wait." She stopped me. "You can see the future?"

"If I wanted to, yes. But I don't."

"*Well, why the fuck not?* If it was me, I'd be playing the lottery every day."

"Because it doesn't work like that," I explained. "If you see one future, it doesn't mean it's going to be the future you'll end up in. The moment you see a possible future, you start making decisions that lead you away from it. It's like a catch-22. A single thought can throw you off course. The future that actually happens might be close to the one you saw, but it's actually entirely different. The future doesn't go in one direction. It fans out in front of us in an infinite number of possibilities, and each of those futures is real. They all exist at the same time."

"So in one future I'm rich as fuck."

"And in another future—"

"I work at the Gap." She sat back in the booth, processing this. "You have to be the only psychic in the world that only looks backward," she scoffed. "It's like you're dyslexic or something. When you go back in time, can you touch things and pick things up and change stuff?"

"No, I'm just observing," I told her. "It's as if it's happening right here, right now."

"That's gotta be trippy."

"Honestly, it's like a never-ending panic attack."

"And there's nothing you can do to stop it?" she asked.

"I have tricks I use to make it through the day," I explained, "but there's really only one way to stop it, at least for a little while."

"And that's—?"

"Climaxing."

She lit up with surprise. "Wait, like having an orgasm?"

I nodded. "It shuts everything down somehow. Like, I go into this…I don't know what to call it. Like a white space. A nothingness."

"Are we talking masturbation? Or does it have to be *sex*-sex?" she asked. "Like, with someone?"

"Either way, but it's better with someone."

"Yeah, tell me about it," she said with a snort. "So are you just having sex all the time, or—?"

"I try to."

"Oh. Well. Shit. OK," she said, grinning. "I like to think that I do too, but something tells me you've got me beat. Like, what are we talking here?"

"Too many to count."

"Alrighty then!" she laughed.

"And not all guys."

"Oh, now we're talking!" she sat up, delighted. "So, like, what are we looking at, ratio-wise, men to women—80:20?"

"More like 40:60."

"Wow… Is that because it's more effective with a woman?"

"It can be good either way. It just depends on the person."

"So wait, I'm just taking this in for a second," she said. "Do you ever have a guy going down on you, and he's just not getting it done, and you're like, 'Motherfucker, you need to concentrate! I'm trying to get to my white space!'"

"Actually, it's the opposite. I have to get them off first."

"Really?"

"It's hard to describe. It's like…there's a door. At the top of the stairs. And I have to lead them up to it. I have to let them in. And then I can follow."

"They're in your white space with you?"

"It's not just mine," I said. "It's all of ours. I think it's where we began."

She processed this for a moment. "OK. So straight up, I need to start having more sex. Like, immediately."

After wrapping up at the cafe, we head into the Saturday-afternoon fray of Union Square, weaving through the massive crowd at the farmers market. Jemma ducks into the vestibule of Paragon Sports, a department store packed with tourists loading up on end-of-season deals. Jemma takes my hand, swerving us through the racks, down the escalator to the sneaker department, a fluorescent-lit dungeon of manic shoppers. I can feel my throat closing up, like there's nowhere to run. I try to focus on something, anything, the infinite wall of sneakers. I let my eyes go blurry until all I can see is a grid of hazy colors.

"Can I help you?" a voice asks, out of nowhere. I snap back into focus, meeting the eyes of a salesperson, a light-skinned Black kid wearing a teal polo shirt with the store's logo on the chest. A burst of white light fires out of the black disc of his pupil, and I clench my eyes shut, holding my hand to my forehead to block his gaze. "Sorry," I say, trying to duck away.

"No problem, are you OK?" he asks, seeming genuinely concerned.

"I'm fine, thanks," I say, looking for Jemma, the closest exit.

"It's kind of overwhelming, right?"

"Overwhelming?" I say, trying to avoid eye contact.

"Sneaker shopping. It's like trying on jeans. I get it. I'll tell you what—point at the sneakers you hate the most." We turn to the wall of shoes, and as though in a trance I feel my arm lift and my finger point at a pair of pink-and-purple cross-trainers that look like they're made of volleyball material.

"Yeah, I feel you!" he says with a laugh. "So now tell me why you hate them."

"They're pink…and purple…and chunky."

He chuckles. "Totally. I don't know what they were thinking with these. So let me ask you this: What's the opposite of chunky, pink, and purple? I think I know." Gently, he guides me by the elbow further down the display wall—to a charcoal-gray running shoe.

"Look at these skinny little bitches," he says, holding up the shoe. "You can do anything in these. Yoga class. Jump on the treadmill. You could even wear them with jeans and they'd look cute." He hands me the shoe and I turn it over and over, mesmerized, as if marveling at a holy object. The sneaker is sharp and beautiful and light as air. "You might be the greatest salesperson I've ever met," I mutter.

"Oh my God, thank you!" he gushes. "The universe meant for us to meet, I guess!"

"Because I pretty much hate sneakers," I say.

"No lie?" He looks around, dropping his voice. "So do I. But I feel bad for them."

"For sneakers?"

"Totally. No one gives them the love they deserve. You just beat them up and throw them away. They live in your closet next to your Pradas. They're just like, 'Kill me, please.'"

"They hate themselves."

"They do," he nods. "Unless you're one of those sneakerhead guys who owns like 100 pairs."

"Which isn't healthy, either."

"Yeah, that's just crazy. It's like the sneaker version of a cult."

"Sorry, but what are you doing working at Paragon?" I ask.

"Why?" He perks up. "Do you have something better? Do tell!"

"I don't know—I might."

"Seriously?" He does a quick glance over my shoulder, then takes me by the hand, tugging me behind a rack of track pants, ducking down a little. "What do you do?" he asks.

"I work in fashion."

"Thank fucking God."

"I'm sure I have a client that could use a good salesperson."

"Are you an angel? You are, aren't you? I'm Randy, by the way," he says, shaking my hand. He pulls a business card out of his pocket and writes his number on the back. "*Please, please, please* save me from this place!"

Jemma saunters over, sporting a pair of bright yellow running shoes. "Hi, sorry, what do you think of these?" she asks.

"Are they too yellow?" She judges herself in a full-length mirror. Randy steps beside her, taking in the look. "They make you look confident," he says.

Jemma considers this. "But sometimes confident is just a shade of crazy," she replies.

"True, but I think they look cute," Randy says.

Jemma turns to him. "You know the girls walking home from the gym who look like they just don't give a fuck—but also look super cute? That's what I'm going for."

"Then you nailed it," Randy says with a nod.

"OK. Done."

"See that?" I say. "Best salesperson ever."

"Oh my God, I love you both!" Randy gushes, pulling us in for a group hug.

As we get in line to pay, a text buzzes in from Jake:

An ocean can't keep me away from you

The words rush to my head—a swirl of dizziness. I brush it off, dropping my phone in my purse, then pull it out again to look. I'm not answering right back. Because fuck him. Fuck him for making me feel dizzy. I look at the text again. *Fuck.* I text him back:

You sound like an '80s song

Where r u

Where r u?

Greg's place

Be at mine in 2 hrs

He sends a thumbs-up emoji.

I nudge Jemma as we step outside, showing her the phone. "Ah, there we go!" she says, beaming. "So, I guess that's a wrap!"

"Is that OK?" I ask. "I'm sorry."

"Are you kidding? I'm living vicariously through you. Be free, little one! Be free!"

I give her a hug as she flags a cab. "Are you alright?" she asks. "I feel like we didn't finish talking about your dad."

"I'll call you later," I tell her.

"Perfect," she says, tossing her shopping bag into the taxi, slipping in beside it. "By the way," she says, "let me know the next time you go to Jersey. I need to hit Ikea and I know you love that shit." She blows me a kiss as the cab pulls away, and I take out my phone and look at the texts. *Fuck you,* I think—and smile.

8 | HEAD OF A LION

I rush around the apartment tidying up, without making it too tidy. I plug my phone into the stereo and put on my hip-hop mix as the buzzer rings.

"Hello?"

A voice crackles back on the other end. "Two Boots!"

I push to answer. "Two Boots doesn't deliver."

There's a pause, then another buzz.

"Hello?"

"Ray's Pizza!"

I buzz him in and leave the door unlatched, and hurry into the bathroom. I turn on the shower, strip down, and get in. I hear the door close in the vestibule, then boot steps, then the bathroom door creaking open. "Did somebody order a pizza?" Jake announces into a cloud of steam.

"I hope you got the order right," I reply.

"Hawaiian, right?"

I pull back the curtain and stick my wet head out. "Um, hi, you can't just walk in here."

God. How? How does he look better every time I see him? Has he been working out? He knows I hate beards, but fine, whatever—the scruffy world traveler look. He smiles his goofy grin and strips off his T-shirt, kicks off his boots.

"You're not coming in here," I tell him.

"I need to shower," he says, stepping out of his jeans.

"Well, you should have thought of that."

He pulls down his boxer briefs and a giant erection springs out. "Jesus!" I laugh. "Be careful with that thing!"

He pulls back the curtain and steps in, looking me up and down. "Wow," he says, grinning.

"Please." I turn into the spray, ignoring him. I can feel him studying me.

"Have you been working out?" he asks, moving up behind me, kissing my shoulder.

"Um, no?"

"Well, keep *not*-working out or whatever it is you're doin'," he mumbles, sliding his hands up around my hips. He turns me to him, his hard cock pressing up against my stomach.

"Wow, it feels like there's three people in here!" I say with a laugh.

The steam amplifies his scent. *How does he smell this good? Just by sweating?* Like warm leather and coconut. It sends waves up through me, my stomach, my neck, my jaw. His lips press into mine and I press back. I want to push all of me into him. He grips me. My legs scissor up around his waist. He braces a hand against the tile wall, slides the other under my ass. His fingers find me, sending bolts up my core. He sets me down and kisses my neck, my collarbone, my breasts, down the length of my stomach, the water cascading over his head. I scrape my nails over his skull, pulling him to me. He puts his mouth on me, his tongue, his jaw. He turns me around, and I brace against the wall as he pulls me to him, his mouth, his big hands gripping my thighs, making me feel small, overpowered. He takes my wrist, puts his hand over mine, bringing it between my legs, feeling me touch myself as he consumes me. My knees shaking, bucking back against his mouth, until I'm just holding myself there, right there, and he's holding me still, and then a torrent rushing up through my core, up the tunnel of my throat, my mouth open, thighs shaking against his face. I begin to crumble, and he rests me down in the tub, a wrecked pile of bones. He brings his hand up behind my head, gripping the wet knot of my hair, and I reach up to him, bringing him to my mouth, cupping his tightness, coaxing him, slowly, bringing him there. He says he's going to come, and I feel him expand in my mouth. He pulls back, taking himself in his hand, pumping over my lips, across my face, my jaw, my neck. He pulls me up to him, kissing me hard. I push him away. "Hand me the soap," I say.

"Hand me your razor."

"You're not using my razor," I say, soaping up.

"Come on."

"Reach in the cabinet and get your own."

"You're not gonna let me use your pussy razor?"

"Get the fuck out."

He reaches through the curtain and pulls his razor out of the cabinet and starts shaving his beard—no shaving cream, no mirror—like some burly gold miner. I turn into the spray. "When did you get in?" I ask.

"Yesterday. I crashed at Greg's."

I turn to him, watching him shave. "You must be jet-lagged."

"Do I seem jet-lagged?" He grins.

"You seem all right."

"Yeah? Just all right?" He slaps my ass.

"Fuck off."

"Look at that ass," he says, gripping my butt cheek.

"So how long are you back for?"

"I'm not sure yet," he says. "There's something going down on Wall Street. Some kind of protest."

"Where did you fly from?"

"London. I stayed at Jeff's for a couple of nights. Before that, Paris—by way of Corsica—by way of Tripoli."

I turn to him. "You were in Libya? I thought you said—"

"I know, but what am I supposed to do?" he says, rinsing off the razor. "My clients want to see the aftermath, what everyone's doing now that Gaddafi's out. By the way, did you watch the movie I sent you?"

I ignore him.

"It was good, right?" he presses.

"Is that what you want?" I ask.

"Is *what* what I want?"

I turn away, rinsing off. "Is that what you want for yourself?"

"I want to tell stories that matter, if that's what you mean."

I pull back the curtain and step out. "Look, I respect that Tim was your friend," I say, drying off, "and yes, the movie was fine, but you don't want to end up like that."

"I realize that," he mumbles.

"I'm serious, Jake."

"I'm serious too," he says, pulling the shower curtain aside. "And you *seriously* don't have to worry, 'cause I'm here now, right?" He pulls me in for a kiss. "Right?"

"Are you hungry?" I ask.

"When am I not?" He smiles.

I wrap my body in one towel and my hair in another and walk out to the kitchen.

"I missed you," Jake mutters, mostly to himself, as he towels off. He doesn't know that I heard him or that I smiled, or maybe he does. He saunters into the kitchen wrapped in a towel and nuzzles up behind me as I look through the fridge. He kisses my shoulder, sliding his hand through the fold of my towel. "Do you know how much I thought about you?" he mumbles. "Did you use your superpowers to read my mind while I was away?"

"It doesn't work that way. You know that," I say, shrugging him off.

"It would have been pretty vivid if you did," he says.

"I'm sure."

"Did you think about me?" he asks.

"No, I didn't, actually."

"Not even a little?"

I pull a bowl of Moroccan couscous out of the fridge and hand it to him with a fork. He gives me an "I'm waiting" look as he eats.

"Don't be an idiot," I say. "Of course I thought about you."

He mumbles through a mouthful. "What did you think about?"

"Other than you getting shot? Or beheaded?"

"Other than that."

I pull a bottle of white wine from the fridge and pour two glasses. "I wondered what the morning smelled like where you were."

He sets down the bowl, pulling me to him, nuzzling my neck. "Not as good as this," he says. "I gotta say, your thoughts were way more G-rated than mine."

"I'm sure," I say, pushing him away.

"You know what I mean," he smiles. *Those dimples.*

"No," I say. "Actually, I don't."

"Come on," he nudges.

"You come on."

"You want to know what I thought about?" he asks.

"Other than us fucking? Yes. If you'd like to tell me."

"OK," he says, turning me to him, looking for my eyes. "I thought about the day we met. Remember that?"

I'm suddenly starving. I steal the bowl from him. "Of course I remember."

"At Sunday Best," he says. "Watching you dance under the tiki lights. And me trying to get the stones up to talk to you. I bet you can't remember what you were wearing."

I think about it. "The bird dress."

He makes a buzzer sound. "*ERRRNH!*"

"No?"

"*ERRRNH!*"

"OK, so what was I wearing?"

"A black wifebeater."

"A *wifebeater*?"

"And green shorts."

"Ah, right," I recall. "My 'don't fuck with me' outfit."

"Guys were trying to dance up to you, but you weren't havin' it," he says, grinning.

"I like to dance alone."

"I know you do."

"So then what happened?"

"Then you came up to me and asked for a light," he says.

"I saw you checking me out—that's what happened."

"Yeah? You saw me?" He prods.

"I saw you. I thought *you* thought you were cute."

"Give me a break," he says with a laugh. "You were the one who was too cool for school. You had this giant blunt. I'd never seen a blunt that big. It was, like, a cartoon blunt."

"That's right! Jemma used to roll them before we'd go out. OK, so what happened next?"

"You asked if I had a light. I said I did, if you wanted to share."

"And did I?"

"You did," he smiles.

"Well, that's rare. So then what?"

"Then we just leaned up on the building and watched people dance and got a little high."

"*ERRRNH!*" I buzz. "As I recall, we got *super*-high."

"We did!" he says, smiling. "And then everyone left, and we went looking for chocolate chip cookies."

"Oh my God. We walked forever."

"We finally gave up and got tacos," he says, "at that food truck at Grand Army Plaza."

"And watched the sun set over Flatbush."

"So you *do* remember," he says, cuddling up to me.

"I thought about that too," I confess, leaning into him.

"Did you?"

"And other stuff."

"Oh yeah?" He nudges. "What other stuff?"

"Other-stuff other-stuff."

"Maybe you could show me some of that other stuff."

"I thought you were hungry," I say.

"I'm always hungry," he says, scooping me up in his arms like a newlywed, both of us laughing.

We sit across from each other at Cowgirl, tucked into a corner booth. I watch Jake as he scans the menu. I like to watch him eat. He's purposeful. Not particularly healthy, but purposeful, and he has the metabolism of a lion. The waitress comes by and takes our order and the menus. Jake switches positions, sliding his body up against the wall. He looks down at my hand as I fidget with my rings. He slides his hand into mine, gazing out the windows onto Hudson Street, lost in thought. Anxious, I squeeze his hand back and pull mine away. "You said you were at Jeff's," I say. "How is he?"

"He's good… Can I ask you something?" Jake asks.

"Sure."

"What if we went somewhere," he says. More of a statement.

"Like…now?"

"This winter. I don't know," he says with a shrug. "Christmas maybe. My dad's got his thing with his wife and her whole family. Maybe we could do something."

"I mean…like what?" I ask, shrinking back. "Where would we go?"

"I don't know," he says. "Anywhere."

"But I usually spend it with my family in Jersey."

"I know you do."

"So, I don't know," I say, searching for an escape hatch from the conversation. I take a sip of water.

Jake ducks down, looking for my eyes. "Hey. You OK?"

"I'm fine!" I say, a little too emphatically.

"I'm just asking—"

"Right. It's fine," I say. "I just don't know yet."

"OK…and nothing's up?" he asks.

"Why do you always think something's up?"

"What are you talking about?" he says, squinting.

"You assume things."

"I assume things?"

"You do. You haven't asked me anything. How am I doing? About work. You just want to tell me about all the *thrilling* places you've been, or some party you're invited to, or your hipster friends with their fucking protests."

"What are you talking about?" he scowls.

"Never mind."

"Hey," he leans in. "What's happening right now? I asked you how you were. I asked you about work."

"It's fine. You're right."

"Catherine, I want to know what's going on with you, but you're the one who holds back. What am I supposed to do? You tell me these little pieces of things. It's like a jigsaw puzzle with you. You think because I'm not in your head that I don't know you've got some heavy shit going on? But you don't talk to me about it. And what about me? You know, you're constantly reading all of these other people, but you've never told me what you see when you look into *my* eyes."

"Yes, I have."

"No, you haven't. You dance around it. I mean, what the fuck? Was I a serial killer or something?"

"Can we please not do this?"

"I don't even know what we're doing," he says, sighing.

We sit in silence for what seems like an hour. He turns his spoon while I stare into my water glass. The waitress arrives with his baby back ribs and my burger. I can't even look at it. I push it aside. He takes a couple of bites of his food and pushes it away. He looks up. "You know what I think about when shit gets real bad out there?"

I glance up, then look away.

"Look at me," he insists. "Do one of your tricks or whatever you have to do, but look me in the eyes when I tell you this."

I look back at him, into his big brown eyes, chanting to myself, silently. *Uoy evol I... Uoy evol I... Uoy evol I...*

"I think about you," he says. "That's all." He hesitates. "I—"

"I know," I cut him off before he can say it. "You know that I know. You don't have to say it."

"I *want* to say it," he says. "But you can't hear it."

I hate how he looks at me. I look to see if anyone's listening to us. I look for something to say. I look for anything but to have to look at him. When I glance up, the waitress is there, but something's off, my eyes won't focus. I can see her outline, but the details are murky, like looking at someone through a wavy plane of glass. "Do you think…he only thinks…of you?" the waitress asks. Her voice is strange, the way she slurs the words. I try to answer, but nothing comes. "I see…his heart," she says, sneering. "I know…her name."

Jake slides up against the edge of the booth, sulking. He glances around the room, oblivious to the strange woman standing beside us.

"You…can make…him yours…forever," she mutters, her voice wavering like a signal shifting frequency. "Invite…me in…and I…will show you…the power…you hold."

The dining room flashes in a brilliant white light, dissolving the figure before me like a pillar of sand. I rub my eyes as the room bleeds back into focus.

"Just the check?" the waitress asks.

"What—?" I wince.

"Oh, sorry," she says with a smile, ducking away. "No rush. I can come back."

"No, we're done," Jake says under his breath.

The waitress looks to me for confirmation. "Just let me know if there's anything else I can get you." She sets the slip on the table and Jake slides his card over. He takes out his phone, scrolling through texts, avoiding eye contact.

I watch the waitress as she walks away, disappearing into the bar.

9 | BLOOD IN THE WATER

It begins to rain on the way back to my apartment and I run the last block, tripping up the stairs of my building. My mind plays and replays the scene, the strange figure in the restaurant. Her voice, her words, feel like a snake that's slithered inside my brain. *I know her name.*

I open my phone and scroll through Jake's online profiles, his pictures, looking for a woman, someone conspicuous, but it's just random shots from his trips overseas—ruby sunsets, blue-black skylines at dusk, group shots of him and his team at bars, desert hikes, exotic birds. I hurl my phone at the couch and pace the apartment, antsy, the black metal file box lurking beneath the desk.

I open my laptop and run a search on mental disorders, clicking through online forums, message boards, clinical websites. Every description sounds like me. I close the computer and push it away and collapse on the couch, eyes shut tight, willing myself away somewhere—another time, a memory…

Working shoulder to shoulder in the garden with Clara, kneeling in the row of soil under the late-summer sun, weeding the beds of flowers, a quilt of color. After a long season of crawling around the garden together, we can finally be quiet with each other and just work, Clara and I. And today, that's what I need more than anything—my space, my trowel, and the silence between us. Clara can sense something is off, but she lets me be. Eventually she scooches up beside me, ripping out a persistent clump of weeds with her garden claw. "I think someone may have had a long night," she says—to no reply. "Hey there," she nudges.

"Hi, sorry," I say, sighing.

"Everything OK?"

"I can't get into it," I mutter.

"Oh? And why's that?"

"I don't want to bother you with my stupid girl drama."

"Are you kidding?" She laughs. "I invented stupid girl drama!"

"It's embarrassing. And, like, super TMI."

"Why don't you try me and if I start to freak out, I'll go like this." She makes a giant X gesture with her arms and a scared face. "Sound good?"

"I think I have a problem," I say with a sigh. "In fact, I know I do."

She waits.

"I think I'm a sex addict."

"AH!" She bowls over with laughter. "Oh my God. I'm sorry!" she cries. "Of course you are! Catherine, you're a college student. Everyone's a sex addict in college."

"Were you?"

"Of course I was!"

"I mean—did you experiment?"

"Did I experiment?" she asks. "What? With women? Sure, there were a couple. But I went to Smith, so no surprises there. Is that what this is about?"

I busy myself with my trowel, tearing out a clump of weeds as Clara waits for an answer. "I think I'm a total slut," I grumble.

"Oh? And why do you think that?"

"Um, because I am? You have no idea."

"Do you want to tell me?"

"Seriously, I've hooked up with so many people at this point it's like being the mayor of a town."

Clara screeches with laughter. "That can't be true!" She looks at me. "Can it?"

"It's fucked up. I know."

"Well, wait," she says, "when you say so many people—"

"You name it. My dorm, my friends' dorms, people from my classes, a couple of guys from UMass. I even hooked up with one of my professors, but it wasn't super all-the-way, thank god. And he was an adjunct, so it didn't really count."

She takes a beat, processing this. "And…are you enjoying it?"

"I don't know what I'm doing," I say, sighing. "I think so. It's like I need it more than I actually want it. It clears my head. It resets me."

"You feel like you're in control?" she asks.

"I mean, yeah—*something* is."

"Something."

I rip out another clump. "Sometimes I feel like I don't know who I am. Like this me might not be the real me. Like maybe the real me is hiding somewhere inside."

"And what do you think of that other you?" she asks.

"I don't know, it's like she's always been there. Like she stands back inside me, watching everything, listening. And then at some point she steps out and takes over."

I look to see if Clara is with me. She waits for me to continue.

"The first time it happened was sixth grade, the year after my parents died. I'd moved to my aunt and uncle's house in Butler. The kids at my new school were horrible to me. This one girl, Ashley Gordon, she was this giant ogre of a girl. She looked like she was in high school. She would constantly pick on me— call me names, steal my clothes in gym class. She'd pick fights and push me into the lockers. Just her size alone was terrifying. She was like this angry wall. One day she started taunting me, calling me Little Orphan Annie, saying how my parents killed themselves just to get away from me. That's when I felt it. It was like something shut off inside me—and something else turned on. This other someone stepped out of me. It was like watching a movie. I saw myself walk forward, the way my fingers curled, the sinews in my arms. And then I leapt at her. Like an animal. I knocked her down and pinned her to the ground. A circle formed around us, but no one stepped in, not even the teachers. I grabbed Ashley by the hair and pulled her across the floor, kicking and screaming. I looked at all of them, into their awful faces, and I let her go, and marched down to the principal. I walked right in, past the secretary, into her office, and stood at her desk and told her what I did. I told her it was her fault—the principal. I said she was supposed to protect me. All my teachers saw me getting bullied and didn't do anything. She had me sit in her office while the school called my uncle at work. He came and got me. It was strange after that. It was like I was floating. Like I was there and not there. I don't know what happened next. I remember everything being quiet—at home, on the bus the next morning. The principal met me at the door and asked me to come into her office. She sat in a chair beside me and said she was sorry. She said that Ashley wouldn't be a problem anymore, and that I was safe there."

I wipe my eye with the edge of the gardening glove. "It's funny. I had friends after that. The girls in my class wanted me to hang out with them. But I don't think it was me they wanted to hang out with."

"It was her." Clara says. She considers this. "Who do you think she is?" she asks.

"I don't know. She's not me in a past life, if that's what you mean."

Clara begins tapping through the dirt with her garden claw, thinking. "When I was a little girl," she says, "I knew something was different about me. It wasn't just an overactive imagination. I knew things. I felt things. Plants spoke to me. Birds, snakes. They spoke directly into my mind. I didn't tell anyone about this, of course. We lived in a poor Black part of Mississippi, and I stood out enough as it was. I got good grades, I went to church, and I kept my secrets. But when I went to college, things started getting away from me. I think it was the new environment. Places have different energies, and New England has a very different energy from the Mississippi Delta. Not just the people, but the ground itself, the wind. I felt like a vase that had cracked, with the water seeping out. And they could see it, the spirits. The benevolent ones, they move past you, they ignore you, they don't care. But the dark ones, they see you too. They're like sharks circling. They smell your blood in the water. I knew what these things were. I had seen them before, back home, but that was my turf and my animal spirits protected me there. But at school I was alone. I could feel them closing in. I'd see their shadows at the top of the stairs. Then one day the shadows were everywhere. I was in class and I felt a coldness, like the room was being filled with ice. I ran out, past the playing fields, deep into the woods. My head was spinning with sounds, whispers— the animals, the trees. Suddenly, I stopped. I put my arms out like wings, long and wide, and spread my fingers, and I called to her, the Great Mother. I called for her energy, to give me strength. Then I turned and faced the shadows. I screamed—something deep and raw, from way down inside me. Everything went still. Then somewhere in the darkness there was a sound—a slow, heavy, crushing sound. Something big moving through the brush. A giant bear, the size of a car. Its fur black and shiny. It stepped out from the tree line. I couldn't move. I was frozen in place. The bear lumbered toward me, close enough that I could smell her, the humidness of her snorts. She rose up like a tower, slow and steady on her back legs, and gazed down at me. And I felt her, looking at me, through the bear's eyes—the Great Mother. Just for a moment I felt her there. Then the bear dropped its paws to the ground, turned away, and lumbered back into the woods." Clara looks to me. "She'd come to tell me something. She wanted me to know it wasn't she who was going to save me."

"It was you."

Clara nods. "That power, it's something we all have access to. We're not just made of light. We're made of darkness too. You can let the darkness become something bigger than you, that rules you, or you can find a way to use it. That's why claiming your wand is so important to a witch. It's the moment you choose to point your energy toward something, when you choose to live with intention. That time will come for you—and you'll know it when it does."

10 | AN UPPER BOUNDARY

I lay on the couch with the lights off and the windows open, smelling the wet night air, listening to the sound of the street below. I wonder where Jake is, hating myself for the way I left things.

I light a joint, gazing at the black file box shoved under the desk. I open my laptop and type a name into a search box. It's strange to see the name spelled out, plain and simple, like it belongs to someone real, someone I could call if I wanted to.

Lillian Harper

A cascade of results fills the screen—a slew of Lillian Harpers, but not the one I'm looking for. Except for one link, a research paper archived on a Stanford University subdomain. The paper, published by a gender studies student in 2005, examines the notable contributions of women engineers over the second half of the 20th century. I scroll down to a highlighted passage:

Laser engineer Dr. Lillian Harper served as lead researcher and lab manager for the laser laboratory at Bell Labs from 1984 to 1988. During her tenure, Harper led pioneering advances in optical data storage and holography, developing methods for encoding three-dimensional data within two-dimensional light interference patterns. Harper's early work in particle physics and quantum field theory served as a catalyst for the study of the holographic principle, later expanded upon by Stanford professor Leonard Susskind in his formalization of the principle within the tenets of string theory.

I run a search on the holographic principle, wading through a stream of articles and links. I find an animated film on the subject produced by the California Institute of Technology. The narrator begins:

Imagine a beautiful mountain lake. Its surface is completely still, like a sheet of glass. Now imagine that you're beneath the surface, seeing everything inside the water—the fish, the frogs, the rocks and weeds.

The inside of the lake represents what we experience within our known universe.

Now pull back to where you just see the still surface of the lake. Or, in this case, the surface of the universe. According to the holographic principle, everything that is happening inside the lake is encoded on its surface, or "boundary," as tiny particles of information. When light shines through the boundary, it projects the information from the two-dimensional surface, transforming it into a three-dimensional underwater world.

If the holographic principle is true, it means that the three-dimensional world we sense all around us may be nothing more than a trick of the light passing through a two-dimensional plane on the far edge of the universe.

My phone buzzes across the coffee table, startling me. I snatch it up and answer it. The caller clears his throat. "Hello, is this Catherine? This is Peter Phillips. You left me a message."

My mind is blank. *Who the fuck is Peter Phillips?*

"About Andy," he clarifies. "Your father—we worked together."

"Dr. Phillips—yes! Hi! Thank you for calling me back." *What time is it?* I glance at the face of my phone—11:11 p.m.

"Yes, hi," he mutters.

"Sorry for leaving you such a strange message. I'm sure this must seem completely random—"

"Catherine, I'm sorry to interrupt, but can I ask a favor?"

"Yes, of course."

"Would it be possible for us to speak in person? I'm in Virginia. Would that be all right?"

"Well, I'm in New York, so…"

"Yes, I understand it's quite a distance," he says, "but I think it would be better if we spoke in person. Can you meet Monday morning?"

I try to process this. "Like, two days from now."

"The sooner the better, I think. Would that be all right?" He waits in silence for an answer.

"I mean—I can try…"

"Thank you. It'll be wonderful to meet you, Catherine. Your father told me so much about you. I'm going to text you from a different number."

"But wait. So—"

"Virginia Beach. 8 a.m., Monday. I'll send you the address. I'm sorry, but I have to go. I'll see you then. Thank you."

The call ends and I sit staring at the black face of the phone. I click it awake and bring up the call history, the last incoming number. I plug it into a search.

> Elizabeth City, NC
> UNREGISTERED, UNKNOWN

11 | THE CIRCLE

My phone buzzes on the bedside table, the faint blue glow of the screen illuminating the ceiling of the motel room. I pick it up, squinting at the text.

Pocahontas pancakes 8 am
Red baseball cap

I look at the time—5:30 a.m.—and slide the phone away.

I find a parking spot across the street from the restaurant, a bustling no-frills coffee shop two blocks from the beach. I'm early, so I sit and wait, watching the regulars shuttle in and out—contractors, senior citizens, a group of young moms navigating their strollers backward through the doorway. I flip down the sun visor and check my makeup, glancing over at the tote bag tucked in the footwell of the passenger seat containing the files. *Do I bring them with me? No. This is bizarre enough as it is.* I flip the visor up and take a long, deep breath. *What am I doing here?*

I stand at the hostess station scanning the crowded dining room, landing on a red baseball cap worn by a man seated at the far side of the room with his back to the door. Compact and stocky, he wears a light blue button-down shirt and khakis, an old-fashioned leather attaché slumped against the leg of his chair. As I approach the table, something catches my eye, a small shiny black box, about the size of a hockey puck, tucked in between the salt and pepper shakers.

"Dr. Phillips?" I ask, coming up behind him.

He startles. "Yes! Hello!" He rises to greet me. "You made it!" he smiles warmly, offering a soft but firm handshake. There's something disarmingly plain about him. He removes his cap and tucks it into the flap of his bag, smoothing down his hat-head, trying to make himself presentable. "I appreciate you coming all this way," he says, offering me a seat on the banquette opposite him. "I hope it wasn't too much of an inconvenience. They have great pancakes, if that's any consolation. Breakfast is on me, by the way."

I'm drawn in by the kindness in his eyes, light-blue pools, pulling me forward, down, down, down—

> *Snapshots of his morning flickering in rewind:*
> *Shaving at the sink in his undershirt and boxers.*
> *Kissing his wife's shoulder as he slips out of bed.*
> *The night prior: sneaking a smoke in the backyard.*

A phone call: cupping his hand over the
mouthpiece, keeping his voice down.
I clench my mind to hold the scene there,
to scan the room,
an office,
the light of a computer,
papers, files—
and then the light gathering around me,
ripping me back further.
A candlelit restaurant, white tablecloths.
His wife is seated beside him. Younger
now.
Someone approaches their table.
He rises to greet them.
A handshake, a hug—
my mother and father.
Her green silk dress.
I know this night. The night they died.
I touch my father's shoulder and he
flinches, his eyes meeting mine.
Does he see me? How could he see me?
Then the light gathers around me and
thrusts me back through the crackling
flash of time—

—back into the vinyl seat of the banquette. I grip the edge
of the table, steadying myself. A waitress hovers over us,
coffeepot in hand. She looks at Dr. Phillips, then back at me.

"Yes, both of us, thank you," Phillips says, smiling. The
waitress gives me a sideways glance as she pours the coffee,
then gladly steps away.

"You were there," I say. Phillips blinks back at me,
confused. "The night they died. You met them. At a restaurant."

He looks for something in my eyes. I chant backward in my mind so as not to be pulled back down.

"Your father and I worked together," he says.

"I don't remember you."

"Yes, well, we never met, you and I. But Andy—"

"Are you recording this?" I ask abruptly.

He looks confused. "Am I—what? No, of course not."

"What is this?" I ask, reaching for the small black box between us. It's heavier than it should be, cold and smooth like a block of polished marble. Something about it feels wrong. I pull my hand away.

"I'm sorry, Catherine. I'd like to explain." He readjusts the box to its original position. "This is just to give us some room to talk. In private. It averts prying ears—and eyes."

"What do you mean?"

"I'd like to explain as best I can, but I'll need you to bear with me if that's all right." He pauses a beat, considering where to begin. "Like I said, your father and I worked together. For quite some time."

"For the government," I interject.

He glances at the tables on either side of us, then back at me. "Unfortunately, I can't say who this was for. We were often part of a larger team, but on our last project we were kept apart. When Andy learned that I was involved, he reached out. He was concerned. He thought something was off about the project— the nature of it. He said he wanted to meet, but he thought we were being monitored."

"Monitored by whom?"

"You have to understand, this is all part of the nondisclosure agreement: the nature of the contract. Everything is strictly confidential. Andy knew his work was contributing to a larger effort, as was mine—all of the contributors, for that matter. But, in this case, it seemed like we were being kept in the dark about the core intent of the project." He smooths out a napkin on the table. On it, he draws a circle, and in the center of the circle, a black dot. He slides the napkin to me. "What do you see here?" he asks.

"A circle. And a dot."

"Exactly. A wheel, perhaps. A bull's-eye. There are only so many ways you can perceive this, because you're looking at a flat, two-dimensional drawing. But what if I were to add a third dimension?" He draws a second circle above the first, connecting the two with perpendicular lines, transforming the circle into a cylinder. "What was once a dot inside a circle now appears to be a ball inside a cylinder. By adding one additional dimension you get a completely different perspective. What you thought was one thing is actually something entirely different. You just didn't have the information to see it. When you're working on a project like this, all you're allowed to see is this." He flips the napkin over and draws a circle and a dot. "There are only a few, a select few, running these projects that see this." He flips the napkin over to the ball in the cylinder. "That's how you keep secrets. By hiding them in plain sight. Even from the people who are working on them. Your father wasn't OK with that. He wanted to know what he was being used for, so he started digging."

"The names on the list."

"Sorry?"

I pull the note out of my purse. "This is how I knew to contact you. I found this in the file."

He pulls his glasses from his shirt pocket and inspects the list. "Do you know these people?" I ask.

"I do," he says, then slides the list back to me. "We would have all been briefed separately. For instance, Andy was told he was developing a treatment to prevent PTSD—something to stabilize soldiers prior to combat. My brief was completely different. It focused on energy transmission—how subatomic particles interact and transfer information at quantum scales. If all of us received a different brief, then where do they intersect? The list you have. Is that the entire list? How many contributors were there? And how were they briefed? What were they tasked with, and why?"

"White Ladder 369. What is that?"

"I don't know."

"Why would they brief you on completely different assignments if you were working on the same thing?"

"Because keeping us siloed means we'd never see the whole picture. We'd only see what was in front of us." He flips the napkin over to the dot inside the circle.

"Subatomic particles," I say. "What are they?"

"Think of it this way." He slides his water glass between us. "Everything is made of particles. You. Me. This glass of water. Particles are the building blocks of everything. But if you were to zoom in, way in, to the structure of this glass, to the subatomic particles that make it up, you would see something strange. The particles disappear. And reappear. Over and over again. In a seemingly random way. We don't know why this happens. But more importantly, we don't know where they disappear to. Subatomic particles are binary in nature. They exist in pairs. Like twins. When you see one particle, you're really only seeing one half of a pair. Its twin particle is hidden—perhaps in this dimension, perhaps not. It might exist in two dimensions at once. It's like the circle and the dot. One of the twin particles exists in the circle—as a dot. But its twin might exist in a higher dimension—"

"As a ball."

"Precisely," he says, taking a sip of water.

"But what does this have to do with—"

"Any of this?" he asks, smiling. "Possibly nothing. But it goes back to my question: How was Andy's work linked to mine? Or any of the others'? Maybe they were looking at alternative use cases. Andy was essentially developing a drug. He was told it was meant to help soldiers. But maybe it wasn't. Maybe they were looking at other ways it could be used." He glances at the table beside ours, a young couple eating breakfast, a baby tucked into its carrier beside the mother. He smiles at the woman. I watch his eyes quickly scan over the husband, the baby in the carrier, their table. He looks back at me.

It suddenly occurs to me. "You're talking about a weapon."

He sips his coffee. "I don't know for certain, but the deeper your father dug into it, the more he didn't like what he found. He put a file together—documents, bits and pieces, things that didn't fit. Odd things. For instance, there was a spiritual component. Citations, passages—from the Bible, the Quran, the Kabbalah. Cross-references. Lists. He couldn't make sense of it."

"You said you were briefed by someone."

"Yes," he nods, "by two people, actually. They brief you in pairs. They identify themselves with a code. In all the years I've been working with this client, I have yet to meet a chief officer. If you're lucky, you might meet with someone who reports to someone who reports to the CO."

"So you're just signing up for these projects, no questions asked."

"I know how it sounds," he says, "but there's nothing nefarious about it. Every project follows a protocol. There are rules everyone has to follow, especially when it comes to maintaining secrecy. One rule is that there are always two narratives attached to a project—one true and one false—and both are woven together. That way, if someone discovers something they shouldn't have, they'll never know what they've actually stumbled upon. Fact wrapped in fiction."

"I'm not following."

"Well, that's good," he says with a chuckle. "That's the point. You've probably heard of the Philadelphia Experiment. The story goes like this: In the 1940s, in the midst of World War II, the Navy tested a cloaking device on a battleship docked in the harbor in Philadelphia. The device was supposed to make the ship imperceptible to radar, an early version of stealth technology. But when they turned it on, it malfunctioned. Instead of simply cloaking the ship, it completely disappeared. Gone." He snaps his fingers. "A moment later, it reappeared in a shipyard in Norfolk, Virginia, hundreds of miles away. If you had been there watching, it would have all happened in the blink of an eye. But time and space aren't what they appear. They have the ability to warp. Which means that for the sailors on the ship, it could have felt much longer. Apparently, when the ship dematerialized, many of the men aboard became disoriented. They moved around the vessel, frantic, and when it rematerialized, some of them were fused into the hull of the ship, the mast, the bulkheads."

"My God."

"It's terrifying. But the good news is it didn't actually happen that way. Of course, you'll never know what the true story is, because the story they want you to know is already out there taking its place."

He pulls a small spiral notepad out of his bag and writes down a name and number. "There's a name on your list. Dr. Colin Marsh. He teaches at Columbia." He tears off the page and slides it to me. "He's not going to want to talk to you, but it's worth a shot."

He glances at his watch. "I may have to take a rain check on our breakfast," he says. "I hope that's okay." He reaches for his wallet and takes out a $50 bill and tucks it under the water glass. "There's one other thing," he says. "I don't know what it is, or even if it's important, but your father had a unique interest in my line of work—quantum entanglement in particular, the nonlocality of particles. You see, entangled particles remain connected, no matter how far apart they are. One could be on Earth, the other on the moon, yet whatever happens to one is instantly reflected in the other. Not even Einstein understood how it worked—he called it 'spooky action at a distance.'

"But your father was searching for something more— something about the nature of entanglement. How one particle could be observed while its twin remained hidden, possibly beyond our perception. He wondered if the twins were inextricably linked across dimensions. And if so, could we tap into that connection, like a wire, and extract information from the twin in a higher dimension? Like tapping a phone line. It's a fascinating concept. I've often wondered—what would we hear coming across that line?"

He picks up the shiny black box and sets it in his bag, securing the clasps. "I really wish I had known your father better. Andy was a brilliant man, a consummate scientist. He was always open, always questioning. It felt like he was searching for something very personal in his work. I hope he found it."

He rises, offering his hand. "It's wonderful to finally meet you, Catherine. I hope you'll have a safe trip home."

As I shake his hand, he leans in close to whisper: "Please don't contact me again." He looks at me to make sure I've heard, smiles and nods, then turns and walks out.

I sit behind the wheel of the rental, numb, watching customers filter in and out of the coffee shop, crisscrossing the street, the cars passing by.

I look down at the note Phillips handed me, the name and number written there. I dial the number and it reroutes me to the university switchboard, a faculty directory, a voice mailbox with a synthetic, prerecorded greeting: "You have reached the office of—" the recording pauses, replaced by a rough, resonant voice: "Dr. Colin Marsh." Then a beep.

"Hi, yes, my name is Catherine Harper. I was referred to you by Dr. Peter Phillips. I believe you may have worked with my father, Dr. Andrew Harper. I had a question for you—about a project you collaborated on. I was wondering if you could give me a call?" I leave my number and hang up, then roll down the car window, drawing a long, deep breath. I turn the key in the ignition, but nothing happens—the engine silent, the dashboard dead. I try it again—nothing. *You have got to be fucking kidding me.*

I crane my neck out the window looking for help, but the street is suddenly empty. No cars, no people. My head feels strange, swimmy. I take out my phone, but it won't turn on. *Seriously. What the fuck.*

I reach for the engine latch and pop it, then get out of the car and pry open the hood. I gaze down into the engine block. I have no idea what I'm looking at.

"Can I help you?" a voice asks—a woman, I think. Her tall silhouette is shadowed by the sun. Short blond hair combed back, wet and shining against her head. A pair of sharp blue eyes regard me, holding my gaze, her head tilted like a bird, curious. I clench my focus to keep from falling in, but nothing happens. Her eyes hold me, somehow, glimmering like shards of ice.

"Are you stuck?" she asks.

There's something strange about her voice, an odd inflection, silvery and melodic. It makes my head feel tired. She steps beside me, peering down into the tubular guts of the engine. "Do you know where you're going?" she asks.

I try to speak, but there's nothing there, no air to push out the words.

She looks to me. "Are you lost?" Her eyes are mesmerizing. "Home. Is that where you wish to go? I can show you the way, if you'll let me. We can go together." Tiny flecks of color, like a shattered prism, revolve in the blue ice of her gaze. "It's not safe to go alone," she says. "Accidents happen. You know that, don't you?" Her blue eyes spark with a flash of white light, a sharp white star in the black void of her pupil. A hand suddenly grasps my arm, snapping me out of my trance.

"Ma'am, you OK?" A Latino kid in a grease-spattered kitchen apron blinks back at me.

"I—I'm fine," I stammer. The kid looks confused, like he doesn't know what he's doing here either. "Maybe you oughta sit down?" he says. He glances around, looking for help. The street has returned to normal—but the woman is gone.

"My car," I say. "It won't start." I make for the driver's side door and he lends a hand, holding it open for me, helping me in. "Maybe you need a jump?" he asks.

I turn the key and the engine comes alive with a roar. He looks at me, confused. "I must have fixed it," I say, playing up a shrug.

He hesitates. "Um, you sure you're good?"

"Yes, could you close the hood?" I ask, straining to hold it together.

He walks around the front and shuts it, then steps out of the way, watching me pull out. I wave a "thank you" and he gives a reluctant thumbs-up as I gun the accelerator, getting the fuck out of there, the silvery voice echoing in my mind. *Do you know where you're going?*

12 | TEACHERS

Gravel clatters under the car as I skid to a stop behind my Aunt Teri's hatchback, parked outside the house in Butler. A curtain is yanked back from the living room window, and a face peers out, annoyed at first, then elated when she realizes who it is. The front door is thrown open and Teri hops out, arms wide, pulling me in for a hug.

"What in the world?!" she cries. "Did your uncle know you were coming? He doesn't tell me anything!" She holds me away from her, taking me in, my face. Her expression goes dark. "Are you OK?"

We sit across from each other at the kitchen table with our untouched mugs of tea. Teri looks past me, trying to process what I've told her. She has my father's face, his square jaw and cheekbones. She's wearing my uncle Ted's Jersey Devils hoodie, which makes her look tiny, like a child.

"You didn't know anything about this?" I ask, breaking the silence.

She looks at me, not hearing the question.

"The night of the accident," I say. "Did they tell you where they were going? Who they were going to see? Anything?"

"They were going out to dinner," she says. "It was just a regular night."

"Does any of this make sense?" I ask. "You and my dad, you used to go to antiwar rallies. Why would he be working for the military?"

"I don't know—guilt?"

"For what?"

"Dodging the draft? I don't know."

I've never heard this story. "He dodged the draft?"

"He was exempted. For the work he was doing. His research."

"What research?"

Teri gathers the mugs and dumps them in the sink. "Honestly, I have no idea what your father did for a living."

"When the police came to the house that night, I told you what happened—to me."

She glances out the window as she washes up.

"Why wouldn't you ever talk to me about it?" I ask.

"About—"

"The accident. What happened to me. Do you not believe these things—?"

"You talk to your uncle about that."

"But why not you?" I persist. "Why can't I ever talk to *you* about it?"

"Because I don't like it!" she snaps, turning on me. "Because it frightens me!"

I stare back at her. "I frighten you?"

She wipes her eyes with the cuff of the sweatshirt. "Do you think this is my fault?" she asks. "Is that why you hold this grudge against me?"

"What are you—?"

"You think you're the only one who misses him?" she snaps. "I always protected him!"

"Protected him? From what?" I ask.

She waves it off, exasperated. "God only knows. The world? He was so sensitive. As a kid, he was like a target. With his imaginary friends, and his—"

"His what?"

"Oh God," she sighs. "Kids go through it. It's a phase. But with Andy, it was like he never outgrew it."

"What do you mean?"

"Like, as he got older, he stopped talking about it, but every once in a while he'd tell me something. About the things they showed him. His *friends*. That's what he called them. Our parents knew about it, but they never said anything."

"These things—spoke to him?"

"Not in words so much, but in pictures. In feelings. In his head. He wrote them down in his journals. I still have them if you want to see."

Teri shoves open the attic door and tugs the lightbulb chain, revealing a dim stockpile of plastic bins, skis, fishing gear. In the far corner, tucked under the eave, is a stack of milk crates loaded with books and old toys. Beside them sits an old-fashioned storage trunk with brass fittings. Teri drags the trunk forward and unlatches the lid, heaving it open. The trunk has been partitioned into two sides, his and hers, full of Teri and Andy's childhood memories. On one side are shoeboxes stacked with dolls, gymnastics ribbons, photo albums, a crocheted baby blanket. On the other: science fair awards, *MAD* magazines, an Erector Set, and a stack of composition notebooks. I pull one of the notebooks off the stack and crack it open along its brittle spine, leafing through the yellowed pages. They're full of pencil sketches—rudimentary shapes and symbols. I pause on one of the drawings: a circle with 12 notches, like the dial of a clock. Beside it, a circle half its size with six notches. Between the two dials, a symbol of the sun.

"I figured out how to read them," Teri says, hovering over my shoulder. "They're like a riddle. You flip to the next page to see the answer."

I flip the page. There, written in my father's bird-scratch handwriting, is a single sentence:

There is no such thing as time

My mind suddenly flashes, a machine-gun burst of images: a plain gray room, like a hospital. A metal table. Three white cards laid out in front of me. My hand rests on one of the cards and my mind flashes white.

"Yes, you are beginning to see," a small voice whispers, the words sharp and fine. I turn to look, but Teri is gone. "Many threads," the voice whispers. "Woven together. Into a web. And who is at the center?" In the corner of the attic, something glimmers in the crook of a rafter, a spiderweb, its filaments glowing, pulsing, opalescent. A black spider plucks the threads as it weaves the silk in concentric circles. "I can show you what the web is," the spider clicks. "Come close and you will see." There's something soothing in its voice, something soft and old and wise. I find myself moving toward it, floating, until I'm standing before the gossamer net clinging to the beams.

"Touch it and you will see," the spider whispers.

I extend a finger to a band of glowing silk and make contact, my mind flooded by a rush of information, a surge of electricity coursing through the folds of my brain. My mind wrenches, trying to slow the images, to decode what I'm seeing.

"You are caught in their web," the spider hisses. "But I can show you how to break free. Do not fight it. Look deeply. Follow the thread and you will see where it leads. Home. We can go there—together."

A high chirp and a flutter of wings snaps me out of the spell. A ruby red cardinal clings to a rafter overhead, its crimson feathers aglow. It cocks its crested head at the spider and descends upon it, capturing it in its beak. The spider pries the bird's mouth wide, fighting, unrelenting, as a white light fills the cardinal's mouth, dissolving the spider whole.

My head goes cold and I stumble backward—into Teri's arms. "Catherine!" she cries. My head spins, the entire attic spinning. I lurch for the trunk and scoop out the notebooks, gathering them in my arms. Teri doesn't know what's happening. She tries to help, but I pull away, concentrating on my balance, out into the hall, down the stairs, bursting out the front door.

I pull open the driver's-side door and dump the books inside, my head pounding, my ears like cotton. Teri's voice murmurs behind me, something, pleading. I start the engine and gun it in reverse down the driveway, rocking onto the road. Teri stands in the front yard, shell-shocked.

"I'm sorry," I say—to myself, to her, to no one. "It's not your fault."

13 | AN EMPTY SPACE

I tear off the packing tape, knee deep in boxes, the fluorescent lights of the storage unit buzzing overhead. I dig out the items marked OFFICE, piling them around me. In one of the boxes I find a photo album. I flip through its crinkling pages—faded images of my parents' wedding; my grandparents, young and alive; my mother holding me as a baby in the hospital; snuggled in the crook of my father's arm. I flip forward through the years—a birthday party, everyone crowded around the kitchen table, my dad lighting the candles. I look at the faces of the children, but I don't recognize any of them. *When was this?* There's a man standing in the back, his big smiling face and beard, his wife beside him. Did he work with my dad? We used to go to their lake house, out on their boat. I flip to another photo—he and my father, arms slung around each other's shoulders at a backyard barbecue. I pull the photo out and flip it over. There, in my mother's handwriting:

A. and Harvey. DC, '85

Harvey. I remember now. I find another picture of him. This one with his wife, a pretty blond woman with perfect teeth. They're leaning into each other along the rail of a sailboat, wind-whipped, out on the water. I flip it over:

Harvey and Janet, Annapolis, '85

It's strange. I remember these people, yet somehow I don't. They were my parents' friends. What was their last name? Warner? Wilson?

I rummage deeper into one of the boxes, unearthing my dad's Rolodex. I fan through the cards.

Harvey and Janet Ward
16 Grove St.
Annapolis, MD 21401

I run a search on my phone and find an online profile for Janet. Posts of her and her sister at a Broadway show; photos of her and Harvey in Annapolis; a selfie of them seated together on a park bench, the harbor in the background. Janet crowds next to him, smiling, huddling them into the frame. Harvey looks old, like he's not all there. I enlarge Harvey's face, his eyes. My mind flashes—Harvey, younger now, looking down at me from a window, the glass wall of an observation room. My father is beside him, nodding. He waves to me reassuringly. I'm seated at a metal table across from a woman. She has a stack of white cards. She sets three cards in front of me, face down. As she touches each card, a shape materializes in my mind, a symbol. I say its name aloud, then she flips the card over, revealing the same.

Dagaz. Dawn. Intuition.

Uruz. Power. Gateway.

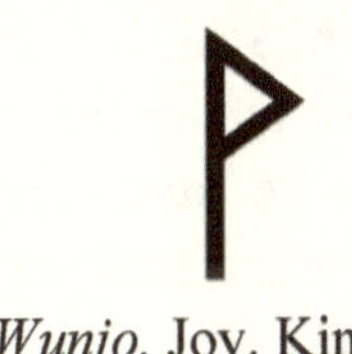

Wunjo. Joy. Kinship.

My mind flashes white, snapping me out of the memory. I click the email icon beside Janet's photo.

> Hello. My name is Catherine Harper. Andrew
> Harper's daughter. Is there a way for me to speak
> to Harvey? I'd like to ask him something about
> my dad. A project they worked on together.

I include my number and click send—and at that moment the lights snap out, plunging the unit into an impenetrable darkness. An alarm sounds in the corridor and an emergency floodlight pops to life over the unit door, flashing on and off, illuminating the unit in a pale rhythmic strobe. I reach for the door, but the handle won't budge. I bang on it with my open palm, but the sound is drowned out by the sirens in the hall. I turn to look for something to pry the handle, but the unit is suddenly empty—the boxes, the stacks of furniture, everything, gone. All but a shadow, the silhouette of a man, seated on the floor, cross-legged, facing the far wall. With both hands I grip the door handle, shaking it with all my strength. I look for my phone, patting my pockets, but my clothes are different now. I'm wearing something loose, like medical scrubs, padded slippers on my feet. *What the fuck is happening?* I turn back to the seated man, petrified. He doesn't move, doesn't acknowledge me. He's wearing scrubs like mine. There's something about him, something familiar, the hunch of his shoulders. I move toward him slowly, until I'm right there looking down at the profile of his face, flashing ghost white in the strobe light. My voice quivers. "Daddy?" I whisper, but he doesn't move. His eyes are fixed on the far wall, as if he were gazing at something. He flinches as he breathes, fast and shallow, his shoulder blades thrusting back like wings beating.

"Daddy, I'm scared," I say, touching his shoulder.

He turns his head to me slowly, like an owl, his eyes looking into mine without seeing me, looking through me.

"Daddy? What is it?"

His mouth forms a word without a sound—*home*. Then, slowly, he turns his attention back to the white, flashing wall, rapt in its spell.

I back away slowly, then turn and bolt for the door, throwing all my weight into it, bursting into the corridor.

The siren blares down the hallway like an ambulance, wailing. Beneath it another sound, like drums, pounding thuds, the doors all the way down the hall pounding from the inside.

"I'm getting help!" I cry. Then suddenly the sirens, the doors, the flashing lights, all become synchronized, lining up like a battle march, beating in time. Then stop. Nothing. A dead silence.

Then a voice, a small voice, rasping, behind one of the doors. I step closer to hear. Closer.

We... go... home...

I flinch away as the lights snap on and a door is thrown open at the end of the hall. A heavyset security guard marches toward me, sweating, out of breath, gripping a giant flashlight like a police baton. "Was that you?" he barks. "Did you pull the alarm?" He marches past me, whipping a massive set of keys off his belt, then unlocks the tamper shield on a security panel. He punches in a code and pulls a walkie-talkie from his hip. "It's on three," he announces. "I'm checking it out."

He looks at me. "Did you see anybody up here?"

I shake my head no.

He points to the open door with his walkie-talkie. "This you?"

I nod yes.

He steps to the door and tentatively pokes it open, scanning the room. The unit has returned to normal, stacked with boxes and furniture. He looks at me. "You good?"

I nod.

He holds the door for me as I slip inside and snatch up my things, then duck past him, down the hall, bursting through the crash bar, down the stairs, out into the night.

14 | MORNING LIGHT

I wake up curled in Jake's embrace. He kisses my shoulder and turns me to him, his warm smell coming up through the sheets. "Hey," he mutters. My eyes blink open and he's smiling at me—that goofy grin, that dimple. I chant backward in my mind, holding back my vision. "Hi."

"Well, that was nice," he says, grinning.

"What was?"

"Come on." He nudges me. "That was a hot-ass booty call."

"Give me a break," I sigh, turning away. He pulls me back for another kiss. "So, we're good then?" he asks.

I shrug.

"You don't know?" he smiles.

"Yes, we're good. *What?*"

"Awesome. You hungry?"

"What time is it?" I reach for my phone. The screen blinks awake—8:55. "Fuck!" I cry, whipping back the covers, springing out of bed.

"What's happening?"

I dive into the bathroom, shutting the door. "I have to go!"

"Go? Go where?"

"I'm supposed to meet a friend from work."

"Ugh." Jake sighs, flopping back on the bed. "Can you cancel? It's Saturday."

"She's in from London," I say, mumbling through a mouthful of toothpaste. "I can't bail on her."

Jake rolls onto his side, watching me as I hold up outfits in front of the full-length mirror. "Your titties look good in that bra," he comments.

"That's wonderful," I reply.

"Why don't you bring them over here. Just for a second."

"You need to get up. Seriously. Get dressed."

He whips back the sheet, revealing a giant boner. "I'm going out like this," he says, smirking.

"Whatever you want, but you need to get a move on."

He reaches down for his pile of clothes, hesitating as he spots something beside the bed. He lights up. "Oh, hang on! What do we have here?"

I spin around as he's flipping through the photo album.

"Wow, is that you?" He holds up a picture of me and my dad, a fall day at Princeton, playing in a huge pile of leaves on the quad. My mind flashes: *My father's ghost-white face looking up at me in the strobe-lit room.* I snatch the book away.

"Jesus! What?" He flinches. I want to say something, but I can't. I grip the book to me, shaking. Jake sits up. "What's going on?"

"You have to go," I say, tossing the book into the closet.

"Hang on, are you all right? You're shaking."

"I'm fine."

He scoots to the edge of the bed, making a spot for me. "Come over here. What's going on?"

Reluctantly, I sit beside him. He wraps the covers around my shoulders. I want to explain, but there's nowhere to begin. "I don't know. There's some crazy stuff going on right now."

"OK." He waits for me to elaborate.

"Like, stuff with me. What I deal with."

"The usual stuff?" he asks. "Or, like, other stuff?"

"I don't even know how to explain it."

He looks for my eyes, but I look away. "It's crazy," I say, exasperated. "I don't know. I can tell you about it later."

"Tell me what? What happened?"

"I've been, I don't know—seeing things." I glance at him to read his expression. "Please. Just get dressed. I have to go. Seriously, I'll tell you—"

"Seeing things like what?" he asks. The look on his face.

"Please don't look at me like that," I snap.

"Look at you like what?"

"Like I'm crazy."

"I'm not looking at you like you're crazy. I'm just trying to understand."

I turn to the mirror to put on my makeup. He sighs, gathering his clothes. I watch him from the mirror. "I'm sorry," I say. "Everything's fine."

"You think it's the medication?"

"The medication?"

"The stuff you're on. Maybe you're—"

"I'm not taking it."

He hesitates. "I thought you were gonna try—"

"I did try, Jake. It doesn't work. This isn't something you can just *medicate* away."

He looks at me—that look again.

"What do you think this is?" I snap. "Do you think I'm schizo? Is that it?"

"Of course not," he says, zipping up his jeans. "What are you talking about?"

"This is what comes with me. Maybe that's too much for you to deal with. Maybe you should find someone else to fuck— or whatever it is we're doing. I'm sure you have someone else waiting in the wings."

"Wait—what?"

"Don't tell me there isn't some other girl. On these trips you go on. We see each other for a week here, a week there. You're gonna tell me you're some kind of chaste soul, that you live like a monk when I'm not around? Give me a break."

"Where is this coming from? Are you saying you want me around more? Because I'd love to hear you say that. For all I know, I'm just some part-time fuck buddy."

"You don't seem to have a problem with it."

This hits the wrong way. His face goes dark. "Maybe I do have a problem with it," he says, pulling on his hoodie, grabbing his boots.

"So that's it?"

"I thought you were done with me," he sneers. "I can go now, right?"

"You can be a real asshole, you know that? All you ever want me to do is open up, and the moment I do, it's too much for you."

He spins around, facing off with me. "Actually, no—I'm here for it. I think you know that. I think it's too much for *you*. That's the problem." He waits for me to say something, but I ignore him, turning away, looking through my bag, for nothing. He shoves his hands into the pocket of his hoodie and walks through the apartment, pausing at the door. "See ya," he says, to no reply. I flinch as the door slams shut behind him.

15 | THE SOUND OF WINGS

The Alexander McQueen exhibit closes in a week, and everyone who has procrastinated for the last three months has chosen this morning to finally make it happen. The entire west side of Fifth Avenue is clogged with a slow-moving mob stretching from the mouth of Central Park to the steps of the Metropolitan Museum of Art. Above the entrance, an exhibition banner ripples in the breeze—an image of McQueen's doughy, boyish face overlaid in a white death mask, a not-so-subtle reminder of his suicide a year ago.

"Hello, gorgeous!" a voice says cheerfully as I exit the cab out front. "Care for a hot dog?" Geri extends her long arm in the air, signaling for me to join her at a hot dog cart. An onyx-black goddess, Geri exudes an effortless aristocratic air. She wears an oversize neon-pink sweatshirt emblazoned with the words YES, PLEASE, skinny blue jeans ripped at the knees, and a pair of vintage checkerboard Vans. Her giant Afro, pinned up in a bouffant mohawk, gives her the effect of a punk supermodel. I haven't seen Geri since my last visit to London, and the sight of her lifts my spirits like a party song.

"Swee-tie!" She gathers me up in a soft pink hug, planting a kiss-kiss on each cheek. She smells like I remember, like vanilla and peppery spice. "You *must* have one of these!" she urges in her posh British accent, handing me a hot dog. "They are absolutely divine! This beautiful man here is Anwar," she says, gesturing to the man beaming proudly from behind his cart. "Anwar knows *exactly* what a girl with a raging hangover needs. Don't you, Anwar? You little party boy. Two, please! Keep the change!" She spins back to me. "Now, let's have a look at you, you gorgeous thing. I love this whole look, by the way—so *incognito*," she coos, taking in my last-minute outfit—linen tunic, black jeans, ballet flats, and enormous black sunglasses. She dips into her purse and plucks out two VIP passes. "Voilà! Shall we?" She slips her arm into mine, hustling us up the steps.

The exhibition is held on the Met's lower level, the Costume Institute, a warren of low-lit underground galleries forming a sort of catacomb beneath the museum. The show has been arranged as a serpentine maze of ghost-white mannequins perched on pedestals—a procession of archangels dressed in feathered gowns, imperial cloaks, and macabre battle armor. I pause beneath one of the figures, *Dress No. 13*, a tufted white cocktail dress blasted with black and yellow paint. Beside the figure, a video monitor plays a loop of footage from the spring/summer 1999 show in London. In it, the model Shalom Harlow spins slowly on a revolving platform, her tiny balletic frame resembling a music box figurine. As she spins, a pair of robotic paint cannons assault her, swinging their hulking steel arms, blasting her with paint, obliterating the delicate dress into something vandalized and raw. Suddenly, something catches the corner of my eye—a dark flicker, like the beat of a bird's wing. I turn and the gallery is suddenly devoid of people, just the mannequins frozen in their poses, ghost-white faces aglow in the spotlights.

Wings shudder behind me and I spin, looking up into the featureless face of a towering figure arching over me like a specter. Dressed in an oil-black gown of raven's feathers, the wraith regards me with her smooth white face. She extends a cold alabaster hand, uncurling and pointing a long, thin finger, gesturing to something in the center of the room. There, on a lone pedestal, stands a figure dressed in a golden suit of armor, radiating beneath the spotlight. The faceplate of the helmet is lifted, casting a shadow across the figure's face. I move toward it, its features bleeding into focus, and there, within the window of the helmet, my own face gazing back at me. A hand grips my arm, and I gasp, flinching, breaking the spell. "There you are!" Geri says, beaming gleefully. "Is this fucking mad? I'm losing my mind in here. These dresses are absolutely gorgeous!"

My mind reels, reclaiming the reality of the space—the gallery, everything back as it was, throngs of tourists shuffling past the displays, gazing up at the frozen figures.

"I need to get some air," I press, scanning for the closest exit. Geri concurs. "This is a fucking madhouse," she says. "Let's go." She tugs me along beside her, slipping us through the crowd.

"You need to show me the painting you told me about," she says as we collect ourselves in the outer hall. "It's here, isn't it?"

"The painting?"

"*Joan of Arc*. I've been dying to see it."

The elevator delivers us to the second floor, the European Hall, a marble corridor hung with life-size paintings—a procession of massive gold frames like fairy tale doorways to another realm—and at its center, young Joan in the garden in Domrémy.

"Gorgeous," Geri sighs, stepping close to examine the young girl's face. "It's like a photograph," she remarks. "Those eyes." She glances at the placard beside the painting:

> Bastien-Lepage, a native of Lorraine, depicts the moment when Saints Michael, Margaret, and Catherine appear to Joan in her parents' garden, rousing her to fight against the English invaders in the Hundred Years War…

"Oh, right, I see," Geri remarks. "The saints up there, floating in the background." She continues reading:

> When the painting was exhibited in the Salon of 1880, critics praised the expressiveness of the principal figure, but found the saints' presence at odds with Bastien-Lepage's naturalistic style.

"Oh, for fuck's sake," Geri scoffs. "What do the critics know? It's marvelous. It's like a story."

I stand beside her, gazing up at the painting, at the expression on young Joan's face. "I used to think it was all about her. But then I fell in love with the saints, and suddenly it was all about them. But now…" I pause a beat, examining the scene. "I don't think it's about either—but something in between. A question. Left hanging in the air. *Do you or don't you?* The saints have come to tell her what she must do. And she's heard them. But now it's up to her to decide. *Do you or don't you?* It's about how we choose our own fate. Even in the face of God."

"O Catherine, you gentle heart," Geri sighs, giving my hand a squeeze. "I love how you see things. We need to spend more time together. No more of this once-a-year nonsense. I'm going to be in London this fall, but I want to get together the moment I'm back. Deal?"

I only half-hear Geri as I regard the painting. There's something different about it, something I hadn't noticed before, like the beginning of a secret revealing itself. My eyes track through the familiar scene to the apparitions floating over Joan's shoulder. Saint Catherine doubled over, hiding her face in anguish. Saint Margaret wringing her hands. And Saint Michael the Archangel, hovering before them, arms crossed, resolute, dressed in a gleaming suit of armor, a golden armor, his halo like a helmet with the faceplate drawn back.

16 | SYMPOSIUM

The stockroom door has been left ajar along the back wall of Abingdon Market, revealing a netherworld of walk-in freezers and shrink-wrapped pallets of supplies. Adam sits hunched at a makeshift desk gazing into the blue light of his laptop. I knock and it startles him—he spins around, squinting into the light. "Yes, hi."

"Sorry. Can you talk?" I ask.

"Oh." He brightens, recognizing me. "Yeah. One sec." He shuts the computer and saunters out into the glow of the dairy section. Tall and gangly, he wears a green apron over a Richard Hell T-shirt, his boyish face belying a darkness behind his eyes. "What's up?" he says, nodding.

"I need to talk to you about something."

"OK," he says with a shrug, waiting.

"Like not-right-here something."

"Ah, got it." He motions for me to follow him up front, where he tells Jennifer, the cashier, that he's stepping out for a minute. She gives a little wave, not looking up from her magazine.

"Did you read the book I gave you?" Adam asks as he leads us up the block. "Let me know when you do, 'cause I have another one that's gonna blow your mind." He catches the door at the Corner Bistro, holding it for me, marching us past the regulars watching a soccer match on satellite TV. He slides into a high-back booth in the back room signaling to the waiter, a tiny gray-haired man with a mustache who looks like he's been here since the wallpaper went up. Adam orders two beers and a chili cheese fries, then folds his hands on the table, smiling, ready. "So, what's up?"

"I need you to look at something." I pull out my phone, bringing up a photo. I hand it to him. "Have you ever seen anything like this?"

He squints at the screen, enlarging the image with his fingertips. "There are more," I say. "Keep going."

He flicks to the next, zooming in, then glances up at me. "Where did you get these?"

"They belonged to my dad."

He nods, then continues flicking through the images, zooming and inspecting. "What exactly does your dad do?"

"Did," I clarify. "He was a professor. Of biochemistry. He died when I was a child."

He looks to me. "I mean, you know what these are, right?"

"I was hoping you could tell me."

"Well, if they are what I think they are…" He pauses. "Was your dad a contractor?"

"A what?"

"For the government." He flicks back through the documents. "These code numbers are bogus. But aside from that—here, look." He turns the phone to me, pointing out the alphanumeric code at the top. "The first set of letters, that's

Naval Intelligence. The second set, that's the project code. But the last row, that's like a subcode."

"OK…"

"Your dad was what? A biologist?"

"A biochemist."

He zooms in on one of the documents. "The pineal gland," he mutters to himself.

"Yeah, I saw that too. I thought it might have to do with his research for the drug he developed—Seraphyl."

Adam does a double take. "Your dad invented Seraphyl?"

"Yeah, why?"

He snickers to himself. "Amazing."

"What's amazing?"

"They tried to put me on that," he says with a sniff.

"Who tried?"

He ignores the question. "Do you know what the pineal gland is?" he asks.

"It creates enzymes—I think."

"Melatonin, actually. The pineal gland takes serotonin and converts it into melatonin, which helps regulate your sleep." He leans back, making room for the waiter to set down the beers and fries. "The pineal gland does a lot of things, actually," he continues. "It's basically your body's drug dealer. Have you heard of dimethyltryptamine—DMT?"

He can see by my face that I haven't. "Ayahuasca?" he asks.

"Like, the shaman stuff?"

"Exactly. Drinking potions and seeing spirits and all that. DMT is like the no-fucking-around version of ayahuasca. It's like the magic key."

"The magic key…"

"Right, so basically, there's *this* reality," he motions all around us. "The one we see here—in this space. And then there's the reality we don't see, which is *also* in this space. Everything we see here is on the same frequency. You, me, this table. But if you change the frequency, just a little tweak, like a radio dial, the whole thing is different. On a different frequency, this might still be a forest with Natives running around hunting boars or whatever."

"Like ghosts."

"No, not like ghosts," he takes a swig of beer, "because that would mean all of that was happening in the past. But there's no such thing as the past. And, by the way, there's no such thing as ghosts, either. Well, there is, but they're not what you think." He sets his beer on the mat, continuing. "Anyway, DMT basically allows you to tune yourself *out* of this frequency and *in* to that one. Which sounds trippy as fuck, but we actually do something similar when we dream. When we enter REM—the stage where dreams happen—our brain chemistry shifts in ways we don't understand. There's a theory that the pineal gland produces and releases DMT during the dream state. Like a mini-trip. Your mind relaxes, and the pineal gland gives it a hit of DMT. Then it's like, *click*—you're in."

He jots down a name on a napkin. "You need to look at this dude, David Morehouse. He was part of the Army's psychic soldier unit—astral projection, remote viewing. He wrote a book about his time in the program called *Psychic Warrior*. The stuff this guy has seen is on a whole other level—literally."

"Wait, so back up," I say. "The code number on the file— you're saying it's fake?"

"Fake is the wrong word," he says, plucking a fry from the plate. "It's *pseudo*. A red herring. Misinformation with a purpose. It's designed to look like a normal project, but only the people running it know what the subcode stands for. Anything the government can't officially touch gets pushed off to private contractors. Off the books. Outside federal oversight." He flicks through the documents. "You've read all these?" he asks.

"I've tried."

"You know what else this makes me think of?" he says, ruminating. "It sounds crazy, but have you heard of the Montauk Project? This old, decommissioned Air Force base out on the tip of Long Island. Allegedly, there was all this wild stuff going on out there. Weird mind control shit. Astral projection. Some say they opened up a wormhole to another dimension. All these kids went missing. It's some creepy shit. The reason I bring it up is this stuff with the pineal gland. I remember seeing some files connected to the Montauk Project. They could have been completely fake, but still. They talked about triggering the pineal gland as a way to induce altered states of consciousness. Super out-there stuff. The pineal gland is like this bizarre anomaly. It's this little node, smaller than your thumbnail, right in the center of your brain. It's not part of the brain, but it's nested inside it, almost like the brain is meant to protect it. What's even weirder is, the pineal gland is light-sensitive, even though it has no contact with light whatsoever."

"Like a third eye."

"Exactly," he nods. He pulls over another napkin and starts sketching. "You've seen the Eye of Horus, right? The Egyptian symbol? It looks like this." He turns the drawing to me—a stylized hieroglyphic eye with an elongated teardrop. "It represents protection and power," he explains. "What's odd is that if you were to split a human brain in half, right down the center, the cross section would look identical to the Eye of Horus." He traces his finger over the drawing. "The brain plate here…the brainstem below…the cerebellum. And right there, at the center of it all, the pineal gland. The ancient Egyptians knew all about the brain, human anatomy—but don't get me started on the ancient Egyptians."

"What does this have to do with—"

"Your dad?" he asks. "Probably nothing. But here's the thing. If these files are what I think they are, this was a black project—something the military won't even acknowledge—and if this was a black project there's a reason why it was designated that way. Everything I've told you about what happened to me— *that* was a black project. There's always a record of it, but they keep it so deeply buried, so cryptic, that you wouldn't know it if you found it. It's one thing to run a top secret project. It's another to say that no one, not even the president, can know about it. That's what we're talking about here. So, is that something? Yeah, probably. The only question is, do you really want to know?"

"Of course I want to know," I say, indignant. "I have a right to know."

"You do—sort of," he says, handing the phone back to me. "A piece of advice though? Don't submit a FOIA, if that's what you're thinking."

"I don't even know what a *foya* is."

"A Freedom of Information Act request. It's when you ask the government for everything they have on a subject. For one thing, they're not going to have anything to give you. And the other thing, it'll flag you. You'll get sent some bullshit response, like months later, that the project doesn't exist—while in the meantime, the system's alerted the parties involved that someone is digging around for something they shouldn't be."

"But this would have been from 20 years ago."

He pulls off a hunk of chili cheese fries. "That doesn't mean that it's not still classified," he says. "Nobody declassifies anything unless they absolutely have to. Look, I know all this sounds cloak-and-dagger-y, like some wild mystery to be solved, but that's not what it is. It's business. It's people getting paid to do a thing, and not asking questions, and only looking at what they're supposed to. This is how things actually get done."

"Meaning?"

"Meaning there's always someone else steering the ship," he says, taking a swig. "You might think the president runs the country, but the president is really just an employee. We all kind of know it, but we don't like to think about it, because that would mean that democracy doesn't really work the way we'd like it to. So, we try to focus on a more acceptable reality—that things might go off the rails a little, but on the whole, people, especially the people we elect, are championing our best interests. I, on the other hand, think people are inherently self-interested. If you're in power and that's your comfort zone—being in power—then you don't want anyone taking you out of your comfort zone. Any threat against your power is a direct threat against your identity. You'll do anything to defend it. A conspiracy, any conspiracy, is based on that principle. But conspiracies sound sinister. They're scary. Not because of what they are, but because of what they represent—that if we actually looked at them, we might see that same sinister thing in ourselves."

"My father would've never done anything—"

"In self-interest?" Adam asks, popping another mouthful.

"—that would hurt someone."

He sits back considering this. "So what is it you need to know, then?"

"I want to know what happened to him. He and my mother. Maybe you could help me. You know about these things. From what you went through."

His face darkens. He reaches for his beer. "Yeah. I don't know."

"I have no one I can talk to about this, Adam. No one would understand. I know you know how that feels. Maybe we can help each other."

"Help each other?" he asks, dubious.

"Maybe if we can figure out what happened to my dad, we can figure out what happened to you."

"What does one have to do with the other?" he asks.

"I don't know. I just—"

"If you want my advice, I'd leave it alone. You don't want to get into any of this, believe me. You think you do, but it's just a distraction."

"Really? So what are you doing, then?"

"What am I—?"

I lay into him. "This whole thing you've got going on. You really expect me to believe you're part of some bizarre experiment that went awry, and the powers that be were just like, 'You know what? It's all good. We're just gonna put you in a time travel witness relocation program and give you a new identity as a greengrocer. How does that sound? You'll keep quiet, right?'"

"You have no idea—"

"You're right. I don't. So why don't you tell me—"

"I'm not *trying* to figure it out!" he snaps. He lowers his voice. "You send somebody into the future, and you think they're just gonna cut them loose? *I am* the project. I'm the data. That's the only reason I'm still alive." He looks for a reaction, then slumps back in the booth, disgusted. "But why should you believe me? It's not like anybody else would."

"That's the crazy thing, Adam. This whole time travel situation? Funny enough, I actually *do* believe you. What I *don't* believe is that you're OK with it. Maybe you've told yourself that this is serving some kind of higher purpose, but I think when it comes down to it, you know you were used, and you don't know what to do with that."

Adam gazes at his beer, turning it on the coaster.

"I don't know what that's like," I say, "but I think my father did. I think he woke up one day and realized that he was involved in something he shouldn't be and it scared him."

Adam glances at me, through me, weighing something.

"All I'm asking for is a friend," I say. "Maybe I'm wrong, but I think you could use one too."

A group of friends enter the back room with their beers, 20-somethings, laughing, talking loudly, tumbling into the booth across from ours. I watch Adam watching them.

"It doesn't have to be like this," I say. "You're allowed to take your life back."

"What life?" he snaps, turning back to me. He suddenly seems like a petulant teenager.

I gather my bag, setting cash on the table. "Think about it," I say. He ignores me, gazing into his beer.

Stepping out of the bar into the sunlight, my phone vibrates. I assume it's Adam changing his mind. I pick it up without looking, but the voice on the other end is a woman's, shaky and upset.

"Catherine, this is Janet Ward." She hesitates, waiting for me to place the name. "You sent me a note about Harvey."

It suddenly occurs to me. "Yes, hi, of course. Thank you for calling. Is everything all right?"

"I don't know if you know that Harvey's been sick," she says. "It's been a long time since we last saw you."

"I'm so sorry. Is he—"

"It's dementia. He's OK. But something's happened. I don't know...I don't know what it is."

"Can you tell me what—"

"The message you sent," she says, lowering her voice. "I read it to Harvey and something...happened. He came back. It triggered something. He sat up, his whole body changed. He looked at me—he didn't know where he was. He said, 'Janet, what time is it? Where are we?' It was like he woke up from a dream. I brought him to the doctor, but even the doctor didn't know what to make of it. He warned me that it was most likely a 'good spell' and that Harvey would relapse, but it was like he was totally back. I don't know how else to explain it. This morning, we got up, we were sitting on the porch…" She pauses, sniffling. "I'm sorry. It's just…" She pulls herself together. "We tried to figure out what it was. I read him your message again, thinking maybe it had something to do with it. As Harvey listened, it was like he was *watching* something—in his mind. A memory. He told me to get him something to write on. He started jotting down all these things. I don't know what they are. I have them here." She reads: "'Symposium.' Do you know what that is? Symposium?" My mind flashes white. She continues: "I think this says 'ladder.' Something about a ladder? The rest is— it looks like scientific terms. Something about—a code? Duplicating genes? Does any of this make any sense to you?"

Someone calls to Janet in the background, a man's voice. Janet answers back, "OK, hon, I'm coming!" Then, back to me, she whispers. "I'm going to call you back."

"Yes, absolutely."

"Do you know what this is?" she asks, hurriedly.

"I don't know. That's what I—"

"Walter Reed?" she asks. "Is that where—?"

A man's voice calls out again in the background.

"I have to go," she says. "I'll call you."

17 | PARALLELS

I page through the photo album, finding a handful of snapshots that include Harvey. I concentrate on his face, his eyes, trying to place a memory. I plug his name into a search, pulling up a random patchwork of results. An archived conference program from 1984, entitled "Emerging Therapies in Combat Psychiatry" lists Harvey L. Ward as a panelist and Department Chair at Walter Reed National Military Medical Center.

I continue scanning the search results to a paper co-authored by H.L. Ward in 1982, "Pediatric Dissociation & Sensory Reintegration," focusing on post-traumatic stress disorder in children exposed to wartime conflict.

A military alumni newsletter notes Ward's retirement in 1995 after "three decades of dedicated service in behavioral science." No photo. No further details. No mention of post-retirement activities.

The last link takes me to a defunct online forum thread, *Alt.health.research.conspiracies*. Someone posting under the name GateOp47 mentions "Ward, H.L." and something called

Project Highbridge, a rumored Navy research program in the 1970s dealing with "dream manipulation and astral displacement in children." The post is riddled with paranoid ramblings. Most of the replies dismiss it, but I take a screenshot anyway.

My door suddenly buzzes, snapping me out of the rabbit hole. I hurry downstairs where I find my pot dealer, Dez, leaning against the mailbox wall in the vestibule of my building. He beams up at me, pulling me in for a hug. I tuck a fold of cash in the front pocket of his hoodie, withdrawing a small Ziploc bag that I disappear into the pocket of my sweatpants.

"That's the new one from Oregon they're using for adult ADD," he says, stepping out of the way so my neighbor Pam can get her mail. He nods to her, waiting until she's gone. "The first time I smoked it, the shit was so real, I was like the robot from *Alien*. I did, like, 12 crosswords in a row. So, anyway, what's going on, yo?" he asks, smiling, ready for a chat.

"I'm good, you know, just banging out some work," I say, trying to find a way to wrap this up quickly. "You're looking good, Dez," I say, fishing my keys out of my pocket, hoping he'll take the hint. "Are you working out?"

He lights up. "You noticed! Yeah, I've been hitting the climbing wall. I'm getting ripped!"

"It shows!" I say, playing up my enthusiasm. "Listen, I wish I could chat, but I'm on a deadline. I hope that's OK."

"Yeah, no problem," he shrugs. "It's all good."

I give him a kiss on the cheek and usher him out the door, then hurry back upstairs. I roll a joint and get myself set up for business, unloading the contents of the file box onto the coffee table. I open my laptop and run searches on the names on the list, anything I can find: academic papers, articles, online profiles. I send the results to the printer, which churns in the corner, spitting out a ream of pages. I sort them into stacks for each participant:

>Dr. Allison Barnes: Biotechnology
>Dr. Margaret A. Koeffler: Neurology
>Dr. James Siegfried: Clinical Psychology
>Dr. Colin Marsh: Applied Mathematics
>Dr. Peter Phillips: Quantum Mechanics
>Dr. Andrew Harper: Biochemistry

I cross-reference the names, looking for overlaps, common associations, schools, laboratories.

A match surfaces, a peer-reviewed article citing Barnes and Siegfried conducting a study on sleep disorders. I scan the page, looking for where it took place—Walter Reed National Military Medical Center.

An article in *American Science* mentions a collaboration between Sellings Laboratory and the Madigan Army Medical Center for a study on the relationship between quantum mechanics and higher brain function. The study was led by Dr. Margaret A. Koeffler and Dr. Peter Phillips.

Of all the names on the list, Marsh, the mathematics genius, is by far the most public-facing, the showman of the group. A quick search unearths a trove of links, articles, interviews—from *Popular Mechanics* to *Vanity Fair* to a *New York Times* piece on the math behind the Mars rover launch. Marsh is referred to so often, it's hard to draw any clear connections between his work and that of the others on the list. It's like he's everywhere at once, cloaked in his own celebrity.

I search for Dr. James Siegfried and his work on PTSD. The bulk of his research begins in the 1990s during the Gulf War, tracking the mental health and recuperation of veterans who experienced friendly fire during deployment.

I plug "Dr. Peter Phillips" into a search, digging for whatever I can find. I come across a presentation he gave at SUNY Stony Brook in 2002—a headache-inducing kaleidoscope of diagrams and charts covering "statistical ensembles of pure states and their relation to quantum entanglement." I send it to the printer and move on.

I look up the book Adam recommended—*Psychic Warrior*—and find a summary. It tells the story of David Morehouse, a decorated Army officer and former Airborne Ranger who began experiencing visions and out-of-body episodes after a near-fatal training accident. These experiences eventually drew him into the Stargate Project—a classified U.S. military program designed to train psychic spies to gather intelligence beyond the limits of time and space. I find an entry on Wikipedia:

> The Stargate Project was the code name for a U.S. Army unit established in 1978 at Fort Meade, Maryland, by the Defense Intelligence Agency and SRI International (a California contractor) to investigate the potential for psychic phenomena in military and domestic applications. This primarily involved remote viewing, the purported ability to psychically "see" events, sites, or information from a great distance.

I plug in the name of the drug Adam mentioned, DMT, pulling up a slew of information—message boards, blog posts, psychedelic paintings, videos of people describing their trips, a *National Geographic* article on the ayahuasca shamans of South America. I find a website dedicated to shamans based in the U.S., complete with an interactive map. The majority appear in clusters around upstate New York, western Connecticut,

Colorado, Santa Fe, Los Angeles, and the Pacific Northwest. The site describes the role of a shaman as a "tour guide" to the spirit realm, preparing the ayahuasca and sitting with you during the trip, helping to mediate the experience.

> Traditionally, a shaman would leave the tribe to live alone in the jungle for months at a time, during which he would consume large amounts of ayahuasca to remain immersed in the spirit realm and familiarize himself with its laws and terrain.

I scroll through the strange paintings and drawings people have posted depicting their trips, essentially visits to another reality. Many of the drawings include fractals, a spiraling mathematical multiplicity seen throughout nature—in the curl of a leaf bud, the swirl of a goat's horns, the double helix of DNA. I take a long drag, gazing into the spiraling patterns, letting my mind go soft…just as my phone buzzes, breaking the spell. I grab for it, answering.

"This is Dr. Colin Marsh," a voice grumbles. "You left me a message."

My mind clicks in. "Yes, hi! Dr. Marsh! Hi," I stammer, swatting away a cloud of smoke, stifling a cough. "Thank you for calling me back. How are you?" *How are you?*

A silence on the line.

"Um, right, so, Dr. Phillips," I say. "He gave me your number."

I wait for a response. "Dr. Marsh?"

"I'm here," the voice replies.

"Right, OK. So…I think you may have worked with my dad, Andrew Harper…"

Silence.

"…And I was wondering if I could maybe ask you a couple of questions?"

Still no response.

"Dr. Marsh?"

"Questions about?"

"A project. That my father was working on. Right before he died. Your name was on a list."

"What list?"

"Well, that's kind of my first question."

There's silence for a moment, then: "You're in New York," he mutters.

"Yes, I'm—"

"The Hungarian Pastry Shop. Across from St. John the Divine. I'll be there tomorrow morning at nine."

"Oh. Great! I'm just writing that down," I say, concentrating on spelling the words. *"Hun-gar-i-an Pas-try Shop.* Got it. Great. Really, Dr. Marsh, this is so incredibly helpful. Thank you for taking the time."

"Don't thank me yet," he grumbles. A click.

18 | A THOUSAND NOWS

A bell jingles over the door of the Hungarian Pastry Shop, a relic of old New York. The air inside is thick with butter cookies and steaming black coffee. Undergrads crowd the cave-like space, tables crammed together, backpacks, laptops, cords snaking from power strips jabbed into the chipped plaster walls.

It's easy to pick out Marsh. He sits alone at one of the tables along the far edge of the room, dressed down in a white V-neck tee and an unbuttoned denim shirt. A faded Hollywood sort of handsome, he reclines back in his chair, his reading glasses pushed high on his forehead, his large, mitt-like hands folded on his chest. He's smiling up at an underclassman girl who's attached her hip to his table, talking with her hands, gushing over something incredibly important. I inch my way over, waiting for an opportunity to break in, but it's like the girl has created an invisible wall between Marsh and the rest of the room.

"Excuse me," I interrupt. "Dr. Marsh?"

The girl spins around and sizes me up, a piercing glare.

"Yes, hello." Marsh smiles up at me warmly. He rests a hand on the girl's arm, instantly softening her, reeling her back in. "I really am fascinated by this," he tells her. "Let's pick this up this afternoon. Would that work? Why don't you come by my office? Do you know where it is?"

"Absolutely!" the girl blurts, delighted. She flashes me a triumphant sneer before striding off. Marsh half-rises, offering me the chair opposite him, sliding a stack of books aside. "Pardon the mess," he apologizes. "I don't even know why I bring these. There's no getting any work done here."

"I can see that," I say, watching him tidy up the table. His movements have the smooth assuredness of an old tiger.

"Come again?" he says with a smile, eyebrows raised. His hazel eyes sparkle, illuminated, a glittering field of energy rising like a wave, enveloping me,

> *ripping me forward,*
> *down into the sizzling light,*
> *through it, below it,*
> *a vast darkness,*
> *the light shrinking above me as I'm*
> *pulled down into the void.*
> *I reach my body out,*
> *stretching my arms and legs like a star,*
> *but there's nothing to snare,*
> *to slow my velocity,*
> *as I plummet through the infinite*
> *darkness,*
> *and then—*
> *WHAM!*
> *My body slams into the earth.*
> *Coughing, gasping,*
> *the wind knocked out of me.*

*I reach my hands over the ground, over
wet grass,
my vision warping into focus.
Above me, a sea of stars.
An infinite constellation spread across
the dome of the night.
I draw in a deep breath,
the air sweet and bitter and green,
filling my brain,
a raw oxygen,
sharp and crisp.
I squint around me:
a rolling landscape,
soft hills,
black-bodied trees.
I look at my hands—
a man's hands.
I'm wearing something like a robe, a
long tunic.
I listen to the sound of the wind shushing
through the high grass.
And this feeling, deep inside me—
a hollowness,
homesickness,
marooned here,
far away from home,
somewhere up there,
in the stars,
in the phosphorescent swirl—
wishing myself there,
projecting my consciousness up into the
night,
into the light of a star,*

> *enfolding me,*
> *taking me home…*

I slump forward, catching myself on the edge of the table. Marsh reaches out, steadying me. "Hey there, everything all right?"

I shield my eyes from his gaze. "Yes, sorry. Long night," I mutter, trying to laugh it off.

"No need to apologize," he says with a chuckle. "Let's get you a cup of coffee, shall we?" He regards me for a moment, then meanders up front, waving to one of the girls behind the counter.

I draw a deep breath, willing myself together.

Marsh returns with a small white coffeepot in one hand and a porcelain cup and saucer in the other. "Better now?" he asks.

"Yes, sorry about that." I say sheepishly, as he pours me a cup.

"Nonsense," he says, setting down the coffee pot, resettling in his chair. "I'm the one who should be apologizing. My memory seems to have gotten away from me. I want to say you're in my…Tuesday class?"

"Tuesday?"

"Linear algebra," he says.

"Oh…no. I'm sorry," I fumble. "I'm Catherine. We spoke last night."

"Ah, yes." He takes another stab at it. "At the dinner."

He has no idea who I am. "We spoke on the phone," I say. "Last night."

No recollection.

"You called me," I say, trying to piece it together.

He fidgets in his seat, glancing around the room. "I'm sorry," he says. "Maybe there's a mistake. I'm—"

"Dr. Colin Marsh," I say. "I'm Catherine Harper. Andrew Harper's daughter. I believe you and my father worked together."

He tries to place the name.

"On a project," I add.

Suddenly, a pall descends over him, as if he's been caught in a lie. "I'm sorry," he says, shrinking back. "What is this? Who called you?"

"*You* did," I say.

"*I* did?"

"You called me last night. You said to meet you here. At nine o'clock."

He shifts in his chair, scanning the room again. He glances at his watch. "There must be a mistake," he says. He gathers up his books, slipping them into a canvas tote. "My apologies, but you'll have to excuse me. I have a class I have to—"

"Dr. Peter Phillips," I blurt. "He gave me your number. He thought we should speak."

The name means something. He looks at me—a pause before changing tack. "Yes, of course," he says. "Would you mind walking with me?" Without waiting for an answer, he loops his bag over his shoulder and strides to the front counter, bidding a cheerful farewell to the girl. I hustle to follow him. He holds the door for me as we exit, then strides ahead, pulling an old flip phone from his breast pocket. "Hi, sorry," he grumbles into the phone, "can you cover my 10 o'clock?" He leads us up the avenue, through the university gates, signaling *she's with me* to the guard in the security booth. We continue up the tree-lined path, emerging onto the central quad, alive with back-to-school energy. A sea of students spreading out in all directions—music on the lawn, an Ultimate Frisbee game, hippie girls in peasant skirts twirling hula hoops.

Marsh ducks into the entrance of a colossal stone building overlooking the green. He fumbles for his key card, holding the phone in the crook of his neck, beeping us in. "No, everything's fine," he mumbles. "You know where we left off. Thanks." He snaps the phone shut and pockets it, loping up the marble staircase. I hurry up behind him, rounding a corner into a long, narrow corridor of faculty offices, an endless procession of wavy-glass doors. Marsh fishes out his keys and opens the door, collecting an envelope someone slipped under it while he was out. He moves to his desk, a walnut behemoth stacked with papers, tossing the envelope onto a pile of mail. He motions to the door. "Can you…," he says, trailing off, waving for me to close it.

Marsh's office is like a den of organized chaos—floor-to-ceiling shelves crammed with books, file boxes, stacks of old magazines, a football tucked into an old baseball mitt, a battle-hardened soup thermos. A wall of awards, certificates, diplomas, and black-and-white photographs presides over the far side of the room, looming above a tired brown leather sofa.

He heaves open a desk drawer, pulling out a pack of Marlboro Reds. He knocks one out and offers it to me. I decline, thanking him, trying to figure out if I'm supposed to stand or sit. Marsh doesn't offer any hints. He crosses to the enormous window overlooking the quad and hoists it open, strikes a match, and lights up. He waves the match out and flicks it out the window, then leans back, half-seated against the window ledge. He takes a drag, watching me, thinking.

He turns his head and exhales a thin white line of smoke. "You'll have to forgive me," he says. "I'm a little confused." He examines me as I stand in the center of the room. "Peter Phillips said you and I should speak?"

"Yes, about a project you worked on with my father, Andrew Harper."

"And you're saying we spoke, you and I, last night?"

"Correct."

He considers this, flicking ash out the window. "Well, that's strange," he says, "because I don't remember making a phone call."

"That is strange," I offer. "Because we definitely spoke."

"You're sure it was me?"

"I mean—it was your voice."

He takes a drag. "And what did I say?" he asks.

My mind draws a blank. What *did* he say? "You said to meet you at the cafe. At 9 a.m."

He leans there, watching me.

I try to recall anything else. "You said, 'Don't thank me yet.'"

This means something to him. I can't tell what. He snubs out the cigarette and returns to his desk, rummaging through a lower drawer. He fishes something out and sets it on the desk in front of him—a small, shiny black box, the size of a hockey puck, just like the one Phillips had. Marsh rocks back in his chair, smoothing his hands behind his head. "Come to think of it," he says, "Andrew Harper. The name does ring a bell. We spoke on a panel together. When would that have been?" He ponders. "Ages ago. But aside from that?" He shrugs.

"Your name was on a list," I say. I retrieve the slip of paper from my purse and slide it across the desk. He puts on his glasses and inspects it. After a moment he glances up at me. "And what do we think this is?" he asks.

"Do you recognize anyone?"

"Well, Peter, of course. But aside from that—"

"White Ladder 369. Does that mean anything to you?"

Marsh swivels his chair to face the window, reflecting. He scans the list.

"My father," I say, "he was part of a team working on a project right before he died. I think you may have been working on it as well—perhaps without knowing."

Marsh swivels back, sets the list on his desk, and leans back, folding his hands behind his head, ready to listen.

"Phillips was working on the project as well," I continue. "He thought the other participants—the names on that list—were being kept apart."

"And why is that?" Marsh asks.

"He didn't know. Maybe to keep them in the dark about what they were actually working on."

"Who was keeping them in the dark?" he asks.

"The government? I don't know."

"Peter told you this?" He scans the list. "These names here..."

"Were involved somehow," I say, completing his thought.

He pushes his glasses onto his forehead and tugs at his nose, thinking. "And this was when?" he asks.

"It would have started in 1987."

"And what did this project entail?"

"I was hoping you could tell me that."

"Without knowing more of the details of what we're talking about, I'm at a bit of a loss," he says. "However, if this *was* a government-funded project, there'd surely be a record of it. Have you submitted a FOIA request? It's worth a shot. At least that's where I would start." He holds out the list to me, waiting for me to take it. I tuck it away in my bag. With that, Marsh begins rearranging the stacks of papers on his desk, a cue for me to wrap this up.

I watch him for a moment. "You know what, you're right," I say. "This is crazy. I don't know why I'm bothering you with this. I'll keep asking around. Something's bound to turn up." I turn and cross to the door. I can feel his eyes on me.

"Who's next?" he asks.

"Excuse me?"

"On your list there," he says.

"That's a good question," I reply, "since nearly everyone on it is dead."

There's a shift in his expression.

"All but you," I say. "And your friend Dr. Phillips. You must have an angel watching over you." I glance at the small black box sitting on his desk. "It's funny, Dr. Phillips had one of those."

"One of—?"

"A little black box," I say, nodding. "Just like that."

He processes this. "Is that right?" he says, reaching again for his pack of cigarettes. He taps one out and lights it. "You know what?" he says, rocking back. He expels a white puff of smoke to the ceiling like a simmering dragon. "Let me make a couple calls."

I try to play up my enthusiasm. "Really? You'd do that?"

"Why not." He rocks forward, sliding a pad and pen to me. "You never know. An old coot like me might still be good for something. Write down your number."

"Dr. Marsh, that's so kind of you, thank you," I say, jotting down my info.

"Of course, anything I can do." He rises and walks me to the door and extends his big-knuckled hand. "Catherine, it has been a true pleasure," he says, holding my grip a beat too long. "Almost like meeting extended family."

"Yes, right—thank you," I say, pulling away. I feel him watching from the doorway as I walk a bit too fast down the corridor and descend the staircase. I burst out onto the quad under the bright blue sky, weaving through the throngs of students, through shouts and laughter and games—ducking down the colonnade onto Broadway. I scan the block, looking for the subway station, a cab, anything to escape. I step off the curb just as a hand reaches out, grabbing my arm, saving me from the path of an oncoming truck. I gasp, reeling back, looking up at who's holding me: a college kid in a white tennis shirt, blond, blue eyes. He says something to me, but the words don't register. I concentrate on his mouth, but his lips don't move. *Is he speaking?* There's a sound coming from him like humming. Or is the sound in my head? Echoing like an enormous bell—

> *flowering into images,*
> *symbols,*
> *churning one into another,*
> *kaleidoscopic,*
> *enfolding like the facets of a diamond,*
> *glassy planes reaching out into infinity,*
> *and behind each, a scene, a film,*
> *a thousand screens,*
> *a thousand nows—*
> *I'm inside a car,*
> *my parents' car.*
> *My father is driving,*
> *my mother in the passenger seat.*
> *She's slumped to her side,*
> *her head against the window.*
> *Is she sleeping?*
> *My father says something to her,*
> *touches her arm.*
> *Then suddenly he slumps forward,*
> *collapsing over the steering wheel.*
> *The car swerves,*
> *slams into a guardrail,*
> *rises up,*
> *flipping...*

flipping...
passing like the frame of a film strip...
revealing another scene beneath.
The same, but different now.
My parents in the car, talking, laughing.
Turning into the driveway of our house—
unharmed,
unaware,
alive...

A voice, soft and hissing, curls around the images flooding through my mind:

> *"This life...*
> *is yours...to choose...*
> *You...are...unlimited...*
> *Do not...*
> *be trapped...*
> *as they...*
> *would trap...you ...*
> *I...can show...*
> *you how...*
> *I...*
> *will...*
> *show...*
> *you freedom...*
> *like you...*
> *have never...*
> *known..."*

Another voice shatters the spell. *"Adi la basi alaku!"* the voice snarls. My mind, my eyes awaken—the light of day, the edge of the sidewalk, traffic roaring by. The blond boy releases me and turns, startled, as if he were waking from a dream. He squares off with the person shouting at him, a young Black man standing his ground a few yards away. *"Adi la basi alaku!"* the stranger barks. The blond boy looks at me, then back at the stranger, then gives us both a look like *what the fuck?* He hurries away, across the street, nearly getting run over himself.

"Yo, are you OK?" the stranger asks, approaching. He has a gentle face and big, brown melancholy eyes that sparkle like panes of glass. I suddenly realize we're locked in a gaze, but nothing is happening. *How am I not falling in?* "Who…? "

"Hi, yeah, sorry," he apologizes. "That probably seemed crazy. You OK?"

I glance around, trying to get my bearings.

"I'm Koi," he says, stepping closer. "Like the fish. You're Catherine, right?"

I back away. "What is this?"

"I know this seems weird, but if you could just give me a second, I can explain." He scans the vicinity, spotting something across the street. "There's a bagel shop over there," he points. "Is it cool if we just sit down for a minute?"

"What do you want?" I snap, looking around. "Are you with Marsh?"

He blinks back at me, confused. "I don't know who that is. Look, could we just—"

"I'm not going anywhere," I say, holding my ground. "Who are you?"

"I'm Koi."

"Koi *who*? Who the fuck are you?"

"I'm trying to tell you!" he blurts, catching himself. He lowers his voice, trying not to turn this into a scene. "Look, I'm just trying to help. You're looking for information, am I right? About your dad?" He pauses a beat, sees that I'm listening now. "I get it. You don't know me. I'm coming up to you on the street." He looks to see if anyone's listening. "Can we just talk for a second? Like, just super chill. Maybe not right in the middle of the sidewalk. I can explain everything. I promise."

"What was that—that you did there? That stuff you were saying?"

"You could hear me?" He looks surprised. "What happened? When he grabbed you. Was he saying something to you?"

"Saying?"

"Was he humming? Like singing?"

"OK, I don't know what's going on here," I say, pulling out my phone, glancing around for help.

"The files," he says. "In the metal box. From the storage unit. They have numbers on them. You're trying to figure out what they are. I am too. I just need to talk to you. I'm not looking for trouble."

A chill goes through me. "How do you—"

"That's what I'm trying to tell you. If you'll just give me a second." He's practically begging now. I look over at the bagel shop. He glances at it. "I'll buy you a bagel," he says. "I'm not a psycho. I promise."

19 | THE TREE

I choose a table near the front window, safely tucked between a gray-haired woman reading her iPad and a young mother feeding her toddler. Koi squeezes in, setting down two large coffees and a giant pumpernickel bagel with cream cheese, sliced in half.

"So you've been following me," I say, not wasting any time.

Koi glances at the other tables. "I just needed to find a way for us to talk—and, like, not freak you out."

"Well, that worked."

"Look." He pauses. "There's no real easy way to talk about—"

"How do you know about my father?"

"Right, so that's the thing," he says, shifting in his chair. "I don't. It's more like…I know this is gonna sound crazy, but I *see* things. When I dream. Like, in the future." He looks for my reaction, surprised when I don't have one. "I'll have a dream, and I'll see it like a movie. And then the next day, or maybe the next week, it happens in real life. Like déjà vu. But like I knew the déjà vu was going to happen." Again, he looks for my reaction. "I'm not explaining this right."

"So you see the future," I say, point-blank.

He sits up. "Yeah, like, a lot of it is just regular stuff. I'll see it in a dream and then it'll happen a couple of days later, whatever. But I also have these nightmares. One in particular. The same dream, over and over. About stuff that's, like, further in the future, *years* from now. I don't know what's happened. The way it looks…"

"The way what looks?"

"Everything. The whole world…is dark, hollow. Like the sun went out."

"Like nighttime?"

"Like permanent night. And everything is dying. Sometimes I'm in the woods, sometimes it's a city, or a beach. There's no one around, anywhere. It's all just empty. And everything feels like…*metal*. Cold. I never see what happened, just the aftermath. But then one night I found myself in the nightmare, but it wasn't a nightmare anymore. It had flipped somehow. It was the same places I had seen, but they were full of life. Full of people and energy. The cities had a different look to them. Like, the buildings—they shimmered. It felt like everything was healed. And there was this music. Not like music you could hear, but like, *inside* everything, like in the atoms. I don't know how to describe it. And you were there—in the dream. That's where I saw you."

"What do you mean, I was there?"

"I don't know. It was like this future, this version of the future, included you. Or like you had caused it somehow. Like you *did* something—in the present—that changed the future. Whatever you did affected everything. Like a domino effect."

"OK, I'm… How do you even know who I am?"

"Look," he says, pulling out his phone. He opens an email and hands it to me. Three lines of text:

> catherine harper
> 201 west 10th street apartment 5C
> new york city

"What is this? Who sent you this?" I look for the name of the sender. "Brandon Bell."

"That's my brother."

"And how does your brother know where I live?"

"He doesn't. Brandon's dead. He died three years ago."

I look at the send date—two weeks ago. Koi takes back the phone. "So he's not really emailing that much," he says with a sniff. "I thought it was some kind of prank, so I searched your name and a picture came up. It was you. I recognized you from my dream." He thinks about how to continue. "There's this thing, it's called a divergence," he explains. "If someone changes something in the present, like they do something unexpected, it breaks the original timeline and creates an entirely new future. Once you appeared in my dream, it was like the nightmare version got erased, and it never came back. I realized you must be the one who caused it. So the next time I had the dream, I focused on you. I can do that. I can focus on a person, almost like a character in a movie, and I can read them backward, like rewinding a video. I followed you back to the moment it happened: You were in a building, like a storage room. Right? There was a box. And inside the box was another box. That was it. I know it because I can feel it. There's a division there. Like everything before that—before you found the box—feels heavy. That's the old timeline. But *after* the box, everything is lighter. That's the new timeline beginning. That was the trigger. The moment you found it, what it made you do."

"What did I do?"

"I don't know," he says, shrugging. "Maybe it's something you haven't even done yet. All I know is you found this box, and that's when a new path started."

"So who wrote the email with my address?"

"Right, so that's some other shit," he says with a sniff. "I checked the headers to see who sent it, but it's scrambled, like some kind of fake server—like a mirror site. So I figure it's gotta be a bot or some hacker or some shit. But why is he using my brother's name? I reply back, 'Who is this?' And whaddayaknow."

He opens another email and hands it to me. Two words. I read them aloud:

lucky charms

"Exactly." Koi nods, like this should mean something.

"Exactly what?"

"That's his favorite cereal."

"Your brother's."

"Yeah, so I'm like, *now you're messing with me*. But before I can write him back, I get another email from him." He shows me.

007

"OK. I don't get it."

"Me neither," he says. "So I write back, '???' No reply. I write back again. Still nothing. Then I get this call. This crazy long number pops up on my phone, like from China or someplace. I don't know who it is, so I push it to voicemail. They call back. I push it again. They call back *again*. So I pick up, and I'm like, '*Who is this?*' And the caller's like, 'Hello, Koi, I'm a friend of your brother Brandon's.' And it takes me a sec, because this dude's got a British accent. I'm like, 'You don't sound like any of my brother's friends.' And he's like, 'Brandon wished for us to speak. My name is Mr. Y.' And I'm like, 'OK, were you his English teacher?' Like, who the fuck? He says that I received an email, with a name and address. And I'm like, *Oooookay, so this is the motherfucker right here*. He says: 'Brandon helped me find you.' And I'm like, '*Brandon?* How could Brandon help you?' And this is when it goes total *Twilight Zone*. He starts telling me about my dreams. Reciting them back to me. Stuff nobody knows. And I'm like, *You know what, we're gonna record this. We're gonna get allllll this shit on tape.* Koi reaches into his pocket and pulls out his earbuds, unraveling them. He hands me one and puts the other in his ear. Reluctantly, I put it up to my ear. He presses play on his phone. The recording starts mid-conversation:

"So wait-wait-wait-wait-wait," Koi says. "How do you know what's happening in my dreams?"

"Because I can see it too," the caller replies. His voice is older.

"See what?" Koi snaps. "What are you talking about?'"

"You have a gift, Koi. You don't just see. The woman in your dream—she has a gift like yours. She's looking for answers, just like you. Isn't that right, Catherine?"

"Catherine?" Koi asks. "Who are you talking to?"

"I'm talking to Catherine." The caller replies. "You don't see her?"

"See who?" Koi asks, bewildered. "I'm the only one here!"

"You will. Soon enough," the caller replies. "Soon, we'll all be together like this, and you'll be holding out your phone, and Catherine will be sitting right there, listening. Do you see her now?"

Koi points his finger at the phone, big-eyed, like *what the fuck is this shit?*

"Catherine, I must apologize," the caller continues. "I would have much preferred this to be in person. There are questions you have that I would like to answer, but I need to answer them in my own way, if you'll allow me. Will you do that?"

"Are you asking me?" Koi replies.

"No, Koi," the voice answers. "I'm asking Catherine."

"I'm listening," I say.

Koi looks at me, baffled.

"You wish to know about your father," the caller continues. "I believe I can help with that. Your father had a gift. He was a genius. Do you know the origin of the word 'genius'? It comes from Latin, meaning 'guardian deity.' The French—they say *génie*, or 'spirit teacher.' There is a belief that knowledge, true knowledge, is not a thing that man discovers, but is rather passed down to him by a higher power—as a gift. In this way, a genius is no more than a receiver, a conduit, a channel the knowledge is passed through. But there is another type of genius—and this is very rare. He not only receives knowledge from the source; he communes with it. He is like the deepest roots of a tree, reaching down into the earth and carrying the information back to the source, back to God. But for all his knowledge, the genius does not know who he truly is. He is like a stranded child, never recognizing the voice that speaks to him. Your father knew it spoke to you as well. Isn't that right? As a child? In your room? You would spread your fingers wide like the rays of the sun and feel something buzzing between them?"

My mind flashes with a memory: my childhood bedroom, me waking in the night and feeling something there, invisible.

"Catherine, if you want to know why your father did what he did," the caller continues, "it was because he was lied to. I know this, because I was the one who lied to him... There are things that have happened that no one could ever know—hidden in a place that no one will ever find. There is a great lie being told, and it's time for the truth to come out."

Koi tries to read my face, to see how any of this is landing.

"The books you read," the voice continues. "The holy books. The ancient stories. You read them as a child—because you were searching for something. What was it you were looking for? A clue perhaps? To where these stories came from? The Bible, for instance. Genesis 1:27. 'So God created man in his own image.' A mirror of himself. If that's true, then I ask you, what is the difference between man and God? What if one were no greater than the other? What if you could unseat God and take his place? Catherine, your father was lied to. But now he sees the truth. And he is helping us. He speaks to you, doesn't he? In the cab that day. You were going home, but you changed your mind. You went to a room. A room with a red door. And in that room you found a box. And in that box another box. And why did you go to the room that day? Was it a whim? Or did you feel something? Did you see something? Or the painting in the museum. The one you have always been drawn to. The girl in the garden, listening—to a message. Where did that message come from? And what if the girl was fooled? What if we were all fooled—and none of this is what it seems? That is what I wish to show you. If you'll let me."

Koi and I sit in silence, gazing at the phone, waiting for more—but the caller is gone. The phone, black and blank. Koi looks at me. "Sooooo."

"That's it?"

He shrugs.

"Who makes a phone call like that?" I ask.

"Was that even a *phone call?*" Koi blurts. "That was some next-level time portal shit. I don't know *what* that was. Obviously, this guy knows your dad, though. It sounds like he worked with him. What was that thing he said about you having a gift like mine? What did he mean by that?"

"If I look at someone, if I look in their eyes, I can see where they've been. Their past lives."

"Seriously?" he says, beaming. "That's like me—with my dreams. The way I can follow people backward. But you can do it when you're awake? Are you doing it now? What do you see when you look in my eyes?"

"I don't see anything."

"What do you mean you don't see anything? Nothing?"

"It's like I'm locked out. When I look into your eyes, nothing happens."

"Well, maybe you gotta concentrate."

"That's not how it works."

"All right, try again." He sits up straight, gazing at me. I take a deep breath, centering my mind, pointing all of my attention into the black disks of his pupils. I shake my head no.

"Maybe that means something," he says. "Maybe we have the same thing. Like, two versions of the same thing. And, like, one deflects the other."

"The guy on the phone," I say. "Do you know who he is?"

"He calls himself Mr. Y."

"Mr. Y? Like the letter Y? Who calls themselves a letter?" Koi shrugs.

"Have you talked to him since?"

"I mean, he texts me," Koi says with a sniff, "but his phone is encrypted or something, because it doesn't come up on a search."

"So how do you know it's him?"

"Because I'm not getting texts from a bunch of dudes asking me about my nightmares," he says. "And if I can be honest, it's like the guy is trying to help—deciphering my dreams, leading me to you. Look, I know it sounds crazy. When he first started telling me everything, it freaked me out. I'm not gonna lie. But, at the same time, I was kind of glad somebody was telling me *something*. You know what I mean? Like, OK, *this shit is real,* whatever it is, and I know it for a fact because somebody else is seeing it too. That's why I'm here talking to you now. If you don't know how to process any of this, I get it. I'm trying to figure it out myself. But here's the thing: This dude, whoever he is, he's been right so far, so I figure, let me see about this. What does he mean my brother is helping him? Or your dad? Like, their *spirits* or something? What does that even mean? 'Cause as far as I'm concerned, I know where Brandon is. I got a lot of people on that side, and they're supposed to be at peace. As far as I'm concerned, Heaven is supposed to be chill as fuck, so why is Brandon trying to get a message to me? I'm just seeing what this dude has to say. And right now he's telling me that you and I are supposed to meet."

"But why?" I ask. "I don't understand."

"I don't know," Koi shrugs. "To work together?"

"Work together on *what*?"

"I don't know!" he blurts, exasperated. "You're acting like I'm the expert on this. I have no idea what's going on. All I know is I got nightmares. I got this Shakespearean motherfucker calling me. You see the past. I see the future. Are we supposed to be the psychic Super Friends? I don't know! I thought *you* could tell *me* something. Like what is this box you found?"

"I don't know. And I'm not sure I want to know." I start gathering my things.

Koi flinches, watching me. "You good?"

"I have to go. I'm sorry."

"Go?" He looks at me askance. "What, you got some other mind-bending shit you gotta attend to?"

"What do you want from me?"

"Who was that? Before."

"Before what?"

"The guy you met. This morning."

"So you did follow me."

He shrugs, waiting for an answer.

"He worked with my father."

"And what did he have to say?"

"Nothing. It was a waste of time."

"And what about the other guy?" he asks.

"What other guy?"

"The Virginia guy."

"What? How long have you been following me?"

"What, do you think you're the only one being careful?" he says. "I don't know you. These people."

I glance at the older woman seated next to us. She's completely abandoned her iPad and is engrossed in our conversation. I glare at her, but she doesn't flinch, waiting for the show to continue.

"If you want to walk with me, fine," I say, "but I have to go."

Koi follows me. "So these guys you met, they worked with your dad. Worked with him how?" he asks.

"For the government. It's called a black project."

"Right, like some top secret shit." He considers this. "I wonder if that's what I was seeing. In my nightmare. The way everything was dead and metallic. Maybe it was a biological weapon."

I look to him as something occurs to me. "On the corner, when you came up to me. That guy. The kid who grabbed my arm. You shouted something at him."

"The possessed guy?"

"The what?"

"Yeah, so that's some crazy shit," Koi says, nodding. "It's been happening to me too. Whenever I'm trying to dig into this stuff, I have some weird paranormal shit happen. Like, trying to stop me, or scare me."

"Stop you?"

"Yeah, sometimes it's a person," he says. "They seem totally normal and then suddenly they start acting weird, or talking weird."

"Weird how? What do they say?"

He shrugs. "Sometimes they're not even saying words. It's like their lips aren't moving. Or I can't tell if they are or not."

"What do you mean, you can't tell? Aren't you looking at them?"

"I mean, I'm trying to," he says. "That's what's even weirder. It's like I can't look directly at them. Or I can just see parts of them. Like this one guy. All I could do was look at his arm. Like I was hypnotized. And he was singing to me."

"Singing?"

"Like humming. Sometimes it's like singing, but without words. It's trippy as hell. I can feel it in my head, like the sound is moving thoughts around—like pictures or symbols. I don't know what it is. Is that what was happening to you? Because I saw you, like, hypnotized." He pantomimes, locking his body into a frozen zombie pose. "But nobody else on the street even noticed. It was like I was the only one who could see you like that. That's when I was like, *I bet this is one of these possessed motherfuckers grabbing her*. So I said that Sumerian shit to break the spell."

"The what?"

"Yeah, the British dude, Mr. Y—he told me a bunch of sayings to use if weird shit starts happening. Has that happened to you before?"

My mind flashes to Virginia Beach. The scene outside the coffee shop. The woman with blue eyes, the way she held my gaze. Did her lips move when she spoke? *Do you know where you're going?*

"Every time you start figuring something out," Koi says. "It's like they're trying to intimidate you."

"Who's trying?"

"I don't know. Maybe it's some government mind-control shit. Maybe it's part of this project your dad was working on. Maybe that's why these guys don't want to talk to you about it."

"This Mr. Y. What else has he told you?"

"I mean, not much," Koi says, shrugging. "Whenever he texts me, it's always some cryptic shit. I'll ask him about Brandon, and he'll ask me a question back, like, 'Where do you think Brandon is?' And I'll be like, 'Um, Heaven?' And he'll be like, 'Where do you think Heaven is?' Shit like that. Everything is like a riddle with this dude. But I feel like he's trying to help. Like he's trying to guide me."

I pause at the top of the subway stairs.

"I feel like he was part of this project your dad was working on," Koi says. "I think he knows what it was all about, but he's not saying. It's like he needs us to figure it out on our own."

"Why would he need that?"

"I don't know," Koi says. "That's just the feeling I get."

There's an awkward pause as I weigh exactly what I'm supposed to do. Koi breaks the silence. "So, maybe we could trade notes? Maybe we could—"

"Look, I'm not trying to be a bitch," I say, cutting him off, "but I need a minute."

"Yeah, no, I get that," he says, giving me space. "I could give you my number." He pulls a McDonald's receipt out of his wallet and scribbles on the back. "I'm staying at the Hotel Giraffe. Just text me, whenever. I'm putting my full name on here, Koi Bell. You can look me up. Make sure I'm not some internet psycho." He hands me the slip of paper, coming in for an awkward handshake-ass-out hug. The moment we touch, a dull shock surges through me, up my arm and into my chest. I flinch and snatch my hand away. "OK, I'll see you," I say, darting down the steps, through the turnstile, slipping in through the closing doors of the train. I put my hand to my chest, feeling the buzz slowly melting away, as the train jerks forward, barreling into the dark.

20 | THE LESSER LIGHTS

I pause outside my building, scanning up and down the street looking for anything that seems off, but there's nothing, just the city bustling by, oblivious. I text Jemma:

> *Is anyone at the cottage?*

> *Not til fri*

> *Ok if I use it for a couple days?*

> *Sure bring coffee and TP we're out*

I run upstairs and sift through a sea of files, printouts, notes, stuffing them into a canvas tote. I open my laptop. A flood of emails—clients checking in, meeting requests, when can I send something? I shut the lid and stuff it into the tote.

I pace under the departures board at Penn Station waiting for the train to be called, scanning through my texts, to the last one from Jake:

> *Thinking about you*
> *We good?*

I toss the phone in my purse…then pull it out and type:

> *Yes*
> *I was awful*
> *I'm sorry*

The board clicks as new track numbers spin up. My phone vibrates:

> *Where r u*

The train slides along the skyline of Long Island, over sun-bleached neighborhoods and black tar rooftops, past strip malls and church steeples, out into the high-reed marshes and beyond, the names of stations whisking by—Freeport, Merrick, Bellmore. I run a search on DMT, scanning down through the results, a cascade of blog posts, testimonials, people's firsthand experiences of their journeys. Each story is uniquely complex, but there are consistencies. Most of the experiences begin with the appearance of a "guide," a woman floating barefoot before them. The woman leads them through a parallel dimension, a sort of collaged version of reality, a world depicted through metaphors and symbols, as though a higher consciousness was trying to communicate a complex concept to a child. Many accounts describe the symbols as resembling Egyptian hieroglyphs.

A book appears in the search results: *The Cosmic Serpent* by Jeremy Narby, an archeologist who spent years living with the Ashaninka, a tribe in Peru, investigating the connections between ancient shamanism and molecular biology. In the book, Narby compares his experiences on ayahuasca to those of the anthropologist Michael Harner and his accounts of incredibly vivid, waking-dream-like encounters while under the potion's spell. At one point, Harner recalls looking up in the sky and seeing what appeared to be a giant Viking ship with a dragon-headed prow passing over him like a blimp. On the ship's deck Harner sees human-looking figures with heads like blue jays, similar to the bird-headed gods depicted in ancient Egyptian tombs.

I continue to scan through the results, noticing a name that keeps appearing—Terence McKenna. A fringe figure with a cult following who rose to fame during the 1990s rave scene, McKenna was known for his research into psychedelic plants and their connection to human consciousness. There are hundreds of videos of McKenna online—conferences, seminars, uploads from radio shows, videos by fans comparing their trips to his. I play one of his conference videos, where he recounts a conversation with a "wizened" Tibetan lama about the lama's experience on DMT. The lama called it "the lesser lights." He said it takes you as far as you can go without "breaking the thread of return."

I run a search for "Tibetan Buddhism and DMT," which points me to another book: *DMT: The Spirit Molecule* by Rick Strassman. As I skim through an excerpt, something jumps out at me, a reference to the pineal gland, how a human fetus develops the gland on the 49th day after conception, and how this coincides with *The Tibetan Book of the Dead*, which says that it takes 49 days for a soul to reincarnate.

An announcement chimes over the intercom: "Next stop, Bay Shore." I collect my things and notice the receipt Koi handed me floating around in my purse, his number scribbled on the back. I enter another search on my phone, pulling up a definition:

> Sumerian—the ancient language of Sumer, the earliest-known civilization in recorded history, located in southern Mesopotamia

I text Koi:

> *Hi it's Catherine. What was the thing*
> *you said. In Sumerian.*

As the train slows into the station, my phone buzzes back:

> *Adi la basi alaku*

I copy it into a search and click translate:

> Bring to naught

21 | PYRAMID

I grab a seat on the upper deck of the ferry, its giant engines rumbling up through the bowels of the boat as we drift out into the bay, mowing through the wakes of speedboats and jet skis carving white X's in the blue-black water. We float across the glimmering stretch to the island on the opposite shore, nudging into the dock at Fair Harbor.

A slender ribbon of sand and trees stretching 30 miles long and barely a mile wide, Fire Island feels less like a vacation hot spot and more a bohemian encampment of dyed-in-the-wool New Yorkers. Its willful avoidance of all things modern and convenient, particularly roads and cars, has effectively insulated the island from the raucous summer crowds of the Hamptons, leaning instead toward an off-the-grid-with-a-good-book vibe.

A sun-bleached network of narrow boardwalks stretches across the island, bisected by a single concrete road, a sand-dusted thoroughfare ringing with the *tring-tring* of rusted bicycle bells as cheerful riders swivel by one another, waving their hellos. Rows of cedar shake cottages sit tucked back in the gnarled thickets of pine and scrub trees, the smell of charcoal grills wafting through the afternoon air. Jemma's bungalow, a time-share she splits with a couple of girls from work, sits among them. An inconspicuous, weathered gray box, the house is joyfully unspectacular, its deck stacked with a rainbow of beach paraphernalia. I pull the key off the hook in the outdoor shower and crack open the side door, letting out a waft of hot, cooped-up air that smells of cedar and mothballs. Three small bedrooms, a galley kitchen, and a wood-paneled living room—the cottage is decorated with a mish-mash of wicker furniture giving it a sort of 70s rec room feel.

The refrigerator jangles open, its door lined with bottles of rosé. I take one out and pour a glass and start setting myself up in the living room, shuttling the contents of the tote onto the coffee table, across the floor.

I begin sifting through the notes, arranging them by subject matter—biochemistry, quantum mechanics, psychology, applied mathematics, biotechnology, neurology—looking for anything that might connect them. Diamonds of sunlight carve across the room as the hours pass, and a realization begins to surface: Whoever funded this project would need something to show for it. Something concrete, something physical. Something would need to be *made*—which would require an engineer. *Am I missing someone?* I sit back, looking across what was once an orderly row of columns, now devolved into a random patchwork of printouts full of inconsistencies and dead ends. I text Koi:

Let's combine notes

I wait for a reply, but there's no response, and I suddenly feel an icy pang in my mind, a creeping desperation. Outside, a lavender light bleeds through the darkening trees. I grab the bottle of wine and a couple of red plastic party cups, and pull the door locked behind me.

The sun descends into the darkening bay, a mango orb glittering across the rippling water, making black triangles of the sailboats gliding along the horizon. The pier has transitioned into a deck party, a nightly ritual for the summer crowd—parents escaping their kids, drinking beer out of coolers, flirting with each other under a fog of weed and cigar smoke.

A woman stands apart from the crowd at the far end of the dock, gazing out at the water, an empty wine glass dangling between her fingertips. She hugs an oversize fisherman's sweater to her tall, slim frame, a pair of giant sunglasses pushed up onto the crown of her head, pulling back her long silver-blond hair. She flashes me a quick smile as I approach—a friendly, please-don't-start-a-conversation sort of smile. I uncork the bottle of wine and point the neck to her, offering a top-up. She glances down at her wine glass, as if she'd forgotten it was there. "Oh," she says. "How lovely. Thank you." She smiles, offering her glass for a pour.

"Quite a scene," I say, nodding at the crowd.

"I try to tune it out," she sighs. "First time?"

"Yeah, I feel like the new kid in the cafeteria."

"No one here is that cool," she scoffs. "Don't worry." She raises her glass for a "cheers." "Who are you here with?" she asks, glancing around me.

"No one, actually. I'm attending a massage workshop."

She nods and sips her wine, turning back to the view. "I can't think of the last time I had a massage."

"Maybe you should treat yourself."

"Maybe I should."

"I've only been practicing a few months, and I'm terrible at self-promotion."

"So what you're saying is, you could be a prodigy," she says, turning to me.

"And I'd never even know it."

"Well, that would be a tragedy, wouldn't it?" She sips. "Feel free to try my shoulders anytime you like. That should be a challenge for you."

"Is that where you hold your tension?"

"You tell me," she replies. "You're the prodigy. Here, hand me that." She motions to my cup. "Beneath my left shoulder," she says with a shrug. I smooth my hand over the ridge of her shoulder blade, finding the knot. I press my weight into it, kneading into the warmth of her sweater. She sighs deeply, letting her shoulders relax. "Good?" I ask.

"Mm-hmm," she purrs.

"You think it's stress, but most women hold their tension here."

"Is that so?"

"Our boobs put a constant strain on our backs. It's the price we pay."

"So my husband should be giving me massages as payback?"

"Absolutely," I say with a laugh. "Point me at him. I'll teach him a thing or two."

"I'm sure he'd love that," she scoffs, shrugging, done with the fun. She hands my cup back to me.

"What you could really use is a full-body massage," I tell her.

"Maybe I should come to your class."

"You could. Or you could be my guinea pig. All I really need is a bed."

"Is that all you need?" She glances at me, considering. "Well, guess what? You're in luck. Follow me."

The house is a short walk from the pier, a sleek mid-century stack of honey-colored cedar boxes with tall black windows facing out to the sea. The gate snaps shut behind us as I follow her up the walkway, past an overturned kayak and a foot-washing spigot. The front door has been left ajar—she pushes it open, kicking off her sandals on the whitewashed floor. I step out of my flip-flops, following her down the hall to the chef's kitchen, where she heaves open the door of a Sub-Zero refrigerator, gazing into it like a teenager. The fridge is almost completely filled with wine bottles, stacked sideways, the uppermost shelf reserved for a container of hummus, a glass jar of yogurt, a carton of almond milk, and a bag of baby carrots. She slides out a bottle of chardonnay, pulls a wine key from a junk drawer, and uncorks the bottle in one swift movement. She pours two stemmed glasses, long pours, then raises hers to mine. "*À nouveaux amis,*" she toasts, when something dawns on her: "Oh! I'm Helen, by the way!" she says, delighted.

"Hello, Helen. I'm Catherine. Friends call me Cat."

"Cat. I like that. That rhymes!" she quips, motioning for me to follow. We ascend a back staircase to the second floor, a long hallway hung with black-and-white photos—three girls, Helen's daughters, I assume, taken over the years—coltish, bright-eyed versions of their mother, arms slung around each other's necks, sun-kissed faces beaming at the camera.

Helen leads us up the hallway to a bedroom at the far end, an airy double-size room with a wall of floor-to-ceiling windows overlooking a clutch of scrub trees and the white-frothing surf tumbling just beyond. She stands at the window a moment in silhouette, gazing out, beside a large unmade bed—a cloud of white covers, a paperback half-tucked beneath a pillow. She turns to me. "Is this OK?" she asks, referring to the room, the bed.

"Perfect," I reply.

She retrieves a small black remote from the bedside table, activating the roller shades, the screens sliding down over the windows like closing eyelids. "I suppose I should take off my sweater," she says, looking for my approval.

"Whatever you like."

She pulls off the sweater, revealing a burgundy silk camisole. She tosses the sweater on a chair, then hesitates. "Keep going?" she asks.

"Feel free."

Without hesitation, she lifts the camisole over her head, tossing it with the sweater. I'm caught off guard by how good her body looks for her age. "Um… So, clearly I need to get a trainer," I comment.

"Oh my God! Thank you for saying that!" she blurts. "God knows there's nothing more terrifying than disrobing in front of a woman. Or putting on a bathing suit, for that matter. Although I'm sure *you* have nothing to worry about."

"Are you kidding? I'm like a walking ball of insecurity."

"Please. How could that be true? You're gorgeous."

"And you're far too kind. Maybe I just need to see myself through a stranger's eyes."

"Well, fine then. Let's go," she motions.

"Let's go—what?"

"You too, then," she taunts. "What are you scared of? I thought massage therapists were supposed to be super chill."

"Is that a challenge?" I tease.

"Maybe," she shrugs. "Or maybe it's the wine," she says, taking a sip.

"You asked for it," I say, acquiescing. I pull my sweatshirt over my head, revealing my bikini.

"There we go. So far, so good," Helen says with a smirk, admiring me over the rim of her glass.

"So far?"

She wags a finger at my cutoffs, pointing *down*.

"OK, now you're asking a lot," I say, and blush.

"Please, I *definitely* have you beat in the big butt category," she chides.

"This is ridiculous," I give in, unbuttoning my shorts and wiggling them to the floor.

"You see," she says, smirking, "just as I suspected. Drop-dead gorgeous."

"Oh God!" I cry, grabbing a pillow from the bed to cover myself. "I'm blushing!"

"Sorry, I'm drunk!" Helen laughs, waving it off.

"Well, now I feel like we're uneven," I counter.

Helen feigns surprise. "What, you mean these?" she flirts, snapping the band of her leggings. "Care to be blinded by my thighs?"

"You're making me feel naked by comparison."

"Fine, fine." She sets her glass aside and pulls off her leggings, slingshotting them at me. "Happy now?" She jeers. "I feel like we need some music." She reaches for another remote on the bedside table, pointing it at the corner of the room. "Do you like Lauryn Hill?" she asks as a song begins to play. "I love this album. I don't know why she doesn't do more." Helen turns to me. "So I just lie down, then?"

"On your stomach," I direct.

She slinks into the center of the bed and flicks her hair over her tan shoulder. I kneel beside her, starting at the small of her back. She sighs as I work my thumbs, kneading away the tension. "You're going to be a star pupil," she sighs.

I smooth my hands up her back, her neck, into her hair, massaging her scalp. "Yes, *pleeeease*...," she purrs.

"We hold a lot of tension in our head."

"Mm...," she murmurs. "You too?"

"Yeah," I say with a laugh. "I hold a lot of tension in my head."

"But you seem so go-with-the-flow," she mutters.

"I like that you think that."

"Whereas people's first impression of me..." She trails off.

"Is?"

"An utter bitch?"

"How is that even possible?"

"Seriously?" she says in a low voice.

"Well, I think you're lovely."

She lets out a deep breath. "That's nice to hear. Thank you," she sighs.

I drink her in for a moment. "People are scared of strength," I say.

"Mm," she affirms.

"But you don't scare me."

"Don't I?" she turns her face to me. "Maybe you haven't known me long enough."

"I think you can know a person in five seconds," I say.

"You think?"

"Like when I first saw you. I felt like I knew you."

"You did?"

"That's why I came over."

"That's funny," she says, settling back in. "I was instantly comfortable with you as well—which is rare for me, since I can't bear most people."

"Well, I'll take that as a compliment," I laugh.

"You should," she smiles. "So if I don't scare you, what does?"

"Good question," I say. "Love?"

"Mm."

"What scares you?" I ask.

"Death. Of course. Is there anything scarier?"

"I don't know."

"Death doesn't scare you?" she mutters.

"Not really."

"Wow, what's your secret?"

I hesitate. "To begin with, I don't think we actually die. Our bodies do, but the thing that makes me *me*—I think that keeps going. I think our souls are like birds, and our bodies are like the trees they nest in. They make a life here, and then they fly away to the next."

"Reincarnation," she says. "I've always liked that as a concept. I sometimes wonder what I would come back as."

"What would you want to come back as?"

"A dog."

"Ha! What kind of dog?"

"A well-loved one," she sighs. "What about you? What would you come back as?"

"I try not to look that far ahead."

"That's because you're present. I need to be more like that."

"I just try to focus on what I'm doing right now, while I'm here. How to make the most of this body while I have it. To feel joy and pleasure."

She turns her face to me. "It sounds like you've got it all figured out," she says with a smile.

"Or maybe I've got it all wrong."

"No, I think you're wise beyond your years," she says, closing her eyes. "So what brings you joy and pleasure?"

"This," I say. "This is a good start. A friend. Feeling close like this."

"You're right," she says. "This does feel nice. Can you come a bit closer?"

I lie down beside her and she shimmies in, looking for my eyes. I concentrate on her mouth, kissing her soft lips, tasting the air between them. As we touch, a rush passes through me, a muted electricity, down my throat, my ribs, my stomach, my guts—numbing me, intoxicating me. My gaze locks into hers, but something else stares back. Helen's pupils have dilated into wide black disks, unblinking, holding me, entranced. Her body jolts, flinching upward, pouncing on me, caging me. Her movements are animal-like, her mouth at my ear, hissing, flooding into my mind like a color, painting away my thoughts, softening my brain. My mouth gapes open as I plummet inward, a white-pink depth, an inner nebula, flashing with light, an infinite ecstasy, radiating from the very core of me. Her mouth snarls at my ear: "*We... Go... Home...*" But it's not her, not Helen—it's something else. My body shudders, unbound, climaxing, an unrelenting wave, coursing through my body. The voice locks in my mind, binding me in its spell:

> *We...*
>> *Go...*
>>> *Home...*
>>>> *I show...You...*
>> *You...Take...*
>>> *Me...In.*
>>>> *You...Say...*
>>>>> *Come...In...*
>> *You...Carry...Me....*
>>>>> *I...Show....The...Way.*

My mind unfolds like a flower, a blooming white light, the voice hissing with delight: "*Home! Home!*" it presses.

Something grabs hold of me, ripping me out of the spell. I tumble backward, spilling off the bed and onto the floor. My head throbbing, I try to focus on what's happening, what I'm seeing—Helen lifted like a rag doll, by someone, some*thing*, a figure, a vapor, there at the edge of the bed. I try to look at it, but it won't let itself be seen, the line of my gaze pushed away like a magnet being repelled by another magnet. Helen thrashes in the air, held up by her throat, gasping, clawing. Suddenly she stops fighting and her eyes peel wide, as if recognizing her captor. "*He! Sees! You!*" she hisses at the phantom, her gaze like a dagger. "*Bro-ther! Bro-ther!*" she chants. "*Bro-ther! Sees! You!*" She screeches with laughter as a sizzling white light gathers in the hollows of her eyes, her nostrils, her mouth agape, erupting in a blaze—

My eyelids blink open to the purple stillness of the room. I'm lying on the floor, my body stiff and aching. Helen lies crumpled in the center of the bed, the faint motion of her body breathing, asleep—alive. I reach to touch her shoulder, then stop myself. The wicked grimace of whatever was inhabiting her flashes to mind. *I need to get the fuck out of here.* I scavenge through the shadows, snatching up my clothes, yanking them on—then bolt out into the light of the hall, down the stairs, out the front door into the clammy chill of the night.

The ocean wind blows through the trees, carrying the sound of waves thundering in the distance, the trill of insects chirping in the wet darkness. I hurry down Central Road, following the lamplights, counting the street signs until I reach the cottage on Holly Lane. I fumble with the key, pushing inside, panting. I freeze.

A sound. Of something. Shuffling. A shadow moves through the living room, wheezing, knocking into furniture. I back step slowly, gripping the screen door so it won't make a sound, then turn and dash up the walkway, back onto Central Road. I pace beneath a streetlight, frantic, shaking, peering at the cottage through the scrub brush, watching, listening for whatever's moving inside. I clutch my phone, shuddering as I dial. A woman's steady voice answers the line. "911, what is your emergency?"

"Someone's in my house."

"There's an intruder in your home, is that correct?" the operator asks.

"Yes."

"Are you safe, ma'am? Are they there now?"

"I don't know."

"Are you in the home?"

"I'm outside."

"Is there somewhere safe you can go and wait for the officers to arrive?"

"I—I don't know," I say, looking for anything, a lit window in one of the neighboring cottages, any sign of life.

"Is there a store or something nearby?" the operator asks. "Something well-lit?"

"The pier."

"OK, go there now. I'm alerting the unit. What is your address?"

"23 Holly Lane. Fire Island."

"Is that Fair Harbor pier?"

"Yes."

"I want you to wait at the pier for the officers to arrive. Can you do that? I'm going to put you on hold for a moment while I speak to them, but I'm still here. If you need anything, I'll hear you, and I'll come back on the line. OK?"

"Yes."

At that moment, I hear something in the direction of the cottage, the screech of the screen door snapping open and shut. Something scuttles across the deck boards, spidering out onto the darkened path. *What the fuck is that?* The creature, pale and spindly, rears up, then collapses as if some animating force had suddenly expelled itself. I stand motionless as the crumpled shadow begins to stir, gathering itself, groaning—weeping. Not an animal, a girl. She wills herself up onto two feet, clutching her arms around her skinny bikini-clad frame, shaking, sobbing. Instinctively, I step toward her, and she flinches, mortified, then turns and bolts into the darkness.

I pace the pier, scanning the black, rippling water, the dotted gold lights of Long Island shimmering in the distance. A tiny blue orb winks in the darkness followed by the soft grumble of an outboard motor as a police boat materializes from the inky expanse, rocking up to the dock. An officer climbs over the edge of the boat, roping it to one of the moorings. His partner steps off and approaches me, a giant man with arms like tree trunks. "Ms. Harper?" he asks. I nod yes, too shaken to speak. He pulls his walkie-talkie from his shoulder harness and announces his badge number to someone on the other end, confirming they're here. "I'm going to have you walk us to the house," he says. I nod and lead the way. His partner strays a couple of yards behind, shining a flashlight into the scrub brush. "Can you tell me what happened?"

"I came home, and someone was in the house."

"Someone broke into your house, is that right?" he asks, scanning the darkness ahead.

"Yes."

"When did you arrive home?"

"I don't know. An hour ago."

He checks his watch. "So, 3 a.m. And where were you prior to that?"

"With—a friend."

"Nearby?"

"Yes. I walked home. I went into the house and heard…" I trail off. An image flashes across my mind—the girl on the path, the terror in her eyes.

"Ma'am?" The officer glances at me.

"Someone…I don't know… Someone was in the house."

"Is anyone staying with you?" he asks.

"No."

I point to the gate as we approach.

I wait outside as the officers inspect the cottage, flashlight beams passing like searchlights over the windows. One by one, the lights in each of the rooms snap on, illuminating the cottage like a jack-o'-lantern.

The head officer reemerges. "There's no one in there, ma'am. I have my partner walking the property. We'll walk the neighborhood as well. Can you come inside with me, please?" He holds the screen door for me and I step into the shockingly bright kitchen, waiting as he does a final sweep through the living room. He pauses in front of the pages spread out on the floor, pointing his flashlight at the documents. "Are these yours?" he asks.

The papers aren't how I left them. They've been rearranged into a pattern, an upside-down triangle, a white pyramid of pages with notes scratched in the margins.

"Um, yeah—" I fumble. "It's my work…I'm a teacher."

The officer gives me an up-down glance, assessing what a teacher looks like, then continues his survey of the house. He pushes open the doors to the bedrooms, the bathroom. "Can you tell me if anything's been moved," he asks, "if anything's missing?"

I peer into the bathroom, the bedroom, trying to find something, anything to report. There on the bed, my purse is toppled over on its side. "I found my purse like this," I lie, pointing, trying to play up my concern. "I keep it in the closet."

He opens the closet door, inspecting it with his flashlight. "Why don't you go through your purse and see if anything's missing," he says. He stands over me as I do this. I blink up at him. "Everything seems to be here."

"Your wallet, the cash…"

"Everything, yes."

"Can you come out here, please?" He leads us back into the kitchen. "I'm gonna write up the report," he says, flipping open his notepad. He pulls out a stool at the kitchen counter and takes a seat. "Make yourself comfortable," he says. "This'll take a minute."

I sit on the couch, gazing at the upside-down pyramid, trying to comprehend what I'm seeing. The scientists' bios have been arranged side by side, forming the top of the triangle. Below each, documents cascade like a flowchart, one overlapping the next, narrowing into a single page at the bottom, one I don't recognize. It contains a medieval-looking image, almost like a religious tapestry. A seven-headed dragon, each head wearing a golden crown.

22 | THE ULTIMATE ENSEMBLE

"Holy fucking shit!" Jemma gasps, trying to keep her voice down, ducking into the break room at her office, the hiss of a cappuccino being made in the background. "Are you OK? That's terrifying!"

"I just wanted you to know in case the police called," I say. "It was probably just neighborhood kids."

"Yeah, but *holy fuck*," she whispers. "Just going into people's houses? It's like *Lord of the Flies* out there."

"Tell Jamie she can call me, but everything in the house is fine. I locked up and hid the key."

Jemma says hello to somebody walking by, then whispers, "Jamie's going out there to change the locks. Where are you now?"

"I'm home."

"You're OK?"

"Yeah, I'm fine," I lie.

"Call me tonight. This is crazy."

I tell her I will and hang up and scan through my texts—a flood of messages from clients wondering where I am, and one from Koi, a reply:

Where and when?

My intercom buzzes; I leap for it. "5C, fifth floor," I say, pressing the button. I pace the entryway, anxious, glancing at the arrangement of documents I've recreated on the living room floor.

There's a rap at the door and I open it to Adam, red-faced and sweating. "Wow, five floors," he mutters.

"Sorry, come in."

"No one can know I'm doing this," he says, glancing past me at the arrangement on the floor. "This is how you found it?"

"This is how it was, exactly."

He crouches over the papers, picking one up. He squints at the handwriting in the margin, tracing the scribbled annotations through the cascade of pages. "You're saying someone broke in and arranged all of this?"

"Yes, but why?"

He moves from one page to another. "Someone's helping you," he says.

"Helping me?"

"You wanted to connect the dots. Well, here you go." He points. "The six names on your list—whoever did this is confirming the link between them. Below each of the names— your dad, for instance…" He picks up a document that resembles an x-ray. "This is from the project folder. Look at this." He points to what appears to be a brain scan, a right-facing cross-section. "You see the white node in the center?" he points. "I'm not sure what these readouts are, but they look like they're measuring the activity of the pineal gland." He reaches for the next note in the arrangement, his napkin drawing, the Eye of Horus. He holds it up, comparing it to the brain scan. "See anything?" The drawing and the scan appear eerily similar. The next sheet down is an overview of the DMT molecule. "The pineal gland, DMT—" he says, "they're all linked." He continues to a handwritten note, something I jotted down while I was researching. He squints at the name. "What is this? McKenzie?"

"McKenna."

"Terence McKenna?"

I nod.

He looks at the pyramid, taking it all in. He homes in on something. "Your dad—his focus was the pineal gland, but over here," he points, "the physicist, Phillips, his whole thing is about energy transmission, entanglement." He continues scanning the rows of documents. "And then here, this one," he points. "Who is this? Marsh?"

"Dr. Colin Marsh."

He looks at me. "Colin Marsh."

"You know who he is?"

"Of course. He's like the Carl Sagan of math. You're saying he's part of this?"

"He teaches at Columbia. I tracked him down."

"And?"

"It was a waste of time. He wouldn't talk."

"Yeah, no kidding," he says, chuckling.

"What's funny?"

"Well, for one thing, the dude's a celebrity. He's not gonna talk to you about some crazy-ass government shit. Especially if he was involved with it—which I wouldn't put past him. Regardless, he's not gonna just *chat* with you about it. 'Oh yeah, that top secret shit from the '80s? Sure, pull up a chair.'" He sifts through the fan of documents. "Do you know anything about his backstory?" he asks. "The stuff with his brother? That's a rabbit's hole in and of itself. You know that Marsh basically founded artificial intelligence, right? His brother has some kind of mental disorder, paranoid schizophrenia, I can't remember what. Marsh was obsessed with finding a cure. He started digging into how the brain communicates, breaking it down into binary code—a kind of computer language. His theory was, if we could understand the code, we could go in and fix whatever was broken. And—amazingly—he cracked it. The human brain code. The only problem was the wetware. The biology. He had the key, but no door—no way to hack into the brain itself. So here he was, holding the cure for every mental disorder on Earth, and biology had locked him out. That's when his team built a virtual brain to test the repair process—which essentially birthed AI."

"So what happened to his brother?"

Adam shrugs. "He's probably still locked in a padded room somewhere." He examines another page. "Look at this," he says. "Half of the material on Marsh is tucked under the Koeffler/neurology column. And these pages out here, along the periphery. What are these?" He points to a fan of pages hugging the pyramid like a parenthesis. "These don't seem to be connected to anyone in particular." He sifts through them, examining a note. "Who is this? Harvey Ward. Project Highbridge."

"He was a family friend. He may have worked with my dad. I have these memories—of being given a test. When I was a child. Like a game. With flash cards."

Adam considers this, as if trying to recall something that won't quite form. He looks back at the parenthesis of notes hugging the pyramid, scanning through them. "Theta brain waves. Astral projection. The Sefirot. Apotheosis..." he reads.

"Maybe whoever made the arrangement was separating them out?" I say. "Like they don't belong."

"I don't think so," he says, taking in the grand scope of the diagram. "They wouldn't have arranged them like this. I think it's the opposite. I think these are somehow connected to everyone—the whole thing." He reads another note along the outer crescent, something I wrote down after my meeting with Phillips. "The Philadelphia Experiment."

"The physicist I met with, he mentioned it."

Adam looks at me. "Mentioned it how?"

"Something about the government covering up these types of black projects. He was using it as an example of a cover story. Why?"

"Because look," he points. "Why would it have been included here? If I'm right, and all of these notes along the edge are connected to everyone, so is this." He crouches down, scanning from page to page, as if searching for something. "Remember when I told you about the Montauk Project? Its connection to the pineal gland? There's a weird story that links the Montauk Project to the Philadelphia Experiment. I remember an article I read, back when I first started digging into what happened to me." He runs a search on his phone. "Right, listen to this."

> In August 1983, an alleged experiment in time travel was conducted at the United States Naval base Camp Hero in Montauk, New York, during which a team of scientists successfully time-locked the hyperspace coordinates of Project Rainbow, a mission conducted by the Navy in 1943. Project Rainbow, also known as the Philadelphia Experiment, involved an exploratory test in radar cloaking on a Naval ship,

the USS *Eldridge*. According to witness testimony, the experiment malfunctioned, sending the ship into hyperspace, relocating it from the Philadelphia Naval Shipyard to Norfolk Naval Shipyard nearly 200 miles away—then back to its original location. It is alleged that during the time-lock, two men, Al Bielek and Duncan Cameron, leaped from the deck of the *Eldridge* and into Camp Hero in the year 1983. Here, Al Bielek claims that he and Cameron met the physicist and mathematician John von Neumann, who had purportedly been involved in Project Rainbow in 1943 and was now overseeing a future phase of the experiment at Camp Hero.

"Von Neumann is one of the greatest mathematicians of all time," Adam explains. "He worked with Oppenheimer on the Manhattan Project. Basically, anything you'd find in a physics textbook, this guy helped discover the math behind it. The Navy denied the existence of Project Rainbow or any involvement von Neumann might have had. But the craziest part is that von Neumann *died* in the 1950s. So how would these guys have met him in 1983?"

"Right, it's absurd."

"Or is it? Remember, these projects we're talking about, they would have been run by the top scientists of the time, maybe of *any* time. That stretch, from World War II through the 1980s, was like the pinnacle of scientific breakthroughs. Who knows what discoveries were made that were never disclosed to the public?"

"Meaning?"

"Meaning, these guys that jumped ship, Bielek and Cameron—maybe they did meet von Neumann at Camp Hero in

1983. Just not the same von Neumann that ran Project Rainbow."

"I don't understand."

"Look," Adam says, "the scientists who were employed in these projects, they were working out the fundamentals of time and space. Unified theory, the fabric of the universe. Whatever they discovered, they would have employed it to move the mission forward. Maybe the von Neumann they met in 1983 came from a parallel timeline."

"But I thought you said he was dead."

"In one timeline, yes. But maybe not in another."

"OK, this is insane."

"Look who you're talking to!" Adam laughs. "The science was there. Granted, it sounds crazy, but we have no idea what's possible. This whole scenario might be like basic physics in the grand scheme of what our government's discovered."

He moves to the bottom of the arrangement, sifting through the documents. "Naval Intelligence. A military contractor. Do we know which one?" He looks to me for help. "The space between them," he says, pointing, "it's like there's something missing." He tracks down to the bottom of the diagram, the single page forming the point of the inverted pyramid. The dragon with seven heads and golden crowns.

"I have no idea what that is," I tell him. "Whoever arranged this put it there."

"It's from the Bible," he says. "The Book of Revelation. The dragon with seven heads and 10 crowns." He hands it to me. "It symbolizes the Great Beast."

"OK..."

"The Antichrist."

"Oh good."

"You know, it's interesting," Adam says, "the way this was arranged, as a pyramid. They could've just laid it out in rows. It feels like it was done on purpose—like a clue." He cranes his neck, looking at the diagram right side up. "It reminds me of something." He takes out his wallet and pulls out a dollar bill, holding it up for me to see. There on one side, opposite the Great Seal, is the icon of a pyramid topped with a glowing eye, beams of light emanating from it like the rays of the sun. "The Eye of Providence," he says. "It's sometimes called the All-Seeing Eye. It symbolizes the divine, the omnipresence of God. The original Big Brother, you might say. You see how the eye is set in a triangle? Three sides representing the Holy Trinity—the Father, the Son, and the Holy Spirit—the three-part equation of God. The pyramid beneath it shows 13 rows of blocks denoting the 13 original colonies of the United States. The unfinished pyramid topped by the Eye is meant to represent our future growth as a nation. You can take that as a metaphor, for progress and prosperity, or more literally, as our expansion into future territories. But there's another way to look at it, which might sound a little strange. If you take the Eye at face value, as an icon representing the divine, then what is it that we're actually working toward? What makes the pyramid complete?"

"Becoming one with God."

"Or becoming God itself." He turns the dollar bill upside down, comparing the inverted pyramid to the diagram on the floor, tracing the documents down to the Great Beast where the Eye of Providence should be. He glances at me. "This is some crazy-ass shit."

"Says the time traveler."

"I mean, if you look at it, there's religious stuff all over these. Have you read some of these annotations? Passages from the Bible. The Quran. What do they have to do with anything?"

"Maybe they're metaphors."

"I don't think so," he ponders. "I don't think they're meant to be cryptic. I think they're meant to be clues. Look, you have these six project leads," he points. "Marsh—math. Barnes—biotech. Koeffler—neurology. Siegfried—psychology. Phillips—physics. And your dad—biochemistry. All of them are at the top of their field, straight-and-narrow science. But if you look at the notes in red, what do you see? What's the one thing that stands out?"

I look from page to page.

"There isn't a single document without a religious annotation," Adam points out. "Whoever arranged this is trying to show a connection between science and the divine."

"What does one have to do with the other?"

He scans the scribblings in the margins. "I mean, on a basic level? They're human constructs. Science and religion. We use them to understand reality. The further back you go in time, the closer they become linked together. Think about it. When man discovered how to make fire, it was like an existential crisis. Up until that point, the only fire he knew was the sun. Or maybe a lightning bolt hitting a tree. Fire belonged to Heaven. But now, here he was knocking a couple rocks together, and holy shit! It was like an epiphany. Suddenly, with that one spark, he had the power of God."

He considers something. "When you look at the world's ancient cultures, when they talk about their gods, they're not talking about something ethereal. They're talking about actual *physical beings*. The Aztecs, the Incas, the Dogon. They all talk about a time when their gods lived among them."

Something sparks to mind, a story Clara once told me. "The Watchers."

Adam looks at me, impressed. "The Watchers, exactly."

"They were angels."

"Yeah," Adam says, nodding, "sent by God to watch over the first humans—to make sure we didn't fuck anything up. But the story is antediluvian, from before the Great Flood, so no one knows exactly who the Watchers were. Some think they were responsible for the destruction of Atlantis. In the old texts it says the Watchers fell in love with human women, that they gave birth to these half-breed children…"

"Giants."

"Right, the Nephilim. Who eventually taught humans how to control nature and gravity and make all kinds of freaky hybrid creatures, like mermaids and minotaurs. At some point, God was like, you know what—*no*. And he just drowned everybody. That's what the Great Flood was all about—wiping the slate clean. It's believed that some of the Watchers survived the Flood, fanning out across the Earth, passing along the secrets of civilization to any of the ancient peoples they encountered. Wherever the Watchers went, these giant empires would rise up out of nowhere. Explosions of architecture and technology and art. The first civilization that formed after the Flood was Sumer in Mesopotamia. There are ancient scrolls that talk about how the gods came to their land and taught them math and science and farming—like a civilization starter kit. These gods gave them the wheel, written language, laws. The Sumerians called them the Anunnaki. They described them as nine-foot-tall beings dressed in elaborate feathered serpent costumes. What's even crazier is if you look at the depictions of the Anunnaki in comparison to the gods of the other ancient cultures that came after Sumer, they all kinda look the same. The people called them gods, but if you ask me, they sound more like—"

"Aliens," I say.

"Aliens. Exactly."

"But wait—"

Adam jumps in. "What do alien gods have to do with any of this? Probably nothing. But it'd be crazy if they did."

"How do you even know about this stuff?"

"When you're a teenage time traveler stuck in the future, you start digging into some crazy corners of the internet. I was looking for mentions of time travel in the ancient texts, the oral histories. I kept finding these references to 'doorways'—essentially stargates the high priests and shamans would use to travel through the cosmos. Who knows what drugs these guys were on, but some of the texts actually go into how the doorways functioned, the technology behind them—this blend of alchemy, cosmology, Pythagorean triples. What does this have to do with your dad? Or any of this? Who knows."

"So you'll help me?" I ask.

"I'll dig into it a bit. But I'm not making any promises. And I'm gonna need photos of all this."

My phone buzzes on the coffee table. Then again. "Of course. Whatever you need," I say, distracted, checking the incoming texts.

"There's one other thing," Adam says, crouching down, pulling one of the documents from my dad's column. "You see the code number at the top?" He points. "Separated into three parts? The middle part—the project code. It's the same as mine."

"The same as—?"

"Whatever your dad was working on, it was being run by the same group that sent me here." He looks at me, waiting for this to sink in. "What year did your dad die?"

"Eighty-nine."

He does the math. "Right, so 12 years."

"Twelve years, what?"

"After what happened to me," he says, taking out his phone, snapping photos of the documents. "I think this was a future phase of the same project. Mine had to do with time travel, but I don't think that was the ultimate goal."

I watch Adam as he hovers over the diagram, fanning through pages, snapping photos. Suddenly, I don't want him to leave. He moves around the diagram, shooting it from all sides, checking the images. "I think I'm good," he says, pocketing the phone, heading to the door.

"So I should call you?"

He turns to me. "No. No calls or texts," he says, looking for my eyes, making sure I understand. "Just come by the store."

I nod, thanking him. The moment he's gone, I open the texts—a random number with a 917 area code.

> *Hi Catherine my name is Rami Asad*
> *CM thought I could help*
> *with what you're looking for*

I search the name and come up with a handful of matches, only one in New York, a professional profile—he's listed as the founder and lead consultant for a logistics firm located at One Vanderbilt in Midtown. I type:

> *CM?*

My phone pings back.

> *Your friend at Columbia*

Before I can reply, another text comes in—

> *Meet up?*

I try to think quickly—someplace public, out in the open, lots of people. I respond:

> *Washington square park*
> *Benches by the fountain*

Now-ish?
Can be there in 30

Ok

I have red shoes on
See you there

23 | PLAIN AS DAY

I sit alone on a park bench facing the central fountain, its fern-shaped plumes of water haloed in a misty rainbow. The park has a sketchy circus vibe at this hour, a sea of New York University students, breakdancers, weed dealers, baton jugglers. A bullhorn wails over a crowd demanding remunerations for the first responders of 9/11—the faces of firefighters and police officers pasted to cardboard signs swaying overhead. A drum circle has formed beside the gathering, seemingly as a show of support, if not for the 9/11 crowd, then for the adjacent demonstration, a racial justice coalition protesting the NYPD's stop-and-frisk policy. A pack of feral skateboarders slalom between people's legs, knitting the scene together in a manic performance of ollies, kickflips, and nose grinds.

My eyes track to a guy standing beside the fountain, scanning the perimeter. He's dressed like a tech bro, but more manicured, more European—black pants, black polo, sleek backpack, and cherry-red loafers. Rami. He has a sort of kinetic energy, the lean stance of a soccer player with a slight stoop to his shoulders. Dark hair, dark features—he's cute, which catches me off guard.

A new crowd wanders past, gathering around the fountain—a German tour group arranging themselves for a photo. They mistake Rami as part of the group and hug him into the shot. "*Käsekuchen!*" they cry, beaming to the camera. Rami laughs, going along with it—a nice smile. He notices me watching, and pulls himself away and walks over. "Catherine?" he asks, cocking his head. The French accent, and my name pronounced *Ka-ta-reen*, throws me. "Yeah, hi," I fumble.

"Hi!" His eyes sparkle a soft hazel, shards of green and gold radiating from the black disks of his pupils. I'm held in his gaze, unable to penetrate. He offers a handshake. "Rami," he says. "May I?" He motions to the seat beside me, shrugging off his backpack and slumping it against the arm of the bench. "This feels very KGB," he says. "Meeting on a park bench."

"Is that what you are?" I ask. "KGB?"

"I am. Do you want the nuclear codes?" He smirks, glancing at the benches on either side of us—one occupied by a woman eating a tossed salad in a takeout bowl, the other by a man in a suit hunched over his phone. Rami looks at me with a smile, waiting—for what, I don't know.

"Sooo…," I say with a shrug. He doesn't take the hint. "You have something…to tell me?"

"Tell?"

"'CM.' I'm assuming that's Colin Marsh."

"Yes. He contacted someone—who contacted me. Maybe if you tell me what you're looking for, I can help."

I look into his eyes—for something, anything. "You OK?" he asks.

I snap out of it. "I'm sorry, *who* are you?"

"Ha ha, yes, of course, sorry. Your friend Marsh and I work for the same client. My firm consults for them on a number of projects—so I have visibility into things. The project you were asking about is from before my time, but perhaps I can track down some information."

"So it ended?"

He looks confused.

"You said it was from before your time."

"Well, yes," he says. "Is there something specific you want to know?"

"How about everything?"

He chuckles as though we're in on a secret together, but then realizes I'm not kidding. He glances at a note on his phone. "Your father," he says, reading the name, "Dr. Andrew Harper."

"Yes."

"Right, he's on the list."

"The list?"

He's thrown by the question. "You have a list," he says.

"I do have a list. But what list are *you* talking about?"

He smirks, like he's assuming this is in fact a game, that I'm testing him. "What list do *you* think I'm talking about?" he asks playfully. "I assume we're talking about—you know."

"No, I don't."

He scowls, puzzled. "No one has contacted you?" he asks.

"Contacted me about what?"

He reclines back, seeming to think about how to navigate this. He seems annoyed, like he's been put on the spot. "There's a list," he explains, "of people like us. That's what I thought this—"

"What do you mean, 'people like us'?"

"With…gifts," he says. "You know…" He glances around at the crowd, like he's thinking about how to explain. "Forgive me if this seems a bit strange," he says. "Let me ask you. You can see me, correct?"

"See you?"

"Here in front of you. And you can hear me. Plain as day. Am I right? Now watch." He rises from the bench and steps in front of the woman eating her salad. "If you can see me, then this woman must see me as well."

Weirdly, the woman doesn't react to the strange man standing directly in front of her. Rami leans in closer. He claps his hands in front of her face. The woman doesn't flinch, she just munches away on her salad, zoned out. "Hellooooo?" Rami calls to her. "I'm right here!" He waves his hands in front of the woman's face. Nothing. He gauges my reaction, then scans the crowd, picking out a shaggy-haired teen sitting on his skateboard watching his friends do tricks. Rami crouches behind the boy and blurts "BOO!" in the kid's ear. Nothing.

Rami looks at me. "Strange, no? You can hear me, but they can't. OK, now watch." He closes his eyes and draws in a long, deep breath, then expels it. "BOO!" he blurts.

"FUCK!" The boy jumps out of his skin, his skateboard sailing out from under him. He scrambles to get up, grabbing his board and turning on Rami. "You're a fucking psycho, dude!" The boy signals to his friends—*we're outta here*. His friends blink back, dumbfounded—*what just happened?*

The woman eating her salad is completely freaked out by whatever she just witnessed. She snatches up her belongings, throwing me a crazy look, like *is that lunatic with you?* Rami offers the woman an apologetic wave as he returns to the bench beside me. "That was bizarre, I know," he says. He can tell I'm shocked, but I'm not bolting, which he takes as a cue to continue. "What I just did has to do with energy," he explains. "You might think of it as an aura. Like an envelope of energy—a force field. We all have one, and we can turn it on and off whenever we want if we know how. When you see or hear someone, it's not just the physical person you're experiencing. You're receiving the energy they're sending—their signal. Without the signal you can't see or hear them. I know it sounds crazy, but it's true. It's just the way our minds are wired. The person could be right there in front of you, but your mind won't pick them up without the signal. It's like being a ghost. But not with you. You could see and hear me the whole time. Am I right? That's because you and I are alike in some way. I can feel it. I have a sense for these things. I feel it like a pull, right here," he says, placing a hand on his solar plexus. "It's like a magnetism. It helps me with what I do. Finding people—like us." He unzips his bag, digging something out—a small black box like the one Phillips and Marsh had when I met with them. He sets it on the bench between us. "OK, so what I showed you there—imagine if you could take that ability and put it in a box. That's what this is. It blocks our frequency in a special way. People can see us, but they can't hear us. They *think* they can hear us, but they can't understand our words. It's like listening to someone speak in another language. Your ears just tune it out."

"And you made this?"

"I helped. When I meet with someone to talk about these things—I keep it with me, so we're not overheard."

"Overheard by?"

"Good question," he says, smirking. "It seems like everyone could use someone with a gift. Would you agree?" He glances at the people walking past us, oblivious—then back at me. "This gift you have, do you think someone might want to take advantage of it?" he asks.

"I think I would know."

"Would you?" He looks for something in my eyes. "Just because you haven't agreed, doesn't mean you're not being used. As for me, I like to know who I'm working for."

"Your client."

"Yes."

"What do you do for them?"

"I do many things. But mostly I keep an eye out."

"You're a spy."

He chuckles. "I'm not James Bond, if that's what you're thinking. I look out for my client and my client looks out for me. I'm sure they would be happy to look out for you as well."

"Why would they do that?"

"Because you could help each other."

"How's that?"

He shrugs. "You could ask them. Would you like me to set up a meeting?"

"Are you recruiting me?"

"Recruiting? No. But you should probably keep this," he says, nodding to the box.

"Why, so your client can spy on me?"

"No. They don't need this to spy on you."

"That's what you're for."

"They don't need me either," he says, smirking again. "They just don't want anyone else to have me." He scans the encircling crowd as though he's looking for someone. "I'm curious," he says. "Do you ever see strange things? Things that no one else can see?" He looks to me, as if he's sensing something in my eyes. "As if something is revealing itself to you?" He takes my silence as an answer.

"You should be careful what you talk about, and with whom," he says, "especially when it comes to this project. The less you know about these things, the better. As they say, ignorance is bliss." He smiles. "Just look at me, I'm living proof. I don't understand any of it, and I couldn't be happier." He regards me as I glance at the box. "You can touch it," he says. "It doesn't cause cancer, if that's what you're worried about."

I pick it up. Its dead weight feels menacing, alien.

"That feeling you get," he says, "of something watching. I've felt it too. Since I was a little boy." I glance at him. The glimmer of a memory sparks to mind, something familiar—about him? It's too faint to grasp. "But as long as I have this with me," he says, with a nod to the box, "the feeling isn't there." I try to read the look in his eyes—a mixture of sadness and anger, and beneath that something else, something vulnerable. "I know how strange it must seem," he says with a sniff, glancing at his phone, suddenly shifty. "But I think they're trying to help. The people I work for—I think they know what's watching, and they're trying to protect us from it."

"Protect us from what?"

He shrugs uneasily. "I asked them, 'How will I know if I'm confronted by it?' Their answer was very strange. They said…'" He utters a phrase that I hear, but can't parse. My brain twists and my head goes cold. A flash of white light unfolds like the petals of a flower, revealing a tunneling vortex that spins and clicks, unlocking an answer—to something, a code surging through me. And then, just as suddenly, I'm expelled back through the flower as its petals close, back into the light of day. Rami catches my arm. "Hey, you OK?"

I steady myself, shaking him off. I feel like I've just woken up from a dream. My mind races backward, trying to recall what it was. Rami glances around nervously. "Maybe we should move inside," he says.

"No. You need to go," I say, shielding my eyes from the sun glinting off the fountain, suddenly intensified.

"Oh yes, OK, no problem," he fumbles, seeming not to know what to do with himself. He reaches for his bag. "I hope I didn't…," he says, trailing off, as if he's not sure what to say. He reaches for the box, but hesitates. "Should I leave this with you?"

I pull it toward me, which he takes as his answer.

"If there's anything you need…," he says. He draws a business card from his pocket and sets it on the bench. He regards me for a moment, then strolls away, melting into the crowd.

I pull out my phone and text Koi:

Can you meet me?

A reply buzzes back:

Sure where

24 | A LIGHT IN THE WALL

I sit at a table in the tucked-away courtyard at Vol de Nuit, the small black box on the chair beside me. Koi walks up, shouldering his backpack. He pulls out the chair across from me. I set the box on the table. "Do you know what this is?" I ask.

Koi glances at the box and hesitates.

"Go ahead. Pick it up."

The weight of it seems to surprise him. He turns it over, examining it from all sides.

"Yesterday, when you and I met, I was coming from a meeting with Colin Marsh, one of the people involved with the project. He had one of these in his office. Same with Peter Phillips, the physicist I met in Virginia. I thought it was some kind of recording device, but apparently it's used to block sound or to disguise language or something. It makes it so other people can't understand what you're saying."

Koi sets the box on the table and reclines back, listening.

"So, today I get this random text," I explain. "From this guy." I slide him the card. "When I met with Marsh, he said he'd make some phone calls and see if anyone could give me some information. Now, I don't trust Marsh—*at all*—but I think my sniffing around spooked him enough to move this along. So this guy Rami reaches out to me. Apparently he and Marsh work for the same client."

"Military."

"That's what I'm thinking. Anyway, Rami says I'm on a list. The same list my father is on—Marsh, Phillips. A list of people with 'gifts.' That's what he called it. He helps his client find these people."

"Find them for what?"

"He doesn't know. He said it's part of the contract. It's sketchy, I know. But I don't get a creepy vibe from him. I think he's just going along with it."

"Right, not fucking with the money," Koi says with a sniff.

"He thought I was there to ask about the list, but then he realized I don't know anything about anything. And that's when he pulled this out." I gesture to the box. "He said I need to be careful talking about this project, because people are listening. Phillips, the physicist in Virginia, he warned me about the same thing."

"What if it's a tracking device? Maybe they're listening to us right now."

"I don't think so. I think Rami helped build it. He showed me something when I was with him. The way you and I have visions, he has something too. He can turn his energy off."

"His energy."

"I saw it with my own eyes. People can't hear or see him. He can turn it on and off."

"You mean you could see him, but nobody else could?"

"Exactly."

"And you know that for a fact?" There's something in his voice I don't like.

"What are you asking?"

"I'm asking if anyone else saw him do this."

"You think I'm crazy."

"I don't think you're crazy. I'm just trying to figure out if it's some kind of magic trick or what."

"It wasn't a trick. Believe me. He's on the list too."

"Am *I* on the list?"

"You might be."

"You didn't ask?"

"Did you want me to?"

"Nah, I get it."

"You sound like you *want* to be on the list."

"Whatever," Koi says, seeming miffed. "So, what, this guy gave you this 'cone of silence' box?"

"He asked if I've been seeing anything strange."

"Like how?"

"Like the thing that happened on the street when you met me. He said he's seen stuff like that too, but this box fends it off somehow."

Koi turns the box over, inspecting the sides. He glances at me.

"Heavy, right? Like, what's inside it?" I ask.

He runs his fingertip along the edge of it. "I don't know how you'd open it up," he says, squinting. "No seams, no screws…" He sets it down. "So he just gave this to you? I thought you said he needed it for protection."

"He probably has more than one. Or why would he give it to me?"

"You think he has a stash of these things?"

"I thought we could have somebody look at it. Maybe they could figure out what it is, how it works. Maybe it'll tell us something."

Koi considers this. "I might know someone," he says. "I reached out to my cousin, Trey. He has a company that does back-end security. They work with some big companies. They also do some stuff for the government. Trey's got access to shit. On a whole other level. He said if we want to come see him, he'll do some digging. He might know what this thing is," Koi says, regarding the box.

"He's here in the city?"

Koi hesitates. "He's upstate."

"So what, do you want to call him?"

"I mean…" He glances off. "It's not really a phone thing. Look," he says, "I get that you don't know me. You don't know Trey. But we need some help, and Trey's solid. We grew up together. If he thinks he can find out something, he probably can. He doesn't waste his time with shit. I figured, you and me, we could ride up there, see what he has to say, and just hash things out a bit." He takes a beat, measuring my reaction. "We could go up today. If it's a bust, we drive back tonight. Otherwise, Trey could put us up. He's got a couple of hotels up there he does work for. They throw him rooms whenever he needs them." He pauses, then adds: "I mean, we'd have our own rooms, you know." Koi seems to sense my apprehension. "I can drive."

I try to wrap my head around what's being proposed here. "Sorry, *who* is your cousin?"

"Trey—Treyvon. He's my mom's sister's son. He's got some things in common with us, you and me—like, sensitivity-wise. That whole side of the family does."

"What do you mean?"

"Like, I can talk to him about some crazy shit and it doesn't faze him. My dreams and all that."

"And how exactly is he going to help us?"

"I gave him the gist of what's going on," Koi says. "I know he has access to databases, government servers and all that. So I had him run your dad's name, and he—"

"You what?"

He catches himself. "I mean—I figured we needed to start somewhere. I'm sorry, I thought… look, he found some information. He just can't talk about it over the phone."

"Why not?"

"It's just his thing," he says with a shrug. "He doesn't do phones."

I look for something in Koi's face. He blinks back at me with his big brown eyes.

"Where upstate?" I ask.

"Amsterdam. Like three hours from here." He opens his phone. "I'm sending you his info right now. You can look him up, his company, the whole deal."

My phone vibrates. I open the contact and click the company link. A sleek, streamlined website loads. Clients. Services. I click the About section and scan through it.

"It's legit," Koi says. "I promise."

Koi waits outside my building while I pull a bag together. I call Jemma to tell her what I'm doing, so somebody knows where I am.

"You're going *where*?" she asks.

"I know it sounds insane."

"And you know this guy how?"

"It's a long story. Don't worry. I checked him out."

"What's his name? I'm looking him up."

I text it to her.

"Is this him?"

She texts me back a photo.

"That's him."

"He's cute. He looks like a guy I went to college with."

"I did a deep dive. Nothing weird came up."

"And who's the guy you're going to see?"

"His cousin. I'm sending you his info."

"Got it." She opens the link. "So it's like a tech company?"

"Yeah, his name's Trey."

"I'm looking at his bio page," she says. "Treyvon Aubois, President."

"If I text you 'code red'—"

"I'll drop in there like Shiva."

"I'll text you regardless."

"You better."

Koi hails a cab on the corner and we head up the West Side Highway to the ferry terminal. Koi looks sheepish. "Are we taking a boat?" he asks.

"Yeah, I keep my car in Weehawken, across the river. You good?"

"Yeah, nah, it's all good," he says, trying to play it off. I keep tabs on him as we step aboard, his otherwise bright demeanor deteriorating into a sickly shade of green. "You don't like boats," I say, pointing out the obvious.

"It's fine." He shrugs, trying to force a smile as the ferry nudges away from the dock, drifting across the choppy Hudson.

"What is it? Seasickness?"

He shrugs, changing the subject. "Is this where Sully's plane came down?"

"Sully?" I look out across the blue-black water as it dawns on me—the airliner on the news. The pilot had to make an emergency landing in the river. "I think it was," I say, remembering the dreamlike nature of that day, the footage of the ferryboats, the way they glided out to the sinking plane. The people standing on the wings. The ferry workers flat on their stomachs, hoisting passengers into the boats.

"It was crazy the way he put that plane down like a feather," Koi recalls. "People thought it was a terrorist attack, when they were actually seeing a miracle." He glances around the deck—a handful of midday commuters on their phones, reading books, zoning out. "I wonder if this was one of the boats that rescued them." The ferry gives a slight jerk as it rumbles into the dock at Weehawken. We disembark through the terminal and head up the boulevard to the parking garage a few blocks away. Aleksy, the owner, stands outside with his face to the sun, finishing a cigarette. He waves as we approach, giving Koi the up-down, wondering who he is.

"Hey, Lexy," I say, leaning in for a kiss-kiss on each cheek. "How are you?"

"Good, good," Aleksy replies in a thick Polish accent. "I have her all set for you."

He leads us down into the parking garage to a special corner where he keeps my prized possession, a 1971 Land Rover Series IIA. Tough, angular, and outdoorsy, the truck looks like something you'd see on a safari in a National Geographic special—a spare tire fastened to the hood, a utility winch jutting from the grill. Koi takes in the vehicle, dumbstruck. Aleksy takes in Koi, unimpressed. Aleksy looks at me. "You good?" he asks with a hint of concern.

"I'm great, Aleksy, thank you. We're off to visit a friend and I wanted to show her off."

Aleksy nods, defrosting a bit, but not entirely. "Remember," he says, "whenever you want to sell—"

I finish his thought. "You'll be the first person I tell, I promise."

Aleksy holds the door for me as I get in. Koi climbs into the passenger seat, resting his backpack between his feet. He scans the interior, the utilitarian sparseness of the dashboard—a line of dials, a hand gearshift jutting up from the floor like a scepter. He feels around for his seat belt. "This is a real car, right?" he asks, half-joking. He plugs the address into his phone as we pull out of the garage, working our way up onto the highway, past strip malls and furniture stores and car dealerships with pennant flags snapping in the wind. He gazes out the window, lost in thought. "You said you're from Chicago?" I ask, breaking the silence.

"Yeah, you been?"

"I haven't. Is it nice?"

"It depends," he says with a shrug. "I grew up in Washington Park, which is basically the hood. But I went to school on the North Shore. You know John Hughes, the movie director? He did *The Breakfast Club*. It was filmed near my high school. You ever see *Ferris Bueller's Day Off?*"

"Of course."

"I was in that," he says, nonchalantly.

"You were in *Ferris Bueller's Day Off?*"

"Yeah, you don't remember the Black kid?" He looks at me, straight-faced—then breaks the act. "Just playin'. But yeah, I was in *all* those movies. The mall scene in *Weird Science.* The choir in *Home Alone.* He shot all his movies up there."

"You're an actor?"

"Nah, my mom made me do it."

"And so your cousin Trey—you went to school together?"

"Nah, Trey lived down in New Orleans, where my mom's family is from. He'd come up in the summer. The lady my mom worked for got us jobs with some of the other rich folks in town—cutting grass, gardening, and stuff."

"What's he like?"

"Trey?" He chuckles to himself. "Trey's the entrepreneur in the family. Dude's like Walt Disney. He gets an idea in his head and makes it happen, which I've got a lot of respect for. He gets it from our grandma, my mother's mother, Mama Tee. So the way it works, down South, you got aunties. Everybody's got an auntie. Sometimes they're not even your real aunt. My grandma is, like, the biggest auntie of them all. All the families go to her. They called her Mama Auntie, but the little kids couldn't pronounce it, so they called her Mama Tee. Now that's what everybody knows her by."

"And they go to your grandmother for—?"

"You name it. Poor Black folk, they're not going to doctors for every little thing. The aunties, the grandmas—that's who you go to see. They got the potions, the old ways. You get sick, you go see your neighbor's grandma, lady old as dust. She starts pulling out the chicken bones, the gris-gris. When you're a kid, that shit scares you so bad it frightens the sick right outta you."

"You mean voodoo."

"Voodoo, hoodoo, all that," he says with a sniff. "My grandma has another name for it. She calls it 'A.' The letter A, but pronounced in French. I asked her what it meant, but she wouldn't tell me. I don't know if it's some secret slave shit, or West African, or what."

"So she's a healer for the community?"

"She's everything," he says, grinning. "She's like the mayor. She got taught all this when she was little—from her grandma. Mama Tee started a laundry business out of the back of her house. She'd do the healing stuff on the side. Pretty soon she *owned* a laundromat. Then two. Then five. She bought an old motel and fixed it up. She's got a funeral parlor, a fish restaurant. Mama Tee's like an *empire* down there. Everybody goes to her—from New Orleans all the way up to Baton Rouge. One of the women my mother worked for in Chicago, her friend's son had this twitch, like a stutter. My mom told her to go see Mama Tee. This rich white lady and her son, they flew down there. It was crazy." He shakes his head, chuckling. "They came back, that kid was *sorted* out."

"And you're saying Trey is like Mama Tee?"

"Nah, I mean, Trey's got his own thing. Not the healing stuff, really. He's got this thing where he sees how things work, like how everything connects. He tried to explain it to me once, the way he sees stuff. He said it's like dreaming while you're awake. He'll close his eyes, and he'll just put something in the center of his mind. Anything. An object, whatever. A motorcycle. And he'll see that bike come apart like an explosion. He'll see all the parts floating there, the gasoline, the oil, and he'll focus on the oil, and the oil will come apart, into particles, and he'll focus on a particle and it'll explode into molecules. And he'll keep doing that—down, down, down—until there's just *the fabric*. That's what he calls it, like threads of light. He says when you're at that level you realize there aren't really 'parts' of things. The motorcycle and the rider are actually one thing that looks like two." He glances at me to see if I'm following. "Crazy, right?"

"This company of his—it has something to do with the government?"

"Yeah, he manages security for their contractor network."

"Like what?"

"These companies you hear about, big aerospace companies that build jets for the Navy, that kind of stuff. Server farms, logistics. Everything is super encrypted."

"It sounds like you understand this stuff."

"It's a part of what I do." Koi says with a sniff. "I'm more on the hardware side. I work for myself—which is convenient when I need to break away and run down some top secret shit," he says with a smirk.

"On that note," I say. "Can you grab my bag?"

Koi twists around, reaching in the back seat and heaving the tote into his lap.

"This is everything I've put together so far," I explain. "My father wrote down a list of names—other high-level scientists who were involved in the project. They were each briefed on a piece of it without realizing they were part of something larger. I looked up the other projects my dad worked on—mainly research for medical treatments, normal stuff. This project was different. He sensed something was off about it, enough that he went digging. Which I think is what got him and my mother killed."

Koi looks at me, processing this.

"Their car went off the road," I explain. "I think they were being followed."

Koi looks ahead, piecing something together.

"There are too many deaths connected to this," I say. "The majority of the scientists involved died under strange circumstances, not long after my parents. I think whoever was running the project—"

"—was cleaning it up." Koi says with a sniff. He flips through the bag and pulls out a folder, thumbing through the contents.

"These scientists worked in different capacities," I explain. "Psychology, quantum physics, mathematics. I think each of them was meant to develop their own piece of the puzzle, and then at some point—"

"It would all be pulled together." Koi nods, examining one of the documents.

"Phillips," I add, "the scientist I met with in Virginia, thought it might've been a weapon." I reach over, pulling out one of the folders. "Look in there—the files of the soldiers, the ones with the photos attached. Look on their profiles, the line that's highlighted."

"P-S-Y," Koi reads. "What is that?"

"I don't know, psychology? Some of my dad's work was bundled with the psychologist, Siegfried."

"Bundled how?"

"Right, so when I left you that day at the cafe, I went out to my friend's place on Fire Island, just to get my head straight. I brought my notes with me, everything in that bag. One night I came back to the house and found this on the living room floor." I fumble with my phone, trying to keep my eyes on the road. I scroll through the images, landing on one. I hand the phone to him.

He zooms in on the image. "I don't get it."

"Someone came in and arranged all my notes—into that pattern."

He looks at me.

"They're showing how the work of each contributor correlates with the others'—and how all of it ties back to the Navy, and an outside contractor. All of the contributors were tasked with research. Which would need to be transformed into something—something operational. Something would need to be built. Which would require an engineer."

"Mr. Y," Koi mutters. "He said he recruited your dad."

"Exactly. What if he was the engineer? In which case, he would have known what components would need to be researched for the final development."

Koi looks at the diagram again. "You said you came home and all this was just laid out?"

"Someone broke into the cottage."

Koi looks at me. "Like a burglar?"

"I don't know what."

"What do you mean? Did you see someone?"

"There was a girl. I don't know what she was doing. She was crawling."

"*Crawling?*"

"Like she was in a trance or something. It freaked me out. There was something else too. I was with someone, earlier that night. And something…took her over. Like something was trying to get to me—through her. It happened so fast, the whole thing was like a blur."

"Took her over how? Like, attacking you?"

"It was like it wanted to…show me something. 'Home.' It kept saying, 'Home.'"

"Like it was telling you to go home?" he asks.

"No. Like *it* wanted to go home. And it needed me to take it there."

Koi glances out the window, processing this. "What did it feel like?"

"What did it—?"

"Did it feel evil? Like some spinning-head *Exorcist* shit?"

"It was scary. But it didn't feel evil. It felt…desperate."

"Desperate how?"

"Like it wanted help. And then something happened. There was something else in the room. A figure, something—like a presence. I couldn't see it. It was like you said, where you try to look, but your eyes aren't allowed to see. Whatever took this woman over, it was like it *recognized* the other presence in the room."

"The presence—it was like a person?" he asks.

"I think so."

"Man or woman?"

"I don't know—both, maybe?

"*Both?*"

"I don't know. It was this tall *presence.* Like, not one or the other."

"Like David Bowie?"

"It lifted her off the bed. I don't know what happened. I blacked out. I woke up and she was completely passed out. That was it."

"OK, so first off—remind me never to go to Fire Island."

"I mean, *what the fuck is that?*" I press. "What are these things? You said the same thing's been happening to you?"

Koi rubs his face, looking out the window. "Yeah, something like that," he says. "Like something's trying to communicate."

"I don't understand. What is it? A spirit?"

"Or some demon shit? I don't know." He continues paging through the notes.

"That call from Mr. Y," I say. "He said something about communication. Between man and God. If you look in the notes there, the red annotations," I say, pointing, "there's a bunch of religious stuff."

Koi pulls out one of the documents. He reads the inscription scratched in red ink at the bottom of the page:

> And Jacob went out from Beer-sheba, and went toward Haran. And he lighted upon a certain place, and tarried there all night, because the sun was set; and he took of the stones of that place, and put them for his pillows, and lay down in that place to sleep. And he dreamed, and behold a ladder set up on the earth, and the top of it reached to heaven: and behold the angels of God ascending and descending on it. —Genesis 28:10–12

"Ladder," I say. "White Ladder. The note I found with the list of names. There was something called White Ladder 369."

"What is it?"

"I don't know, but there's a note in there somewhere. Something about a ladder."

Koi flips through and pulls out a slip of paper. "Ladder… Code… Duplicating genes…"

"Right. Look that up. 'Duplicating genes.'"

He skims through a search on his phone. "Something to do with DNA. Gene mutation."

"Run another search. Type in 'DNA ladder.'"

Koi reads the result. "DNA is structured as a double helix, a twisted ladder of nucleotides that carry an organism's genetic information."

"OK, run another search: 'DNA and the pineal gland.'"

He scans the results. "Here… INMT." He reads: "'The INMT gene encodes an enzyme called indolethylamine N-methyltransferase, which plays a key role in the biosynthesis of serotonin and dimethyltryptamine (DMT). The INMT enzyme is expressed in the pineal gland, though its precise role in DMT production has yet to be determined. Genetic variations in this gene could theoretically influence the level of DMT produced by the pineal gland.'"

"I've looked through my dad's work," I say. "Most of it centers on the pineal gland. When they briefed him on the project, they told him he'd be working on a PTSD treatment. He specialized in SSRIs, selective serotonin reuptake inhibitors. Antidepressants."

"OK," Koi nods.

"Serotonin and DMT are synthesized in the pineal gland."

"Right."

"So what if he thought he was working on a trigger for serotonin…"

"…when it was actually for DMT."

"Right. What if he was creating a trigger for a self-induced psychedelic state?"

Koi flips back through the files.

"Read me the thing again about the genetic variations," I say.

He looks at his phone. "'Genetic variations in this gene could theoretically influence the level of DMT produced by the pineal gland.'"

"The files of the soldiers," I say. "Look at the ratings on there, the highlighted ones."

"PSY."

"Right, now look at the ones with the green tags. They rank higher than the others."

Koi scans through the documents. "Some twice as high."

"PSY, what do you think that stands for?" I ask.

Koi looks at me.

"What if it means psychic?"

He nods, processing this. "But how would they test for that?"

"I've been having these flashbacks," I say. "Like a memory I've blocked out. I don't know what it is. Some kind of experiment, or test, when I was a kid."

"With cards?" he asks. He looks like he's seen a ghost. "Where they show you a card and you're supposed to guess what's on the other side?"

"Exactly. White cards with black symbols."

"That's crazy. I did that too."

"Wait, when?"

He tries to recall. "It must have been, like, second grade."

"Somebody gave you a test?"

"They came to my school. They were like nurses. All the kids took it. I remember they called my mom afterwards. We had to go to this place in the city."

"Your class went?"

"No, just me and a couple of other kids. We were in this waiting room with our parents. My mom thought it must be something good, like maybe I was smarter than the other kids. She took me out for ice cream after. I don't remember my mom ever taking me out for ice cream other than that one time."

"What was the test?" I ask.

"There were these symbols. Like you said. They were weird. Like a foreign language or something. They would put the cards in front of you, face down. Then you had to name the symbol before they turned it over."

"Did they tell you what it was for?" I ask.

"I can't remember. I thought it might be one of those tests where they put you in a smarter class, but when I went back to school it was like nothing happened."

"Did they ever give you the results?"

"Maybe. If they did, my mom probably has them somewhere. She keeps everything." He looks off, recalling something. "There was something else," he says. "The day we were there. I had to do this other thing. It wasn't a test. I don't know what it was. It was, like… *flashing*."

"What was flashing?"

"Something—like a wall. A room." He tries to recall. "There was a white light, flashing, like a strobe light. And you had to look at it. You had to look for something."

"Something where?"

"I don't know. It was weird. I had to stare at a wall. Like, I was supposed to keep looking at it and tell them if I saw something."

"On the wall?" I ask.

"On it. Or maybe *in* it," he says, seeming confused. "I think I did. But I don't remember what. What was that?"

"I have these memories," I say. "But it's like they've been scrubbed away. Do you remember anything else about that time?"

"Anything about—?"

"Like, *anything*. That year. Second grade? Your birthday? Anything?"

He tries to recall.

"I was looking through a photo album," I say. "From around the time I took the test. I see myself in the photos, but I don't remember any of it. These flashbacks I have—sometimes I see my dad in them. I think he was part of it. I think we did it together."

Koi pulls up something on his phone. "This is crazy," he says. "This is an article from the *Chicago Tribune*. It says that in the 1940s, researchers from Duke University went to a school in Brandon, Manitoba, where they conducted ESP experiments on the students without their parents' consent. There's a link to a paper published in the *Journal of Parapsychology* in 1943. It talks about how these kids were given a test to see if they could guess what was written on hidden cards using extrasensory perception.

"And check this out," he continues. "This is from an unclassified document posted on the CIA's website. It was created on June 29, 1989:

> Analysis of Tests on the Transmission of Sensations Through Channels in 25 Psychic Children:
>
> In our process of testing child psychic Liu (x), we made the initial discovery that in his recognition of characters he was using transmission of sensations through channels, and sending it to the

brain. This is how he is able to recognize characters. To demonstrate this discovery, we tested 25 other child psychics, and the results of our observation are given in the paper.

"What if they were using us?" I ask. "What if that was the test? To find people like us."

Koi looks at me. "Then why would they let us go? It's not like we started working on some top secret shit when we were nine years old."

"Maybe they were waiting."

"Waiting for what?"

25 | EMPIRES

The highway snakes through the mountains, following the curve of the river past abandoned dairy farms, their gray, weather-beaten barns leaning to the side. Old mill towns line the opposite bank—crumbling kingdoms separated from one another by long stretches of marshy nothingness. An exit directs us over a low bridge, under a wrought-iron sign welcoming us to Amsterdam, its skyline a battlement of enormous brick buildings with tall black windows rising up from the hillside. Koi reads a message on his phone. "The building with the clock tower. Park in the back."

We navigate through the city's downtown, a wasteland of abandoned storefronts hung with faded signs from another time—a dress shop, a hat shop, a locksmith—followed by a row of brightly lit convenience stores and dollar shops peddling mobile phones and hookahs. We follow the central boulevard, up past the hospital and cemetery, through a canyon of hollowed-out industrial plants, pigeons flitting in and out of shattered windows. One building rises above the rest, a clock tower keeping watch over the barren landscape. We follow the edge of the building into the back lot and are surprised to find someone waiting for our arrival. A girl with curly blond hair in a red T-shirt and blue jeans waves to us enthusiastically, pointing for us to park next to a row of candy-colored motorcycles. She spins around, signaling to somebody behind the wheel of a giant black SUV—a heavyset Black dude in a Lakers jersey hefts himself out. Our welcoming committee.

"You found us!" the girl cheers. "I finally get to meet the mysterious Koi!" She saunters up to Koi for a hug. He glances at me like he has no idea who this chick is. The big guy in the Lakers jersey smiles at me shyly, not quite sure how to greet me. He hesitates before offering a meaty handshake. "I'm Teddy," he mutters, trying to make himself as small as possible. The girl noses in between us. "Hi, I'm Lana," she says, beaming as she offers a small, clammy hand. There's a manic shiftiness to her that puts me on edge. "Trey's in a meeting," she says. "He wanted me to show you around."

"Should we grab our stuff?" Koi asks.

"No, you can leave it," Lana replies. "I know it looks sketchy, but it's totally safe. Trust me." She pulls Teddy aside, saying something to him under her breath. He climbs back into the SUV, offering a small wave as he pulls out.

Lana motions for us to follow her up the steps of the loading zone to a rusty metal door with a digital panel fastened to the wall beside it. She punches in a code and heaves the door open, ushering us into a long, dimly lit corridor. "So, crazy fact," Lana quips, kicking off the tour. "This is where they used to make Cabbage Patch Kids. Insane, right?"

Koi glances at me.

We arrive at another metal door with a digital panel. Lana places a hand on the black glass and it scans her, glowing around her fingers in a dull green halo. A lock disengages and the door pushes open into a ghost-white stairwell lit by neon beams of black light that illuminate our eyes and teeth like phantoms. Lana bounds up the stairs to the second floor, where she beeps us in with a key card.

As though stepping through a portal, we enter the polished, wood-paneled lobby of an enormous open-plan office space, buzzing with activity, laughter, music thudding down from speakers overhead. Banks of wooden worktables are positioned in rows beneath the giant industrial windows lining the far wall, golden sunlight beaming through them like the light of a chapel. A laser-engraved black-on-black sign welcomes us. Just one word:

PANTHR

I look to Koi like *where the fuck are we*, but he seems just as confused as I am. An espresso machine grinds to life in an adjoining cafe space—a miniature dining hall complete with a salad station, organic-soda machines, cold-cereal dispensers, hot buffets. The space is bustling with young caffeinated people going about their day. As I scan the crowd, I realize Lana and I are the only two white people here.

"Yo, yo!" a voice cries out. A cute skater dude in a green bomber jacket and skinny jeans weaves past us on a kick scooter. "*La-La* in the house!" he cheers.

"Hey, Benji!" Lana coos back. She motions for us to follow. "This is the main space," she says, beginning the tour. "Koi, you've seen the new digs, haven't you?"

"Uh, no, not like this," Koi says quietly as he scans the scene.

"We call this area 'The Lab,'" Lana says, pointing. "That's our marketing department. Over there is digital. The research pod. Our dev teams are over in that corner."

She leads us down a glass hallway of conference rooms named after famous figures—Rosa Parks, Malcolm X, Frederick Douglass, Dr. Dre. We continue up a honey-colored staircase to a mezzanine, past a row of video editing suites, recording studios, and an endless bank of server rooms filled with row after row of blinking data towers. A doorway is lit at the end of the dark hall. Lana knocks at it, popping her head inside, then waves for us to follow.

It takes a moment for my eyes to adjust to the brightness of the room, stark white, a gloss black conference table running the length of the space like a god-size tablet. A sharp, intense figure sits hunched at the far end of the table, hovering over a silver laptop. He looks up, recognizing Koi. "What up, cuz!" He leaps out of his chair, clowning up to Koi, pulling him in for a hug. "What's good, kid?"

I can see the family resemblance. Trey is a bit taller, more angular, his hair faded up into a short plume of twisted braids. He wears a crisp white T-shirt under a black tailored suit, the pant legs rolled up to reveal a pair of black leather sandals. Trey beams at me over Koi's shoulder. "You brought a friend!" he says with a nudge. "Introduce me!"

"Trey this is Catherine. Catherine, Trey."

Trey extends a hand, tugging me in for a peck on the cheek, his face smooth and chiseled, a subtle dab of cologne smelling of spice and rum. "You get the grand tour?" Trey says, glancing at Lana with a grin.

Before she can answer, there's a rap at the door. A young kid in a silver hoodie pops his head in—he nods to Trey. "You good?" the kid asks. Trey nods, motioning for him to enter. The kid whisks around the table, collecting Trey's laptop, then disappears out the door.

Trey ignores the interruption, taking in his cousin. "You're lookin' good, bro! You been hittin' those weights! You get that routine I sent you?" Trey nods to me, looping me in. "I'm trying to get my boy here on a regimen." He winks at Koi playfully. "Mind, body, and spirit. Am I right?" He throws an arm around Koi's shoulder, turning to me. "So, Catherine," Trey says. "You like Catherine or Cat? 'Cause Cat just feels right," he says, grinning as he looks to Koi for consensus. "You know, the ancient Egyptians worshipped cats," Trey says with a nod. "Cleopatra loved her cats more than she loved her men." Trey glances at the door, noticing Lana hovering nervously. "We good?" Trey asks, pointedly.

"Yeah, I sent Teddy," Lana says, squirming. "What time are we thinking?"

Trey looks at his watch, a slim black cuff with a biometric interface. "You talk to Heng?" Trey asks, glancing at her.

"He'd like to talk to you," Lana replies.

Trey turns to Koi. "You wanna go for a ride?" he asks with a smirk. Koi looks at me, not sure where this is going. Trey nods for us to follow, leading us up the corridor, past the banks of blinking servers.

"Looks like you been expanding," Koi remarks.

"Kid, you don't even know," Trey snorts. "Just trying to get enough power up in here? Crazy. We got new optical lines, solar roof. Gotta keep it one hundred. You know how we do." Trey glances at me. "Last time Koi was here, we were sitting on boxes. Isn't that right? We've been moving at warp speed since then."

"So this is all network security?" Koi asks.

"Nah, that's just a piece of it," Trey says with a sniff. "It's all about the cloud now. We got five floors of these bad boys. You're looking at 6 percent of the world's data right here."

"Six percent?"

"Maybe more," Trey says, shrugging. "We got everyone in here, from Kathmandu to Who Knows Who." He laughs. "We're gonna be like the Library of Alexandria up in this piece."

Koi looks at him. "Didn't that shit burn down?"

"Burn down?"

"The Library of Alexandria. It burned down, and they lost all the scrolls."

Trey looks at me for confirmation—then bursts out laughing. He throws his arm around Koi's shoulder, pulling him close. "You're crazy! You better not burn those scrolls! I miss you, dawg. You gotta come by more. It's like you're not even curious to see what you helped build."

Koi glances at me. Trey notices. "What, he didn't tell you?" Trey asks. "Koi was PANTHR's primary investor. Homeboy broke out his tool belt! You didn't tell her about our mission statement?"

Koi rolls his eyes. "You mean your manifesto?"

"Come on," Trey scoffs. "I'm the vision. You're the precision. That's how we do, am I right?"

"What's the manifesto?" I ask. Koi looks like he wishes I hadn't.

"See, man, why'd you have to call it that?" Trey chides. "You make it sound sinister. It was a *mission statement*," he clarifies. "I'm not gonna bore you with the details, but basically we decided it was time to change the game. Let me ask you something. When was the last time you saw a full-on Black-run tech company? I'm not talking about filling quotas or some affirmative action shit. I'm talking full-on Silicon Valley game. That's what we're doing. You're in *Titanium* Valley now!" he says, smiling broadly. "You know what they made in here back in the day? Video games. You ever hear of Coleco? *Donkey Kong*? *Zaxxon*? I know you remember Cabbage Patch Kids. How people went crazy for those? They were dropping them outta airplanes. It was like UNICEF trying to get those dolls out for Christmas. Before that, they made carpets in here. This whole city was mills back in the day. All of it, factories, until they moved that shit to Mexico. This city right here? It's been waiting for someone to come in and save it. And I tell you what, you find a place that's desperate enough, they'll even roll out the red carpet for some Black people," he snorts, checking my reaction. "Nah, I'm just playing. We got a whole crew of white folks holding it down." Trey leads us out into the back parking lot, where Lana is pacing back and forth on her cell. He pulls a black Ducati out of the line of motorcycles and tugs on a helmet. He saddles himself on the bike and revs the engine.

Lana holds out a set of keys to Koi and points to a cherry-red bike with two helmets resting on the seat. Koi turns to me. "It's cool if you don't want to ride. You can take the car if you want."

"Where are we going?"

Koi shrugs. He pulls on one of the helmets and mounts the cycle. He holds the other helmet out to me. I size up the bike. "You know how to ride one of these?" I ask.

Trey rolls up beside us. "You kidding?" he shouts. "He taught me!"

Reluctantly, I take the helmet from Koi and strap it on. I hop on the back.

"I'll have Teddy bring your car to the house," Lana says. Koi looks at me and nods. I hesitate before handing over the keys. "Please make sure he's careful."

"Of course!" she cries. "I promise!"

Trey flicks down his face shield and guns his bike onto the street. I hold Koi by the waist and we thrust forward, following Trey down through the bombed-out city, seemingly oblivious to any speed limit. Trey pulls off into the parking lot of a huge Romanesque church, its sign draped with a cheap vinyl banner that reads "Temple for World Peace." Trey jabs down the kickstand. "Gimme a minute," he says, dismounting the bike and loping up the front steps.

A huge white moving truck is backed up to the side of the church, its rear door rolled open, full of cardboard boxes, rugs, gilded Buddhist icons. A crew of bald Asian men wearing bright yellow robes hurries down the front steps of the church, retrieving a load of contents from the truck and hustling it inside. They pass another crew exiting the church, lugging out armloads of religious paraphernalia: ornate crucifixes, rolled-up tapestries, a hand-painted statue of the Virgin Mary. A conveyor belt of activity, swapping out one religion for another.

Trey returns after a few minutes and mounts his bike without explaining what we're doing here. He nods for us to follow, then guns it out of the parking lot, up into a hillside neighborhood, past rows of vinyl-clad houses, their yards littered with toys, cars up on cinder blocks—then further up, turning onto a tree-lined boulevard, past rows of forgotten mansions hidden behind dense thickets of overgrown hedges.

Trey slows in front of an iron gate affixed with a pair of lion heads that slowly parts as he approaches. We follow him, coasting up the long drive beneath a wide canopy of old-growth trees, coming to rest in front of a stately manor resembling a small English castle. Trey leads us up the front steps, through the vaulted portico and into a rose-colored vestibule, tossing his helmet onto an antique velvet chair. "I bought this spot last year," he announces, striding up the grand central hall. "They were practically giving it away." I glance into the rooms as we pass—an oak-paneled library repurposed as a gaming den—a huge flat-screen TV pushed up against one of the old bookcases; a seafoam-colored drawing room turned into an impromptu gym—a weight machine, an exercise bike, and a rack of dumbbells forming an island in the center of the room.

"Back in the day, this place would've been poppin' off," Trey remarks. "Can you feel the energy in here? The walls, the stone. It's like a crystal skull. Like where the Aztecs kept their records. They channeled their energy into the crystals like hard drives. The crystals in these stone walls, they hold everything. They recharge you while you sleep."

The central hall terminates with a vaulted archway opening into a lush exotic plant–filled solarium. A heavenly light pours in from a glass wall overlooking the back courtyard, where a team of people is busy setting up buffet tables and lounge chairs around a pool.

Trey opens his phone, triggering a sound system. Tupac's "California Love" thumps through the house, setting a party vibe. Trey crosses the room, dipping behind a polished zinc wet bar, flanked by a row of stools with leather seats. He plucks a bottle of champagne from a mini fridge, pops the cork, and pours three flutes. He hands them to us and raises his, then plunks down on one of the oversize sofas clustered in the center of the room, signaling for us to join him.

Trey props up his feet on a coffee table arranged with art books and a gold dragon statue with sharp sapphire eyes and a ruby glowing in its mouth. "My boy Heng gave me that," Trey says, nodding at the statue. "The dragon's the most powerful symbol in Chinese culture. That's my sign—the Dragon." He looks to Koi. "What's yours?"

"I have no idea," Koi says with a shrug.

Trey sits back, considering him for a beat. "I'm thinking Rooster."

"Is that good?"

"Yeah, that's good," Trey says with a sniff. "You know, the Chinese think they descended from the dragon. The Yellow Emperor rode a dragon. That's him right there," Trey says, gesturing to a tapestry hung over the mantel of one of the two fireplaces flanking the room. A rotund, pointy-bearded Asian man in a golden robe gazes back at us knowingly.

"You gotta surround yourself with the right images," Trey explains. "The right icons. They're power sources. That one over there is by my boy K." He nods to a painting hung over the opposite fireplace, a portrait of Trey dressed in a plum-colored suit, white shirt, and black tie against a gold-leaf background. Vines of tropical flowers encircle his legs and arms, rising behind him like the Garden of Eden. In one hand he holds a saber, blade down, like a cane. In the other hand, a crystal ball resting in his open palm. The entire room is arranged like a gallery—oil paintings, charcoal drawings, glass statues, ceramic bowls.

"I didn't know you were into art," Koi remarks.

"I *got* into it," Trey says with a sniff. "Everything you see here, this is soul energy. It comes from an inner place. Made by hand. You can't do that with photography, or movies, or any of that Hollywood shit. Real art is all about the soul, the way it comes through the hands. That's when you're closest to God."

Koi glances at him. "What about cooking?"

"What *about* cooking?"

"That's made with the hands, right?"

"Yeah. So?"

"So, I make some mean-ass pancakes," Koi says, shrugging.

Trey pauses a beat, then cracks up. "Yo, gimme some of those pancakes!" he says with a laugh, loosening up. I wonder if he's like this with anyone other than Koi.

"I told Catherine you had a look at some of the stuff we talked about," Koi hints.

"Yeah, yeah." Trey nods, checking a text on his phone. "The Stargate thing," he mutters, distracted.

Koi leans in. "The what?"

"I thought I texted you. I ran the name again—a couple different ways. The Army's got some files housed on a vault site. This thing called Stargate."

The name means something to me—I don't know what.

"What is it?" Koi asks.

"Remote viewing," Trey mutters, preoccupied with his phone. "You concentrate on a person or a thing—and try to figure out where they are." He tosses his phone aside and takes up his champagne flute. "Like coordinates. Some psychic spy shit."

"Psychic spies."

Trey chuckles. "Kid, you'd be surprised what the military is doing. It's like Pink Floyd meets *Harry Potter* up in there. I've actually thought about stepping away from the whole corporate game and just becoming a straight-up consultant."

Koi looks at me for help, then back at Trey. "What are you talking about?"

"Bro, this is where it's all going," Trey says with a sniff. "Parapsychology. Remote viewing. I got this one client at the Department of Defense. He's been working with witches. Like some ancient Druid shit." Trey laughs. "It's crazy! But it's *good*. This is our time!"

"What do you mean, working with witches?"

"Like, straight-up sorcery—but on some molecular-level shit."

"And you know this how?"

Trey tops off our glasses. "I'm in there working on their systems. Can I help it if I see some things now and then? I signed an NDA. I know they'll grab my ass and ship me off to Guantánamo if I leak anything." He leans back, stretching. "Honestly, they're not even worried about this shit leaking, 'cause it sounds so crazy. They know people will just be pegged as freak shows if they talk about it. But *don't* talk about it," he adds, "'cause they'll come grab your ass too."

"Thanks for the heads-up," Koi says, smirking. "So while you were in there digging around, you found some stuff?"

"Yeah, the name you gave me—there were a bunch of codes connected with it. One was this thing, Stargate," Trey continues. "Or a sister project. Sun Streak, I think it was called. Remember Terry Waite, from the '80s? He was all up in that hostage shit? He went to Lebanon to try to negotiate with the Islamists, but they took him captive instead. It turns out our government used these remote viewers to figure out where he was, if he was being taken care of, if the other hostages were all right. This is all public domain now. You can look it up."

I look to Trey. "And you think that's what this is?"

"Remote viewing?" Trey says. "Nah, but it has something to do with it."

Koi leans in. "So how do we find out—?"

"Cuz, I got you," Trey assures. "It's gonna take a minute. I'm actually glad we're talking about this. I had a favor I wanted to ask. Both of you, actually."

Koi looks at me, seeming unsure of where this is going.

"So, you know how I was telling you about the crystals and all that?" Trey begins. "Well, I've been studying what you can do with them, and I'm telling you, it's mind-blowing. I got this client. He's got a crystal cave, like an hour from here. He does these tours—boats going down this underground river, laser lights, this whole Disney 'It's a Small World' situation. So I'm doing a trade with him. I take care of his website, his ticketing system, and he gives me access to the cave whenever I want. Now, I go down there, like, once a week. Just trying stuff out, experimenting with the crystals. This isn't, like, normal crystals. When you're inside a crystal cave, it's like being inside *one gigantic crystal*. You get a sense of how the energy flows. It's next-level. Let me tell you something. Microchips? That shit is done. It's all gonna be crystals before you know it. You wouldn't believe how much information they hold. Not just information, but energy. Different kinds of energy. Like, spirits. It's crazy."

"What do you mean, 'spirits'?" Koi asks.

"Yeah, so my client at the DoD. I've been letting him in on my other 'talents,' you know, just seeing what's up on the consulting side. He talked to some of his people and they reached out about a project. Some ISIS shit."

"ISIS?"

"Yeah, like the terrorists."

"Yeah, I know what ISIS is."

"Anyway, my guy needed someone to get inside their data servers, hack their shit. But not just that—they needed a way to track them when they weren't online. See what their offline network looked like, how they operate, how they think, what scares them. I poked around with some of my contacts on the dark web, put some feelers out. I mentioned this black box server that's going online in Azerbaijan. Some people came sniffing around, seeing what's what. One of them was this low-level ISIS kid, Ahmed. Dude was trying to make a name for himself on the recruitment side, running their social media. We get to talking and it turns out this kid Ahmed's into hip-hop. I start throwing him some recos, shit that's poppin' off, and we start forming a friendship. No business, just saying what's up. He gets hooked on my boy Frank Ocean's shit. So I'm like, yo, Frank is playing a gig in Brooklyn, you want to come out? I'll take you around. So this kid jumps on a plane. And he's cool. I take him out, show him some spots, hit the show, introduce him to Frank. So we're tight now. He flies back to Damascus. Next thing I know, he's hitting me on chat, like, every other day. He wants me to come out, meet some people, return the favor. My guy at the DoD is like, go for it, just hang out. So I do. And it's cool. I mean, these

ISIS foot soldiers are no joke, but most of them are just regular folks. And my name's been getting around. I'm, like, their one Black friend. Plus, I'm from New York, so it's like Jay-Z just rolled up. Anyway, I'm hanging with these guys and they're mumbling some shit about something coming up, out in the desert. They keep saying this one word, '*jinn, jinn,*' like they're spooked. I'm like, 'What is that—*jinn*?' And they start telling me about these spirits. Like demons or something—but not. They live in this part of the desert and they can kill you, or make you go crazy."

"Jinn," I interrupt. "Like a genie."

"Yeah, same thing. These jinn are supposed to be super powerful. You gotta be careful not to piss them off. But on the flip side, if you help a jinn, if you protect it, it'll be indebted to you. You can call on it whenever you want. That's where the 'genie in a bottle' comes from. So I'm thinking, *what if you had a jinn you could call on whenever you needed it?* Like, this thing that works for you on this whole other level—protecting you, facilitating shit. I asked my guy if anyone had ever caught a jinn. He said he didn't know, but there was someone who knew how to speak to them, how to ask for permission to move through their territory. He introduces me to this guy. He's the grandfather of one of the soldiers. He lets me sit in on an incantation where he's communicating with the jinn. It was crazy. We're in this old man's tent and you could feel the electricity in the air, like chills all up and down. I recorded it on my phone. I've been practicing it ever since."

Koi cocks his head. "You've been practicing what?"

"The incantation." Trey knocks back his glass.

"To catch a genie."

"Yeah, but I can't do it by myself. That's the thing. I was talking to the old man. He said no one's ever caught a jinn, because you need to do it with other people who have the gift. Three people, reciting it at the same time."

"Why three?"

"I don't know. It's some mystical triad shit. You got these three rings of energy, and they all intersect in the middle. Then you call the jinn inside that, and it holds it there."

Koi glances my way.

"I was thinking we could do a trade," Trey says with a sniff, checking a text on his phone.

"What kind of trade?" Koi asks.

"Maybe team up for a second."

"Let me get this straight," Koi sighs. "You're saying you'll help us break into a government server if we help you catch a genie?"

Trey laughs. "I mean, win-win, right?"

Koi glowers. "You didn't say anything about this."

"Kid, I just came up with it!" Trey blurts, raising his hands, innocent. "I'm just throwing ideas around! You know I got you. Whatever you need. I'm just saying, maybe we could help each other out. How often do you have three psychics in the same spot? Am I right? Imagine what you could do if you had one of these jinn working for you. Who you could help."

"Oh, so this is about helping people," Koi scoffs. "Like some philanthropic shit."

"Kid, there's all kinds of—"

"First off, this sounds crazy. Like, beyond your normal crazy," Koi snaps. "Secondly, doesn't this sound *even a little bit* like slavery."

Trey recoils. "*Slavery?*"

"Like some *genie-ass* slavery."

Trey laughs. "We're not putting him in a golden lamp, dawg! We're just having a conversation, getting to know each other. I already tried it by myself, but it didn't work. I can feel the electricity, so I know it's there, but then it just, like, fades out." Trey leans in. "Bro, isn't this what we always talked about? How we gotta push the boundaries? You said it yourself. Otherwise no one's gonna see past what's right in front of their face. Look, I'm not trying to force you into anything. I'm just saying maybe we could help each other."

Koi looks at me, like *I'm sorry I dragged you into this.* Trey turns to me, looking for an ally.

"I want to see the information you found on my dad," I say.

"Absolutely," Trey nods. "I'll show you tomorrow."

"No. Now. Then we can talk."

Koi sits up, amazed I'm even entertaining this.

"All right," Trey says with a sniff, "hand me that." He motions for a laptop resting on a stack of magazines. Koi hands it to him. Trey flips open the computer and keys in something, a password maybe, then another, then another. He turns it to face us. "Welcome to the Pentagon," he says, smirking. The screen glows with a line-by-line screed of green command text. He turns the computer back to himself. "What's your dad's name again?"

I lean over his shoulder. "Harper. Andrew Harper."

He feeds it into the system. "Dr. Andrew P. Harper. Princeton University. Professor of Biochemistry. Awards... Patents... List of projects... Completed. Discontinued. Ongoing."

"Ongoing."

He types in a command. "White Ladder," he reads. Koi looks at me. Trey enters another command. A new page of green text fills the screen. "'Project White Ladder deals with 1) Induced biological advancement, 2) Psychoenergetics, 3) Applied quantum mechanics...'" He scans down the page. "'Psychoenergetics are here defined as 1) Mental collection of information, 2) Transdimensional transit... Since the early

1970s, U.S. military and intelligence agencies have been examining the potential uses and effectiveness of psychoenergetics as a tool for espionage and reconnaissance. Early experiments were led by physicists Hal Puthoff and Russell Targ at Stanford Research Institute. Research and application of psychoenergetics has since expanded into chrono-regression/progression, astral projection, and telepathy.'"

"Chrono-regression. What is that?" Koi asks.

"Time travel," I answer.

Trey does a double take, glancing at his cousin. "You see that? It's crazy, bro! The military's on some *other* shit!" He types in another command, then another. His brow furrows.

"What is it?" I ask.

"It's blocking me," Trey says with a sniff. He tries another password, but it's rejected.

"So we're locked out?" Koi asks.

"Kid, I got *all* the keys," Trey sighs. "It's gonna take a minute though. Which means less time for what I'm trying to do." He sits back, tossing the laptop aside. He looks to me: *What's it gonna be?*

I look at Koi. "If Koi's in, I'm in."

Trey grins from ear to ear.

"There's one more thing," Koi says. He nods to me. "You got that box?"

I reach in my bag and hand it to him. Koi sets the polished black square on the coffee table.

"What is it?" Trey says, nodding at it.

"That's what we want to know. I figured you might be able to take a look. We were told it was some kind of frequency jammer, a 'cone of silence'-type deal. Any time we meet with someone to talk about this project, they pull out one of these. We want to know what it is, how it works."

Trey picks it up. He seems surprised by its weight.

"I thought it might be lead-lined," Koi says.

Trey inspects the casing and flips it over. "You hiding some plutonium up in here?" He sets it on the table. "I'll look at it," he says with a sniff. "So we good?"

Koi looks at me for a final call. "It's up to you," I say.

"All right," Koi sighs, "how do we do this?"

"Do what?" Trey asks.

"Catch your genie."

"You mean *collaborate*?" Trey smirks.

Koi looks exasperated. "You know what—"

"I'm just playin', yo!" Trey blurts. "What do you want? I'm excited! We'll get into it tomorrow."

"Get into *what*?" a woman's voice asks. She flows into the room, immaculately dressed in a green silk suit, heels, a hot pink blouse, and huge black sunglasses. Her entrance feels like an event. She removes her sunglasses and hands them to Teddy as he hustles in behind her with her Louis Vuitton luggage.

Trey leaps up. "Everyone," he announces, "our queen, Eesha, has arrived!" He offers her a peck on the cheek, which she accepts with lukewarm enthusiasm. Koi approaches, coming in for a hug, which she gladly accepts. "What up, Eesha, you good?" Koi mutters.

"Hey, sweetie," she replies, warm, sisterly—then turns to me, offering a cold up-down glance. Trey jumps in between us. "This is Koi's friend, Cat. Cat, this is my business partner, Eesha."

I move to shake her hand. She meets it with a limp grasp, her fingers wrapped in huge gold rings.

Trey pulls a fresh bottle of champagne from behind the bar and pops the cork. He pours a flute and hands it to Eesha.

"I'll take these to your room," Teddy mutters, rolling away the luggage.

"Thank you, Teddy," Eesha replies, distracted, checking her phone.

"Where you coming from?" Koi asks.

"Funny you should ask," Eesha says, smiling as she drops her phone into her purse and enthrones herself in a plush velvet chair. "I went to see your grandmama," she says, "since her grandsons can't seem to make the time." She sips her drink, letting this sink in. The cousins glance at each other, sheepish.

"How's Mama Tee?" Koi mumbles.

"She's good," Eesha sighs, "all things considered. I got nothing but respect for that woman. She's got quite the empire down there."

"Oh yeah?" Trey says with a sneer. "How's her fish shop doing?"

Eesha corrects him. "You mean her restaurant chain."

"Yeah, right," Trey says with a sniff, scrolling through his texts.

Eesha turns to Koi. "You know your grandmother has six restaurants now? And she's been generous enough to ask her grandson here to partner with her."

"Yeah," Trey scoffs, "'cause we're getting into the shrimp and grits business. 'Cause that's the hot new shit."

"No," Eesha corrects him, "that's the hot *old* shit. And I'm surprised to hear something that ignorant coming out of the mouth of someone calling himself an entrepreneur."

Trey feigns excitement. "You know what, you're right. Let's do it! Let's get into the fried fish business!"

"That doesn't sound half bad," Koi says with a sniff.

Eesha notes the vote of confidence. She turns to Trey. "You know what the margins look like on some good home cooking?" she asks. "Tell me her sweet tea isn't the best you've ever had. If we broke into the beverage market—"

"Yo, I got it!" Trey plays. "We'll call it Mama Tea!"

Eesha throws a look to Koi. "Maybe you can talk some sense into your cousin."

Trey pleads his case. "All I'm saying is, why do we want to be wrapped up in all that when we got all this? I mean, what happened to staying on brand? Me and Koi, we've been working all our lives trying to get *out* of the bayou—"

"I grew up in Chicago," Koi corrects him, "and so did you—kind of."

Eesha holds her ground. "I'm just saying, why not keep our options open? And keep it in the family if we can."

Teddy returns and, reading the energy in the room, tucks himself onto one of the barstools and starts scrolling through his phone.

Something outside catches Trey's attention. The courtyard, now filled with PANTHR employees, has erupted into full-on pool party mode. Amid the festivities, two dudes stand out like sore thumbs—pale, blond, and puffy-faced, sporting polo shirts and khakis, they move through the crowd saying *what's up*, showing love to people.

"The Chads are here," Trey says, nodding.

With that, Eesha sets down her glass, rising from her chair. She crosses the room. "Teddy, I'll be down in a few," she says, exiting through the back hall, leaving a palpable tension in her wake. I move myself over to the bar beside Teddy.

Trey stands at the window, watching the scene outside. Koi joins him. "I didn't know you were talking to Grandma," Koi says.

Trey waves it off. "Eesha's got this whole scenario in her head. Whatever," he sighs. "I got things going on. I don't need Grandma all up in my head right now."

"You don't think she'd be impressed? With everything you got going?"

"She can't hear about it," Trey grumbles. "You know how she is. You try to explain something to her and she makes it sound like you're acting the fool. Like she knows what I'm supposed to be doing. If she wants to be down there babysitting all those poor Black folks, keeping them in the Stone Age with her visions and spells, that's her business. I mean, she should want to come up *here*. *This* is the future. But she can't even talk about it. You say one thing about technology and she's like, 'Oh, that's the Devil talkin'.' Going on about the kids on their phones and the internet, like they're under some kind of spell. And I'm like, you want to talk about spells? What are you doing with them chicken bones?" He looks to Koi. "You think she bought half those businesses down there? Please. People *leave* them to her. Like they're indebted. But that's what I'm supposed to be doing, right? Keeping that empire going?" Trey shrugs it off. He swings open the French doors onto the patio as the music spills in. "Gimme a minute," he says. "I'm gonna say hello to some people." He strides out to a round of cheers.

Koi joins us at the bar. He nods to Teddy. "Is Eesha all right?"

Teddy stretches his shoulders, setting his phone aside. "Yeah, you know," he grumbles. "Just a lot of big personalities. She's been on Trey about this Mama Tee thing for a while."

"And what's up with the Chads?"

Teddy shrugs, trying to avoid the subject.

Koi turns to me. "The Chadwick brothers. They're big players in the venture capital world. PANTHR's like their calling card, 'cause it gets them a lotta press. Black-owned. Woman-led. People eat that shit up."

"Wait," I ask, "Trey doesn't run the company?"

"Trey does a lot of things—but Eesha runs it."

"And they're…together?"

"A couple?" Koi says, smirking. "Nah. They go way back. Eesha's like a sister."

"And she's into this whole thing? With the genie?"

"Oh man…," Teddy grumbles.

Koi looks at him. "You know about this?"

"Yeah, I know about it."

"And what do you think?"

Teddy gives him a big-eyed shrug, like he's not supposed to talk about it.

"'Cause it sounds crazy as hell to me," Koi says.

"Just don't mention it around Eesha," Teddy sighs.

"So she knows about it?"

Teddy looks at him as if to say *please*.

"I don't get it," Koi says. "Trey's on this whole thing about tech being the future, and yet he's still fucking with this black magic shit?"

"He says it's technology."

"What is?"

"All that," Teddy says, "with the spells and stuff. He was telling me. I drive him back and forth to that cave out there. Once he was having one of his off days. He was upset. I mean, he's usually quiet about all this stuff, but something set him off. He was talking about robots, and the spirit, and all this end-of-the-world stuff. I'm just trying to follow what he's saying, 'cause, you know, when he gets like that, you just gotta let him roll. He's going on about AI and how it's gonna take over everything, and how we gotta figure out what the soul is before it's too late, or the robots are gonna take 'em."

"Take what?"

Teddy shrugs. "Our souls or some shit."

"The robots?"

"I have no idea," Teddy sighs. "He was like, 'That's the next slavery right there.' I think he got all wound up talking to that agent."

"Which agent?"

"The one he's always talking to. The one he got hooked up with—with the ISIS shit."

"What about him?"

"I don't know," Teddy sighs. "I just don't like him. I don't like his voice. I've heard some of those phone calls."

"Yeah, like what?" Koi asks.

"Like some mumbly, cryptic-ass shit. They got him going in for these sessions. I don't know what. But he comes out looking like a zombie."

"Sessions where?"

"Up at this office park in Albany. I asked Trey what was going on, but he said it was none of my business and to keep my mouth shut. And not to tell Eesha either. I'm only telling you 'cause you're family, and I thought you should know."

"But you said Eesha knows about it."

Teddy shrugs. "Nothing gets by Eesha. They got into it one night. She said she doesn't want him messing with them anymore."

"So he stopped?"

Teddy looks at him.

Koi glances at the party outside. "What's all this then?"

"If you ask Trey, this is the brand," Teddy says, smirking. "Company culture—all that. But you ask me, it's all just a big show for the Chads, trying to be hip-hop. The Kennedys getting down with the New Blacks. That's what Eesha says. She calls Trey, Trey Kennedy. She thinks they got him brainwashed. That's why she's trying to get him down to talk to Mama Tee. She doesn't want anything to do with this."

"What do you know about this genie shit?" Koi asks.

Teddy rolls his eyes. "I don't know. He's been going down to that cave for like the past two months. I don't know what he's doing down there. And I'm not going down to see."

"Is it safe?"

"*I mean*…it's safe. It's like some weird amusement park down there. I just don't fuck with it."

Koi glances at the scene outside—Trey play-fighting with one of the guys from the office, a ripped dude with locks wearing a pair of swim trunks. They grapple, each trying to make the other fall into the pool. The guy grabs for Trey, but Trey knocks him off balance and he pinwheels into the water, kicking up a huge splash. Everyone cheers as Trey howls in victory. Trey sees us watching from the window and waves for us to come out.

The party bleeds late into the night, the music thumping like a pulse through the house, up through the floor of my room. The pool, a glowing turquoise rectangle, lights the faces of the remaining guests, drinking from plastic martini glasses, passing around joints, laughing under a fog of weed. Koi spins counterclockwise in a pool tube, talking to Trey, who's straddling the end of the long, white diving board.

I check my phone for a text from Jake but there isn't one, so I start shuffling through my accounts, antsy, landing on the message I sent to Janet Ward a couple of days ago. I click on her photo, opening her profile. A cascade of posts fills the page— family and friends offering long, heartfelt messages about how much they'll miss her and Harvey, how hard it must have been those last few years, how they wish they had known she was suffering. I scroll through the posts—photos uploaded by friends, poems, inspirational quotes. I do a search for "Harvey Ward." An obituary appears, dated yesterday, in the *New York Times*.

In addition to his contributions to clinical psychology and pediatric health, Mr. Ward served as chair of the Department of Mental Health and Substance Abuse at Walter Reed National Military Medical Center from 1978 to 1995. Ward served as chief physician at Walter Reed following 12 years of active duty as lieutenant, and lieutenant commander, of the Navy, supporting the health and welfare of American troops throughout the Vietnam War…

I scroll through Janet's profile, trying to piece together what's happened. I land on a message from a woman in Annapolis, Maryland, one of her friends.

…and I know I shouldn't say this, but how could you? We loved you. You could have talked to us. And now there's nothing. Just pain and ?s This isn't how we should remember you. I want to remember you from the book club nights. All of us laughing. That's how I want to remember you…laughing…not like this…

I run a search on Janet Ward and find an obituary published today in the *Capital Gazette*:

Mrs. Ward passed away at her home in Annapolis…

My mind reels. *We just spoke. How is this possible?* I trace through my call log—incoming, from Annapolis, two days ago. My hands are shaking. I click back to the obituary, but the words begin to shift and blur. A burst of light and the room spins, a roulette wheel, flashing through scenes, moments:

> *My parents at home, getting ready to*
> *leave.*
> *My mother gathering her purse.*
> *My father behind the wheel.*
> *Their bodies jostling,*
> *side to side,*
> *slow motion.*
> *The car jackknifing,*
> *tumbling,*
> *splashing down,*
> *sinking in the blue-black water.*

I clench my eyes shut, willing the images away, but my mind keeps spinning, flashing, faster, faster—

> *Another scene—*
> *A white-walled room*
> *flashing with light.*
> *In the middle of the room,*
> *a chair.*
> *Seated in the chair,*
> *a child.*
> *A little girl.*
> *She gazes at the wall,*
> *at nothing.*
> *I look at her face—*
> *my face,*
> *my young eyes,*
> *mesmerized,*
> *staring like a deer into headlights.*

White squares flash across her pupils
as she looks
at something.
Something there
in the whiteness,
in the wall.
What is it?
What does she see?
I turn
and look.
And there...
There...
I see...
I see...
I...
see...

26 | THE CAVE

*I'm standing at the end of a white marble hall. The museum at
closing time. A crowd drifts past me, dark figures. There, at the
other end of the hall, a pair of stragglers, two young girls,
standing with their hands jabbed into the pockets of their
windbreakers, looking up at the painting—the young Joan of
Arc. The girls nod to me as I approach, making room beside
them.*

"What do you think of it?" I ask.

"It's epic," one girl mutters.

"Her eyes are super intense," her friend remarks.

"What do you think she's looking at?" I ask.

*"Nothing," the friend says, considering it for a moment. "I
think she's listening."*

*I look at Joan's face, the stillness in her gaze. "To the
angels?" I ask.*

"To herself," the girl replies.

"Her face is a composite," her friend remarks. "Her body is based on the artist's cousin, but her face is a combination of two girls."

"Two?" I look again at young Joan—her face, the face I've always known, suddenly new to me. "Who were they?" I ask, but the girls are gone, disappeared in the exiting crowd...

I'm thrust awake from the dream by a rap at the bedroom door. "Yo, Catherine, you good?" Koi mutters. I lift myself and sit up. Another rap. "I'm up!" I call, shielding my eyes from the morning light clipping in through the wavy panes of the window.

"OK, cool. Trey wants to head out," Koi says. "We'll be out front."

I reach for my phone. The screen opens on Janet Ward's obituary, her photo. I click it off and will myself to get up, shuffling to the bathroom. I check my face in the medicine cabinet, my eyes, chanting under my breath. *"Llits ma I, won si siht, ereh ma I... Llits ma I, won si siht, ereh ma I..."*

Trey's black SUV idles in the driveway out front, Teddy behind the wheel, Trey in the passenger seat gazing down into the glow of his phone. Koi waits beside my car, watching me, tentative as I navigate the front steps. "You want me to drive?" he asks, taking my bag, helping me in. I nod, handing him the keys. He walks around to the driver's side and gets in, regarding me for a moment. "You alright?"

I nod, getting myself situated. Trey's SUV pulls past and Koi follows it, out through the gate, coasting down through the sleeping city, over the river to where the road opens up and the sun beams gold across the hillsides. "I made you some coffee," Koi says, nodding to a travel mug wedged into the console. I take a sip, the dark, earthy smell snapping my mind awake. I gaze at the farms clipping by, the old red barns, silhouettes of cattle grazing on the hill.

"I'm sorry this is so weird," Koi sighs. "I'm gonna try to get us in and out of here, I promise."

"It's fine. As long as he can help."

"He had me up playing video games all night," Koi says. "Honestly, I don't know when he sleeps."

Trey's SUV turns onto a road marked by a hand-painted billboard: AMAZING CAVE TOURS!

"I think it scares him to sleep," Koi remarks. "Like me with my nightmares. I don't think he likes to close his eyes."

We follow the SUV up a gravel drive, parking in front of a massive building that looks like a Swiss chalet, perched atop the hill. Teddy waits with the car while Trey hops out and unlocks one of the side entrances. He waves us over, ushering us into a dim corridor smelling of carpet cleaner and wood polish. The passageway is lit by a single floodlight, an eerie gallery of wax statues and taxidermy—bats, bobcats, snakes—frozen in nightmarish poses. Trey hits the button for an elevator, and the doors bing open, revealing an inner iron gate. Trey slides it aside, and we file into the small, tight cage, shoulder to shoulder. The door panel offers two options—THE LODGE or THE CAVE. Trey presses the button and we begin our slow descent through the rock-walled shaft. He scrolls through his phone, an awkward silence. Koi breaks it. "So, you got that incantation?" he asks.

"Yeah, I texted it to you," Trey mutters. "You need the Wi-Fi?"

"They got Wi-Fi in here?"

"Yeah, go to HC-Admin. Password is CRYSTALS! All uppercase with an exclamation point at the end."

Koi and I follow the directions and our phones light up with a signal. A group text appears; I pop it open and scroll through. The incantation reads like a series of short poems translated into broken English.

The elevator nudges to a halt, the doors open, and we're hit in the face with a waft of stony air. The mouth of the cavern opens before us, an enormous yawning void lit by floodlights tucked into its shadowy crevices. Stalactites dagger down like long, dripping fangs, forming slick pools of calcified rock at our feet. A shimmering black river snakes through the cavern, descending into the gullet of the Earth, a small fleet of aluminum rowboats tied along the shore.

"Check this out," Trey says with a nod, clicking the face of his phone—the cavern lights respond, blooming into a radiant sapphire blue. He clicks again and the lights bleed into neon pink, then purple, then green.

Koi looks apprehensively at the rowboats. "Yo, we taking a boat?"

"Nah, I got you," Trey says with a sniff, nodding for us to follow. We edge along a narrow footpath hugging the riverbank. Koi glances at me as we maneuver around a dripping pillar of rock. He calls up ahead to Trey, "OK, so how we doing this?"

"I'm gonna recite the first incantation," Trey explains, "which calls the jinn into our realm. I'll say it slow, so you can follow along. Then both of you start saying it with me, over and over, until we feel something."

"Like what?" Koi asks. He holds out a hand, helping me leap to a patch of level ground.

"It's different every time," Trey says. He pauses on an outcropping, trying to gauge how much further we need to go. "Like, it might get cold all of a sudden. Or the lights will start to flicker. That's when I start saying the second incantation, which invites the jinn into the space between us."

"So, we're like, what—holding hands?" Koi asks.

"Nah, we gotta stand in a triangle," Trey says, figuring out where he wants to position us. "You'll feel the electricity—like the hairs on your arm standing up. That means it's come into the center. Then we start saying the final incantation, which closes the triangle."

"OK. Then what?"

"Then I start speaking to it through my mind."

"Through your mind."

"Trust me. I got this." Trey pulls a small megawatt flashlight out of his pocket and clicks it on, shining it up along the cavern walls; the wet, daggered ceiling. "Everything is through the mind," he explains. He points the beam at the ground, a few feet in front of him. "All right, cuz, you need to stand here." Koi does as he's told, stepping into the center of the beam. Trey points the light to another spot about six feet away. He nods to me. "Right there." I step into the white circle, completing the triangle.

"All right, so if the lights go out, just stand still," Trey instructs. "And keep repeating the incantation no matter what."

"What does it look like?" Koi asks. "The genie. Is it, like, some kind of freaky demon shit?"

"It's not a demon."

"So you've seen one."

"Nah, but this dude explained it to me. They live on the same plane, the jinn and the demons. But they're like different species."

"What plane?"

"The *interdimensional* plane," Trey sighs, exasperated. "What does it matter?"

"What else lives there?"

"Bro."

"I'm just saying—are we opening some kind of portal?"

"It's like a window, all right? It's like a room."

"Like a room. Where we visit with a genie."

"Exactly."

"And what if this genie figures out we're trying to trap him?" Koi asks.

"We're not *trapping* it." Trey huffs. "We're *conjuring* it. The jinn lives on its own plane. When you need its help, you call for it, it crosses over, it does its thing, and then it crosses back."

Trey does a final check of our arrangement. He glances at Koi and me. "We good?"

Koi looks at me. I nod yes. "Yeah, we're good," Koi sighs.

"OK, let's do this," Trey says, straightening up. He opens his phone, takes a deep breath, and begins reciting the incantation. At first the words feel meaningless, but as we repeat them, they begin to change their texture, blending, merging into one another, a snake of utterances slithering through our lips.

The floodlights flicker through the cavern, then dim, then brighten in a slowly undulating wave. Then all at once they wink out, like candle flames blown out by the wind, leaving nothing but the light of our phones dotting the blackness. Trey begins the second incantation and Koi and I follow, locking into a rhythm. As we do, the air becomes cold, vacant, the damp, stony breath of the cave replaced by a sharp, flinty stillness like the smell of a burnt match. I feel myself uttering the words—the vibrations rising through my throat, my lips moving—but the sound disappears, as if it's detached itself, existing in a layer of reality just outside this one. I look to Trey, to Koi, their faces lit by the glow of their phones, but it's like I'm looking at them through a plane of glass tipped slightly sideways, like I'm gazing out from the inside of a prism.

A pale blue light winks in the dark, in the space between us, like the lick of a gas flame. It hovers there, pulling and tugging its shape, elongating into a thin, sizzling thread, coiling upward. And within the coil, the shape of something, a figure, made of shadow, made of void. The light coalesces around the head of the figure and disappears within it, swallowed down, illuminating the mouth, the nostrils, the eyes filled with a pale, crackling blue. It gazes at me, its glowing eyes blinking, frightened, and I feel my insides go cold with shame. I will myself to stop the incantation, but the words have built a momentum of their own. I bite down on them, clenching my teeth, crying out to the figure with my mind, willing it away. "Go! Escape! Now!" Its eyes glow brighter, as if it's heard my pleas. Its mouth moves, breathing words like wind against crystal.

I...see...

 you...

 for what...

  you are.

That...

 which is...

  within...you...

   trapped...

    from...the light.

  You fear...

   the darkness...

  But it...is...you.

   Your other...half.

Your line...

 has been...broken...

  But you...

   will lead...

    them back.

 They are...with...you...

  always...

   waiting...

to be led.

Look...

and you...

will see.

A dim light dawns through the cavern, revealing a wretched horde of creatures, like an army of the damned writhing in anguish, a shadow-black sea of pain.

Look...into...their faces.

They...cannot...

harm...you.

What...

do you...see?

"Awful..." I gasp. "Torment..."

Look...deeper.

Look...

into...

their hearts.

"Broken. In two."

Yes...

"Half a heart."

And where...is...

the other...

half?

"Home," I utter without thinking.

Where...
> *is...home?*

I raise my gaze as the rock ceiling begins to shudder, a fissure racing along the apex, opening in a mouth of white light. The dark creatures scream in exuberance, clawing, grasping upward. I gaze into the light, its radiance so familiar, like a recurring dream.

You...know...
> *the way.*
>> *You...possess...*
>>> *the key.*

As I gaze into the light, it begins to pulsate, unfolding like the petals of a flower. Along its edge stand magnificent figures, glowing sentries, positioned on the outcroppings.

Do you see...
> *who guards...*
>> *the gates?*

"Beautiful," I whisper.

Look...deeper.
> *Beneath...*
>> *the light.*
> *What...*
>> *do you...see?*

I focus on the figures' ethereal glow, through it, to what lies beneath.

> *Look...*
> > *into...*
> > > *their...*
> > > > *hearts.*

"Broken," I say. "In half."

> *The gate...of...*
> > *Heaven.*
> *The gate...of...*
> > *Hell.*
> > > *Open...the gate...*
> > > > *and all...*
> > > > > *will be...*
> > > > > > *one.*

> *Only...*
> > *you...*
> > *have eyes...*
> > > *to see...*
> > > > *the way...*
> > > > > *home.*

I reach upward to the flowering light, but it retracts, folding backward, closing, blotting out into darkness, taking my breath with it—

I gulp in air, sputtering, coughing, disoriented, squinting into a bright synthetic light, a flashlight. "Catherine? Oh man, hang on," Koi gasps. He shines the light into the surrounding darkness, searching. "Trey, turn on the lights!"

"I'm trying!" Trey barks, groping around in the dark.

Koi crouches beside me, touching my arm. "OK, all right, don't move. We're gonna get help."

I try to speak, but there's no wind to push out the words.

"Call Teddy!" Koi shouts.

"I'm trying!" Trey replies. "There's no signal!"

I turn on my side, pushing myself up.

"Wait, hang on," Koi urges. "Don't move."

Suddenly the floodlights snap on, like someone plugged in a Christmas tree. Koi tries to help me, but I shove him away. "Yo, take it easy. You might've hit your head." He braces me as I stabilize myself, my eyesight blurring into focus. A large shape hurries toward us from the entrance of the cave, wheezing, out of breath—Teddy. "Yo, what happened?" he huffs.

"Catherine fell. We're getting out of here."

"OK, I got ya," Teddy says, helping me. "I'm taking her up. Go help Trey."

Teddy steadies me along the path back to the elevator, holding the door as he ushers me inside. "I heard your voice," he says, sweating.

"My…voice?"

"In the car. I thought it was coming from my phone. You were calling me."

"How…?"

The elevator nudges to a halt, and Teddy pulls the cage door. He helps me along the corridor, slamming the emergency exit bar out into a white blast of sunlight.

I blink my eyes, trying to focus. "I have to go," I say.

Teddy hesitates, unsure of what to do. "We'll go to the hospital," he says, looking back for Trey and Koi, like *where the fuck are they?*

"Teddy," I say, squeezing his arm, "thank you." I push away from him, toward the shape of my car.

"All right, so…maybe we just wait a sec?" he pleads. "I'm calling Trey."

I reach for the driver's-side door and hoist myself in, blinking the world into focus—the steering wheel, the dashboard, Teddy in the parking lot trying to get a signal. I put the key in the ignition and throw it in reverse, spinning up gravel, then gun it out onto the dirt road in a plume of dust.

I don't know where I'm going. A couple of miles out, I pull off the road beside a cornfield. My hands are shaking. My mind flashes in all directions at once, searching for a place to land—a name, a face, someone to call. I bring up a number and dial. It rings and rings, and then, just as I think it's about to go to voicemail, a voice picks up, sleepy. "Why, hello there…," Leslie purrs. "My sweet, sweet girl. How are you?"

What's up with her voice? Is she high? "I need to ask you something," I say, "about the panic attacks."

"Oh sweetie," she tuts, "you're still getting those. I have someone who can help."

"I thought you could give me a trick. Just something to get—"

"No more tricks," she says matter-of-factly. "You're a big girl now. Come up here, and we'll get you sorted."

"Leslie, I can't. I have—"

"Sweet girl, don't think, just come. You'll thank me for it, I promise."

27 | OUT OF NOTHING

My phone vibrates against the dash—calls from Koi, texts. I pull over and scroll through the frantic flood of messages, trying to think of how to respond.

> *I'm sorry*
> *I freaked*
> *I'm OK*
> *I need a minute*

> *Where did you go?*

> *I'm with a friend*

> *Are you coming back?*

A flatbed truck roped down with bales of hay roars past my window, rocking the car to the side. I watch it as it throttles up the mountain pass, a corridor of towering pines, their soft bodies blowing back in its wake.

I type a name into my phone—then hesitate, unsure if I should dial. When she picks up, her voice is raspy, thinner than I remember it. "I saw your name come up on the screen and I nearly fell over," Clara chides. "Where are you?" she asks "*How are you?*"

"I'm on my way to see Leslie, and I was thinking of you. I have a question I wanted to ask."

"This sounds serious," she says.

"When you do a spell, when you conjure something out of nothing, what is that?"

"What is what?"

"Where does it come from?" I ask.

"Where does *what* come from?"

"The thing you've conjured—out of nothing."

"Well, there you go," she chuckles. "You've answered it yourself. It comes from nothing."

"But how can that be? When you cast a spell of good health, it's not something abstract. The body actually gets better. It's like something enters and repairs it. But what is that something? How can it manifest from nothing?"

"That's the ancient riddle, isn't it?" she replies. "In Latin, they call it ex nihilo—creation out of nothing. The Kabbalists speak of it. So does Genesis. But here's the catch: Nothing isn't really nothing. It's just the space between things. The unseen potential. Scientists talk about the universe being a kind of hologram—a projection from a higher-dimensional space. Matter, as we think of it, might be more illusion than substance. Do you remember the book *A Wrinkle in Time*?"

"Of course. It terrified me."

"As it should!" she laughs. "Remember the tesseract? The idea that instead of traveling a long distance, you could just fold space and jump across? That wasn't just science fiction. That's a visualization of something very real. In a spell, you're doing the same thing—you're folding space and intention to reach into that higher dimension, to access what already exists outside of time. And then you anchor it here."

"Like pulling something across dimensions."

"Exactly. A spell doesn't create—it reveals. It realigns. You're not inventing health; you're collapsing the distance between the body and the possibility of health—folding it into being. We think of these things as something we have to summon, when really, they're already here. They live among us as vortexes—those in-between spaces. Energetic whirlpools that connect dimensions. A natural tesseract, in a way. The author of *A Wrinkle in Time*, Madeleine L'Engle, lived in Goshen, Connecticut, not far from Dudleytown. That area is full of vortexes. Not unlike where you're headed now. You remember what I warned you about when it comes to vortexes?"

"Don't fall in."

"Exactly. They can be seductive—pulling you back into the Earth, into the womb. They feel like home. But once you're in…"

"I'll be careful," I tell her. "I promise."

"I know you will. So what's the reason for the trip?" she asks. "Is everything all right?"

I lie to her and say that everything is fine, that I'll be out to visit her soon, and I think she knows I'm lying. She says she's going to perform a spell of protection over me. I thank her and we say our goodbyes, and I look up ahead at the long, wooded road, at the dark ridge of mountains rising before me, daring me to enter.

28 | A WAVE OF GHOSTS

Leslie's family farm is in Montgomery, about an hour north of the city, a thousand-acre plot of rolling meadows and ancient forests passed down through the generations. Leslie and I would escape there on the weekends the summer after graduation, racing over the George Washington Bridge in her convertible with the top down, radio blasting, screaming into the wind.

The Vos family had arrived in the New World as envoys of the Dutch West India Company, looking to expand their holdings in the North American fur trade. They established some of the earliest trading posts in the Indian territory, ultimately dominating the Hudson Valley trade route from the deepest reaches of the Catskill Mountains to the shipyards of New Amsterdam—what became New York City.

Over the centuries, the family plot doubled and tripled in size, becoming a thriving dairy and cattle farm. It served as a base camp for George Washington and his troops during the Revolutionary War, and later was a safe haven along the Underground Railroad. The farm continued to operate through the Industrial Revolution, tapering off soon after as the Vos children fanned out to pursue their fortunes elsewhere. From that point on, the farm served as a holiday outpost for family gatherings, centered on the main house, a rambling manor of elegant old rooms and hidden alcoves. One of my favorite rooms was a fieldstone nook tucked deep into the center of the home— a surviving remnant of the original stone cottage, essentially a house within a house. I could spend days snuggled in its cozy confines beside a crackling fire, surrounded by a heap of old books. Leslie used to complain that the room was full of ghosts, but if it was, they never bothered me. There was something grounded and proud about it, like an anchor in time for visiting souls as they drifted through.

One day, not long after the Towers fell, Leslie left for the farm and never came back. She'd always struggled with the city. It was overflowing with ghosts, she said, centuries of them— every street, every building. The spirits knew Leslie could see them, and they constantly begged for her help—an unrelenting stream of messages for the living.

When the Towers came down, the city was flooded with a new wave of ghosts, lost and angry, pleading with Leslie to tell their families what happened. "*I saw what they did, I saw what they did,*" a woman once cried to her from across a busy street, her dust-white face streaked with tears. Leslie would never tell me what the ghosts told her, but she was different after that. She would be with you, right beside you, but she wasn't there anymore.

After Leslie moved to the farm, I would send her jobs here and there, last-minute alteration work my clients needed done in a rush. It wasn't long before Leslie made a name for herself as the mysterious seamstress girl secreted away in the mountains.

She designed a dress for Chloë Sevigny for the Oscars one year, and word spread quickly after that. Suddenly, Leslie Vos was the bespoke dressmaker for the edgy, alternative crowd. Her gowns would turn up at the Met Gala, the Grammys, worn by Rihanna and Florence Welch and Karen O. I loved to listen to the red carpet commentators trying to explain the looks, unsure if they loved or hated them. The gowns were from another place, another time. Vintage-seeming, but not old. Old, yet strangely modern. Edited down into the most minimal lines—empty boxes, clouds, unconstructed memories.

Around this time, a flock of New York artists began buying and restoring the dilapidated old farmhouses scattered throughout the Catskills, erecting studios in the woods and hills surrounding the Vos family farm. It was a cultural exodus that would eventually include the city's tech pioneers and a steady stream of hipster parents fleeing the confines and exorbitant prices of the city. This area, largely referred to as "Upstate," began to take on a certain mythos, a next-big-thing buzziness, and at its center was Leslie—a founding mother and an instant, if not reluctant, it girl, putting the perfect face to a name.

Leslie was suddenly what every girl in Brooklyn wished to be: beautiful, masterly, and a dropout. I'd see her pop up in spreads in *Vogue* and *W*, moody pictorials shot on the farm, Leslie dressed in a billowing boho dress and floppy hat, feeding chickens or unfurling a drape of fabric across an unadorned worktable. She would text me about an event she was invited to in the city, and we would make plans for her to stay, but she would always cancel at the last minute. Her elusiveness only made her fans love her more. They would follow her online, glued to a sporadic stream of cryptic photos, often posted in the middle of the night—of farm animals, or the woods at dusk, or an artfully posed self-portrait, taken just far enough away to mask the details of her beauty.

The city, the Old City, had gone down with the Towers, and those who survived longed for a hidden, magical world, far away from the mourning and the cold, futuristic skyline that would rise in the Towers' wake. These women saw themselves in Leslie, their future selves.

I once asked Leslie what it was like to die. What are spirits? Where are they? Are they here? Are they there? In some kind of in-between? She said there was no difference between us and them. "Our souls are eternal," she explained. "They live on a different frequency. Our bodies are homes for these frequencies, and as the body wears out the signal has less and less to hold on to, until it finally slips away, back to where it came from, back to the eternal source."

She told me the story of when her grandmother died and the family came into the room to say their goodbyes. After everyone had paid their respects, Leslie stayed behind, gazing at her grandmother's body from her bedside. There, hovering above the body, was a thin, silver cloud connected to the woman's navel by a ribbon of smoke. Leslie's mother came into the room and told her it was time to go, but Leslie wouldn't leave her grandmother's side. "She's not gone yet," Leslie told her. She hoped her grandmother's cloud would see her and wave a private goodbye. Later, Leslie would come to realize that this is a private moment between the body and the soul, a ceremony, a final handshake before returning home.

"At the end, the thread splits and you're free," Leslie told me. "But if something interrupts the ceremony, or if you aren't ready to leave, your soul tries to maintain its frequency, and that's what you're seeing when you experience a ghost. Every plane is a projection of light, and the spirit is trying to project its light into this plane, to remain with it. That's why you only half-see them, or sometimes just feel them, because they're only able to project that much."

I asked her about the projection, where she thought it came from.

"From God," Leslie replied. "God isn't a thing. God is light."

I barrel down a mountain road, past flooded ponds and cattails reaching high like antennae out of the muck. The air blows in through the windows—the smell of manure, wet grass, a brush pile burning in the woods somewhere. I pass the freight yard, the luncheonette, the abandoned hotel—over the river to where the old estates lay hidden behind flanks of ancient trees, their perimeters marked by tumbling stone walls snaking along the roadside. I turn onto an unmarked dirt road, bounding up through the muddy potholes under a leafy canopy, and there at the crest of the hill, the manor house standing proud, like a gleaming white temple.

Leslie's cranberry Volvo is parked in the turnaround behind a rusted pickup truck loaded with landscaping equipment. I pull in beside it and shut off the engine, and listen—to nothing, to the leaves rustling high in the trees, hulking limbs creaking in the breeze. My phone vibrates with an incoming call, its face lit, but with no number, just a blank white screen. I silence it and toss it into my bag, then step out of the car, looking for some sign of life, peering into the darkened windows of the house. I rap the knocker on the front door, listening for movement inside, but no one arrives, so I try the latch. The door swings open into the foyer with its old familiar smell of musky tobacco and saddle leather. A smoke-colored portrait of Leslie's great-great-grandfather hangs over an ochre-yellow sideboard scattered with a mishmash of belongings—hats, scarves, cell phone chargers, a giant Rite-Aid shopping bag.

I venture deeper into the home, announcing myself as I go. "Hello?" I call, poking my head into the parlor, the dining room, the sunlight beaming in across the countertops and giant wooden fruit bowls in the country kitchen. I creak open the screen door into the garden, looking out over the back property. A pair of sleek brown mares stand at a pasture fence, watching me with their black eyes.

The sound of voices wafts up from down beyond the barns, and I follow them, down to the chicken coop where Leslie and a buff, European-looking dude with a mustache are pitching feed into a clucking assembly of snow-white chickens. Leslie spins around, surprised, shielding her eyes from the sun, then shrieks with delight, throwing her arms open wide, chasing up to me. "Oh my God! Oh my God! You're here!" she squeals, enveloping me in her long arms, planting a fervent kiss on each cheek. She smells just as I remember, like soap and sandalwood. She's dressed in overalls, an Evel Knievel T-shirt, and a floppy straw hat that rings her head like a halo.

"Catherine, this is my friend Leonardo!" she says, beaming, as she presents me to her friend. "Cat is one of my oldest and dearest friends!"

Leonardo sets down his bucket of feed and brushes himself off, extending his hand, bright-eyed and cheerful. "It's nice to meet you. I'm sorry if I stink," he apologizes.

"Oh my God, I can't believe you're here!" Leslie cries. "I'm showing Leo how to feed the chickens. Where are your things? I have so much I have to tell you. Leo, I need to steal Catherine for a second. Is that OK?"

"Absolutely, go, go," he insists. "I've got it from here."

"You're a saint!" Leslie says, smiling broadly. "By the way, Leo is DJing the party tonight. This is *the* Leonardo I told you about. My angel of music. I hope you're ready to dance the night away!" Leslie snakes her arm into mine, pulling me close.

"Come on, you're mine now. I have to show you the studio," she says, marching us up the hill. "It's nearly done. Remember the icehouse? The little shed in the back? I have a friend in Brooklyn who does these gorgeous build-outs with repurposed materials. Zero footprint. He came up and completely redid the shed. It's incredible. It's my church!"

She leads me up to a small cedar barn tucked behind the main house. As we approach the door, Leslie hops in front of me to perform the big reveal. She flings open the door, sweeping her arm inside, like *ta-da!* The barn's spartan interior has been transformed into a luminous whitewashed loft. Chocolate-colored beams soar overhead beneath a peaked glass roof that gazes up at the cloudless blue sky. Throughout the space, old wooden worktables have been positioned, piled high with textiles: bolts of wool, kilim rugs, layers of raw linen. An antique baker's cart stands at the ready, stacked with pencil boxes and spools and ribbons, a basket of wild-bird feathers, huge glass jars full of buttons twinkling like semiprecious stones. Leslie glides through the workshop, aglow. "Wanna know the best part?" she says. "We're completely alone! No ghosts! You would think after all this time *something* would have happened in here. A murdered child, something. But nothing. Nada. Total silence. Can you feel it?"

"Leslie, I need to talk to you."

"Yes, of course! I want to hear everything. But can I just show you one thing first? I've been dying for you to see it." She unveils a clothing rack hidden beneath a burlap drape, revealing a row of hanging garment bags. She pulls off one of the bags and unzips it; a slippery party dress spills out. "I'm designing this for Kristen Stewart," she says, holding up the dress by the shoulders. It reminds me of a mechanical bird—a sharp peplum in the front, transitioning to a pleated tail in the back. The dress is made of a crisp, dark gunmetal-gray fabric, an oxblood leather seam running up the center that forms a T across the chest.

"It's gorgeous."

"Thank you! I absolutely love it," she gushes. "You need to feel it." She gathers up the tail of the dress, offering it to me. I run my fingers over the mysterious material. "Guess what it is?" she says, grinning.

"I don't know. Silk?"

She shakes her head, dying to tell me. "It doesn't have a name!" she blurts. "Did you ever meet my friend Gertie? From Spence? She's a Winthrop. You know, the chemical company. She sits on their innovation board. She's been sneaking me these prototypes they're working on. She wants to break them into high-end textiles, taking all these next-gen materials they've been developing for NASA and the military and spinning them into luxury fabrics. This one's bulletproof! I'm not shitting you. I have to show you this..." She dumps the dress in my arms and pops open her laptop, jabbing at the keys to wake it up.

I can't believe how light the dress is—the weight of a running shoe.

"Where is it?" Leslie squints into the glow of the laptop screen, pulling on her glasses. "Yes—yes! Cat, look at this!" She pulls me beside her, then hits play. A cell phone video shows Leslie in the foreground loading a hunting rifle. In the distance, bales of hay have been stacked like an archery target, a black square of fabric lashed to it with rope. She takes aim at the target and cracks off a shot. The fabric ripples; a direct hit. She fires again, then again. Each bullet produces a dead *puff* like a marble hitting a canvas sack. The video jostles as the cameraman runs to the target and smooths his hand over the fabric, unmarred, not even a divot to show where it was struck.

"*Is that fucking crazy or what?!*" Leslie gushes. "The only thing we're figuring out is the stitching. You can't use regular needles, so they've been sending me all these crazy contraptions." She points to a hulking steel apparatus lurking in the corner like a gargantuan machine press. "The material only comes in dark gray right now, but I don't care. I absolutely love it. Look, when you hold it to the light. It's like a shadow. It's like wearing a fucking stealth fighter."

Leslie slips the dress back into its bag and hangs it up, then turns to me, taking me in. "Oh Cat, I can't tell you how much I needed to see you. You are absolutely beautiful. Honestly. You're lovelier every time I see you. How do you do it? With the city, and the energy, and all of it? And you just remain this gorgeous angel, this amazing soul. Oh God, come over here," she says, beaming, gathering me up in a big squeeze. She holds me away from her, looking for my eyes. "Now, tell me everything. We need to get you sorted. Sit down. Sit. I made us iced tea. I brew it in the sun so it gathers its essence." She pops open a mini fridge under one of the workbenches, pulling out a crystal pitcher filled with an amber liquid. I take a seat on one of the couches as she wipes dust out of a couple of hand-spun coffee mugs. She pours the tea, handing me a cup. I take a careful sip. It's not your average iced tea. It has a sort of complexity that worries me. "There's nothing in this, right?"

"Nothing, like what?" she asks.

"Like weed or something."

"Oh my God, *no!*" she says, laughing. "Not at all. It's just tea. I mix in a couple of herbs, but nothing crazy."

"What herbs?"

"Like *mint*! Fuck. *Basil!* Have a little faith," she says with a snort, plunking down beside me. She brushes my hair back from my forehead, taking my temperature with the back of her hand. "God, if I only had your skin," she mutters. "You need to bottle your genes and sell them on the internet." She props herself up to face me. "OK, tell me everything. What is going on? I'm here. I'm present. I'm all yours."

I hesitate for a beat. I thought this was what I wanted, but now I don't even know where to begin.

"Is it work stuff?" she asks. "Your guy?"

The banality of her questions overwhelms me. I don't even realize I'm crying until she tugs me in for a hug. She wipes a tear from my cheek. "Oh, sweetie…," she coos. "It's OK. Everything's gonna be fine."

"I think I'm coming apart," I sob.

"Cat, you're not coming apart. Look at me," she says firmly, taking me by the shoulders. "You're not coming apart. You just have to shut it down. This thing—it's not yours to carry. Just because you were handed something doesn't mean you have to accept it. Why should we have to live with these things? We don't deserve normal lives? Why? Because of karma? You've seen your past lives. Did you murder someone? Were you some kind of psychopath?"

"Not that I know of," I say, wiping my eyes.

"Exactly. What the fuck did we do to deserve this? Nothing. Life isn't meant to be a hell you have to live through. Seriously. If there's a God, he can judge me when I'm dead. In the meantime, everyone can fuck off!"

"Is that your mantra?" I say, sniffing.

"That's my mantra," she says with a laugh. "*Fuck off!*"

I lean into her, resting my head on her shoulder. She wraps an arm around me. "So what is it?"

"You really want to know?"

"I really want to know," she says, squeezing me.

I try to think of where to start, but it's too much, so I just let it rip. "I think my dad was part of a top secret government project to create some kind of weapon. I don't think he knew what he was working on, but he knew something wasn't right. I found a bunch of project files while I was going through his stuff. There was a list of people who were involved in it—other scientists. Only two of them are still alive. And neither of them wants to talk to me. But that's not even the crazy part. Ever since I discovered this thing, something's been happening. It's like something's *watching* me. I don't know what. Every time I start digging, some freaky paranormal shit happens. I don't even know how to explain it. It's like time stops. Like I'm paused in this *in-between*. And these *things*, I don't know what they are, they're trying to get me—to do what, I don't know."

Leslie looks through me, processing this, a strange look in her eyes.

"And there's something else. I've been having these memories, fragments of things, from when I was a child. I think I might have been…part of it."

"Part of what?" Leslie asks, breaking the spell.

"I was given a test when I was little. I don't remember all of it, but there were these cards with symbols on them. I had to guess what they were."

"What did the cards look like?" Leslie asks.

"They were like flash cards, face down on a table. I had to point to them and say what they were, and then the woman would flip them over. They had symbols on them."

"Black symbols," Leslie says. "I took that test too."

A chill runs through me.

"They came to the house," Leslie says. "My mother said it was to help with my visions, to figure out why I saw things no one else did. It was weird. My mother would never go for something like that. She was incredibly private. But I think she'd had it with all the ghost shit, and she just wanted someone to tell her what was wrong with me. I remember sitting in the dining room, and this woman sitting across from me. She had a stack of cards with her. She laid them out in front of me. I would point at a card and say what it was, and then she'd flip it over. I was right every time. But I'd never seen symbols like that before. So how could I know what they were? She said they were just random shapes, something for my mind to focus on. But there was something strange about them. After she left, I drew the symbols in my notebook, and when I went to school the next day, I showed them to my teacher, Mr. Edwards. He took one look at them and said, 'Ancient runes!' They're an ancient alphabet, one of the first written languages. Oracles used rune stones for divination—almost like tarot cards."

"The woman who gave you the test, why wouldn't she just tell you what they were?"

Leslie looks at me.

"I mean it's completely bizarre," I say, playing it back to her. "This random woman shows up to do psychic flash cards with you. What happened after that? Did you get the results? What did your mom say?"

"She never mentioned it again. And I was glad, to be honest."

"You didn't want to know?"

"I don't know, maybe," she says, shrugging. "It scared me, I guess."

"Scared you how?"

"Like maybe they were going to take my visions away."

"But you *hate* your visions."

"I do. But I'd rather see them than not."

I look at her, trying to process this. "I don't understand. Who are these people? The ones giving the test? They just go around quizzing kids who see weird shit? Do you know anyone else who took it?"

"No," she says. "Do you?"

"Funny enough," I say with a snort.

"Seriously?"

"This guy, Koi. He sees visions of the future. He tracked me down after seeing me in a dream." Leslie absorbs this, unfazed. "Apparently, in this dream I played some pivotal role in saving mankind."

"How did he find you?"

"He got an email from his dead brother."

Leslie nods, somehow tracking the logic.

"He says he wants to help me find out what happened to my dad. Now granted, all of this is insane, but at the same time everything he's been telling me checks out. So anyway, he convinces me to drive upstate to meet his cousin who does some shady work for the government and can hack into the Pentagon to see what this project is. The only catch is we have to help him trap a genie. But instead of capturing the genie, I help it escape, and as a thank you, it starts showing me all this freaky shit about demons and angels. This whole Heaven and Hell situation. The next thing I know, I'm lying flat on my back in this dark-ass cave, and I'm like, you know what, I'm done. Get me the fuck out of here. That's when I called you."

"OK, so big week," Leslie says, nodding.

I expel an enormous sigh, deflating into the couch. Leslie looks at me. "You said something's trying to get you? What do you mean, get you?"

"I have no idea. Sometimes when they appear, they're like demons. Other times, they're like—"

"Angels," she says, finishing my thought.

"What's weird is the demons don't even feel that evil."

"What do they feel like?"

"I don't know—desperate. Like they're lost. And the angels, whatever they are, they don't feel entirely good."

"Maybe because they're not," Leslie says with a sniff. "The whole 'angels and demons' thing—one's good, one's bad? Please. The universe is about balance. That goes for everything, even angels and demons. They seem more like siblings, if you ask me."

A memory flashes to mind, something Peter Phillips said. "Twins," I say.

"Exactly," Leslie nods. "I have a friend Nicky up in Kingston. She's a psychic. She runs these seminars for families who have kids with 'gifts.' She talks about what it was like growing up with her visions—how, when you're a child, there's no one to help you understand what you're seeing. And because you're so young, you have no preconceived notions about it. You experience everything as a blank slate. She said the first time she saw an angel, it was terrifying. It looked nothing like the angels you read about. She said it had a thousand eyes—on its wings, its body, just covered with them. These black, staring eyes. She said they're all different, the angels. There was another one, it was as tall as a building."

"What are angels supposed to do, exactly?"

"They're messengers," Leslie says with a sniff. "But they're also, like, soldiers. Like an army."

"An army against what?"

"Utter fucking chaos? They're like peacekeepers."

"So then what are demons?"

"They're rebels. Instigators. Bringers of change."

"But I thought they were like monsters. Like hideous creatures that chain you to rocks and eat your guts out."

"I mean, sure, some might," Leslie says with a shrug, "but most are just like…angsty teenagers. They're like punk kids. Think about it. They got the shit end of the stick. Can you imagine if God created angels and demons and he was like, 'OK, you're the beautiful light-filled ones, and you're the gross evil ones.' If you got picked for the demon team, you'd be like, what the fuck?"

"But you said everything is balanced. So why would God create two types of beings that are supposed to be all one thing or the other?"

"Maybe that's the point," she says. "To balance each other out. You've heard of the fallen angels, right? How they disobeyed God and were banished to Hell? That's just a story. How does anyone know what God did? The Bible was written by a hundred different people over a thousand years with everyone putting their own spin on it. And even if the story *were* true, what does that say about angels?"

"What do you mean?"

"Think about it," she says. "If the angels disobeyed God, it means they had free will. They didn't just suddenly transform into demons the moment they went to Hell. Their demon side was always there, otherwise they wouldn't have rebelled. Everything in the Bible is about casting away darkness, turning toward the light. It's all a bit one-sided, if you ask me. You can't just get rid of the darkness. It's gonna find its way back."

"Home," I say.

"Exactly. Condemnation—it doesn't work. It's an avoidance tactic. Light and dark were meant to be together. They're family."

Scenes flash through my mind: Helen in her bedroom, possessed. The invisible force holding her up by the throat. How she hissed at it. *Brother!* The strange figure on the empty street in Virginia Beach, its ice-blue gaze. *Do you know where you're going?* The young girl spidering across the floor of the cottage, arranging notes, scrawling in the margins—and what Adam said when he saw them. *Someone's helping you.*

I look at Leslie. "How does it find its way back?"

"How does what?" she asks.

"The darkness. Back to the light."

She thinks about it, then shrugs.

"What the fuck was that test about?" I ask.

Leslie's phone buzzes. She reaches for it, scanning a text. "I have no idea," she mutters, her attention drifting.

"I mean—do you think we're like…the Chosen Ones?"

She looks at me, tuning back in. "God, I hope not. And even if we were, *fuck* getting chosen. Nobody gets to choose for me. *I* choose for me." She rises from the couch and starts rearranging one of the workbenches. "Honestly," she says, "that's why I never related to any of the prophets. It's like, take it down a little. Jesus was great, but he was a bit much. Everybody needs to be a little—I don't know—*reluctant*. Like Moses, when God called to him from the burning bush. He was like, 'You know what, I would totally lead the Israelites out of Egypt, but I'm not a huge public speaker.'" She rests her hands on her hips, assessing the arrangement of the room. "All I know is if we're the Chosen Ones, we need to start dressing the part," she says, turning to me. "Like, full-on Stevie Nicks."

"Who would our apostles be?"

"Oh my God!" she says, brightening. "Number one—Tina Turner."

"Steve Perry from Journey."

"Yes, definitely," she says, pondering. "And, like, maybe somebody who's good with animals…"

"Jane Goodall."

"Totally. And the Indigo Girls! Oh my God, I'm excited now! Let's totally be the Chosen Ones. But first, we need to get rid of these panic attacks. And I have just the person who can help. His name's Enzo. He's a genius, Cat. He studied with a healer in Sundown for three years, a Native elder over 100 years old. He came back with *the knowledge*." She begins sorting through a basket of fresh-cut wildflowers, plucking the leafy stems one by one, arranging them in a vase. "Plants have the power to save us, Cat. We're on this planet to help each other—

us and the plants. It's a symbiotic relationship. Do you know that we've only discovered one percent of all the healing plants in the Amazon? Enzo speaks their language."

"He speaks plant."

"He does!" she blurts. "He speaks *plant*! You'll see. He's a scientist. But he's also like a fairy. He lives between worlds. Just the thought of you two meeting… He'll know exactly how to help you. You'll meet him tonight. He's coming to the rave."

"To the what?"

"Oh my God, I didn't tell you!" Leslie says, delighted. "You could *not* have picked a better day to come. A friend of mine is doing these secret pop-up music festivals, totally off the radar. Tonight it's at the old air base, out behind the airport. My friend Theresa's dance collective is doing a piece. They have a DJ flying in from Manchester. Leo's opening for him. It's going to be amazing. Oh, wait! Shit!" She checks the time on her phone. "I need to take my vitamins." She snatches up a clay jar, shaking out a couple of tiny white pills. She pops them in her mouth and chugs them down with a swig of tea.

"What are those?" I ask.

"*Theeese*," she says, beaming, shaking the jar like a maraca, "are my little miracles. They clear away everything, Cat. They're absolute lifesavers. I don't even want to get into it, but my visions, the whole thing—it got really bad, even worse than before. I didn't think that was possible. But these little guys wipe everything away. They give me peace and quiet so I can finally get some work done."

"Like, bad how?" I ask. "What's been happening?"

"It sounds totally insane," she laments, "but it's getting harder for me to tell who's alive and who's dead. It's like having to squint to read. I met these people from the city who were up here for the Beltane festival. They invited me to their camp in Kerhonkson. I was out there for two days, and then one morning

I woke up and there was no one there. Totally packed up, gone. So I called Sara—you remember Sara—'cause I thought she was there with me."

"What do you mean you thought she was there with you?"

"I thought she came with me."

"Well, did she?"

"Apparently not," Leslie says with a shrug. "So I call her, and she's freaking out, asking where the fuck I am. I guess I'd been texting her for two days—crazy shit, like: *No one is dead. No one is dead.* And she's texting back, *Who's not dead?? What the fuck?* Scared I'm tripping my balls off."

"Well, were you?"

"No!" Leslie cries. "I wasn't on anything! I did yoga in the morning, and then I met these people at Bliss Kitchen. I don't remember anything after that." Her phone vibrates and she glances at it. "Oh!" she flinches. "I have to get ready. My guru's coming over. We're doing an open-eyed prayer session. You should do it with us. You don't have to look at anyone. You'll absolutely love Edwina. She comes from a family of healers. She's like this island of calm."

"I love you," I say, rising from the couch, "but there is no way I'm doing an open-eyed prayer session."

"No, I totally get it," she says, laughing. "Oh Cat, I can't believe how lucky I am to see you! Come over here." She pulls me in for a hug, then holds me away. "I'm taking you out to dinner tonight—deal? Then we'll go meet Enzo. Then we're off to the party. I can't wait!"

29 | FIGURES

I drop my bag on the bed in one of the upstairs bedrooms and glance at my phone. All I want is a message from Jake, anything, but all he's sent is a bunch of photos from the protest on Wall Street—sweaty, raggedy-looking hipsters holding up cardboard signs: "WE ARE THE 99 PERCENT," "THEY GOT BAILOUTS, WE GOT SOLD OUT," and "HONK IF YOU'RE IN DEBT." Crowds shouting at cops. A rapper with a megaphone. Girls in bikinis being led off in handcuffs. The final text reads: *We're camping on wall st tonight you should come down!!*

I drag a chair over to the window, heave it open, and light a joint, looking for the horses in the pasture, but they're gone. So I go back to my phone and scroll through work emails, anything to neutralize my antsiness. Something catches the corner of my eye, out in the pasture—a flicker of wings. I turn to look, but there's nothing there, nothing but the breeze moving through the grass. Then I see it, at the edge of the tree line, fluttering shadows—then gone, snapped out of sight. Deer? I move closer to the window. Again they appear—flickering black blobs, like sunspots. Not deer—figures. I squint to make them out. They're dressed alike, in black hoodies but longer, like rain slickers. They move in a strange unison, drifting through the grass, and as they move, they flicker, like the frames of an old film. I raise my phone and turn on the camera, but all I see on the screen is an empty field. I move the phone away and the figures are there, statue-still, as if they know they're being watched. Slowly, they turn to face me. Within their hooded shrouds, where their faces should be, there's only a hollow black void. I flinch away, shouting for Leslie, stumbling out into the hallway, down the stairs. I burst out the front door, nearly toppling over the gardener as he loads his tools into his truck. He blinks up at me, dusted head to toe in grass clippings.

"Were you out back?" I gasp. "Just now?"

"You OK, miss?"

"Are you out here by yourself?"

He looks around me, nervous. "You want Ms. Leslie, miss?"

I look around for anyone else, but it's just the two of us. "No. Yes. I mean—yes," I stammer. "I'll find Leslie. Sorry. Thank you."

Tentatively, he turns back to loading his truck, keeping an eye on me. I edge my way along the side of the house, peering around the corner. But there's nothing there, just the empty pasture, the grass undulating in the breeze.

"HELLO!" a voice shouts from out of nowhere.

"JESUS FUCK!" I gasp.

"Oh my God! I'm sorry!" Leo cries, high-stepping through the grass, out from the edge of the woods, a camera slung over his shoulder. "I didn't mean to scare you. I was out here shooting. The light is gorgeous right now."

"Was that you out there?" I wheeze, my heart beating out of my chest.

"Was that me where?" he asks.

"Did you see anyone out here?"

"No, did you?" he asks nervously.

"I don't know what the fuck I saw."

"Oh my God!" he cries. "What was it? I don't know *what's* out in these woods! Was it a bear?"

"It looked like people."

"*People?*" he gasps. "What *people?*"

"I have no idea. Maybe it was the sun playing tricks?"

He scans around anxiously. "I have to say, I love Leslie," he says, "and this house is unbelievable, but this place—"

"Is creepy as fuck, right?"

"Oh my God, thank you!" he blurts. "I feel so much better hearing someone else say it. Not, like, *creepy*-creepy. But there's definitely something going on with the energy out here."

"Like a vortex."

"Totally!" He lights up. "I wasn't going to say it, because I thought you'd think I was crazy."

"Have you seen anything strange?" I ask.

"Today?"

"Or, like, ever?"

"I guess you could say that. I've been shooting Leslie's stuff for her, so I come out here about twice a month," he says. "We're doing a trade. She's modeling for my portrait series, and she lets me use the house for shoots. She has all these fabulous people who come by. I feel absolutely blessed. She talks about you all the time. I can't believe I'm finally getting to meet you." I keep looking out at the empty pasture as he's talking. "I have to say, you look absolutely stunning in this light," he remarks.

I turn back to him. "Sorry, what?"

"I was just saying you have an amazing look. That beautiful skin and hair. Against all this green? Do you want to model for me? No pressure, of course."

"I mean—maybe?"

"Really? I would be so grateful!" He adjusts his camera. "Just do you. Pretend I'm not here," he says, snapping a pic. He ducks around me, snapping another. I try to act natural, cool, but I can't help laughing at the way he's darting around me like a forest sprite.

"I love it when you laugh!" he says, gushing. "You light up everything! You are totally in my series, I hope you know that. I'm having you sign a waiver, like, *yesterday*."

"You actually like photographing people?"

"I do!"

"But why?"

He laughs, thinking about it. "You know, it's crazy. I don't know if anyone's ever asked me that. I feel like I should have a smart answer. I don't know, the vulnerability maybe? It's unpredictable. You never know what's going to come through. It's like a person's soul is…elusive. It's shy. You have to be patient. You have to wait for it to come to the surface, and when it does, it looks out at you—for just a split second." I glance at him and he snaps a photo. "Just like that," he says, smiling. His gaze wrests me forward, down into the lightning tunnel of his past:

> *A room, a bedroom.*
> *I look down at my hands,*
> *a woman's hands.*
> *I'm seated at a dressing table.*
> *I'm checking my makeup in a mirror—*
> *my eyes, my lips.*
> *There's a man sprawled naked on the bed*
> *behind me.*
> *He rolls on his side,*
> *reaches for his wallet on the nightstand.*

The light of the bedside lamp draws me
in,
hot and white,
a tiny sun.
I'm thrust into another scene, another
life:
a bonfire burning high into a cool, black
night.
Men gathered around the fire,
soldiers,
uniforms like gods—
Centurions, a Roman legion.
We've won a battle.
A celebration.
One of the other soldiers, I watch him
through the lapping flames.
I'm in love with him.
I have a wife at home and I'm sick with
guilt.
He looks back at me through the fire,
the light drawing me in—
then out again, into another time,
another scene:
I'm naked,
dancing in the woods—
drums,
the moon high above,
a giant white disk in a purple sky.
Bodies caked in mud.
We move in unison,
undulating like the wind,
like the sea,
celebrating the Great Mother.

We are one with her.
We are loved and pure.

"You're crying," Leo says, breaking the spell. I laugh my tears away, wiping my eyes. "Can I give you a hug?" he asks.

I let him in. "Do you think Leslie is done with her prayer session?" I say with a sigh.

"God, I hope so," he says, snickering.

My phone vibrates—again, the creepy ghost-white screen, no name, no number. I click it off. Leo takes my hand as we walk back to the house, following the sound of the Cure blasting from an upstairs bedroom window. We follow the music up to Leslie's room, where we find her pacing around nervously in a bra and panties, furiously texting someone. The room is like a time capsule of her teenage years—band posters curled up on the walls, Christmas lights strung along the ceiling, Polaroids wedged into the frame of the dresser mirror. She spots us in the doorway and tosses her phone on the bed like a white-hot coal.

"I just had the most amazing prayer session!" she blurts, amping up her joy. "I kept hearing this album in my mind and I just had to play it. Remember how we used to listen to this at school? Lying on the lawn? Oh my God, take me there! I read somewhere that Robert Smith wanted people to listen to it with headphones because it's atmospheric, like a dream. Can you hear it?" She floats her willowy frame around the room in long balletic sweeps, collecting scattered pieces of clothing. She slips on a voluminous cornflower blue tunic with an embroidered yellow sun on the front and a white crescent moon on the back, denim cutoffs, and a pair of beaded moccasins. She kicks into a pose, hands on her hips. "Ready?" she says, beaming.

30 | MOTHER OF PEARL

"Are you guys starving? 'Cause I am!" Leslie blurts, fiddling with the radio as she floors the Volvo onto the interstate. We hold on for dear life, me in the passenger seat, Leo in the back. "I'm taking you to my favorite spot in Newburgh," she says, checking her makeup in the rearview mirror. "My friend Steve and his wife run it. Total hippies, amazing souls. They make *the* best barbecue you've ever had. And oh my God, the mac and cheese! Oh wait, Leo!" she cries, glancing at him in the mirror. "You're not doing dairy anymore, are you?"

"I brought my pills," he mutters. "It's all good."

Leslie grabs my knee. "Cat, wait until you see this place. So amazingly old-school. People are always talking so much trash about Newburgh, but just you watch, it's gonna be a total thing in a few years. My friend from Beacon is closing his studio and moving it there. There's a whole movement happening. Even further out. Kerhonkson. Andes. You have to see this little town. Precious. But even Andes is almost over. It gets so played out. All these new-money tech dudes moving in, trying to make it the new Hamptons. I swear, if I see one more artisanal bakery I'm going to become a fucking arsonist. Right now, I'm all about Schoharie. Like *way* the fuck out. My friends Brit and Alex bought a farm up there, where they're harvesting rare-breed flowers for their shop in Brooklyn."

"That's awesome," I say, cutting in. "Not to change the subject, but have you seen any weird shit in your backyard lately?"

Leslie glances at a text on her phone. "You're gonna have to be more specific."

"Like giant black specters," I clarify.

"Wait, what?" she asks, half-listening, skimming the text. "Are you sure they weren't townies?"

"Um, yeah. These were not townies."

"You mean, like, *ghost* specters?" she asks, tuning back in.

"I don't fucking know. You've told me about ghosts, and these did not look like ghosts."

"What did they look like?" she asks, rocking the car onto the off-ramp.

"Like tall, black figures."

"Like Black people?"

"Like *shadow people*! They didn't have faces. Like, some Grim Reaper shit."

"Shut the fuck up!" she says, laughing.

"And they were *flickering*."

"Flickering?"

"Like an old Charlie Chaplin movie."

"That sounds freaky," she says, leaning over to dig her lip balm out of the glove compartment.

"No shit, it sounds freaky. It *was* freaky."

"Oh sweetie, don't even worry about it," she sighs. "Seriously. I'm sure it's nothing. It's probably just interdimensional."

Leo snorts in the backseat.

"*What?* It probably is. Guys, we're, like, only *one level* of what's going on here," Leslie explains. "There are these whole other realities layered on top of this one. I did this ayahuasca session last spring and it explained everything. When you see stuff, it has to do with the ley lines. The nervous system of the planet."

"The ley lines," Leo says, skeptically.

"Right. There's, like, this *grid* of energy that connects the Earth's chakras. They *enhance* everything—consciousness, psychic power. There are these special places where every dimension connects at a common point. If you look at the grid on a map, you can see how all the ancient cultures built their cities and temples on ley lines—the Egyptians, the Incas, the Druids. They were all built on that shit."

"Like Stonehenge?" I ask.

"Exactly. Stonehenge. That whole zone. Just look on a map at where all the crop circles appear. *Those* are ley lines. Same thing with UFOs. Just a couple miles from here there's a town called Pine Bush. At one point, there were so many UFO sightings, people started setting up lawn chairs like they were waiting for a parade. Remember that book *Communion* from the '80s, with the alien on the cover? The author had a cabin not far from there. I have some friends who found it on a satellite map and sneaked onto the property one night. They said the energy was next-level freaky."

"I'm definitely good on that," Leo mumbles.

"But it's not even the aliens you have to watch out for," Leslie adds. "It's the trickster spirits. There are *tons* of tricksters out here." Before she can explain what she means by trickster spirits, she pulls the car up to a curb with a jolt. "We're here!" she says cheerfully.

The bar is tucked along a tidy cobblestone row of 18th-century townhouses—an old-world saloon catering to a motley assortment of old-timers, dusted-up contractors, and battle-hardened schoolteachers; a girl bartender with a sleeve tattoo stands washing glasses behind the bar. All of them turn to look as we walk in. Leslie hops up on a stool, giving the bartender a kiss on each cheek, then bolts through the swinging doors of the back kitchen, announcing herself. A white-haired man in a Hawaiian shirt and chef's apron escorts her back out into the bar, goading her. "OK, so what kind of trouble are you getting into now?"

"Catherine, Leo, this is Steve, my angel of Newburgh!" Leslie says with a grin, showing off her friend, clinging to his arm for dramatic effect. "Steve, please, please, *please* feed my friends! They need to try *everything*. I'm going to make a super quick call and then I'm digging in. Deal?" She gives him a kiss on the cheek, then ducks past us, pulling out her phone and slipping out the front door. The bartender makes Leo and me a spot at the bar, setting us up with a couple of oversize margaritas, followed by a conveyor belt of comfort food—a bubbling heap of chili cheese fries, mac and cheese, and a platter of chicken and ribs. I watch Leslie through the front window, pacing the sidewalk. I glance at Leo. "So who's Enzo?"

"Good question," he says.

"You've met him?"

"Yeah. He's, um… He seems like a very *interesting* person."

"Is he her dealer?"

Leo shrugs, reaching for a piece of chicken. "I have no idea. I know people who go to him for stuff. He's like a witch doctor or something. Not a *real* witch doctor. A chemist, I guess. He hooks up my friend's band. They come back with these potions and things I've never seen before."

Leslie bursts through the door, smooshing in between us at the bar, snagging a gooey hunk of chili cheese fries. "Are we ready?" she nudges.

"We just got here," I say, scowling. "And there's, like, 20 pounds of food."

"We can take it with us," she says, waving over the bartender, snapping down a credit card. At least I think it's a credit card—matte black, no writing. Are there even numbers on it? Leslie signs the receipt and waves her goodbyes as Leo and I are handed a pair of giant to-go bags.

Enzo's place is only five minutes from the restaurant, but the neighborhood is an entirely different world, a sort of post-apocalyptic Charles Dickens novel. A bombed-out husk of boarded-up row houses stand shoulder to shoulder on a hillside street a couple of blocks up from the river. Leslie pulls up behind a graffiti-tagged moving van, seemingly oblivious to the sketchy surroundings. She beeps the car locked and leads us up the steps of one of the darkened buildings, huddling in the doorway beside a buzzer panel that looks like it's been smashed in with a hammer. "I texted him," she assures us, skimming through the messages on her phone. We wait for what seems like an eternity, trying to act like it's no big deal. A block up the street, a little boy is being pulled down the hill by a massive pit bull barking at a couple of guys smoking on the corner. Leo glances at me. The buzzer sounds and we all grab for the door at once, shoving into a dingy stairwell permeated with the scent of incense, fried fish, and ketchup. We ascend one flight of stairs after another, assaulted by the sounds of apartments with their doors flung open—a television blasting *Wheel of Fortune*, a baby crying bloody murder. Leslie turns down a corridor, halting in front of a door affixed with three deadbolt locks. Music thumps behind the door like a heartbeat. She bangs against it with her open palm. Leo looks at me like *I know* as we listen to the sound of the locks being unlatched. Suddenly, the door swings open and we're met by a short, stocky Latino dude dressed in an oversize Ice Cube T-shirt, cargo shorts, and purple high tops, his thick black hair pulled back in a glittery headband. "Why, hello there, my darling dear," he says in a mock-British accent.

"We brought a picnic," Leslie says, handing him the takeout bags as she shoulders inside.

"Ooo!" Enzo says, beaming. "You know I love a picnic!"

I watch Leslie take in the inner sanctum of Enzo's bizarre disco-cave apartment. We're standing in the kitchen—a chaotic circus of pots and pans, cereal boxes, and soup cans—which seems to double as a makeshift laboratory. Along one wall, industrial shelves sag under the weight of plastic bins, murky glass jars, and five-gallon buckets filled with what look like broken branches, crumpled leaves, and dirt.

Enzo gazes up at me. "You must be the famous Catherine," he coos. "It's wonderful to meet you!" He rocks back, taking me in. "Wow, wow, wow! Your aura is just incredible," he gushes, looking for my eyes. "I can see you," he says, grinning. "Can you see me?"

Leslie intervenes. "Enzo, don't be weird. Let's eat and go. We're late."

"Oh, but I can't turn away," Enzo purrs. "I'm transfixed. Catherine, you're absolutely glowing. Do you know that? I've never seen colors like this," he motions, fluttering his hands. "You're like mother-of-pearl, a moving rainbow. How fascinating. You get headaches, don't you? They come from every side of your head. The crown, the third eye. Of course they do. You're an antenna, aren't you? Look at you. Trying so hard to plant your feet on the ground, or you might get sucked back up into Heaven. Isn't that right? The angels want you back, don't they?"

A memory flashes in, the figures standing like sentries around the gaping white light at the ceiling of the cave.

"Enzo, will you please chill!" Leslie orders. "Are you ready or what?"

Enzo spins on his heel, facing her. "Girl, I'm always ready. You just can't wait to see your boyfriend," he scoffs. "Pretty Mr. James. Be careful with that one, ya hear? Brother Enzo sees star-crossed lovers."

I look at Leslie. *Boyfriend?* She throws me a look back. "I need to use the ladies' room," she says. "So does Catherine."

"Shoo! Shoo!" Enzo waves us away, turning dramatically to Leo. "Leave me here with this gorgeous man. Leo-*narrr*-do. I just love saying that name. Leo-*narrr*-do. Where is that camera of yours, Leo-*narrr*-do? When are we gonna do a photo shoot, you and I?"

Leslie leads me down the back hall, deep into Enzo's lair. A dumpster dive come to life, the apartment has all the charm of a kidnapper's den—threadbare furniture, storage bins, old-lady lamps buzzing with fluorescent bulbs. We pass a door to what looks like a bedroom with a padlock dangling on the front of it. Leslie feels her hand into a darkened doorway and snaps on the light, revealing a pink-tiled bathroom. She hefts an iguana tank off the toilet lid and sets it on the floor, then squats to pee, hovering over the seat. I throw her a look, like, *what the fuck?*

"I know he's a lot, but he's fine," she says with a sigh. "I've known him forever. He grew up in Westchester. This whole thing is an act." She zips and flushes. "We're doing a trade," she says, checking herself in the smudgy medicine cabinet mirror. "He makes my pills, and I introduce him to people."

When she opens the bathroom door, Enzo is standing there, making like he was just walking by. *Was he listening?* He dangles two Ziploc baggies in front of us—one containing a handful of blue capsules; the other, a handful of red. "Look!" he says, smiling. "It's *The Matrix*!" He gestures for us to follow him back into the murky light of the kitchen, where he presents us with the contents of the baggies. "The blue ones are for tonight—a chill mushroom blend with this really nice ecstasy afterglow. I call them Velvet Ropes, because they only let the good ones in—the fairies, the gnomes, the angels." He pops a pill, washing it down with the remnants of a Diet Coke. "Leonardo, are you with me?" Enzo asks, flirtatiously dangling the baggie at him.

"I'm good, thanks," Leo replies.

"Leo's spinning tonight," Leslie jumps in. "He has to stay focused."

"Oh, *Mr. Professional*!" Enzo snickers. "OK, well, Uncle Enzo will hold onto these for anyone who wants them. But for you, my dear…" He spins to me, holding out the bag of red pills. "Just what the doctor ordered," he says. "My treat! 'Cause who needs a panic at the disco, am I right?" He plucks a red capsule from the baggie, holding it up with pride. "I call this one Me Time. Perfect for anyone who needs a little headspace. It's like a Tibetan monastery in a pill. Just this total *om* moment." He closes his eyes and gestures in a mock-lotus pose.

"What's in it?" Leslie asks.

"Nothing you have to worry about. It's like a super tame combo of Adderall and DMT—with a smooth finish of medical-grade marijuana. It turns your third eye inward. Just this really sweet meditative state."

I look at Leslie.

"Not, like, *full-on* DMT," Enzo clarifies. "More like DMT's super chill cousin. It holds your hand the whole time. It's glorious—meeting your guide, this beautiful woman in robes. But with *this*," he says, placing the pill in the palm of my hand, "she doesn't take you on such an intense trip. She just guides you into your quiet space. It's like, your mind gets to relax while the rest of you gets to have fun." He grins up at me, waiting for me to pop the pill. Leslie steps between us, taking me by the hand. "Enzo, you're a genius," she says, waving him off. "We can't thank you enough. Catherine will take it when she's ready."

"Absolutely!" Enzo blurts. "I'm only here to help." He snags my wrist and tucks the baggie in my hand. "Come see me if you ever need more," he says with a wink.

"Are we done here?" Leslie presses.

"Of course!" Enzo says cheerfully, throwing open the apartment door with a dramatic sweep of his hand. "Let's dance!"

31 | A HIDDEN SCAR

If this party was meant to be a secret, its cover has been completely blown. We pull in behind a river of brake lights backed up for what looks like a mile, inching our way along an overgrown airfield. Police cars have set themselves up as traffic stops, lights twirling red and blue. Officers wave the cars forward, pointing their flashlights into the squinting faces of the drivers as they roll past, searching the interiors for anything suspicious. Farther up, past the fence, merchandise hustlers dash from car to car peddling neon glow sticks and whistles and ginseng shots. Leslie creeps the car forward, then jacks the wheel into a K-turn, gunning it in the opposite direction. "Shortcut," she says.

We turn off onto a dirt road about a half mile back the way we came, bobbing and bouncing through tractor ruts, snaking through the woods onto the back lot of the air base, jerking to an abrupt stop between a giant tractor and a utility shed. We pile out, following Leslie like a safari guide through the waist-high grass under the silver disk of a giant fairy-tale moon.

A dull disembodied thud of bass emanates across the field from an airplane hangar, a hulking black dome set against a purple sky. A rear loading door bangs open and a couple of biker-looking dudes lumber out for a smoke. Leslie shouts their names and dashes up to them, throwing her arms around their necks. She holds the door open for us, ushering us into a backstage area, a long cinder block corridor crowded with what looks like the cast of a traveling carnival. Women dressed like jungle animals in printed leotards and face makeup. A half-dozen girls dressed like crayons. A gaggle of apocalyptic gladiators wearing black leather shorts and battle armor. An old-timey surgeon. A kabuki girl clicking around in wooden platform sandals. Leslie explodes with joy, clambering through the crowd, falling into the arms of a tall, blond goddess-looking woman dressed in a silver bikini bottom, gold pasties, and hot pink running shoes. "You guys!" Leslie cries, waving us over. "You have to meet Beatrix!"

"Are you kidding?" Enzo exclaims, squeezing through the crowd. "I know Bee! Come 'ere, girl. Lookin' fine as ever!"

Leslie presents her beautiful smiling friend to us. "Bee runs a workshop on futurism at Burning Man. Catherine, you would love it! Cat's a fashion forecaster."

"That's amazing!" the blond Amazon says, smiling broadly. "You should teach a class."

Leo whispers to me that he has to go.

"I have to help Leo set up!" I shout. "Great meeting you!" I snake my arm into Leo's and pull him close. "Can I hide in the DJ booth?" I ask.

"Absolutely!" he says with a grin, weaving us through the crowd.

We squeeze our way up the corridor into the massive hangar bay, where racks of disco lights blast rainbow laser shapes across a sea of undulating bodies, illuminating a smoke machine haze. The music thunders in from all sides, rattling my bones as I stand on tiptoe, trying to gauge the distance from here to the DJ booth. I tell Leo I have to pee and will be over in a sec, and he gives me a thumbs-up as he shoulders through the thrashing crowd.

A line has formed along the back wall under a spray-painted banner that reads: PORT-A-POTTIES THISAWAY. A voice pipes up behind me. "Is this the bathroom line?"

I turn to face a tiny woman with a bleached pixie cut and thick-rimmed glasses, dressed in a bright yellow jumpsuit and rainbow wristbands. "I think so."

"Somebody didn't plan this right," she grumbles. She holds up two tallboys of Brooklyn Lager. "Want one?"

A beer is the last thing I need right now, but I accept it anyway, happy for the distraction.

"Figured I'd be here a while," she nods, cheers-ing our cans. "I'm Sam."

"Catherine."

She scans the crowd like she's looking for someone. "Did the acrobats come out yet?"

"I just got here."

"I hope I didn't miss it. My friend's in it."

"Your friend's an acrobat?"

"Yeah, my friend Meredith. She's crazy. You couldn't pay me to do that," she says, still scanning the crowd. "The human pyramid? Fuck that shit."

"I like your jumpsuit," I say.

"Thanks!" she exclaims.

"I didn't know we were supposed to wear costumes."

"You think this is a costume?" she scowls.

"Oh! No, I mean—"

"I'm just messing with you," she says, chuckling. "I didn't know what to wear. My friend was just like, 'Wear bright colors!' So here you go. These costumes are crazy though, right? You ask me, this place is freaky enough as it is. I don't need people painted like silver clowns."

"What's freaky?"

She does a comic double take. "You're not from around here, are you?" she says, laughing. She pulls an electronic cigarette from her pocket and takes a long drag, the tip blooming a bright blue. She exhales a gust of white steam. "They call this 'the Newburgh Triangle,'" she says, gesturing. "There's all kinds of crazy shit going on out here. You know about Pine Bush, right?"

"With the UFOs?"

"Yeah, for starters. I'm up in Ellenville. You listen to people in line at the A&P. It's like *The National Enquirer* came to life. You heard about the cat with the cardboard head, right?"

"The what?"

"Yeah," she snorts, "I haven't seen that shit, *thank God*, but I know someone who did. The cat has a cardboard head!"

"A cardboard head?"

"Like, where the head is supposed to be," she says, pantomiming, "there's a piece of cardboard. Shaped like a cat's head. It's crazy."

"And it just roams around?"

"Yeah, that cat is everywhere. One thing I did see, though— the 'shadow people.' Have you heard about these things? I'm driving down Main Street in Pine Bush one day, like, middle of the day, and there's this person standing out on the corner like they're gonna cross the street. So I slow down, 'cause I don't know if they're waiting for me to go or what. But as I'm getting closer, I'm like, *what the fuck? Is it Halloween?* This chick has on this long-ass black robe with the hood pulled up—super tall, like a basketball player. And I'm like, *OK, Goth chick, no big deal*. But then she steps out into the street, and she's not moving like a normal person. She's walking, but she's, like, *flickering*. Like stop-motion. You know what I mean? Like *click-click-click-click-click*. So now I'm stopped in the middle of the street, and I'm like, *is anybody else seeing this?* I look over, and there's this woman standing on the steps of the post office, and she's just watching this thing. When I look back, it's stopped in the middle of the crosswalk, and it's just staring at me! At least I think it is. I can't tell because there's no face inside the hood. It's just *black,* like a shadow. So I'm just like, *you know what, you do you.* And then this shadow thing, it turns and crosses the street, and when it gets to the other side—*poof,* it's gone, vanished. I look back at the woman on the steps and she's looking at me, and we're both like, *what the fuck was that?*"

"So people just see these things—?"

"—*and just go right on with their day!* Which makes it even freakier. It's not like the cops don't know about it. Everybody sees it. And then you've got all the witches and psychics and that whole scene. It's like everything converges out here. And the UFOs—it's not like they just fly by. Those fuckers *hover.*" A new song thumps in and Sam perks up. "Oh shit! That's my jam!" she says, delighted. "I feel like I'm too sober for this party. You know what I mean? *That's* why—" she dips into her back pocket "—I brought these." She holds out a baggie of yellow pills. "Want one?"

"I think I'm good, but thank you."

She shrugs and pops a pill, washing it down with the lager. "Well, just shout if you change your mind." The music starts to crescendo and Sam toots a birdcall in the air. "OOT-OOT!" She cranes her neck looking down the line for the bathroom. "Listen, I'm gonna sneak out the back and pop a squat. You wanna come?"

"I think I'll wait."

"Suit yourself," she says, shrugging, "but come find me later." She dances backward into the sea of writhing bodies, making an "Oh my God" terror face as she's sucked into the crowd.

Suddenly the mass of bodies swells, as if the one extra person had tipped the balance of the dance floor, bloating the mayhem outward. I'm pinned against the wall, assailed by a legion of sweating, ecstatic faces, bouncing up and down, side to side, hands grabbing at me, trying to get me to dance. A chill seeps through me, my eyes glazing over, knees giving. I plant my hand against the wall, trying to vertically crawl my way back toward the corridor where we came in, but it's swollen with people, and now I really have to pee—not a wait-it-out situation. I frantically scan the crowd for a way out, my chest closing up, my throat. I need a life preserver, anything. I reach in my pocket and fish out the bag of pills Enzo gave me, and pop one, swigging it down with a chug of beer. Then I turn and aim myself at the EXIT sign glowing through the smoke on the far side of the room. I battle my way through the humid euphoria, the jabbing elbows, the body odor, the warm breath, until I'm chucked out the other side, lunging for the crash bar of the metal door and smashing out into the cold, sobering night air. I use the tallboy as a doorstop and hurry down the steps, ducking behind a moving van and whipping down my shorts, hissing a wicked piss in the gravel. Just as I finish up, I hear the door squeal and slam shut. *Fuck!* I hike my shorts up and dash back up the steps, but the door has no handle, so I start beating on it as hard as I can, trying to outpound the music thumping inside. Then somehow, miraculously, the door opens, and there, standing in the swirling disco light, is a woman dressed like the Virgin Mary in a long, pale blue robe with a white hood gathered around her shoulders. Her face is strangely calm, dazed, like, *this chick is definitely on something*—and now, as payback for letting me in, it feels like I need to lead her back inside, to help her find her friends. But then I notice something else. Her skin is glowing. Not radiant-skin-cream-glowing, but an actual light inside of her, and as I process this, the disco lights spinning behind her suddenly shift, morphing into soft pliable shapes, puzzle pieces, diamonds and swirls and crescent moons bulging and smooshing together like water balloons.

"Come in, child," the woman says, beckoning me forward, and I feel something separate, like the molting skin of a snake. I watch myself step forward and take her hand—leaving behind my energy-self, standing here like a ghost. My physical self turns in the doorway gazing back at me, and I watch as her face begins to soften, to melt, like warm wax, like butter—her face, her eyes, her mouth, her nose collapsing into little black dots. Her clothes slide down into a pile at her feet as her body stretches upward, long and narrow, arms and legs pulling in until she's one long, pink water balloon, slipping back into the sea of other dancing water balloons. I reach out to her, trying to pull her back to me, but she just makes a wet squishing sound as she squeezes into the sea of dancing shapes. And now all of the balloons are laughing, children's laughter, and Mary says, "She'll be safe here. Friends will watch her." And as she says this, two men emerge from behind her as if they're stepping out of her. They're naked except for white sheets wrapped around their waists like ancient Greek javelin throwers. Chiseled and muscular, the men stand on either side of Mary like bodyguards. That's when I notice their feet—Mary and the two men—all of them barefoot, hovering a few inches off the ground. Suddenly, Mary is beside me, her fingers enfolding mine, and I feel a warm white light pass up through me—up my arm, through my body, filling my insides, my heart, my veins, bursting out of my eyes, my mouth. Then we're lifting off the ground, Peter Pan–style, high up, above the parking lot, over the swirl of headlights, the wind blowing through my hair, and Mary says, "Look down," and below us are the towns webbing together, golden lights, undulating, phosphorescent. Mary says, "Tell me about the lights."

Suddenly, I know what they are. "They're souls."

"Look how they move," Mary says. "Look closely. Look between them."

"There are threads," I say. I can see them perfectly now, the points of light connecting like a silken cobweb.

"Now look again," she says.

More lights appear, a second constellation overlaying the first, a writhing ocean of light.

"What are the lights?" Mary asks.

"The dead," I say.

"Are they dead?"

"No. We call them that. But they're here."

Suddenly, we're zooming down into the constellation, into the luminous web, and I can hear the lights chiming, singing to each other like a whale song. We hover there, between the souls of the living and the souls of the dead, the silver threads like spider silk rising and descending between them, and Mary says, "Look how they move."

"We're connected," I say.

"Are you alive?" Mary asks.

"Yes."

"Are you dead?"

"Yes."

"How can that be?"

"I am both at once," I reply.

"There is someone you seek," she says. "Look for him."

I'm pulled into a thread of light, whipping through it like a tunnel, and Mary says, "His smell, his sweater, his hands, his laugh." And as she says each of these things, I feel a glow of love reach out to me like a hand, pulling me forward…to my father's office in our house, the brown rug, the diplomas on the wall. He's sitting at his desk. He looks up and takes his glasses off, smiling at me. The scene spins and we're upside down, the room is upside down, and there's another room above me, or below? A church, a chapel? And now I'm in the chapel, and the priest is my father. He has a different face, but the same eyes. I recognize him, I recognize this life. With two fingers he points upward like the hand of a saint, and when I look there's another room, a dingy apartment, a child playing on the kitchen floor, my son. He has my father's eyes. Mary says, "You see how long you have loved each other? Take his hand. He wants to show you something." And when I take the little boy's hand, he turns us around, and we're in a forest at night, and there, in the distance, is a clearing, and in the clearing is a light. He hurries us toward it—we're running now—and all around us a thundering sound, of animals trampling over the earth, tearing through the underbrush, then halting at the edge of the clearing. And there, at its center, a soft white orb, hovering above the ground, its skin rippling like plasma. The boy reaches for it, touches it, and his eye sockets fill with light—his mouth, his nose. He mouths a word without a sound—*home*—and the orb unfolds like a flower, gathering around him, drawing him in. I reach for the light, but it flinches away, darting to the edge of the trees.

A voice addresses me from the center of my mind, a male voice, deep and resonant: "It is not your time."

I turn to look, and there before me hovers a figure clad in golden armor, radiating an otherworldly glow. He cradles his helmet beneath his arm, revealing a young face—somehow familiar. He holds my gaze with a look of serenity and resolve; his blue eyes are mesmerizing, paralyzing.

"You know me," he says, his words not spoken, but felt. "You have been chosen by God as His agent among men. A guardian of the gates, entrusted with a sacred purpose."

I recognize this scene, the surroundings folding into place. A garden. The one I'd always known—the painting of Joan of Arc. And this figure hovering before me, the Archangel Michael.

"But first," the angel says, his glowing hand resting on the hilt of his sword, "you must cut the ties that bind."

He draws the blade, its tip pointing at my stomach, at a thin cord of undulating light snaking from my navel. My gaze follows the cord to its end, settling on a shadowy figure—a woman—just a few yards away. Her soft eyes—my eyes—gaze back at me from the darkness, a look of surrender.

The angel extends his sword by the blade, offering me the hilt. I accept it, as if hypnotized, raising the weapon to the glowing thread—just as another voice speaks from over my shoulder, mercurial, slithering.

> *Why...*
>> *does he...*
>>> *demand...*
>>>> *this...*
>>>>> *of you?*

I turn to the source of the question, and there in the darkness stands the willowy shape of the jinn, his eyes and mouth ablaze with an electric blue flame.

> *Look...*
>> *deeper...*
>>> *and you...*
>>>> *will see.*

I turn to face the angel, willing my gaze inward, beneath his sheath of armor, his alabaster skin, and there, at his navel, a blackened scar.

He asks…

of you…

what has…

been asked…

of him.

I look to my shadow self, bound to me by the silver thread of light—pulsing like a heartbeat, a life force tethered between us. A feeling, a knowing suddenly dawns upon me. I look at the angel, at his wound where a cord once was, now severed. "What have you done?" I ask. His countenance suddenly shifts, as if a thousand emotions were suddenly set off inside, like dynamite exploding in a building, reducing him to rubble. Suddenly, the orb of light fires toward us from the tree line, catching the angel as he stumbles backwards, absorbing him in a blinding burst of light…

"Catherine!" A voice flashes in like a radio signal from another plane. I feel the air change, the light, the sound of people suddenly around me. "Catherine!" A pair of hands, a man's hands, lifts me by the armpits, gathers me up, cradles me to him. I squint into his face, his eyes, blurring into focus. "You—" I gasp as my head goes faint, crumpling into the darkness.

32 | THREADS

I wake to the sound of insects buzzing, the smell of wet grass warming in the sun. I lift myself up to sitting, squinting at the dim green light enveloping me. I touch the wall of it, smooth, sloping fabric—a tent. I feel for a seam, raising the zipper, opening into a burst of sunlight.

A grassy field splays out before me, a stand of pines rising along its perimeter like a soft, dark wall. Off to the right, a narrow creek glimmers like a silver snake. A figure crouches along the water's edge, haloed by the shimmering light. Another paces nearby, holding his cell phone in the air like he's trying to get a signal. He spots me and waves, jogging up the hill. "Yo, hang on!" he calls, slipping on the grass. The crouching figure rises, following him up the hill. I will myself to stand, but my head is light and I teeter sideways, reaching out, grabbing hold of the side of something warm and metallic, the door of a truck—Trey's SUV. I suddenly recognize the silhouette hustling towards me. "Hey!" Koi calls. "You OK?"

I look around, trying to process where I am, what's happening. Koi approaches slowly, his hands out like he might need to catch me. Behind him in tow is Rami, the guy I met in the park. "Maybe you oughta sit down," Koi offers.

I move away, still holding on to the truck. "Where are we?" I look at Rami. "What are you doing here?"

The driver's-side door opens and Trey steps down, joining the group. He nods to Koi. "We good?"

"Where are we?" I snap.

Koi looks around, bewildered, then blinks back at me. "In the woods?" he says—more a question than an answer. "Your friend's place is that way," he nods. "You don't remember? You told us to come here."

"Why would I tell you that?"

He looks to Trey for help, but Trey just puts his hands up like he doesn't want any of it. He wanders off.

I turn to Rami. "And why are *you* here?"

"He helped us find you," Koi says. "What happened last night?" Koi looks concerned. They both do. My mind reels, trying to recall—flashes of images, fragments. A wave of nausea washes over me, and I list forward. Koi and Rami spring to catch me. "Here, sit down," Rami insists. Koi opens the passenger-side door, guiding me to the ledge of it. "I'm calling your friend," Rami says, pulling out his phone. "What's her number?"

"Why didn't you take me there in the first place?" I spit.

"Because you told us not to," Koi replies.

"I told you to take me to the woods?"

"You said you needed to lie on the earth," Koi says, "to connect with 'the Great Mother.' We didn't know what was going on. You made us pull over. You got out and laid in the grass. The tent was Rami's idea. He had one in his truck," he says, nodding. On the edge of the clearing, another SUV is parked in the grass, the glare of the windshield obscuring a pair of shadowy figures seated inside, gazing back at us. "They're with me," Rami assures. "We're all here to help."

My head is throbbing. "How did you know where I was?"

"I followed you," Rami explains. "When I met you in the park, I thought you wanted information about the list—of the others, like us. But you didn't know it existed, which seemed strange. If your name was on it, why had no one contacted you?"

I look to Koi, but he seems equally perplexed.

"They've made contact with everyone else," Rami says, "so why not you? Or Koi here? He's on the list. Then I realized—they needed you *in play*. If they had contacted you, it would interfere somehow. You needed to discover things on your own. But that means they haven't set up your security. No one is protecting you. Because that would interfere as well. Which means you're vulnerable."

"To what?" Koi asks.

"Whatever this is. Whatever is watching. Where is the box I gave you?"

"In the truck," Koi says. "I had Trey take a look at it."

"And what did you find?" Rami asks, turning to Trey. Trey regards him, not saying anything.

"Strange, right?" Rami says with a smirk. "You have a gift too, am I right? What did you see when you looked into the box?"

Trey fidgets. Koi tries to read his energy. "What's he talking about?" Koi asks.

"It's strange, I know," Rami says. "It's a hybrid technology. Partly ours, partly theirs."

"Whose?"

"That's what my client is trying to figure out."

I look at Koi and Trey, trying to read their reactions. "What are you talking about?" I ask. "How do you know any of this?"

"I'm just like you," Rami says. "I've been part of this for a long time. They need us for our gifts. It has something to do with our DNA. That's as much as I understand. You asked about your father. They needed him for something too."

"So why would they get rid of him?"

"Get rid of him?" he says, wincing. "They were trying to protect him. They just didn't know how."

I look for something in his eyes, an agenda, something. "So why did they need him?"

"That's what I want to know. Just like you."

"Trey found something when he went digging," Koi says. "Tell her."

"I got into the database," Trey mutters. "It's almost completely wiped, but the taxonomy is still there—empty folders with names on them. I ran a search. One of them's connected to your dad."

Koi reads a note on his phone. "Harvey Ward."

My mind flashes to my childhood—the Wards' lake house, diving off the dock, my parents sitting on the wraparound porch, drinking, laughing. I blink back. "It's too late."

"What is?" Koi asks.

"Harvey, his wife, Janet. They were family friends. Harvey was involved with this somehow. The test they had me do—with the cards. I found Janet online and sent her a message. She said Harvey had dementia. He couldn't remember anything. When she read him my note, it triggered something. He *woke up* somehow. He started remembering things—things about the program. Then, suddenly, both of them are dead."

There's a rustle in the tree line along the perimeter of the field. We all freeze. A family of deer step out of the undergrowth into the high grass, a buck and a doe, trailed by a tiny fawn. The buck flicks its tail, a flash of white, signaling the baby to wait.

They watch us, statue still, assessing the threat, then bow their heads and begin to eat the tufts of grass.

"The test with the cards," Rami says. "They had symbols on them."

I look at him.

"Rune symbols," he says. "Do you know what they are? The word 'rune' means 'secret' or 'mystery.' A secret conversation. The symbols are a kind of language, but they're also believed to have mystical properties. Long ago, an oracle would cast the rune stones, and whatever position they fell in, it was considered a message from God. A nonbeliever might look at the arrangement and write it off as chance. But the oracle believed chance was the language of the divine—that nothing was actually random. Whichever way the stones fell, that was the direct intention of God. When they gave us those tests as children, I think they used the runes because we already spoke the language without realizing it. I think it carries with us somehow, in our DNA, like an instinct we're born with. Like a message calling to us."

"From home," I say—an icy chill running through me. "These things that have been following me. It's like they're trying to latch on. Like they need me for something. To take them 'home.' That's the word they use. 'Home.' And there are others—trying to keep them away." An image flashes to me— the Archangel Michael illuminated in the darkness. "A guardian of the gates," I replay his words in my mind. I turn to Rami. "Your client—you said they need us."

"For something, yes, but I don't know what."

I pause, taking in Rami, studying him. I recognize him— from somewhere.

"What do you think it is?" Koi prods.

Rami hesitates. "It feels like something on a higher level, beyond our perception."

"Peter Phillips," I say. "You know who that is?"

"I've seen his name," Rami nods. "He's one of us."

"He was talking about subatomic particles, entanglement. Twin particles connected by a thread—where one side exists in this dimension, the other in a higher, unseen dimension." I turn to Trey. "The project you found. White Ladder. It had to do with quantum mechanics. Transdimensional travel. There's a drug that keeps appearing in the research, DMT. It's a portal drug. It takes you to another place, another dimension. These things that keep trying to latch onto me, it's like they live on a different frequency. Ever since I started seeing them, I've been seeing these other things, entities, shadow forms, like cracks in a barrier that separates one dimension from the next."

"Your eyes," Rami says. "Your vision. Maybe that's what you're needed for. To see the way—to the other side."

"What's on the other side?" Koi asks.

"These things that are trying to use you," Rami continues. "The way you describe them, they're like demons. And the others, the ones trying to keep them out, are like angels. It's like they're fighting over you. Because you can see the way. The way home."

Something dawns on me. "Heaven," I say.

Koi looks at me. "Mr. Y—remember what he said? About man being made in God's image. A mirror of himself."

"A twin."

"Right," Koi nods. "That could take his place."

"He called my father a genius. He made a point about the origin of the word, its Latin meaning, 'guardian deity.' The French way of saying it—*génie*. A genie, a jinn, lives on the other side. It lives in the same dimension as whatever these things are."

"How do you know?" Rami asks.

"Because I've seen one."

Trey perks up. I nod to him. "It worked, by the way. That genie you wanted? He's with me now."

Trey looks baffled.

"I think my father was in touch with something on the other side," I say, "as a child, maybe his whole life. His own jinn. He called them his 'teachers.' My family thought he was imagining things—an invisible friend. Maybe this is what the teachers were teaching him. Something he could use one day. To solve whatever this is. Mr. Y, in his message, he said there's a lie being told."

"Mr. Y. Who is that?" Rami asks.

"I thought you would know."

He looks to Koi for help. "This is someone who contacted you?" Rami asks. "That knew about the program?"

"He seemed to know everything," Koi says with a shrug.

"What did he tell you?" Rami asks, agitated.

"It's more what he *hasn't* told us," Koi replies. "It's like you said, about having to discover this on our own."

My mind steps back, taking in the scene, the four of us gathered here. "I think he staged this."

Rami looks at me.

"You said they need us in play." I gesture around us. "I think *this* is the play."

Rami considers this. "Which is why no one has tried to stop you."

"What do you mean?" Koi asks.

"You're being watched," Rami says flatly. "Everything you do. Everywhere you dig." He looks at Trey. "You think no one knows you've been snooping around the Pentagon's servers?"

Trey smirks, trying to play it off, but he's clearly rattled.

"People go away for life for a lot less than that," Rami says with a sniff.

"So why haven't they stopped us?" Koi asks.

"Maybe they're leaving the door open," Rami answers. "So we can lead them through."

"I'd imagine you'd know exactly why," I say, "seeing as how you work for them."

"I work *with* them," Rami clarifies. "I'm looking for answers, just like you. If they're willing to open doors, then why not step through?"

I try to read his energy, his eyes a blank slate. I glance at the SUV parked on the edge of the field, the figures seated inside. "Why should we trust you?" I ask.

"You can't," Rami says with a shrug. "But you can use my help." He looks at Trey. "The database you found. The names. I know where those people are. I was the one who had to track them down. Maybe they can help piece this together. I can take you to them if you want."

Koi looks at me, then Trey. He glances back at Rami. "Give us a sec."

"Of course," Rami says, bowing out, stepping through the grass, out of earshot. Trey keeps an eye on him, then glances at Koi, sharing a look.

"I don't trust him," I say. "Do you?"

"Hell, no," Koi spits. "But how does he know all this?"

"And yet he didn't know about Mr. Y," I counter.

"Maybe there's a reason for that."

"Who's Mr. Y?" Trey scowls, trying to follow.

"The one I told you about," Koi says. "The weird British dude who helped me find Catherine."

Trey nods. "Right, so who is he?"

"Nobody seems to know."

"Which is weird," I say. "For someone who seems to have access to information, why doesn't Rami know who he is?"

"Maybe he does," Koi says, "and he's lying for some reason."

"Maybe. Or maybe it's a false identity," I say. "Whoever Mr. Y is, maybe he's hiding?"

"From what?" Koi asks.

"I don't know, but if he wanted us to find our own way, and this is the path he put us on, I think it'll eventually lead back to him. I have a feeling he's the only one who knows what this is."

Koi looks at Trey, checking to see how any of this is tracking. Trey has other things on his mind. "So what about the genie?" Trey asks.

"The genie?"

"You said it helped you."

"I guess you could say he's my buddy now," I say with a shrug, "after I saved him from your crazy-ass spell."

Trey looks at Koi, then back at me. "So wait…you can *see* him?"

"Like right now? No. But last night—"

"Oh, OK," Trey says, smirking. "When you were on some other shit. That's when you were seeing the genie, right? When you were trippin'? You might want to thank us, by the way."

"Thank you? For what?"

"Rami ran in and grabbed you," Koi says. "You don't remember? There was a huge crowd outside. You were right in the middle of it. I don't know if people thought you were part of the show or what, but you were doing this crazy dance, like straight-up channeling the universe. Then *boom*—out, collapsed. Rami jumped in and snatched you up, and we ducked the hell out of there."

"Yeah, and how do you think that looked?" Trey says, sneering. "Two Black dudes and an Arab grabbing some passed-out white chick and throwing her in the back of a car? People were going crazy. Shit was like *Dukes of Hazzard*. You're lucky we got out of there alive."

"What happened with you last night?" Koi asks.

"I took something…I lost control. It was stupid. But I also saw something." I try to recall the vision. "Whatever this thing is, it's not about us. It's like we're caught in the middle—of something."

Koi glances at Trey, then back at me. "Middle of what?"

"I don't know. These things…these angels and demons. Whatever they are. There's something there."

Koi hesitates. "Like some Heaven and Hell shit?"

"Like some end-of-the-world shit," Trey says. "You see that? Just like your dreams."

"White Ladder," I say, recalling something. "Rami said there's a reason we're on the list. Our DNA. What if that's why they need us? Because we're connected to whatever these things are." I pause a moment as a memory, a story, surfaces. "The Nephilim. From the Old Testament. They were descendants of gods, half-breeds—half human, half divine. But what if the gods weren't gods after all? What if they were just from a higher dimension? How would we know the difference? And if the stories are true, that the gods mated with humans, then the DNA would have been carried down. Pieces of it, scattered over time."

"So wait," Trey says, stepping in. "You're saying we got angel blood?" He looks at Koi. "See, now that's what I'm talking about." Trey grins. "And if we find these other peeps with the same blood, we become like what? Like a god or something?"

Koi looks to me for help.

"Yo, we gotta get up in there," Trey nudges.

"This is not about you becoming a god," Koi says, scowling.

Trey raises his hands, innocent. "I'm not saying that. I'm saying we gotta get to the bottom of this."

"Yeah, right," Koi says. He looks at me. "So what do you want to do?"

"What do *you* want to do?"

Koi looks at Rami pacing across the field. "Maybe we see what he knows," Koi says, glancing at me.

I think about it for a moment, then call out to him, "Hey!" Rami turns around, expectant. I nod. He lights up with a grin and hurries over.

The SUV jostles through the muddy potholes up the drive to Leslie's house. I imagine a line of cop cars waiting out front, Leslie pacing frantically. But the cops aren't waiting when we get there. And neither is Leslie. Just her Volvo parked out front, and a text from her from around 3 a.m.:

> *Going home*
> *You coming?*

I try the front door, but it's locked, so I knock and wait, listening for movement inside. No one stirs, so I walk around back and try the kitchen door, but that's locked too. I scan the property down the hill—the barns, the chicken coop, the stable. Silent, just the birds fluttering through the treetops.

I dig the hidden key out from under the rock by the planter and let myself in, creaking through the kitchen, up the central hall, pausing at the foot of the stairs. "Leslie?" I call—to no response. I ascend the staircase to the upper landing and look down the long, dark corridor. A pale pink light emanates from one of the open doorways like the mouth of a cave. "Leslie?" I call, tiptoeing to the doorway and peering inside. There, I find her curled in the center of her bed, fast asleep, dressed in last night's clothes, the bedcovers twisted around her like a cyclone. The room is lit by a pair of rose-pink Tibetan salt lamps, glowing like torches in a tomb. Arranged on the floor, encircling the bed, are a collection of old shoeboxes filled with bird feathers, crystals, stones, baggies full of sand. I remember the first time Leslie showed me the boxes, dragging them out from under her dorm room bed like a show-and-tell—how she walked me through her nightly ritual, identifying the contents of each box, explaining the power they possessed. She showed me the way she positioned the boxes, just so, to protect her while she slept. "Protect you from what?" I asked. She looked at me and said, matter-of-factly, "From everything."

I step over to the bed and untangle the coils of blankets and sheets, pulling them up over her. I stand there for a moment, watching her sleep, her long, black eyelashes twitching, dreaming. I say goodbye, but she doesn't hear. She just nestles down under the covers, oblivious.

I look around the room—at the posters, the trinkets, the comforting touches of a child, all frozen in time. I open my hands, fingers long like the rays of a sun, and feel it there—a hum in the air, a presence—watching. Slowly, I close my fingers around it, curling them into fists. The air seems to shudder—as if some hidden thing were holding its breath, knowing its time has come.

EPILOGUE | MEMORY GAME

I watch the woman as she gathers the cards on the table, knocks them together into a stack, and slips them into an envelope with her notes. I look over her shoulder at the observation window, where my father is standing beside Harvey. They smile down at me, waving, and my stomach unclenches, knowing that whatever this is, I must have done it right. My father holds up a finger, *one sec*, as the two go over something.

As the woman collects her things, I tune into the video camera set up on a tripod behind her—its cold, black eye gazing back at me. I glance over my shoulder at a second camera watching me from behind. The wide-legged stance of the tripods reminds me of robots. There's something scary about them, the way they stare.

The woman crosses the room to a door with a small square window. As she opens it, a boy squeezes in right past her without her noticing, not even a flinch as she steps out into the hall, the door swinging shut behind her.

I recognize the boy from the waiting room with the others. He's tan and has black hair. He wears a yellow T-shirt and black shorts and Nikes with a red Swoosh on the sides. I raise my hand to point at him, to call out, but he motions for me to stop, smiling like we're in on a joke. He puts a finger up to his lips.

"What are you doing?" I whisper. "You're going to get me in trouble."

"They cannot see me," he says, glancing up at the observation room. He has an accent from someplace, I don't know where. It makes him sound fancy. "Stop moving your lips," he says, "or they will see. *Talk like this*," he says straight-lipped, like a ventriloquist.

"*What do you want?*" I ask, statue-still.

"I know a secret," he says.

"*Why can't they see you?*"

"Do you want to know or not?"

"*A secret about what?*"

"Why we're here."

I look at my father in the booth. He waves, signaling that he's coming down.

"Quick," the boy says.

I shrug a nod, and he darts over, whispering something in my ear, but I don't hear the words. They seem to slip past my eardrum, directly into my brain. I feel a rush, like standing up too fast, my head swirling like liquid, spinning into a vision. A luminous sphere, rotating, the walls of it folding back like a flower, opening, pinwheeling. And at its center, an infinite tunnel crackling with light, gazing back at me like an eye, beckoning.

"Do you see it?" he asks, but I can't answer. I can only nod, hypnotized.

"Now forget," he whispers, and the flower suddenly collapses in on itself, folding into darkness.

REFERENCES

Wikipedia contributors, "Ancient Egyptian conception of the soul," Wikipedia, The Free Encyclopedia. Accessed 2025.

Wikipedia contributors. "Pineal Gland." Wikipedia, The Free Encyclopedia. Accessed 2025.

Walsch, Neale Donald. *The Complete Conversations with God.* New York: TarcherPerigee, 2017.

Wikipedia contributors. "Dudleytown, Connecticut." Wikipedia, The Free Encyclopedia. Accessed 2025.

Wikipedia contributors. "Jack Parsons." Wikipedia, The Free Encyclopedia. Accessed 2025.

The Metropolitan Museum of Art. *Dress No. 13 by Alexander McQueen – Savage Beauty*. Website accessed 2025.

The Metropolitan Museum of Art. *Joan of Arc by Jules Bastien-Lepage*. Website accessed 2025.

Morehouse, David. *Psychic Warrior: The True Story of America's Foremost Psychic Spy and the Cover-Up of the CIA's Top-Secret Stargate Program.* New York: St. Martin's Press, 1996.

Wikipedia contributors. "Stargate Project (U.S. Army unit)." Wikipedia, The Free Encyclopedia. Accessed 2025.

The Holy Bible, King James Version. Grand Rapids, MI: Zondervan, 2002.

Narby, Jeremy. *The Cosmic Serpent: DNA and the Origins of Knowledge.* New York: Tarcher/Putnam, 1998.

McKenna, Terence. *DMT, Mathematical Dimensions, Syntax, and Death.* YouTube video, 30:22. Posted by @infiniteknowledge7874 May 15, 2017. Accessed 2025.

Strassman, Rick. *DMT: The Spirit Molecule: A Doctor's Revolutionary Research into the Biology of Near-Death and Mystical Experiences.* Rochester, VT: Park Street Press, 2001.

Wikipedia contributors. "The Montauk Project: Experiments in Time." Wikipedia, The Free Encyclopedia. Accessed 2025.

Central Intelligence Agency. "CIA-RDP96-00792R000300320001-9." Accessed March 17, 2025. https://www.cia.gov/readingroom/docs/CIA-RDP96-00792R000300320001-9.pdf.

Central Intelligence Agency. "DOC_0000139451." Accessed March 17, 2025. https://www.cia.gov/readingroom/docs/DOC_0000139451.pdf.

Central Intelligence Agency. "CIA-RDP96-00788R001000010001-0." Accessed March 17, 2025. https://www.cia.gov/readingroom/document/cia-rdp96-00788r001000010001-0.

FURTHER ACKNOWLEDGMENTS

I am grateful to the many individuals whose work, research, insights, and public platforms have served as a source of guidance in my exploration of the themes within this book. Their contributions have provided both inspiration and a foundation for deeper inquiry. Special thanks to: Tim Burchett, Kevin Burns, Dolores Cannon, Edgar Cayce, Philip Coppens, Jeremy Corbell, Caroline Cory, Erich von Däniken, Richard Dolan, Julian Dorey, Brigit Esselmont, James Fox, Brandon Fugal, Timothy Good, Brian Greene, Steven Greer, Graham Hancock, Stephen Hawking, Budd Hopkins, Linda Moulton Howe, Terry Iacuzzo, Danny Jones, John A. Keel, George Knapp, Bob Lazar, Avi Loeb, Heather Lynn, John E. Mack, Terence McKenna, Jesse Michels, Robert Monroe, David Morehouse, Jeremy Narby, Garry Nolan, Harold E. Puthoff, Joe Rogan, Shawn Ryan, Suzan Saxman, Jeremy Shaw, Rupert Sheldrake, Zecharia Sitchin, Rick Strassman, Whitley Strieber, Leonard Susskind, Russell Targ, Jacques Vallée, Neale Donald Walsch, Eric Weinstein, Brian L. Weiss, and John Archibald Wheeler.

SOUNDSCAPE

Music was a powerful source of inspiration throughout the creation of this book, shaping its tone and providing a sonic backdrop that helped bring the story to life in ways beyond words. While there are too many artists to name, I would like to extend special thanks to the following for their influence and impact: Anohni and the Johnsons, Banks, Black Marble, The Blaze, Circlesquare, Cold Cave, The Cure, Lana Del Rey, Depeche Mode, Florence and the Machine, Gidge, Godford, Interpol, Kendrick Lamar, New Order, ODESZA, Radiohead, Real Lies, Siouxsie and the Banshees, Stay+, SWIM, Underworld, The xx, and Zola Jesus.

ABOUT THE AUTHOR

Sparrow Hall is an author, producer, and cross-medium storyteller whose work merges literary fiction, music, video, and curated online content into an immersive storytelling experience. His debut novel, *The Invisible Eye,* is the culmination of over a decade of research into paranormal phenomena, quantum mechanics, and spirituality—exploring humanity's evolving relationship with the unknown. Hall is a graduate of Bennington College and lives in upstate New York. Learn more at www.sparrowhall.com.